THE TERMINAL CITY MURDERS

A JOHN GRANVILLE & EMILY TURNER HISTORICAL MYSTERY

SHARON ROWSE

THREE CEDARS PRESS

THE TERMINAL CITY MURDER

A John Granville & Emily Turner Historical Mystery

By Sharon Rowse

Published by Three Cedars Press
www.threecedarspress.com

ISBN: 978-1-988037-24-0

For my friends and family.
With much love, and thanks for your support.

1

MONDAY, JUNE 11, 1900

John Lansdowne Granville glanced up from the sheet of flimsy yellow paper he'd been frowning over and cast an annoyed look at the ceiling fan overhead. It wobbled slightly as it revolved, making a thumping sound and casting odd shadows across the room in the early morning sunlight. His office was warming up, the erratic fan barely creating a breeze.

And the open window wasn't helping at all. It wasn't even eight o'clock yet, but already the air was hot and still. From the street below rose the rattling of delivery carts, the hoarse yells of their drivers and the rank smell of horse droppings mixed with hot tar. Cursing his landlord and whatever idiot had put in the fan, Granville shut the heat and noise out of his mind and turned back to the problem posed by the telegram.

Or maybe it was an opportunity?

He glanced at his desk calendar. They'd only been back in town for a week, and already they had several investigations underway. Most were new clients who had requested their services last month, while he, his partner Sam Scott, and their assistant Trent Davis had been up north, searching for a missing heir. That case had been an unusual one, taking them away longer and much further afield than they'd anticipated, but it had been lucrative. And oddly satisfying.

Being home again felt confining, somehow, after three weeks in the wilderness north of the Skeena River. And spending time in the office felt even more restrictive, like a too tight coat. It had affected the others, too. All of them were a little tense, though they weren't admitting it.

So far, their new cases were bread and butter—background checks on employees and the like—which didn't provide much distraction. Or challenge. None of the new cases would take long, none was likely to hold their interest.

What they all needed was another big case, a gripping one. Like the one they'd just finished. The kind that would take all their efforts to solve. The kind of case that built a big reputation.

He looked thoughtfully at the telegram, and re-read the blurred type for the sixth time. Could this be the answer?

The slamming of a door and raised voices in the outer office put an end to his attempt to concentrate. Granville frowned as he listened to the escalating argument. This was supposed to be a professional office, dammit.

"Trent!" he called out.

There was no answer from the outer office, just louder voices.

Tucking the unanswered telegram under the blotter on his side of the large oak partner's desk he shared with Scott, Granville strode to the door. Clearly he needed to sort things out here first.

He hadn't seen Scott that morning, but Trent was supposed to be in the front office, welcoming visitors. Their growing reputation as investigation agents meant that potential clients expected there to be someone in the office when they came to call. The sounds he was hearing didn't sound very welcoming.

"You can't just barge in…"

It was Trent's voice, far too loud, right on the other side of the door. Who was he talking to?

Granville wrenched the door open.

And had to stop himself from laughing out loud.

Trent was standing—freckled face set and arms akimbo—in front of Mac McAndrews, barring him from Granville's office. A sturdy five foot eight, the lad looked like a bantam cock facing off a stork. McAndrews had to be six foot two, an inch over Granville's own height, but he was thin almost to the point of gauntness. Add in McAndrews' flaming red hair and it was an image from a Gilbert and Sullivan opera. All that was missing was the singing.

But what was McAndrews doing here? He'd met the hot-headed accountant two months before, in pursuit of that missing heir. Their first encounter had been anything but friendly, though once sure that Granville meant his friend Rupert Weston no harm, McAndrews had been both helpful and knowledgeable. He'd also proven incredibly loyal to Weston, and Granville had ended up liking the fellow.

None of which explained McAndrews' current presence, or the stand-off he was engaged in with Trent.

"McAndrews?" he said. Both heads spun towards him. Apparently they hadn't heard the door open. Trent looked annoyed. Their visitor looked worried.

"Granville," McAndrews said. "I'm glad you're here. I need your help."

"Then you'd best come in," Granville said, opening the door wider. "Thank you, Trent."

Trent scowled, glaring at McAndrews, then stomped back to his desk.

Granville waved McAndrews to one of four straight-backed wooden chairs lining the wall beside the door. "What seems to be the problem?" he asked as he sank back into the over-sized leather chair behind his desk.

McAndrews collapsed onto one chair, dumping his hat and briefcase on the chair next to him. "I have a client who's about to be arrested for fraud. And I don't know how to keep him out of jail."

Granville put up a hand. "Whoa. Start at the beginning, please."

McAndrews shot him a wry grin. "That's why I'm here. I'm not cut out for the investigative stuff." He leaned forward. "You know I hoped to set up my own accounting practice?"

Granville nodded.

"Well, I've done so, though it's only part time. My most recent client..." McAndrews paused, shook his head. "Actually, he's more of a potential client at the moment. Because the thing is, I think he should be hiring you, not me."

"And why is that?"

"Because he's being framed."

IF MCANDREWS' client was indeed being framed, Granville could understand why the fellow had burst into the office so urgently. But he was over-reacting.

"Or at least your client says he's being framed," Granville said. "It's usually best not to assume your clients are telling the whole truth. At least at first."

McAndrews smiled at that, but the lines of worry in his forehead deepened. "Which is why he'd be better as your client than mine."

"We'll see," Granville said, opening his notebook. "But first, I need details. Who is this client of yours, and what's his background?"

"Potential client. He's English, born and raised somewhere in the country, but studied at Cambridge and worked in London for a time."

"Not a remittance man, then?"

McAndrews laughed at that. "Hardly. I doubt his family has ever had that kind of money. But he's educated, has an accent not far off your own, and he seems to know people."

He glanced away. "And he was a friend of Weston's. He's the one who told Weston about his brother's deaths."

A warning that had possibly saved Weston's life. Which

explained McAndrews' concern for the case. He wasn't just passing off a client, he really wanted Granville's help.

It also increased Granville's own interest in this case, since Weston had been a client of his. "And this fellow has been accused of fraud? What kind of fraud, and what proof do they have?" Granville asked.

"He's says it's mortgage fraud," McAndrews said. "Because he works for a mortgage company, I suppose. Anyway, he's being accused of writing up deals that pad the company's mortgage rates, and pocketing the difference."

"Who is accusing him?"

"He's not sure," McAndrews said. "But the police have brought him in for questioning. Twice."

"Your client thinks he'll be arrested? Soon?"

"Yes. He's sure he's nearly out of time. He's frantic. That's why he came to me—he seems to have nowhere else to turn."

"And who does he think is framing him?" Granville asked.

"Someone higher up in the company he works for—Vancouver Permanent Investment & Loan. He's not sure who," McAndrews said with a sour look. "They're the firm Weston was going to work for, and I told him not to. Didn't you talk to them, when you were searching for Weston?"

"I did." Granville frowned as he recalled the details. "And I didn't much like what I learned about them. It wouldn't surprise me if someone there had engaged in a bit of fraud. But that's mostly because I didn't like the fellow I met. Which is hardly proof."

"No. It isn't."

Granville glanced at his notes. Mortgage fraud? That was a new one. "So what, exactly, is mortgage fraud?"

As McAndrews started to speak, Granville held up a hand. "In layman's terms, please."

McAndrews paused, grinned. "Okay. It's quite simple, really. You know that banks can't lend money for mortgages, right?"

No, he hadn't known. And since he planned to buy a house for himself and his fiancée Emily Turner to start their life together, these were things he needed to know. "Why not?"

"The government won't allow them to."

"So where does the money for mortgages come from?"

"Mortgage and loan companies like Vancouver Permanent Investment & Loan. Usually they're funded by an investment syndicate, who provide the money up front in return for a higher rate of return than the banks will give them."

Granville's mind went to his unscrupulous elder brother, William, and his fondness for investments that paid a very high rate of return. Which he often couldn't find in England. "Let me guess. The money comes from Britain."

"In this case, yes. Apparently this province is a very popular place for British investors these days. Vancouver Permanent then lends that money to Mr. Joe Homebuyer, in return for a down payment and an agreed to monthly interest."

Granville might need a mortgage soon, but he didn't want to see a single hard-earned dollar going into the pockets of his brother William and his ilk. His interest in this case grew.

"So, there are three parties involved—the original investor, the mortgage company, and the buyer," Granville said.

"Exactly. Fraud can occur at any one of those three points. The buyer can be overcharged or misled about the deal, an employee can defraud the mortgage company—as my client is accused of doing—or the investors can be defrauded. Or some combination of the three."

"So you think that someone at Vancouver Permanent is taking more profits than they are entitled to at one or more of those three points," Granville said. "And framing your client to cover it up?"

"That's exactly right. You sure you never studied accounting?"

"I'm sure." Granville contemplated the ceiling fan—still shaking away—while he thought. As a prospective buyer, he wanted to know exactly what kind of real estate rackets were being run here.

"You know Vancouver's real estate market better than I do," he said. "Which do you think is more likely?"

McAndrews shrugged. "All I do is keep the books. Mortgages are complex because property values and a hot or cold market can affect mortgage rates and terms. I don't know much about land values."

Granville straightened in his chair. He knew someone with an insider's take on land values. And his prospective father-in-law would give him the straight truth.

"On second thought, don't tell me anything more. Let me do a little investigating first, then we can discuss it."

"But you'll take the case?"

"Did I mention that I didn't much care for the fellow I met at Vancouver Permanent?" Or greedy investors like his older brother.

He grinned. "And we could use a new challenge. Yes, we'll take the case."

ONCE MCANDREWS HAD LEFT, Granville telephoned to set an appointment with Emily's father that afternoon, and completed his notes from the meeting with McAndrews. Then he turned back to his telegram.

He hadn't expected to hear back from the Pinkerton's National Detective Agency so quickly. And they were interested in affiliating with his small firm, and wanted to send a man out to meet with him in early August. He hadn't expected so much interest on their part.

Nor their desire to move forward so quickly.

Granville hadn't even made up his own mind about an alliance with the famous agency, much less discussed details with Scott. Financially, it seemed to make sense, especially if they wanted to play in the "championship leagues"—for which the Pinkerton's Agency definitely qualified. And he did want that.

But he wasn't sure his small company was ready—nor how his partner really felt about it.

He scribbled a few quick calculations, then stopped and loosened his tie, ran a finger inside the stiff boiled collar of his shirt. The sun was shining directly into the office now. And all the windows were painted shut. Running a hand through his hair, he let out an exasperated sound when the fan thumped again.

Stupid thing would be completely useless in another month or two, when the real heat hit. Someone needed to fix that, and soon.

As if on cue, the door between inner and outer offices squeaked open. Granville looked up just in time to see a stack of files slamming down on the desk in front of him.

"I can't work like this," Trent said. He planted himself in one of the chairs along the wall and crossed tanned arms.

From the look of him, Trent didn't intend to budge for anything less than a train wreck. Or maybe another murder case. Granville doubted a case on mortgage fraud would do it.

He hid a smile. At least this time it wasn't his partner complaining about the amount of paperwork an investigative business demanded. Trent was their assistant—paperwork came with the job.

Granville tapped the stack of file folders. "You aren't still complaining about the work our office intern did last month while we were away, are you?" He leaned back, watching Trent's face. "How much of a mess can Miss Kent have made of the files, anyway?"

Especially given that all of them, himself and Scott included, would rather be out working on a case than in the office documenting those cases and writing up the reports that got them paid. Their files hadn't been in very good shape to start with.

"Just take a look," Trent said, glowering at the offending files.

This had been building for the last week, but Granville had hoped that Trent would settle down, get over it. He flipped open the top file and glanced at the neat column of entries on the first page. Pulling the file closer, he read it more carefully, then opened the next file. "Are they all like this?"

"Yes," Trent said on a deep sigh. "They are. Every single file has a neatly typed list of the correspondence it contains, in date order, every file is labeled, important documents are flagged—who even has time to do all that?"

Granville suspected that any professional office did exactly that.

"She took my system apart and now we have—this." The boy looked as if he'd been given warm black coffee. Which he hated.

"I can't work that way. And…" Trent glared down at his feet. "Well, she must have spent days doing this. How can I just tear it apart?"

Granville remembered that Emily had said something about their files needing attention when she'd hired her friend and fellow business student to mind the office while they were away last month. He should have paid more attention. He knew Emily well enough by now that he should have anticipated something like this.

"So what would you like me to do about it?" he asked his irritated assistant.

"I don't know," Trent said, "I suppose it's done, now."

He ruined that surprisingly mature statement by rocking backwards on the chair's two rear legs, balancing against the wall, and chewing on his lower lip. He brushed in an irritated manner at the poorly cut strands of brown hair that had fallen over his forehead again.

Granville laughed, as much at the situation as at their assistant. Trent glared at him, but his eyes looked hurt.

"I suppose it is time we had proper professional staff in the outer office," Granville said, tapping a finger on the telegram he'd been thinking about half the morning. "I've begun discussions with the Pinkerton's Agency about working with them as an affiliate on certain cases. They're interested, but if we want this to go anywhere, we'll have to prove we can be as professional as they are."

"Really? Pinkerton's?" Trent said, slamming the chair back to the floor and leaping to his feet.

Then his face fell. "But what about me?"

"You? What about you?"

"If you're getting someone 'professional'," Trent said bitterly, "you won't be needing me, will you? What am I supposed to do?"

"You'll work as our assistant, of course. Just without the paperwork."

"I will? And no paperwork? But that's—that's..."

"If we can find someone that will suit. Someone we can afford." Which might not be easy. They were doing well, but the firm was still very new. They hadn't yet made a name for themselves on the scale he hoped to reach one day.

Trent whooped.

"And I still have to talk to Scott," Granville said. "So don't say anything."

That quieted him. "Not a word. But Mr. Scott won't like it. He hates spending money."

"And he's even less fond of being broke than I am," Granville said.

"But..."

"And I don't want to hear about gold mines," Granville added.

Not being able to freely spend the money they'd earned earlier that year in finding a lost gold mine—which had to remain a secret—was a lingering sore spot for Trent. "This business has to pay for itself, remember? We don't spend money we can't explain by way of our profits."

"Yeah, yeah." Trent gathered up the files, turned to go. "I'll just take care of these. Make sure we have everything in order for our new clerk."

Granville held back his grin until Trent had left his office and closed the door behind him, but he was whistling softly as he went back to figuring out how to help McAndrews with a fraud case, of all things.

2

An hour later, Granville leaned back in his prospective father-in-law's comfortable visitor's chair and surveyed the view. Angus Turner's fourth floor office, with its view of the bustling train yards and the busy harbor beyond, was several degrees more opulent than his own, but then Turner's managerial role with the Canadian Pacific Railroad trapped him behind the mound of paperwork that covered his desk.

"Mortgage fraud?" Emily's father repeated. He tapped his pursed lips, then leaned back in his high-back leather chair, pudgy hands relaxing on the carved oak armrests. "Interesting you should be asking about it."

Granville wished he would hurry up. Turner was genial enough, but he was one of those who doled out information as sparingly as they did their personal fortunes. "Why so?"

"Well," Angus Turner said. "It's like this. Land became a good investment again when the money started flowing in from the Klondike gold rush as well as the silver mines in the Kootenays."

Pretty hard to miss the screaming ads proclaiming the latest real estate deals. And Granville happened to know that the CPR had been given ownership of a good chunk of the best properties.

All part of their deal for choosing Vancouver as the terminal city when they brought the railroad across the continent.

Which accounted for Turner's smugness. But ignorance often got more answers than knowledge. "Oh?" Granville said.

"Hmmm. Houses selling as if they were jewels and at similar prices. Most wage-earners can't afford them, either," Turner said. "So they go to the mortgage syndicates for the money, then spend years paying them off at rates that would give them nightmares if they ever thought about it."

"Are their lending practices legal?" Granville asked, watching with interest as Turner straightened and leaned forward. This was evidently a favorite topic.

He made a mental note to ask Emily if her father had any interests in real estate, aside from what was likely a substantial amount of CPR stocks.

"Supposedly. It's creating a lot of opportunity for fraud, though. Especially since prices are rising so fast," Turner said.

"What's driving the price increases?" Granville asked, leaning forward. This was information he'd need before he went house hunting.

"Prices softened a little last year with the end of the Klondike rush, but they have more than recovered this spring. It's a crazy thing," Turner said. "Prices are rising and the cost of borrowing money is falling, so people buy more than they can afford on credit. It can't last. Some are saying we're overbuilt now and with all the projects underway, it can only get worse."

"Indeed?" Granville said thoughtfully.

"It's what happens when you have unregulated syndicates lending money to greedy fools."

Granville wondered if those syndicates ever lost money on the greedy fools. No doubt the railroad made money either way, since there would always be buyers and those who wanted to lend them money. "What role would a young English gentleman have in such a syndicate?"

"Most of the money is coming from England these days. If this young man has any connections, he could be invaluable in raising the credibility of the firm he represents."

From what little McAndrews had told him, Granville wouldn't have thought his potential client would have those kinds of connections.

"If the young gent were personable, he might be set up as a front man, someone who talks the gullible into doing business with them," Turner was saying, oblivious to his future son-in-law's thoughts. "He'd be paid a percentage of the business he brought in. Could do quite well."

Then why was McAndrews' client being accused of fraud?

Given the amount of money that had to be involved in the scenario Angus was talking about, though, anything was possible. Granville's interest in taking on this case had just deepened. "How would I talk to the investors in such a syndicate?"

Shrewd eyes considered him. "You'd be hard pressed to get anyone to talk. If you give me the young gentleman's name, I can make a few discreet enquiries for you."

He might have to rethink his view of Emily's father after all. "I'd appreciate it, but I haven't agreed to take the case yet. Let me get back to you."

Turner nodded. "Just let me know."

"Thank you. I will."

"Will you join us for supper tonight? I know Mrs. Turner would be pleased to have you. And Emily too, of course."

The thought of Emily's company and the good food was tempting, despite the rather cramped formality of dining with Emily's family. His fiancée would be intrigued by this case.

And he wanted to hear her thoughts on the wisdom of adding a clerk to their office. He suspected she'd suggest her friend Miss Kent, who was the girl who had organized the office while they were away and so offended Trent.

He shook Angus' hand firmly. "Thank you, I'd be pleased to do so."

"Good. We'll expect you at seven."

"I'll be there."

<hr>

AFTER A FOUR-COURSE DINNER, which had been prepared and served by the Turner's Chinese cook, Emily and Granville went for an evening stroll along Georgia Street, then turned down towards the harbor. It had been a warm day, but the breeze over the ocean was cool, and Emily drew her light wool wrap more tightly around herself. Granville shrugged out of his jacket and draped it around her shoulders, and she smiled up at him in thanks.

"It's a good thing I don't eat like that every day," Granville said, smiling back at her. "I sit behind a desk too much these days."

He was looking particularly dashing this evening, dark hair windblown and that gleam in his eyes. And no shortage of muscles.

She took his arm. "Not that you spend much time there, except in between getting shot at," she said lightly. "Which reminds me. Laura was asking if you were pleased with her work?"

"Laura?"

"Laura Kent? My classmate? The poor woman who had the task for sorting out the mess in that office of yours last month."

"Ah, Miss Kent. It's a very timely question."

"Oh?"

"Indeed. I'm very pleased with her work," he said. "Trent, however, is not."

"What?" Emily shot him an irritated look. "That ungrateful—the only reason he was able to be part of your last investigation is because of Laura. What exactly did he find to complain about?"

"He doesn't feel he can live up to the standards your friend set."

"Oh. Oh, I see. Laura is exceptionally meticulous in her work." Emily tugged at her bonnet, which the breeze was trying to pull askew. "Don't tell Trent, but I'm not sure I could live up to her standards, either."

"Not that I'd want to, you understand," she added with a quick grin. "Why does Trent want to?"

"It's not so much that he wants to match her standards, as I understand it. It's because there's too much of a gap between his way of doing things and how she set up the files. Her methods either have to be maintained, or the whole thing has to be taken apart and redone."

"Oh. I never thought of that," Emily said. She felt terrible. She'd never meant to cause a problem.

They walked a few paces in silence, then she pulled on Granville's arm to bring him to a stop facing her.

"I'm sorry," she said. "It seemed like such a good idea and I just didn't think about what would happen when Trent got back. How can I fix it?"

EMILY LOOKED REALLY UPSET. Granville had to fight back the urge to hug her. She might appreciate it, but her neighbors would be scandalized, and her mother would never let her hear the end of it. "Actually, I think you've done me a favor."

"I have?" Her eyebrows drew together. Then she pulled her hand from his arm. "You aren't going to let Trent go, so you can hire someone who knows what they're doing, are you?"

"Funny, that's exactly what he said. And you're both half right."

"Which half…?" She met his eyes, and started to smile. "You're going to hire someone to run the office, aren't you? But you're also keeping Trent."

"That's it. Now all I need to do is find someone who can match the standards your friend set. Whom we can afford. And why are you glaring at me?"

"Why can't I run the office? It's what I've been training for, after all."

And there it was. "Emily, you have your typewriting classes."

"Our first semester just ended in May. Now we have the option of spending a full semester, or even two semesters, as interns, working in an actual office. Like yours."

How to point out to her that she hated the routine of an office? She'd be bored in a week. "So Miss Kent will also have that option available to her?"

"Yes, she will. And if you mean you'd rather hire her than me..." She seemed to run out of words and just stared at him for a long moment. Surely that wasn't a glint of moisture in her eyes? "I know it's not professional, and I'm supposed to be business-like, but I thought you loved me."

"I do love you. And I need you too much to see you locked away in an office all day."

"Oh, pshaw. That may be romantic and all, but what exactly do you need me for? Planning our wedding? That's two years away, and besides, Mama is going to be arranging all of that. And don't even think of trying to interfere with her. It wouldn't be worth it."

"I'd like to hire both of you," Granville said, which seemed to deprive her of words again.

Before she could think of any, he continued, "You're an excellent investigator, and I think your photographs are going to prove to be more helpful than either of us can envision now. I need you free to work with me—or with your friend Clara Miles, if she'll agree—when an investigation raises questions a man can't easily ask."

"Really?"

"Really. There are already two desks in the outer office—you and Laura can work together at times when you're not out on a case." So he'd know if Emily was getting herself into danger again. "If Miss Kent would be willing to work for us, of course."

"She'd be thrilled. I don't believe she's found a permanent placement yet, and she needs the work—she's helping support her family. It isn't easy yet for women typewriters to find work in town, you know. Most businesses like to hire male clerks, and have them do all the typewriting too."

"Then it's settled. Would you ask Miss Kent to come in and talk to me about terms one day this week?"

"Of course I will," Emily tucked her hand back into his arm and began walking again. "But what about Trent?"

"I thought we already settled that he'd continue to assist with investigations."

"No, I mean where would he sit?" She walked more slowly, head half-turned so she could see his face. "There are only two desks in the outer office, and the partner's desk in your office. Where would he work?"

"We'd have to see if there are additional rooms available on that floor."

"Rent more space? For Trent? Nonsense. It's a waste of money," Emily said. "You have a perfectly good storage space that's far too large. It can be divided to make space for Trent. I'll speak with the landlord on Monday."

"Good thinking. Maybe you can get him to fix the overhead fans, too. And unstick the windows in Scott's and my office." She'd make a holy terror of an office manager if she ever decided she wanted to be one, he thought with an inward grin, careful to keep any hint of it out of his voice.

"It does get too hot in there, doesn't it?" she said, distracted for a moment. "I'll see what I can do about it. But Granville—can you really afford to hire another person, let alone two? I mean, Laura and I will only be making partial salaries, of course, as it's an internship, but still, it raises your costs substantially."

"Oh, I think we can manage."

She gave him a suspicious look. "You're not just saying that? I don't need charity, and neither does Laura."

"No, you don't. And this isn't charity, or if it is, you are the ones taking pity on us," he said with a grin. "I suspect you'll both be horrified at our operations, and have us sorted out and earning well in no time."

He'd never planned to hire Emily, had hoped to keep her as far away from the dangers of his business as he could, and his impulsive offer had surprised him as much as it had her. And now he was surprised again to realize that he meant every word. In fact, he suspected that his surprising fiancée was likely to turn into a major asset for their business.

Emily was giving him a suspicious look. "There's something you aren't telling me," she said.

He had to grin. Five months engaged, and already she knew him too well. "You're right. There is another reason, one I haven't even shared with Scott yet. I got a telegram this morning."

Her hand tightened on his arm. "Granville! Not Pinkerton's?"

How had she guessed? "Yes. They're interested in affiliating with us, want a meeting in August, in fact."

Emily let out a little squeal of excitement, then covered her mouth with a gloved hand and looked horrified at herself. Seconds later she was grinning at him. "But that's wonderful. And no wonder you want to make the office more professional. It will have to be, won't it? I mean, if you partner with them."

"Affiliate," he said absently, intrigued by how quickly she'd guessed his news and understood the implication. "And yes, we'd definitely be playing for bigger stakes if we worked with them."

He glanced at her excited face and smiled, wishing he didn't have the questions he did. Was he looking to grow too fast? "But please keep it to yourself until I have a chance to talk to Scott," he said. "I'm not sure he's persuaded of the advantages of a business arrangement with them."

"I'll keep quiet," Emily said. "And don't worry. Scott will come around. You'll see"

He hoped she was right.

TUESDAY, JUNE 12, 1900

The following morning, Granville strode into the steamy interior of Mary's cafe, shaking the rain from his hat and coat. He could smell bacon and hash browns frying, fresh bread and coffee. His stomach rumbled, despite how well he'd eaten the previous night.

Granville scanned the room for McAndrews' red hair, spotted him sitting in a rough wooden booth against the far wall and made his way through the crowded, noisy restaurant. As he passed the wood-planked counter, every stool full, he saw Mary herself behind the battered wooden cash register. He gave her a nod and a smile.

She looked up at him—a long way up from her five foot nothing to his six foot one—and shook her head at him. But his coffee would be on its way before he sat down.

"Granville," McAndrews said. "Good morning. I got your message."

Granville clapped McAndrews on the shoulder and they gripped hands. "Glad you could meet me here. Have you ordered?"

"Just the coffee."

They both looked up as Granville's coffee landed in front of him with a thunk. "Thank-you, Jean," he said with a grin. "And two breakfast specials. McAndrews?"

As the other nodded agreement, their waitress winked at them and left.

"So who is this client of yours?" Granville asked, pitching his voice so McAndrews, and only McAndrews, could hear him under the raucous noise of a popular cafe.

"You educated on mortgage fraud now?"

He grinned, drank some of his coffee. "I am indeed. Interesting system you colonials have going."

"I'll have you know I'm an American."

Granville gave him a skeptical look, and McAndrews laughed. "Don't be deceived by the Scottish accent," he said. "I took ship to Boston first, then settled in Chicago for a few years. When the Klondike madness hit, I came this far north, and decided my talents were best served here."

That was a surprise. Granville put his cup down. "Ever have dealings with Scott when you were in Chicago?"

"Your partner? No, I can't say that I did. It's a big town."

Of course it was. But he'd check it out with Scott all the same. "And your client?"

"Fellow named Sinclair."

"And you said that this Sinclair knew Weston?" Granville asked, then sat back a bit as their breakfasts were delivered. Bacon, eggs and toast, with hash browns fried in the bacon fat on the side. His mouth watered at the smell, and he picked up his fork. "Dig in."

McAndrews didn't need to be asked twice. "According to him," he said, forking up a mound of scrambled eggs and shaking hot sauce on it, "He's the one who told Weston about his brothers drowning last January. It's why he came to me when he realized he was in trouble—he knew Weston and I were friends. Apparently he decided he could trust me. He's pretty suspicious at the moment. Doesn't trust many people."

"And for good reason, if his story is true," Granville said. "So what role does this not-quite-client play for Vancouver Permanent?"

"He sells mortgages. Spends a lot of time finding potential buyers who are looking for mortgage money."

Granville watched McAndrews shake more hot sauce on his toast before eating it. "I've never known a Scot to eat toast with hot sauce."

McAndrews laughed. "Told you I was an American."

Granville shook his head. When you had toast with bacon, who needed anything else? "But surely finding buyers with money can't be easy for an expatriate Englishman in this city?"

"I thought it odd too. But it seems he's good at it."

"So why are the police questioning him?"

"The police seem to be accusing him of selling mortgages in bad faith. Apparently a number of his clients have complained." McAndrews said.

"And how true is that?"

"He's heard nothing but praise from any of his former clients. And the police won't give him names."

"What do you think? Any truth in the accusations?"

"I spoke with several of his former clients—he gave me a list of everyone he's dealt with, and I chose names at random. All were very pleased with the deal Sinclair made for them." McAndrews shrugged. "That's when I realized the case was too big for me, and decided to ask if you'd take him on. There's more going on than the fraud Sinclair is being accused of."

"Why does Sinclair think he's being set up?

"Sinclair is personable and a good listener, and his colleagues have talked more openly than perhaps they meant to," McAndrews said. "He says what he's doing is exactly the same as what all of them are doing. He isn't sure exactly how Vancouver Permanent is set up, but he does know they're financed through an investment syndicate. And he suspects he's being framed to cover up the fact that they're in trouble."

"How bad is it?"

"I don't know how big it might be, or how far it stretches. Bad enough that they needed a scapegoat, anyway. Sinclair is expecting to be arrested any day. If he's telling the truth—and I believe him—someone's deflecting blame on him to cover up what they themselves are doing."

McAndrews drank some coffee, met Granville's eyes. "In my opinion? It could be bad. Major fraud charges bad. The kind with long jail terms."

Granville let out a low whistle. "And your client expects it to come back on him? How likely is it that he'll be arrested, in your estimation?"

"It depends how good their paperwork is. And how crooked they are. If they're slick enough, or connected enough, they could frame just about anyone."

Granville nodded slowly. "I'll need to speak with your client, and soon."

"Of course. But you haven't changed your mind about taking the case?"

"No. But I'm out of my depth on this one. Financial fraud is hardly my area of expertise." He emptied his coffee cup, then gave McAndrews a considering glance.

"What? I didn't have anything to do with it."

That got the grin it was meant to. "Hardly. No, this client of yours…" Granville said.

"Sinclair. Walter Sinclair."

"Sinclair then. You said he was just a prospective client?"

A nod. "Since I'm only running my accounting business on the side for the moment, my time is rather limited," McAndrews said. "This case needs someone who can work it full time. And I suspect Sinclair needs your expertise more than he needs mine."

"So you won't be taking him on as a client?"

"Well—quite frankly, I don't think he can afford both of us."

Granville nodded. "I don't suppose you'd be interested in a part-time contract with us? To provide the expertise I lack on this particular case?"

McAndrews thumped his empty cup on the table and his eyes gleamed. "You want me to work with you to investigate Vancouver Permanent?"

"If we can come to terms,"—and as long as Scott didn't know anything against McAndrews, now that they knew he was from Chicago—"Yes. We need to find out what's really going on there. And I suspect that the numbers will hold the answers that we need. Answers I can't read."

"I'll do it." McAndrews paused, gave him a considering look. "What are the terms?"

Granville grinned and told him. "I think you'll find them fair."

McAndrews beamed at him. "I'll say. Do you need permanent help?"

"I'm afraid not. We may need an accountant from time to time, but the pay wouldn't be as good, since in this case you brought in the client."

"I might consider it anyway. Or bring you more clients."

"Do that. And why don't you set up a meeting for both of us with Sinclair? If he's as legitimate as you say, we'll sign a contract."

"Is tomorrow afternoon too soon? Around four?"

"No, not at all. I'll let Scott know. And then I'm planning to visit Vancouver Permanent. Since I'm in the market for a house these days, they're at the top of my list of firms to visit."

McAndrews stared at him. "You're not serious?"

"Absolutely. They offered such an amazing deal on housing prices…"

"I'll just bet they did," McAndrews muttered. "And I think I'm wasting your time."

Granville laughed. "If you could see your own expression. My apologies. I couldn't resist," he said.

"You mean you're not talking to them about purchasing a house?" McAndrews asked.

"Well, I will be buying a house. And I have every intention of talking to them about it."

McAndrews shook his head. "I don't understand."

"I just have no intention of dealing with them," Granville said with a grin. "You told me two months ago that Vancouver Permanent's finances were questionable. I later talked with their General Manager, Charles Putnam, about the firm. And nothing I heard from him made contradicted what you'd said. Besides, I didn't like the fellow."

McAndrews looked as if he couldn't believe what he was hearing.

"I need to understand more about the local housing market before I sink a good chunk of my future into it. I'm no accountant," Granville reminded the younger man.

"That much is obvious," McAndrews said with a low groan. "Why are you even talking to Vancouver Permanent?"

"Because sometimes the crooks are the ones who understand the system the best. They have to understand it in order to subvert it."

Now McAndrews was simply staring at him. "That makes an odd kind of sense," he said.

"Nothing odd about it," Granville said with a grin. He dropped a couple of dollars on the table to cover their bill, then rose and reached out a hand. "Just ask Scott. It's why he and I are investigators and you're an accountant. Different thought processes."

"I'm beginning to understand that," McAndrews said with a grin. "Once I've talked to my client, I'll call you with the meeting place."

"Fair enough. And if you're asking questions about Vancouver Permanent, be careful."

"Don't worry," McAndrews said, reaching for his hand and pumping it. "Accountants don't take chances."

4

On his short walk to the office, Granville ignored the usual foot and vehicular traffic that jammed the streets at this time of day. Other than putting up his collar against the cool wind and noting that the rain was holding off, he didn't pay any attention to the overcast day, either.

His thoughts were focused on the new case, and the telegram he'd received from the Pinkerton's Agency yesterday. And the fact that he'd still not talked to Scott about either decision. Which wasn't like him.

Was he moving forward too quickly, even for himself?

Climbing the stairs two at a time, Granville flung open the door and dropped his black umbrella in the stand beside the door. He nodded to Trent, who sat at his desk almost hidden behind a stack of paper. The boy still looked annoyed.

Chuckling, Granville strolled into the office he shared with Scott. "Morning, Scott," he said to his partner, who was standing staring out of the window into the busy street below.

"I've been meaning to tell you," Granville said as he sat down. "I think we have a new client. We'll be meeting with him this afternoon to discuss his contract."

Scott turned to face him, his grin wide and white against the thick dark beard. "Oh? You only think we have a client? And have I heard of him?"

"No, this is someone new. A fraud case, fellow named Sinclair. McAndrews came to us with the case the day before yesterday."

"Yeah, I remember you sayin' something about it. But I thought it was McAndrews' client?"

"He's passed him to us."

"We've taken on a fraud case?" Scott snorted and sat down across from Granville. "I hope you're planning to be the one spending your time poring over ledgers, 'cause someone's going to have to."

"McAndrews will be doing that. I've asked him to work for us on this one. But only if…"

"Only if what?" Scott tilted his chair back and glowered at him from under thick brows. "First you take on a case without telling me, now you've started hiring people too?"

The glower wasn't real, but Scott wasn't entirely joking, either. "Only if you agree. And it would only be a temporary contract, if that helps."

"Some. And why wouldn't I agree?"

"Turns out the man's an American."

"Accent says he's a Scot."

"Apparently he spent some time in Chicago, became a citizen. You ever run into him there?"

"Nah. He's still wet behind the ears. My lot would've chewed him up."

"Then I think we should hire him for this case."

"Can we afford him?"

Granville thought of cases they'd successfully closed, balanced them against the expansion he seemed to be planning. Hoped the instincts that had served him so well at the poker tables worked in business. "Yes."

"Fine by me, but why McAndrews?"

"I was impressed by his loyalty to his friend on our last case.

And his ability to read people. This seemed a good opportunity to see what he's made of. Especially since I'm about as fond of ledgers as you are."

"And decidedly worse at reading them," Scott said.

Before he could say anything further, there was a commotion in the outer office, and Granville heard two female voices. One was Emily's, but the other didn't sound like her friend Clara. Who...?

Then he realized who it had to be, and knew he was in trouble. "Uh, Scott?" he began.

Scott gave him a wry look just as the door opened and Emily burst in. Miss Kent—a fragile blonde whose determined work ethic belied her looks—was right behind her, with Trent following noisily behind them.

"Not another new employee?" Scott said.

"Granville, I've brought Laura in, and we need to talk to you," Emily said.

"First they rearrange all my work, and now I'm being kicked out of the office?" Trent said at the same time.

Granville dropped his head in his hands.

"So, what are you planning next?" Scott asked. "You want to take over another company or something?"

This was clearly not the time to bring up his telegram from the Pinkerton's Agency.

EMILY STRUGGLED to keep her expression bland as she looked from Granville to Scott, and back again. There was a tone in Scott's voice that she hadn't heard before, at least not when he was talking to his friend and partner. Surely there wasn't trouble between the two of them?

She watched as Granville calmed everyone down. He explained the new office structure, and ushered Laura and Trent into the outer office to sort out between them who would do what. Then he looked from her to Scott and rolled his eyes.

Scott laughed, but it wasn't his usual hearty bellow, and Granville seemed a little on edge. What was going on? She'd never sensed this tension between them before. They were a team, and she'd seen them back each other up without question any number of times.

"Granville?" she said. "Do you want me to go and join Laura and Trent? They could probably use my help."

Lounging back in his chair, he looked like the lion she'd seen once when her father took her to see the famous Zoo in Chicago—deceptively lazy, but powerful. He looked to where she sat by the door. "You came in wanting to talk to me?"

"I'll get some coffee," Scott said, grabbing his oversized coffee cup and starting to rise.

"No, please," she said, waving him down.

Scott collapsed back into his chair.

"I can tell we interrupted something. I'll go. You need to finish —whatever it is you were talking about."

Her words ran together a bit at the end. It felt as if they were at odds with each other, and it made her nervous. She was afraid of saying the wrong thing.

Granville looked at her, then at Scott. Then he started to laugh.

Scott scowled at him for a moment, then his eyes crinkled up and he let out a guffaw.

Emily frowned at both of them. "What did I say that was so funny?" she asked.

The two men just laughed harder.

Emily considered stalking out, but she wasn't entirely sure they were laughing at her. And she wanted to know what was wrong between them.

"Exactly how big is this team of ours now?" Scott gasped out after a ridiculously long time.

"Big enough to dig from one end of Rabbit Creek to the other," Granville said. Which set them both off again.

Team? Were they talking about Laura? Emily wondered. And did Scott know that she would be working here too? She'd assumed

Granville had talked it all over with Scott first, but maybe he hadn't?

That would explain a lot. And she really didn't want to say the wrong thing now. Finally Emily stood up. "I'm going now," she said. "I'll be out there when you're ready to talk."

"No, wait," Granville said, standing up and walking around the edge of his desk to take her hand. "I'm sorry, Emily. Scott and I need to talk about the business, and I'd like you to be part of the conversation."

He squeezed her hand lightly, then released it and turned to face Scott.

"There's been too much to do and too little time since we got back to town last Friday. A month is a long time to be away. We haven't had a chance to catch up with ourselves, much less plan."

"Plan? We plan?" Scott said.

Granville gave him a wry smile. "Things are changing for us. You know Emily and I have set the date for our wedding. And that we're looking for a house, right?"

They were?

Emily sat down hard, trying to keep her breathing even. It was a shock.

She'd known they'd be looking eventually, but Mama had barely started her planning for the wedding. She was still trying to ignore Mama when she asked what Emily thought about menus and place settings. Granville buying a house was going to make it hard to do so for much longer.

"Yeah, I can see where I'd need to help you plan for that," Scott was saying with a grin.

"And I heard back from Pinkerton's. They're interested in discussing an affiliate relationship with us."

There it was. Emily listened intently, watching their expressions carefully, and trying very hard not to draw attention to herself.

Scott's chair thumped back to the floor and he sat up straight. "What?"

"And Trent is really unhappy with the way the office was run while we were gone."

Scott waved that off. "Ah, he just likes to complain. She did a pretty good job from what I've seen."

"Exactly. The work done by Emily's friend Miss Kent shows exactly the level of professionalism that we will need in the future as our agency grows. And especially if we hope to work with Pinkerton's."

"You're serious about our firm growing?" Scott said.

Granville couldn't read his voice, but he knew it wasn't relaxed. He nodded. "I think so. We're becoming known, and staying the same size will mean turning down requests."

"What's wrong with that?" Scott said.

"Nothing, but it will take someone's time, even to turn people down."

Scott grunted.

"I've learned a little about what happens when small firms need to grow," Emily said. "And it can take more work to stay small than to grow. But it takes resources up front—including more staff—for a firm to grow successfully."

Scott frowned. "So either answer can be wrong?"

Emily felt bad for him. "Yes."

He looked at Granville. "You're serious about growing this team?"

Granville nodded. "I think you and I are the core. And Trent has proven himself as our assistant. It's time to let him out of the office."

Scott let his breath out in a long sigh. "Guess I agree with that. Especially if I try to find something in those files of his."

"I believe Miss Kent is available to work for us for the next six months," Granville said, looking to Emily for confirmation.

"Yes. And perhaps longer," she said.

"So that takes care of the office," Granville said. "But—and this is the difficult part—I'd also like to hire Emily to work with us for the same six months," and he glanced over at her before continuing.

Emily held her breath.

"She would do the same kind of investigating she's already been doing," Granville said. "And she'd take any photographs we need taken. But it isn't my decision alone. We're partners."

"And Emily," he said, turning to meet her eyes. "I'm sorry. I should have talked to Scott before I said anything to you. Scott?"

Scott looked from Granville to Emily and back. He was silent long enough that Emily began to be afraid of what she was going to hear. She couldn't read his expression, either.

"Well, listening to all this—I do have one concern," Scott said at last. He scowled at Granville. "What are you thinking, proposing we hire McAndrews? Not only is he a gambler, he accused you of cheating. And tried to kill you the first time we met him."

Emily felt a wave of relief wash through her. He wasn't concerned about working with her. She'd be able to work here, with them, as part of the team.

That was what he meant, wasn't it? And when had Granville hired McAndrews, anyway?

She glanced at Granville, who was laughing too hard to notice, then back at Scott, who wasn't much better.

She tried for a glare, but it was hopeless—their laughter was infectious. Emily started to giggle.

5

The sun was just beginning its descent as Granville and Scott made their way across the broken boards of the abandoned pier. They still had a couple of hours before twilight, if he was judging it right. The breeze was cold and fresh and smelled of the sea, with a faint hint of smoke and creosote and an underlying reek of mud and river weeds and decay.

In the distance he could hear the rhythmic thump of a steam-driven pile driver, punctuated by the hissing scream of the over-worked engine. Across the railway lines, a few weathered wooden boarding houses sagged, their tin roofs bowed and rusty. A seagull glided overhead, pure white but for the bright yellow feet, a peaceful sight with its raucous cry drowned by the engine.

Two men were walking towards them from the far end of the pier.

Recognizing McAndrews as one of them, he raised a hand in greeting. As they grew nearer, Granville examined the other fellow, who was carefully picking his way beside McAndrews.

The long narrow face and floppy, pale hair said he was English, the thin nose and finely shaped mouth said there was good blood there, somewhere. He was well-dressed, nothing flashy about his dark woolen suit and conservative Homburg. He had long narrow feet, too, Granville saw, and the leather of his shoes was too fine for these surroundings.

"What are we doing out here?" Granville asked McAndrews as soon as they were close enough to hear him over the pile driver. "We're going to have a hard time hearing each other even if we shout."

"There's no-one else to hear us. Which is rather the point," said the long-faced man, stepping forward with his hand held out. "I'm Sinclair, Walter Sinclair, as you must have guessed. And I'm the one suggested this lovely location."

His accent was as English as his voice, Granville thought as they shook hands. He could hear the fellow's middle-class accent under the polish that a good education had given him. So McAndrews had been at least partially right about their new client's accent. "John Granville. Pleased to meet you. And this is my partner, Sam Scott."

"McAndrews here says you two can help me," Sinclair said as he shook Scott's hand.

"I'd like to try, but we'll need to know a little more about your situation. First, how did you know Rupert Weston?"

Sinclair gave a quick nod. "We worked together briefly in England, reconnected on a casual basis when we both ended up here. Shall we walk?" he asked, setting off the way they'd come without waiting for an answer.

Granville looked at Scott and then McAndrews. Both men shrugged. The three of them lengthened their strides. Their sturdier boots made it easy for them to catch up.

Scott and Granville exchanged glances when Sinclair led them along a narrow, rickety walkway that connected with a second pier, even more decrepit than the first. Granville put a hand to his knife. Narrowing his eyes against the setting sun, he watched for any hint of movement.

The place seemed deserted. He hadn't seen even a hint of

anyone else here since they'd arrived. Scott was equally alert. A half-shake of his head said his partner hadn't seen anyone, either.

By this point Sinclair had reached the bank. He turned to walk along what must once have been a boardwalk. It was now a collection of warped and twisted boards that barely held together over the wet mud of the shore.

The four of them walked along the river away from the building site. "What is this place?" Granville asked McAndrews.

"Failed cannery. They're building a new one behind us."

That made sense. Canadian salmon sandwiches were a staple for Sunday teas in England, and he'd been shocked to find that more than half of that market was produced in and around Vancouver. "And why are we meeting here? There are plenty of deserted areas that don't involve long streetcar rides into the middle of nowhere."

McAndrews laughed. "Wait a minute. I'm the accountant. I'm supposed to be the one who doesn't like to go anywhere. You're the fearless detective, remember? Adventure is your middle name, and all that?"

"Don't forget that I'm your employer now."

"Part-time only. It's an easy thing to change."

Before Granville could respond, Sinclair finally stopped, and turned to face them.

GRANVILLE GLANCED AROUND. The area was flat, with no trees and little greenery in sight. Beyond the black mud ran a wide river, flat and muddy. Low, greenish brown banks marked the far side. The wind was cold and smelled of mud and the ocean. He shivered, turned up his collar and tightened his scarf.

"We should be safe enough here," Sinclair said. "And we can actually hear ourselves."

"Who are you afraid of?" Scott asked.

"I don't trust my employers. And I don't know all their connections. I'd rather word of our meeting not get back to Vancouver Permanent. At least not while I'm still employed there. This was the only place I could think of where I'd never run into anyone I know."

Granville glanced around him. "Well, I'd have to agree that you've chosen well, if that's your objective. You're sure you couldn't think of somewhere equally rundown that had four walls and a bar?"

Sinclair flashed a grin that made him instantly likable. Suddenly Granville believed what McAndrews had been telling him about Sinclair being Vancouver Permanent's top salesman.

"I gather you have questions for me?" Sinclair said.

"I do," Granville said. "Exactly what is happening with Vancouver Permanent? And what is it you want me to do about it?"

"I'm not sure what's going on," Sinclair said. "Only that I've been brought in by the police for questioning. Twice now. The nature of their questions suggests it's fraud they're looking at. But that, plus a few rumors I've picked up at the Permanent—that's all I know. And it's making me paranoid. I want to hire you to find out what's really going on. And to help me clear my name if my suspicions prove correct."

Which was succinct, exactly what McAndrews had said, and no help at all.

Granville brought out his notebook, wishing for a moment that he'd worn lined gloves. "Why don't we start with when you were hired, and why."

"I was hired in September of last year, to sell mortgages to men who wanted to buy land before it grew too dear. They told me I was perfect because I was English, and most of the backers—the people putting up the money for the firm, you see—are English too."

Granville wondered again if his own brother, the current Baron Granville, might be one of those backers. It would be interesting to find out. William would like nothing better than profiting from a real estate boom and taking money from desperate colonials. And he'd be none too concerned about legalities, either.

After the ugly case William had last involved him in, it wouldn't bother Granville at all if William lost money. A great deal of it. "So you deal with these backers as well?"

"No. No, I just make sales, mostly to Americans, actually, or sometimes Canadians moving west to set up new businesses or satellite offices."

"And do you know any of the backers personally?" Scott asked.

Sinclair shrugged. "I don't even know who the backers are."

"You've never seen a list of them?"

"No."

"What about the annual report?"

"It's two pages long. And it doesn't list them."

"And none of the backers are on the board of directors?" McAndrews asked.

"I have no way of knowing that," Sinclair said.

"So you have no interactions with them at all?"

"None."

"Then why should it matter that you're English?"

Sinclair looked thoughtful. "I was told that the backers were more comfortable knowing the educational backgrounds of those who worked for the firm. And especially for those negotiating with the mortgagors. But that doesn't make a lot of sense, does it?"

"There are certain fields where it matters very much," Granville said. "And certainly in England your connections and education matter. But out here? In your position? I would doubt it. But then I'm no expert. McAndrews?"

"I'm not an expert in this area, either. But where I've done audits for syndicates, the backers care about the bottom line, and that the numbers on the books match the bottom line." He glanced at Sinclair's worried face. "They leave hiring choices up to the General Manager. And sometimes the board, if there is one."

"No, not in this case," Sinclair said. "It's just the General

Manager who does the hiring. Fellow by the name of Charles Putnam."

Putnam was the fellow he'd met and disliked in April. "And Putnam is the one who hired you?" Granville asked.

"Yes."

"Anyone else interview you?"

"Just Putnam."

Interesting. "And do you report to Putnam?"

"To Putnam? No, no. He's the President and General Manager. I'm a lowly salesman. I report to the Sales Director. Tony Williams."

Granville made a note. They needed to know more about Williams.

"So when did you start suspecting something was wrong?" Scott asked Sinclair.

"Around the time the real estate market softened. Property sales fell off for a time last fall. And there were too many mortgage brokers trying to sell to too few buyers."

"What happened then?" Granville asked.

"First they cut the down payment by almost half. Then they began cutting the interest payments for the first year of the mortgage. I've never worked in a mortgage company before, but even I could see that it couldn't be sustainable."

"And did you talk to anyone?"

"I asked Williams about it and didn't get an answer that made sense to me. I finally went to Putnam himself about it. He was very nice about it, explained that the backers have very deep pockets, and they were long term investors. Everyone expects there to be downturns in real estate."

Granville glanced at McAndrews, who nodded.

"It's a logical argument, but it would be an unusual investment group who would think that way," McAndrews said. "Especially in a colonial boom and bust economy."

Granville turned back to Sinclair. "So when did you start doubting Putnam's explanation?"

"When the market started to take off. They cut the interest rates again. This time the explanation was that high prices were keeping buyers on the sidelines. But when they extended those low rates this summer, then I was sure. Still, the money keeps flowing, and the rates aren't getting any higher. So maybe I'm wrong."

"No, I would say you're probably right," McAndrews said. "Money has to come from somewhere, and presumably they're still paying the investors some kind of interest. So have they cut that too? And if not, where is the money coming from? It almost has to be some kind of fraud."

"Exactly. That's exactly how I was seeing it."

It was clouding over, but despite the poor light Granville could see Sinclair's face tighten with excitement. He could also see that the fellow was young, not long out of university. Perhaps only five or six years younger than himself, but at that age, five years was a long time. And Sinclair was a long way out of his element.

"You suspect that if they're caught, they mean to pin it on you."

Sinclair paled. "Yes. Especially after the police pulled me in, asked those very pointed questions. You'll think me foolish, but to that point, I hadn't connected my suspicions to any threat to myself." He paused, and leaned over to wipe off a patch of mud on his shoes.

And maybe to hide his expression, Granville thought.

"Now I have. There's something wrong with the way I'm being treated. They're too nice, too complimentary, especially Williams, and even Putnam himself. And they're watching every move I make. I have to fill out more forms than ever, but no-one ever signs them. No-one but me."

"You're supposed to have a counter-signature?" McAndrews asked, leaning forward.

"Yes."

"But you don't."

He shook his head. "No. They told me just to put the forms in the clerk's in tray, and they'd be signed. But I checked, one night when no-one was around. The five files I looked up, the most recent ones I'd worked on? Not one of them had a counter-signature."

"Does your Sales Director initial them?" Granville asked.

Sinclair shook his head. "He doesn't even see them."

McAndrews looked at Granville. "He's right. It sounds like a good setup for fraud."

"But how do we prove it? Before they arrest me?" Sinclair said.

He looked from Granville to Scott. "That's why I need your help. McAndrews here says you're willing to help. Will you still take my case?"

———

GRANVILLE AND SCOTT had taken the five o'clock stagecoach back from Steveston, rattling over planked roads and a bridge that looked as if it was held together with wishes. The friendly driver let them off several blocks before their office. Granville had found their excursion intriguing, but it struck him as ironic to see electric lights all up and down Hastings Street, when there was no railway or electric trolley out to the Steveston, which was the heart of the fishing industry. Apparently it was a question of taxes.

He and Scott hadn't talked at all on the trip. Too hard to hear each other over the noise of the stage, and too many ears listening in. Now they were sitting near the fireplace in the King's Arms pub —which made Granville laugh, since Queen Victoria had been on the throne since long before this place was established.

After the damp chill by the water, the fire was welcome, and provided a nice contrast to the cold ale. He'd come to appreciate cold beer in the Yukon, which still shocked that part of him loyal to the memory of his favorite pubs in England, and their room temperature beers.

Granville stretched his feet to the fire and lifted his tankard to his lips, draining off the top few inches of the excellent—and nicely chilled—dark ale.

"So how're you planning on going about sorting out this one?"

Scott said after a bit.

His partner looked—perturbed, Granville thought. Something wasn't sitting right with him, and Granville suspected it was the potential changes to their firm. "Before we talk strategy, what's your take on McAndrews?" he said.

Scott took a deep drink of his ale, thumping the half-empty mug down on the table with a sigh. "Now that's what I call a good beer."

"McAndrews?"

"Uh huh." He picked up the mug again, eyeing Granville as he did so.

"Stop trying to make me suffer and just tell me what you think."

Scott gave him an injured look, which turned into a broad grin. "I like him. And he seems to know his stuff. If he's as good as you say he is on the accounting side, maybe we should just hire him. Part-time, I mean. He could be responsible for our books, 'stead of me having to do it."

Granville smiled back, not sure if Scott was joking. His partner was holding back about something. "That could work. Though we'd need more cases if we want to pay that many salaries on a regular basis."

"Yeah, I figured we'd be gettin' back to that. How serious are these Pinkerton's fellas?"

"Pretty serious from what I can tell. They want to send someone senior out in early August to meet with us."

"Whoa. They're moving pretty quickly, aren't they?"

"They've already got Canadian connections in Toronto and Ottawa, but they've no-one out West. The closest is their office in Seattle."

"Which is where we come in?"

Granville nodded. "Yes. I suspect the fact that William Pinkerton's, Jr., is friends with my sister Louisa and her husband helps, too."

"I'm guessing he doesn't know your brother, the current Baron, though. Or he wouldn't be so interested." Scott grinned again, drained his mug and signaled for another round. Then he turned to face Granville. "You're serious about this business, aren't you?"

"Yes, of course. Why, aren't you?"

"I like it. It's interesting. It's always challenging. And we work well together."

"But...?"

Scott shrugged. "But if you started another business tomorrow, I'd be just as happy working on that one."

Granville felt a little stunned. "You'd change businesses, just like that? Regardless of what the business was?"

Scott slapped him on the back. "Six months ago we were guarding silk trains. Six months before that, we were trying to dig gold out of frozen streams. Six months from now...?"

He shrugged, hefted the fresh pint that had just been slapped in front of him. "Who knows? Cheers."

He was right, at that. Granville grinned at the irony, lifted his own pint. Drank. "So you don't mind if I take a run at building this career into something?"

"Oh, we're talking career now? Aren't we fancy?"

"You know what I mean."

"No. I don't," Scott said. "That's the point. I need money to live, and I hate to be bored. That's about it."

"So what you're telling me is..."

Scott drained his ale, thunked the empty glass on the table. "We're partners, but you're the one with the vision for this firm. And I'm the one's got your back."

"So what's different?" Granville said, watching his partner's expression closely.

"Nothing at all," Scott said. His eyes said something different. "So, about that strategy?"

This conversation wasn't done with, Granville thought. But he'd accept the change of subject. For now.

"First off, I have a confession. I may have an ulterior motive in taking on this case."

Scott tried to look shocked, but couldn't manage it. "Then let's hear it."

"It's time I started looking for a house for Emily," Granville said bluntly. "And if the local real estate market is as crazy as it sounds, the better I understand it, the better the deal I'll be able to make."

Scott raised his beer in a toast. "That's the first sense I've heard you make all day. Here's to you and Emily. Especially Emily."

Granville raised his own mug. They finished their pints, and Scott signaled for another round, which was quickly delivered.

"I still need to hear your strategy for this case, though," Scott said, raising his fresh pint. "Cheers."

"Tomorrow I'm planning to see if Tim O'Hearn can get me into the Terminal City Club," Granville said. "The promise of a story would likely be enough to tempt him. And if you have time between other cases, can you and Trent see what you can learn about Tony Williams?"

"The Sales Director? Seems a good place to start."

"And while you're at it, can you see what you can find out about Sinclair, also?"

"We're going to investigate our client? That's a first."

"I suspect it won't be a last," Granville said with a wry smile. "And in this case, what you learn may well be what keeps our client out of jail."

Scott grinned. "You know I'm in favor of that."

"Thought you might be," Granville said, covering his relief with a light tone. "And I'm serious, here. If Sinclair is being framed, anything you learn that speaks to his character might be of help."

"Not that the police will listen to us."

"No, but they might listen to Sinclair's lawyer."

"Randall? You think he'll take him on?"

Granville hid a smile. Joshua Randall was the best lawyer he'd ever met, and the most devious. And he could never resist a hard luck case. "Oh, I think so."

Scott drained his second mug. "I could use a good steak. You?"

Granville nodded and finished his own ale. "Garrity's?"

"Lead the way."

6

WEDNESDAY, JUNE 13, 1900

It was after four the following afternoon by the time Granville caught up with O'Hearn at the *Daily World* offices. The newsroom was bustling, with voices layered over each other—cheerful, demanding, tense. The air was blue with cigarette smoke, and sharp with the reek of printer's ink. It always amazed Granville that he could just walk right in without challenge.

His eyes scanned the room, looking for that distinctive red hair. Tim O'Hearn was at his desk, arguing with another reporter, judging by the stabbing motions of his pencil as he emphasized a point. Making his way between the desks, Granville amused himself by guessing how long it would take the usually alert reporter to notice him.

It took less than a minute. Part-way through what seemed a particularly strong argument, O'Hearn's gaze focused on him, sharpened. "Granville," he said, and excused himself to his colleague, hurrying over. "What's up?"

"I'm working a complex case and I need your help."

"You have it," O'Hearn said without hesitation. "Any chance there's a story in it somewhere?" he added with a sideways grin.

"Possibly."

"Same terms as before?"

Granville nodded. "You keep it quiet until my case is completed, then any story is exclusively yours. In the meantime, I'll buy you a drink if you're free."

"I'll get my coat."

As they exited onto Homer Street, O'Hearn buttoned his coat against the brisk wind.

"I'd swear that wind comes straight off those mountains," he said, nodding at the steep mountains across the inlet, their peaks still capped with snow. "How is it there are rhododendrons blooming, and I'm freezing?"

Granville laughed. "At least it isn't raining today. Isn't that what you Vancouverites say? Even I know that, and I've only been here a few months."

"Are you saying we're predictable?" Then, with no change in tone, "Where are we going, anyway?" O'Hearn asked as he noticed the direction they were walking. "You have a sudden need to visit the docks?"

"And that's part of the favor. We're headed for the Terminal City Club. I understand you're a member?"

The young reporter groaned dramatically. "Yes, which means everything will end up on my tab. Don't order anything too expensive, Okay?"

"Don't worry, I'll make it up to you."

"I'll make sure of it. Why do you want to go there, anyway? It doesn't seem your kind of atmosphere."

"Perhaps not, but I need to talk to some people. I need to know more about local real estate firms, and particularly an outfit called Vancouver Permanent Investment & Loan."

"Vancouver Permanent?" O'Hearn said in a thoughtful tone. "I know that name from somewhere, but I can't think where. It'll come to me, though. It wasn't a major story, whatever it was."

He was silent for a moment, their footsteps echoing in unison off the board sidewalks. The rattle of a carriage too close behind them had both of them stepping to one side to avoid the spray of water cast by iron-rimmed wheels. It had rained the night before.

"I know a little about some of the mortgage companies, though financial doings aren't my usual beat," O'Hearn added, then hesitated. "I can probably put you in touch with someone, if you'd like?"

It was a generous offer from someone who made his living from being the first with a good story. Granville appreciated the offer, but hoped he wouldn't have to accept it. "Let's see how today goes."

O'Hearn nodded. "And how is Miss Turner?"

"She is well, thank you."

"Not working on this case with you?"

"Not so far. Though I suspect she and Miss Miles will be involved in some way before this is over."

"Ah. I had heard they were traveling, and I haven't seen either lady in some time."

He tossed him a smile. "Brace yourself. The two of them seem to have a habit of calling on you when they need to find out something."

O'Hearn grinned a little. "Yeah. I noticed."

He didn't look like he minded much, though.

***

When they reached the Terminal City Club, Granville was surprised by how familiar it felt. The club was located in an unremarkable office building, but had clearly modeled itself on a traditional English club. Though the stuffed moose-heads in the hallway were a unique touch.

The reception room was heavily paneled and expensively furnished, if deserted. O'Hearn took them first to the reading room. Granville noted it was well-stocked with the latest magazines, but it was also deserted, except for an old codger snoozing over his paper and brandy. Perhaps they'd have to come back later in the evening to find anyone worth talking to.

"This way," O'Hearn said in an undertone. "It's early, so the bar is the only place we're likely to find anyone worth talking to."

The bar was fairly crowded, with prosperous-looking men talking in groups of three or four around small tables. Whiskey and water seemed to be the preferred drink, and the cluster of empty glasses said they'd been here for a while, despite the early hour.

O'Hearn must have sensed his surprise, for he said, "It's an excellent place for business meetings. Many a contract has been signed in the bar at Terminal City."

He sounded like a salesman, which was probably his intent, Granville thought appreciatively. It created a perfect reason for introducing Granville around. Assuming O'Hearn knew any of the other men, that is.

He needn't have doubted him. O'Hearn exchanged smiles and nods with all of the patrons before waving him to a vacant table that was conveniently near the bar. Raising a hand to the nattily aproned bartender, he held up two fingers before turning back to Granville. "Wait until you taste their India Pale Ale," he said. "It's a local brew, and I swear it's better than anything imported from England."

And probably cheaper than whiskey, Granville thought cynically. Until he took a drink of the frothy deep golden brew placed in front of him. O'Hearn was right. It was the best ale he'd ever tasted.

He said so, and O'Hearn grinned. "Yeah," he said, drinking deeply, a look of satisfaction on his face. "Worth joining the club just for this."

Again he was playing to their audience. Granville could do no less. He raised his glass in a toast. "Well, perhaps not just for this."

He drank deeply, grinned. "Tell me about your membership, and who I might expect to meet here. For instance, I met with a fellow named Putnam last month to talk about the local real estate market. Charles Putnam—is he a member?"

"Putnam? I don't believe I know the name." He waved a casual hand. "I'll ask around."

Granville nodded his thanks and drank another mouthful of that amazingly satisfying beer. As he put the half-full glass back on the table, a hand appeared on O'Hearn's shoulder.

"Potential new member is it, O'Hearn?" a jovial voice asked. "Sorry, couldn't help overhearing, and thought I'd see if I could help you make a good impression."

O'Hearn swiveled in his chair and met a broad grin half-obscured by a luxuriant mustache. "Draper! I didn't see you earlier."

"Where else would I be?"

"I didn't know you were back in town."

"Got back yesterday. Going to introduce us?"

"Of course. John Granville, this is Andrew Draper. He's a fellow reporter, with the *News-Advertiser,* for his sins. He's their business reporter. And Granville here is an investigator."

"Pleased to meet you," Draper said. "Are you with Pinkerton's outfit?"

"Not yet."

"Hmmm. Interesting answer. Any chance that's on the record?"

"Again, not yet. But I'll be happy to give you the story if there is one."

Draper nodded. "Good. I hope you do decide to join us, despite this scalawag's lack of salesmanship. And I can tell you that Putnam is a member. As are most of the real estate chaps in town."

Draper glanced around the room. "I haven't seen Putnam today, but one of his colleagues is here. I can introduce you, if you'd like. Are you thinking about buying property here?"

Shrewd eyes assessed him. Granville was willing to bet the man was a top-notch reporter—his insouciance hid a sharp mind. He wondered if this was the reporter O'Hearn had offered to introduce him to, and glanced over O'Hearn, who shot him a rueful look.

"I'm considering it," he said.

"Then you should meet Marshall," Draper said. "I'll just fetch him."

Before he knew it, Granville was surrounded by five jovial,

dark-suited businessmen. Glasses in hand, they pulled up chairs and introduced themselves.

He was pleased to meet two real estate brokers, an investor and a banker. All very knowledgeable about investing in Vancouver properties and businesses. All very pleased to meet him. Clearly Emily had been right when she'd suggested he join this club a few months ago.

He signaled for another round of drinks and sat back to learn what he could.

It took several more rounds before Granville could pry himself away, and then only by promising to submit his application for membership. He had a handful of business cards, several offers to support him for membership and an appointment to discuss real estate opportunities with Marshall.

***

THE SUN WAS ALREADY GOING DOWN and the shadows lengthening as Granville and O'Hearn strolled back towards Homer. "So how do I go about joining Terminal City?" he asked O'Hearn.

"You were serious? You really want to join? Isn't it a bit of a comedown after gentlemen's clubs you must have belonged to in London?" O'Hearn sounded stunned.

The young reporter had a romantic notion of gentlemen's clubs, Granville thought with an inward grin. The energy and camaraderie of the Terminal City Club suited him far better than the refined but subdued elegance and comfort of his father's clubs.

Besides, it was good business. He hadn't realized how important it could be to his new profession, though he should have. Bless Emily for her prescience.

"I need the contacts," he said. "And not just for this case. I'm also going to join the Vancouver Club. I'm sure Emily's father will put me up for membership there."

"And I'll put your name forward here," O'Hearn said. "If your new acquaintances don't come through, I know a couple of fellows who would be happy to support your nomination. It shouldn't be a problem."

"I appreciate it. Thank you." He gripped the other man's hand. "Now, let's see about that steak I promised you. How do you feel about Mary's Diner?"

"That's hardly the payback I had in mind," O'Hearn grumbled.

7

THURSDAY, JUNE 14, 1900

The following morning, Andrew Draper validated the Terminal City Club excursion for Granville when he telephoned with some of the names of Vancouver Permanent's syndicate. Granville was in his office, trying to work out how the information he'd learned so far related to Sinclair's case when the phone rang.

"Morning, Granville," Draper said. "It was a pleasure to meet you yesterday. I hope you found our little club of interest?"

"Very much so. It was a pleasure to meet you, as well. And I've already put out feelers about joining."

"Glad to hear it. It's a helpful place, as you will discover."

"Yesterday made that clear. I have appointments this afternoon with a couple of the members."

"Good, good." Draper paused. "You mentioned a possible story about your firm and Pinkerton's. I don't like to be pushy, but I'm quite interested. Especially since the Pinkerton's were called in for that dust-up at the mines in the Kootenays last year. You have any concerns about affiliating with a firm many consider strikebreakers?"

"From the little I heard about the issues, it was a purely investigative role the Pinkerton's agent played," Granville said. "And the Pinkerton's Agency's reputation for investigative work far outweighs that allegation, in my opinion,"

Draper nodded. "You will keep me in mind if there is a story?"

Granville considered that. The veteran reporter hadn't taken notes when they'd met the day before, for which Granville gave him credit, especially as he suspected the fellow had been itching to do so.

"I'll be happy to," Granville said after a moment. "If there is anything to tell, that is."

"Good, good."

There was a longish pause. Granville leaned back in his chair, swung his feet up on the desk. The line crackled, and Granville wondered what Draper was considering saying. The reporter hadn't struck him as a hesitant sort.

"Look, you mentioned mortgage companies, Putnam's in particular?" Draper said at last.

"Yes. I'll be talking to them later today. Why? Did you have some information for me?"

More crackling.

"Because I like to know a bit about the firms I deal with, and so far I haven't heard the names of the men behind the firm," Granville added. He sensed Draper had reservations about Vancouver Permanent Investment & Loan, but was reluctant to say too much. He'd only met Granville the day before, after all.

Another silence.

"They keep the names close, but I talked to a few sources. There are three local businessmen who did work for Putnam and the Vancouver Permanent group—Smythe, Carver and Ahrens," Draper said after a moment. "My sources suggest that they may also be investors."

He paused again. "Putnam has also done some work with George Gipson, though it isn't clear to me if Gipson is an investor or not, since he's at least partly in the same business. If he is an investor, he's keeping it fairly quiet."

Granville already knew about Gipson's involvement, but Smythe, Carver and Ahrens? All three had been involved with Gipson in his last caper, when he'd blackmailed them into financing a smuggling ring. Only Gipson had been arrested, but Granville would have expected the other three would avoid anything remotely related to Gipson's business dealings in future.

Which was obviously a false assumption on his part. Or perhaps they didn't know about Putnam's connection to Gipson?

"Thank you, Draper. They'll be worth talking to," he said. "Vancouver Permanent must have other investors, though?"

"They do. From what I heard, most of the money comes from investors in England."

"Interesting. What can you tell me of the Vancouver Permanent's reputation?"

"So you are planning on buying through them?"

Granville couldn't tell if the reporter guessed what he was really interested in. Draper struck him as a shrewd man who knew exactly how deals were done here. "I am still considering it," he said.

"Then you might want to consider some of their rivals as well," Draper said.

And that was telling. "Who would you suggest I talk to?"

"B.C. Land and Investment is the largest group, and they've been around the longest. It could be worth your while to talk to them."

"Thank you, I'll do so," Granville said. "And you mentioned that Smythe, Carver and Ahrens all did some work for Putnam. Is there anything you can tell me about the gentlemen themselves or the type of work they did for Vancouver Permanent?"

"Very little, I'm afraid, since none of the three are particularly newsworthy. Presumably Putnam hired them in their professional capacities. Robert Carver is a lawyer in private practice, while Aloysius Smythe and Carter Ahrens are both in insurance. And all three invest from time to time—their names have come up in connection to several rather questionable situations."

After thanking Draper, and promising to be in touch if there were news about his firm, Granville hung up. Dropping his feet back to the floor, he contemplated the notes he'd made.

Well, well. So Gipson's former investors now did legal work and accounting work for Vancouver Permanent. He'd really like to know what kind of work Carver, in particular, was doing for Putnam and his firm.

BEFORE GRANVILLE COULD FOLLOW the thought any further, the sound of the main door creaking open had him looking up, listening. They weren't expecting anyone. Rapid footsteps crossed the outer office, and an unexpected face appeared at his door.

"Emily? I thought you were in your typewriting classes today?"

"We finished early, and so I thought I would come by and see how you are making out with the case." She looked at him. "Why are you smiling?"

He told her about the call he'd just received, and what he'd learned.

"I don't believe it," Emily said.

"Believe what?"

"That these three involved in any way with Mr. Gipson again. I'd have though they learned their lesson about him the last time he was arrested for fraud."

He laughed. "Perhaps they are simply gullible. Or perhaps Gipson's involvement is not illegal this time, despite appearances."

"If that man is involved, I'm sure it's illegal," Emily said. "Though I suppose Mr. Gipson did seem charming enough when I met him. If you didn't look below the surface."

He grinned at the disapproval in her voice. Emily had met Gipson on a previous case, and had not been impressed at all. Perhaps it was simply that she knew Gipson had been trying to have him killed at the time, though they'd never been able to prove it. How the man kept skating clear of the law was a mystery.

Of course, Gipson had money, and most of the local police were thoroughly and rather predictably corrupt, despite the town council's best efforts to remove their Chief. "Or perhaps they are merely more interested in the color of his money than in anything else," he said.

"And which camp would your current client fall into?"

He didn't know. Yet. "That's one thing I mean to discover."

"How?"

"I think perhaps a visit to Mr. Smythe is in order, don't you?"

"Yes, indeed. May I join you?"

It was most unorthodox, but why not? It might be interesting to see how the man reacted to his fiancée's presence. "We could go now, if you'd like?"

"Of course. And Granville? Thank you."

He was nodding acknowledgment as the door burst open. Trent rushed into the office. "There's been another murder."

Scott followed Trent into the room, nodding a greeting to Emily.

"Not another one of our potential informants?" Granville asked.

Scott grinned. "Not this time. As far as I know there's no connection to any of our investigations."

"Some lawyer got shot in his office," Trent put in. "Late last night."

"Did you get a name?" Granville asked.

"Carver. Robert Carver," Scott said, and Emily gasped.

Scott looked at her. "I'm sorry for telling you so harshly. I didn't know you knew him."

Emily smiled at him. "I don't."

"I'm not surprised you don't remember the name," Granville said, grinning at Scott. "Since you were rotting in jail at the time. Carver was implicated in Gipson's smuggling game. Along with Smythe and Ahrens." Granville paused. "And I've just learned that Carver did some legal work for Vancouver Permanent Investment & Loan, and is rumored to be one of their investors."

"And you couldn't have found this out before the man was dead?" Scott said with a straight face.

Trent laughed, and Emily gave him a disapproving look.

Granville shrugged. "Apparently not. I am, however, hoping that Mr. Smythe will again prove helpful. Particularly since he too seems to be involved with Vancouver Permanent."

Scott was shaking his head. "Fools."

"Are the police investigating this latest murder?" Emily asked.

Trent nodded. "Are they ever. They're questioning everybody."

"And do they seem to have any idea who's behind his death?" Granville said.

"Not that I heard," Scott said. "You're thinking this is connected to Sinclair's case?"

"I doubt it. But murder is never a good sign."

"Damn right it isn't. What are you planning next?" Scott asked. "Your pardon, Miss Turner."

She nodded, looking not the least bit shocked.

"Emily and I are hoping to have a chat with Mr. Smythe," Granville said. "Then we'll meet you back here."

"You think it's safe to take Emily?" Trent blurted out, and Emily glared at him.

"Oh, I think I can protect her," Granville said.

Trent went a little pale and tripped over his own words as he tried to explain he hadn't meant to cast any doubts on Granville's abilities. It would have amused Granville, except that Emily was now glaring at him instead of Trent. Now what had he said?

"I hardly think I need protecting," she said. "And perhaps I should have a gun of my own."

"They aren't legal within city limits," Scott told her.

Her eyes went to the gun on Scott's hip, then to the knife Granville carried. "I see," she said thoughtfully.

Granville suspected he hadn't heard the end of this one. "We'd best be going," he said, and glanced over a Scott. "I'll meet you back here?"

Scott nodded. He was grinning broadly, the rat.

ALOYSIUS SMYTHE APPEARED to have come up in the world. He now had an office in the Flack Block, a three-story granite monolith on Hastings Street. Between the ornate arched entrance and the gilded elevator—complete with an operator to open the gates for them—it was an impressive setting.

When Granville and Emily reached Smythe's office on the third floor, however, there was no sign of the man, or his clerk. The heavy door was locked, and there was no notice to indicate when they would be open again. The elevator operator knew nothing, and from outside the building, it was evident that Smythe's office windows were shuttered.

"This is odd," Emily said. "Does he not have a clerk?"

"He does indeed."

"Perhaps Mr. Smythe is out of town, and his assistant ill."

"Or perhaps he has heard about Carver's murder. I think I'll pay a call on Ahrens next. Do you care to join me?"

She tucked her hand into his arm. "Which way?"

Ahrens wasn't available either. His office on Pender was open, but his clerk said he was unavailable, then, when pressed stammered out that the man was ill. Interesting.

Whatever was behind Carver's murder, it seemed to have panicked both Smythe and Ahrens. Granville wondered whether it had something to do with the Vancouver Permanent scheme, or if the three men had been involved in something else as well.

"So where do we go next?" Emily asked as the elevator creaked back down to the lobby. Obviously she was reaching the same conclusions he was.

"Back to the office, I think. I have appointments this afternoon, but we could have lunch sent in?"

"Good idea. The Arlington delivers, I believe," Emily said. "You know, I'm wondering what my father might know of Carver, Smythe and Ahrens. I can talk to him tonight.

She tucked her hand back into the crook of his arm and

wrapped her cloak more tightly around her. "Which reminds me, I did talk to Papa about Vancouver Permanent yesterday. He was none too pleased with me for wanting to know more about the business world. But he was rather scathing about the company," she said.

"Oh? Did he say why?"

"Just that their business practices set a bad example."

"I wonder why he didn't mention that to me when I spoke with him?" Granville said.

"It may simply be that the money behind Vancouver Permanent Investment & Loan is largely British, which the locals sometimes resent. Papa is inordinately sensitive to feelings against the English here, and worried about offending you by mentioning anything even remotely anti-English, I suspect."

Emily didn't seem to have any doubts on the subject, for which he was glad. "Perhaps. It would be helpful to know which practices he had in mind."

"I'll see what more I can find out," she said, giving his arm a gentle squeeze.

8

Real estate agent Grant Marshall had offices on Hastings Street, in a four-story brick building with heavily carved trim that quietly suggested stability and wealth. Marshall's office echoed that theme, while Marshall himself exuded a brash confidence that would either see him wealthy by the end of the decade, or broke. Granville found the contrast amusing. He was curious to hear what Marshall had to offer.

After a round of greetings, both men were seated in well-sprung leather chairs, puffing on cigars.

"I'm glad to see you're thinking ahead, Granville," Marshall said. "This is a great city, and it's going to be an expensive one. Land prices are rising again, and in my judgment, we're just seeing the beginning of what will be an exciting growth. You were in the Klondike rush, I take it? This will be even greater. Those who miss today's opportunity may never get another."

"Tell me more," Granville said.

Marshall was happy to do so. "Prices are rising fast, especially on the best properties. With the increases we've been seeing, you could expect to double—even triple—your purchase price in as little as seven years. You don't want to be left behind in this market, or the house you want will be forever out of your reach. You are looking to buy a home for yourself and your fiancée, I believe?"

"Yes. If it's within my means to do so, of course."

"It's an investment you'll never regret, I guarantee it. And being British, you understand the importance of owning land. When a man owns property, he always has that to fall back on."

"As long as he can pay the mortgage," Granville said dryly.

"For an individual such as yourself, there will be no problems," he was assured. "You have your own business, after all."

Which was not necessarily a guarantee of solvency. It was a dangerous assumption for a real estate agent to make.

"I would want to be sure that I was buying a suitable house, in an area where my future wife would feel comfortable, and would find herself surrounded by her peers," Granville said.

It was the expected answer, but he found himself wondering if he meant it. If he and Emily married, what kind of house would suit them? Would she want to live near her parents? He had to fight back a smile at the thought.

"Yes, indeed," Marshall was saying. "The area just south of Blue-blood Alley is still popular for householders such as yourselves, though of course with the extension of the streetcar to Davie Street, that area is growing quickly. And with the new tramline to the south shore, that is becoming an exciting possibility as well. Some of the more prosperous men are moving to Burrard and Shaughnessy. I'm sure you'd feel at home there, also."

"Hmmm. We—my fiancée and I—would want to look at a number of your listings."

"But of course. Whenever is convenient for you. And while we're discussing real estate, have you ever considered investing in office property, rather than simply renting?"

Now why did that thought appeal to him? Aside from the various annoyances of their current office, that is. Too many gener-ations of landowners in his family, probably.

"You're thinking we'd rent out suites to others, you mean?" Granville said. "It's an interesting proposition. I'd have to see the numbers."

"I'll put something together for you," Marshall said. "You might be surprised by how profitable it can be."

"Before we discuss possibilities any further, I should make arrangements to discuss financing. Mortgages are not something my family has concerned themselves with for hundreds of years and I am having some difficulty understanding how they work here," Granville said. "Whom would you recommend I speak with?"

"I'd suggest Vancouver Permanent Investment & Loan. They are the most flexible."

"I've heard of them," Granville said. "Isn't that Charles Putnam's firm?"

"Yes, indeed. Though you might prefer to do business with Evan Thompson, who is also with Vancouver Permanent. You met him at the Club yesterday, didn't you?"

"Indeed I did."

"Good. You'll find him very willing to consider the client's expectations."

Whatever that meant. Granville nodded, jotted down a note.

"But let me show you some of the listings we have on our books, to give you an idea of what kind of house you might desire," Marshall said.

A half-hour later, rather staggered at the cost of housing here, Granville thanked the real estate agent for his time. "I'll be in touch once I've looked into the financing."

"I think you'll be pleased to find yourself able to buy a far grander home than you might be imagining. A home your wife will be happy in, a home where you can be proud to entertain your business colleagues."

Right. And end up in more debt than he could comfortably live with.

"I look forward to discussing it further with you," Granville said. He was now very interested in speaking with Evan Thompson.

In addition to verifying what he'd heard from Putnam in April, he now wanted to know—exactly how much house could he buy for how little money? And why?

As GRANVILLE PUSHED OPEN the heavy glass doors that guarded the entrance for Vancouver Permanent Investment & Loan, he wondered how he'd best explain his presence if he ran into Putnam. Luckily it didn't happen, and the young man behind the reception desk didn't seem to remember him.

Evan Thompson, who had been only too happy to meet with him on short notice, greeted him expansively. A stocky man, with a neatly trimmed beard and a well-tailored suit, he strode across the expensive carpet with his hand outstretched.

"How nice to see you again, Granville," he said. "Marshall often refers clients to us, and we do our poor best to provide what assistance we can."

He led the way into a well-set up office, waved him towards a deep leather chair. "Please, have a seat. Now how can I help you today?"

"I'm to be married shortly…"

"My heartiest congratulations."

"Thank you. I wish to buy a house suitable to bring my bride to."

"Yes, indeed, a most estimable ambition. I gather you are considering financing at least a portion of the purchase price?"

"Yes, I am."

"Well, you will want the best for your family, so let's see how much we can cover for you." A quick but thorough assessment of his attire. "Which firm do you work for?"

Two could play at this game. "My partner and I have a small but flourishing business. Granville and Scott. Perhaps you've heard of us?"

"The investigation firm? Indeed I have. You've developed quite a reputation in such a short period of time."

Granville was surprised to hear it. He knew they no longer lacked for clients, but hadn't expected Thompson to know him. Had Marshall briefed him? "We plan to continue to build on that."

Thompson was nodding. "Excellent. Excellent. And it is the youngest Miss Turner you are engaged to, I believe? A very lovely young woman."

He hadn't told Marshall that. Thompson must read the social column every evening and make notes. It was a smart business move for a real estate agent. No wonder Marshall spoke highly of him.

"Thank you. Yes, I have that honor. And you understand my desire to bring her home to a dwelling that is worthy of her in every way."

Gads, but he sounded pompous. It wasn't easy to get the words out without grinning. Granville was just thankful Scott wasn't here to hear him—he'd never hear the end of it.

Thompson nodded and scribbled a few calculations. "Hmmm. I think we can arrange things so you can do her proud. How does this sound?"

And he turned the page so that Granville could read the number he'd written down.

It took all Granville's self-control to keep his eyes from widening. "That's—impressive. And will allow me to buy the perfect house."

It would allow him to buy an estate, if he were foolish enough to borrow the whole amount. "What are the terms?"

"Quite reasonable, I assure you. We'll work them out once you've found your new home. How does five percent down with interest at three and a half percent per year sound to you?"

How could they afford to offer rates so low? "Most of my cash flow is tied up in the business at present. Can we adjust the terms to accommodate that?" he said, to see how Thompson would respond.

The other man didn't even pause. "Certainly. In fact, since your credit is so solid, we can adjust the terms so that you pay nothing down."

"Would you need to get approval for those terms? From your manager, I mean?"

"Mr. Williams? That won't be a problem. Once I show him these figures, he'll initial them immediately."

Was Sinclair the only salesman whose deals were formally approved, then? Granville wondered. That certainly sounded like a setup. "And the repayment?"

"Would stay the same."

For a moment, Granville forgot that he was trying to clear Sinclair's name, and saw instead in his mind's eye the mansion he could bring Emily to. Their home. He'd make his mark in this new land in a way he'd never have been able to do in England, as a landowner and respected businessman. Part of the community.

His silence apparently worried Mr. Thompson. "How quickly were you hoping to move into your new home?" he prompted.

It was enough to remind Granville of why he was really there. "I have several business commissions to fulfill before I can really focus on finding the perfect house," he said. "So these discussions are very much preliminary."

"I quite understand, and I commend your forward thinking on the matter. Not many men are so thorough."

Which probably made Thompson's job easier. "I've been told the right house is the key to a happy marriage." He hadn't been, but it sounded like something Thompson would appreciate.

"Words of wisdom indeed," was the response. "But please keep in mind that the Vancouver real estate market is a rising one. A few months from now, you may find yourself wishing you had bought your home at today's prices."

"I will consider it seriously, especially now that I know the money will be available," Granville said. He stood up, held out his hand. "Thank you for your time, Mr. Thompson."

"Excellent," Thompson said, rising to shake hands. "And do not hesitate to contact me if the perfect house seems beyond the amount we have already discussed. I am sure there would be something we could do."

It was all Granville could do not to shake his head as he left.

9

FRIDAY, JUNE 15, 1900

The office door opened, and Emily looked up from the stacks of paper on what was now her desk to smile at Granville. "Good morning."

"Good morning to you. And you, Miss Kent," he said with a nod. He turned to hang up his slightly damp coat and hat.

"I'm glad to see you this morning," he said to Emily.

"Oh? But why this morning in particular? After all, I'm here every morning now," she said.

"But this morning, we need to go and look at houses."

Emily stared at Granville. "What was that? Did you say houses?"

He gave her an infuriating grin, and winked.

Emily glanced over at Laura, who was pretending not to listen and trying to hide her smile, and shook her head. "It's part of the job," she told her.

"Of course it is," Granville said. "And we have a number of houses to see before lunch."

Not entirely sure if he was joking, Emily retrieved her hand bag from the bottom drawer, and donned her cloak and hat. "Are you fine on your own?" she asked Laura.

"Of course," was the answer, delivered with a professional smile.

"We will be back by two," Granville said to Miss Kent. "Can you take a late lunch today? We'll be meeting with Scott and Trent for lunch."

Apparently he was serious about lunch, Emily thought as he whisked her out the door. Was he serious about house hunting as well?

Apparently so. Less than half an hour later, they stood in front of a magnificent Queen Anne style house with ornate brackets at the gables and porch, two turrets and a discreet For Sale sign on a stake driven into the lawn. Emily consulted the list that Granville had handed her just before they descended from the trolley at Burrard Street and walked half a block south along what locals called Blueblood Alley. There were seven properties listed, and this was the first of them.

She took a deep breath. "You were serious."

"Of course. We're meeting our real estate agent, Grant Marshall, inside."

He grinned, and bent to whisper in her ear. "I'm not entirely serious about buying these properties, though. Vancouver Permanent is anxious to lend us entirely too much money, at rates that make no sense to me at all. I want to find out just how far they're prepared to go. Are you with me?"

"In an investigation? Of course!" Then she glanced at the over-elaborate house and back up at him. "Besides, I've always wanted to see the insides of some of these houses. This will be fascinating."

It was even more fascinating to watch him turn a little green, if only for a moment. She grinned at him, and he laughed. "Fascinating indeed."

And his eyes were on her as he said it.

Emily blushed, just a little. She couldn't help it, but she covered it up as best she could by tucking her hand in his elbow and leading the way to the door. "I assume our real estate agent is already here. Shall we?"

FIVE EXPANSIVE HOUSES LATER, neither Emily nor Granville were quite so enthusiastic about this part of the investigation.

"I had no idea a house could be so large," Emily whispered as Marshall led them down another narrow upstairs hallway, pointing out the enduring quality of the carpets and that the wallpaper was a durable print designed to hide dust—features that were in direct contrast to the gleaming quarter-sawn oak floors and embossed wall-paper in the public areas downstairs. Marshall paid particular attention to a lushly planted, glassed-in conservatory and the stables off the back alley.

"I mean, I knew they were big," Emily said. "But there is so much of them."

"And as the future lady of the house, you are expected to take an interest in every niche and cranny," Granville stage-whispered back.

"Shhh. He'll hear you," she said. "But it's true. Just the thought of being responsible for a place this size is enough to make me reconsider marriage."

"To me?" he asked with a grin.

"At all!"

"Well, my bank manager will thank you," he said. "Most women would expect their husband to provide the biggest house in the neighborhood. Which has always struck me as an uncomfortable proposition. Unless there are numerous children, of course."

Emily blushed for real this time. "Granville! We shouldn't be discussing possible children."

"I've never understood why not. Seems eminently practical to me." His eyes were twinkling as he said it.

"Hush. He'll hear you. And we're supposed to be investigating, not planning a family."

At his laugh, she turned even redder. She glared at him, and raised her voice a little. "Now, which of the houses we've seen so far is the most expensive? I know my father will want to be sure you're making an appropriate home for me."

As Marshall pretended he hadn't heard her, Granville gave her an appreciative glance. "Minx," he said softly into her ear.

"After this, you'll have fun trying to talk him out of selling you the most expensive thing on his list," she said.

By THE TIME they'd seen all seven houses, Emily's head was swimming with details, her feet hurt, and all she could think about was lunch. "Where are we meeting Scott and Trent?" she asked as they walked along Georgia. "I'm famished."

"We're nearly there," Granville said. "We're meeting them at Mary's Diner. It isn't fancy, but the food is good, and I think you might enjoy the atmosphere. It will be a change from Stroh's."

"Will my mother approve?"

"Probably not," he said with a sideways glance.

"Good."

He laughed at that. "So what did you think of the houses we saw?"

"I wish I'd thought to bring a notebook, like you did. The details have all run together and I can't remember which house had the dreadful bathroom, and which one had that pretentious parlor."

"Even with my notebook, I don't think I caught that much detail," he said. "I'm more interested in your reaction to our real estate agent."

"Mr. Marshall? I liked him," she said as she thought about it. "He was enthusiastic, and for all his professional patter, he seemed to really care that we find a house that I liked. I didn't expect that."

"Nor did I. And I was glad to have you with me—he was much more honest with you there than I think he would have been if I had seen the houses on my own."

"I'm glad you invited me—I found it fascinating. But do you mean he was pushier when you saw him in his office?"

"No, not pushier. But smoother. His focus was on finding an impressive home for you, rather than one that you could turn into a home."

"Interesting."

"Hmmm. Especially when the house he seemed to like for you—the one you looked at the most closely—was the second least expensive one we saw. So I think that is the one we should buy."

"The—what? Wait!" Emily stopped and stared at him, not sure she'd heard him correctly. "You aren't serious? You aren't really thinking about buying a house now!"

"Well, we are getting married," he said reasonably, stopping as well and turning to face her. "And we will need somewhere to live."

"But these are all enormous. They're far bigger than anything we need."

"But you liked it?"

"Which one?" she said. He meant the second last one they'd seen, she was sure of it. But she hoped she was wrong.

It was such a beautiful house—built in the newer style, tall and narrow, with slender columns supporting the porch, and just the right amount of detail—but it was too much. She wasn't ready to be mistress of a house like that one.

He grinned at her. "The second last one."

He knew her too well. Maybe marrying him was a bad idea, after all. It might be distinctly uncomfortable to have a husband who could anticipate your reaction to things.

"And how would I be able to work with you if I had the responsibilities of a house like that?" Emily said.

"It's big enough to house several servants. They take care of the house."

"And I'd have to take care of them." She'd seen her mother's duties often enough. "Granville, just overseeing the servants in a house like that is a full-time job. I don't want that."

"So we would hire a housekeeper."

"Who would also need my input. Granville, it's still too much house." She paused, glanced at him, then told him the truth. "It's too much for me, and it's too much for the owner of a very new business. If you really wanted to put money into real estate, you'd do better to buy the building your offices are in. And fix the problems it has."

She waited for his response, holding her breath.

He smiled. "I suspect our business will be a roaring success, and that your head for finances will be a big part of that."

She hadn't expected that. "You mean it?"

He nodded. "Marshall suggested something very similar, only he thought I should buy both the office building and a large home."

"With what?" Emily said tartly, then caught herself.

Apparently it amused him. He laughed, squeezed her hand, then placed it in the crook of his arm and began walking.

Emily matched his steps. "So what are you going to do next?"

"Based on what we saw today, I'm going to confirm exactly how much money Vancouver Permanent is really prepared to loan me, and on what terms. And I think I will get the details on our office building from Marshall before I do so."

"May I join you?"

"I wish you could. I would love to have your reaction to the meeting. Unfortunately, it is too unusual for a man to involve his fiancée in such discussions. It might raise questions that we don't want asked at this stage of the investigation."

It was the same story she always heard, but this time it was from Granville. She'd hoped for better from him. Her disappointment must have shown.

"But when we are ready to buy in truth, you will be part of that meeting," Granville added. "And here we are."

He meant it, too, she could tell. Feeling better, Emily looked up to see a weathered wooden sign for Mary's Diner above her. She sniffed the air appreciatively and looked around her with interest. It smelled of grilling steak and mushrooms, and while the wallpaper and the wooden booths were worn, they were scrupulously clean.

"I like it," she said, as she waved at Trent and Scott seated in a booth across the room. "Now let's go and compare notes with them."

10

Late that afternoon, Granville was in his office reviewing the figures Marshall had given him. Based on these, he could definitely afford any of the houses he and Emily had looked at. If he was prepared to trust the interest rates that Vancouver Permanent had quoted him. And there was something appealing in the notion of buying such a grand home for his wife-to-be.

The problem was that he couldn't trust those figures.

And Emily would hate living in such a house.

The phone rang, and he answered absently, his attention still on the page in front of him.

"It's Sinclair," said the voice on the other end. "I have to see you. It's starting."

Granville was immediately alert. "What is?"

"I've just been fired."

Granville opened his notebook. "I'm sorry. What happened?"

"For cause, they say, but they wouldn't tell me what I'd done. Or rather, what I'm supposed to have done."

Sinclair gave a bitter little laugh. "Not that it would matter. They're good, and they have connections. If they intend to frame me for this thing, I'll be in jail before the year is out."

"Just slow down," Granville said, as Sinclair's words poured out faster and faster. "Or better yet, don't say another word."

"Wait—what? You're giving up on me? I thought McAndrews said…"

"Calm down. We need to meet. Where are you?"

"Telephone booth downtown. Don't worry, no-one can hear me."

"You were right. We need to meet in person," Granville said. "Do you have a lawyer?"

"A—no. No. I hadn't thought—I mean, I don't know any…"

"Never mind. I'll introduce you to Randall—Joshua Randall—and you can tell your story to both of us."

"I don't think…"

"Randall's advice is exactly what we need right now. Then I'll buy you a drink. You sound like you need it."

"But…"

Granville ignored him, just gave him Randall's address. "I'll meet you there in ten minutes. All right?"

"Yes, okay. I'll go there now."

Hanging up, Granville strode towards the door, grabbing his coat and hat on the way.

"When Scott gets back, ask him to meet us at Randall's office," he said to Miss Kent as he passed her desk in the outer office.

THIS LATE IN THE DAY, Randall's waiting room was empty, except for Sinclair, who was pacing the floor. Granville took the agitated man by the elbow and sat him down, then went over to speak to Randall's clerk. The man nodded, and disappeared into the lawyer's office. After a moment, he returned and ushered the two of them directly into the lawyer's office.

"Granville? Nice to see you again so soon," Randall said as he came around his heavy desk, hand outstretched. "And this would be your latest client?" he added, glancing at Sinclair.

"Yes, and he is also your new client," Granville said. "Walter Sinclair, Joshua Randall."

It was ironic, he thought as the two men shook hands. Sinclair had started out as McAndrews's client, then became Granville's client, and now the poor man needed to hire Randall as well. And each time, his situation had worsened.

"Please, have a seat," Randall was saying, waving both of them to the upright wooden chairs in front of the desk. Emily would have protested the lack of comfort, but Granville approved the message it sent. Consulting this lawyer was serious business, and not for the weak.

"Now, what can I do for you?" Randall asked, looking from one to the other.

Randall gave no indication that he'd ever heard of Sinclair before, much less discussed him with Granville. His absolute discretion was one of the things Granville valued most about the lawyer. That and his ability to produce legal fireworks when most needed.

Granville glanced over at Sinclair, who sat slumped in his chair, face pale. So he'd take the lead. "My client has just lost his position. He has suspected for some time that his firm was fraudulent, and fears that he will be framed for financial irregularities he had nothing to do with."

Randall was jotting notes on a yellow legal pad. "Go on. Which firm is involved?"

Granville looked over at Sinclair, who sat a little straighter in his chair.

"Vancouver Permanent Investment & Loan," Sinclair said, and proceeded to tell Randall the same facts Granville had already heard from him and from McAndrews.

"Why did you lose your position?"

"I was fired," was the bitter reply. "For incompetence. They said I was incompetent. I'm the best salesman they have."

"Has something happened recently?" Randall asked. "Something different about your job or your interactions with your superiors?"

For a moment Granville feared Sinclair would explode at the word superiors, but the young man mastered himself.

"No," he said quietly. "Nothing at all has changed."

"Are you looking to sue them for wrongful dismissal?" the lawyer said.

Sinclair looked surprised. "I hadn't even thought of it. I'm too worried about being arrested for fraud."

"Is it an avenue you would recommend?" Granville asked the lawyer.

Randall tapped his pencil against the page, now half-filled with his cramped writing. "I'm considering it. We'll discuss the options later. Go on," he said to Sinclair. "Tell me why you're worried about being arrested."

"The police have already brought me in for questioning twice," Sinclair said.

"On what grounds?"

Sinclair grimaced. "It's all very vague. There are no charges mentioned, just innumerable questions about interest rates, and the work I do and the housing market in general. At first, I even wondered if one of them was planning on buying a house and just using the interrogation to get the inside track."

Randall glanced up at Granville, who grinned. It was all too likely.

"I gather you changed your mind?" the lawyer said.

A nod. "The questions got more pointed, and they started asking about how I'd handled specific types of mortgage situations," Sinclair said. "I gathered there had been complaints."

"Hmmm. And the names of the clients who complained?"

"They never told me."

"And the police officers involved?"

"Officers Brickle and Gordon the first time. A fellow named Daniels joined them on the second round of questioning."

"So you've been brought in twice?"

"Yes."

"When was the most recent episode?"

"Ten days ago."

"And no charge was mentioned?"

"No."

"Did they say why they'd brought you in, or what case they were working on?" Randall said.

"No. And when I asked, Brickle laughed at me, told me I was just asking for more trouble. I shut up."

Granville wasn't surprised. He remembered Officer Brickle from their last case, and not favorably. "Did you see a lawyer?" he asked.

"I didn't know who to trust. And I didn't think I could afford one." Sinclair had sunk back into his chair by this point.

"Then why are you here?" Randall said.

Sinclair glanced at Granville. "He brought me. And I'll find the money somehow. I can't just wait for them to arrest me."

"You could just leave town. Disappear," Granville said.

"No. I like being a businessman, and I plan to build a career here. If I run, I'll never regain my good name."

Not surprising, considering his background, Granville thought. "You could change your name. It might be preferable to rotting in jail."

Sinclair gave him a straight look. "That isn't an option. I hired you because I'm proud of who I am, what I've accomplished."

"Hmmm. So being fired for incompetence is a major blow as well," Randall said.

Sinclair went white, looking as if he hadn't even considered that. Perhaps he hadn't. "It means I won't get another job here," he said.

Well, that depended on how flexible his employer's ethics were, Granville thought. But it wasn't information that would help Sinclair right now.

"Not the kind of job you want," Randall said. "Not unless you can prove your innocence. Do you have any proof that your former employer was committing fraud?"

Sinclair shook his head. "I saw a few things, but that's all. I wasn't able to work out what they were doing."

He glanced at Granville, then back at Randall. "It's why I hired an accountant, and then Granville, here. I wanted help in proving what they were up to before they managed to have me arrested. I thought I'd have more time."

"And now you've been fired."

"Yes." He drew in a shaky breath. "I need a lawyer, and I'd like to hire you."

Randall glanced at Granville, who nodded. He'd stand guarantor for Randall's fees.

"I'll take your case," Randall said. "And we're going to sue Vancouver Permanent for wrongful dismissal immediately, before they can move against you. I'll draw up the writ now."

"But how does getting my job back help me?" Sinclair asked. "They're still going to use me as a scapegoat."

"You're not thinking clearly yet," Randall said. "We're not going after your job. We're looking for two things: the first is to clear your name, and the second a significant amount of money as compensation. And in the process, they'll have to give us access to their books."

Sinclair started to smile. "I see," he said.

"Exactly," Randall said. "With Granville's help—and this accountant you mentioned—we'll dig deep enough to prove that they are frauds."

"And it won't be you that ends up in jail," Granville told him.

11

SATURDAY, JUNE 16, 1900

When Granville showed up at Gipson's offices first thing the following morning, Gipson's clerk was quick to usher him into Gipson's office. That made a change. Usually Gipson was happy to let him sit cooling his heels for far too long. What was that low-life weasel up to now?

"I appreciate your time," Granville said, reaching forward to shake hands.

He got an oily smile in return. "You know my curiosity. Now, how can I help you this time?"

"I've been hired to look into the backgrounds of several potential employees. I understand that you've done business with one of the candidates."

"Oh?"

"A Mr. Sinclair. Walter Sinclair."

Gipson's smile widened. "Sinclair? Yes, I've done business with him, but only very occasionally, I'm afraid." He paused, head to one side, as if considering Granville. "He's English, is he not? And with an accent similar to your own. You must know him."

Which only proved that Gipson was not English, and had little ear for the distinctions of class.

"No, I'm afraid not." Granville paused. "I understand his job entailed providing mortgages for those who intending to purchase local real estate?"

"That's correct."

"But is that not the business you are in yourself? I'm confused. Why would you be involved with Vancouver Permanent Investment & Loan at all?"

For a moment he thought the man might not answer, but after a measuring look, Gipson did so.

"It is a minor involvement, as I said. I very occasionally have certain clients for whom the Vancouver Permanent's products are a better match than those I offer. I put those clients in touch with Putnam's firm. In the case of the last few such clients, I put them in touch with Sinclair."

Taking a percentage from every transaction while carrying none of the responsibility himself, he'd wager. Though he hadn't expected Gipson to be so honest with him. "And were they happy with the service he provided?"

"They seemed so."

"So what went wrong that Sinclair was let go?" Granville asked.

He got an elaborate shrug in return. "I'm not familiar with Vancouver Permanent's business in any detail, but my impression was that Sinclair himself never fully understood that business."

Somehow Granville didn't think it was that simple. Not when the police were looking for Sinclair specifically in connection with mortgage fraud. "I gather the money behind Vancouver Permanent flows from an investment syndicate. Would an employee like Sinclair have had any interactions with the investors?"

"It would seem unlikely, but that would be a question for Putnam."

Granville nodded. "Fair enough. Would you be able to tell me who the syndicate members are?"

"I'm afraid I couldn't disclose their names. Even if I knew them."

Right. Especially not when he could inconvenience Granville by not doing so. Which meant he'd learned as much as he was going to here. He thanked Gipson politely, and left quickly. Nothing good could come of prolonging the meeting.

———

BY THE TIME Granville reached Putnam's office, it was nearly ten. When he asked if Charles Putnam was available, the earnest young clerk gave him an odd look. "I'll see if he is in. Who may I say is calling?"

Granville gave his name, then waited impatiently until the clerk returned and showed him into Putnam's heavily elaborate office.

Putnam stood up to greet him from behind a mahogany desk that dominated the room. "It's a pleasure to see you again, Mr. Granville."

A heavy man, with a florid complexion and a damp handshake, he was as prosperously dressed as his office. "I understand you have been doing some business recently with our firm."

"I have indeed," Granville said, shaking his hand and finding it unpleasantly damp. "And the pleasure is mine, Mr. Putnam."

"So, how may I help you? No problems in working with our Mr. Thompson, I hope? Or another missing person?"

"Neither, thankfully. Mr. Thompson has been very helpful, though I am here on a business matter. Not a missing person, though, thankfully. Rather, I have a client with responsibility for hiring several people into very sensitive positions. We've been hired to look into the backgrounds of a number of their potential candidates. And I understand that one of the candidates was an employee of yours."

"Oh?"

"A Mr. Sinclair. Walter Sinclair."

Putnam's eyebrows twitched together. "Ah. Yes. He was indeed employed by us until recently."

"May I ask why he left?"

"It's a confidential matter, I'm afraid."

Granville frowned, brought out his notebook and pencil. He looked up at Putnam. "And what was his role here?"

"He sold mortgages to would-be buyers. In some cases he acted as agent between buyer and seller."

"He would be in a similar role working for my client. Do you have any comment on how he would handle such a position, based on his most recent work? I can guarantee you that anything you tell me will be kept confidential."

"Ah, I see." Putnam looked down at his hands. "In that case—I had such hope for the lad. But we simply couldn't trust him any longer. He didn't have the judgment—you understand."

Granville gave a noncommittal nod. "Go on."

"We lend sums of money, often quite large sums, to people wishing to buy homes. If the buyer over-commits and cannot meet his payments, then we lose money. The ability to judge our borrowers to a nicety is critical. With Sinclair— well, the young man proved to be a gambler, through and through. His actions have injured some of our clients, and they've injured the firm. In fact, confidentially, he has cost our firm a substantial sum."

"Then you would not recommend hiring Sinclair for a similar role?"

"No indeed." Putnam's tone was vehement. "We are a conservative firm. Sinclair extended loans that are far riskier than we would wish. Loans that, if land prices suddenly fell, would expose us to considerable risk. Indeed, some of them have already failed—bad judgment all around. And the worst of it was, young Sinclair couldn't admit his error. He blamed his decisions on the firm, and our business practices."

Now that was interesting. Judging by what Emily's father had told him, it was at least plausible, given the recent rise in the Vancouver real estate market.

Neither Putnam's story nor Gipson's matched what McAndrews or Sinclair had told him, however.

Either someone in his firm wasn't telling Putnam the truth, Granville thought, or the General Manager of Vancouver Permanent was involved in this thing up to his pudgy neck, and telling different versions to strew confusion. He wondered which it was.

He didn't like Putnam, or trust him. But that was no guarantee the man was responsible for fraud.

He'd paused long enough that Putnam leaned forward a little.

"How much did he cost your firm?" Granville asked, expecting to be fobbed off with generalities. "I'm only asking in general terms, you understand."

"Yes. Of course. In very general terms, it is tens of thousands."

"Dollars?"

"Yes," Putnam said.

That was indeed serious.

Granville wondered what the real numbers were, and why Putnam had told him so much. Was the Vancouver Permanent's General Manager being set up? What might whoever was behind this mess have to gain if the firm admitted such a loss now? Was it simply that someone now had a convenient scapegoat to point out as responsible for the loss?

"I see," he said slowly. He really needed to know more about this syndicate of theirs.

"It isn't pretty."

"No, indeed it isn't. I gather the money behind Vancouver Permanent flows from an investment syndicate," he said after a pause. "Would Sinclair have had any interactions with them?"

"No, of course not. His focus was strictly local."

"And your investors are not?"

Putnam gave him a hard look, but his tone was smooth when he replied. "Many of them are English, names you would recognize."

Which was a masterful non-answer. Granville wondered if Putnam would disclose Sinclair's supposed fraud to his investors. Even without McAndrews' opinion and Weston's poor experience with them, Gipson's involvement was enough to make him question the company's honesty.

And Putnam was doing little to change that opinion. He could feel the polite mask he wore growing brittle.

"Thank you. I appreciate your time," Granville said. With a nod, he took his leave. Time to see if news about Sinclair's firing was out, and what Marshall had to say about Vancouver Permanent now.

MARSHALL STEPPED BRISKLY into the comfortable reception area, a puzzled look on his face. "Granville? My clerk said you were here. I wasn't expecting you, was I?"

"No. I took a chance you might have some time free."

"You're in luck, I've nothing for the next half-hour or so. And it's a pleasure to see you again." He gestured Granville into his office. "What can I do for you?"

"My fiancée and I appreciated the house tour on Saturday. Those were some spectacular homes you were showing us."

Marshall smiled broadly. "Weren't they, though? And what did Miss Turner think of them?"

"She loved them, especially the last two."

Marshall nodded, leaning back in his chair. "I was wagering with myself that those would be the ones she liked. So, are we putting in an offer?"

"Not quite. I'm going to need more time with the numbers. And I'm going to make you work a little harder for the sale, I'm afraid."

"Nothing I like better," Marshall said, leaning forward. "What would you like to see? We do have bigger homes available, but I wouldn't have said they were your style. Was I wrong?"

"Not at all. Rather, it's your comment the other day about buying our office space that started me thinking."

It was true. The more he'd thought about the idea, the more intrigued he'd become. And as a bonus, looking into such a purchase would give him more information on Vancouver Permanent's business style.

"You're a smart man. Would you be considering purchasing in your current location?"

"I'd be interested in knowing if the building is even available, and at what price. I'd also be interested in the availability and price of comparable buildings."

"You'd want to be close to the business district, I assume?"

"Yes, I think so."

"Excellent, excellent."

Marshall was practically rubbing his hands together, Granville thought with amusement. Time to take his ambition down a notch. "Of course, such a purchase would mean I'd be looking for a smaller house to start with."

It barely checked the man. "If your fiancée has fallen in love with a home she's already seen, then I'd suggest very strongly that purchasing a different one might make your life—quite difficult."

Granville's lips quirked at the thought. He could just imagine the scenario if he'd been house shopping with Julia, with whom he'd once thought himself in love. Lovely though she was, Julia would never have settled for less than the most opulent house he could afford. Emily, on the other hand…

"It was actually Miss Turner's suggestion," he said. "That we start by putting more money into the business, and a smaller home."

"Then you are a very lucky man," Marshall said. "Marry her quickly, before someone else discovers that a reasonable woman exists."

Granville just smiled. "How long will it take you to come up with several listings to show us?"

"Not long. Two or three days at most."

"Good. In the meantime, I'll do a bit more work on a potential mortgage. Is there anyone other than Evan Thompson that you would recommend?"

"No, he's proven the most flexible in circumstances like yours."

"Even on business mortgages?"

"Oh yes. Vancouver Permanent has no problem with them," Marshall said.

"I understand they've gone through some personnel changes recently. Is that something I should be concerned about?"

"No, not at all. It's a growing market and the firm is growing with it, which sometimes requires a bit of turnover. I haven't heard of it causing any issues."

"And I'm sure you would hear."

"Yes indeed," Marshall agreed, and scribbled down some numbers. "When I talk to Thompson, I'll suggest that you might need a bit of latitude in the total amount you request."

The real estate agent paused, and watched Granville carefully. "Based on rather extensive experience, I'd caution you not to be surprised if your fiancée is not impressed with the smaller homes when she sees them. No matter how reasonable a lady is, it is hard to accept less once she's seen a home she admires."

"I'll keep that in mind," Granville said. He knew Emily, as Marshall did not.

And he was more interested in Marshall's continued recommendations for Vancouver Permanent. Just how flexible were they when it came to very large sums?

And would that have changed in any way, now that Sinclair had been fired?

Emily was sitting behind Granville's desk, engaged in sorting through his papers and setting up a proper filing system. She'd been at it for several hours now, and her concentration was flagging. It was particularly hard to stay focused now that the breeze had shifted. Instead of smelling road dust and fresh manure from the street below, she was being seduced by the scent of roses and the sea.

The sunshine through the window beckoned.

If she listened hard, she could almost hear the clacking of the trolley on the corner. And if she hurried, she could be strolling along the waterfront in Stanley Park in twenty minutes.

Emily stood up, took a quick turn around the office, sipped some water. Took a deep breath. She sat down again, glared at the papers in front of her. How had Granville ever found anything?

She'd just begun sorting through another pile of scribbled notes when she heard the outer door slam open. She looked up immediately.

Laura could certainly handle whoever it was, but things had been quiet all morning. She had hoped for an interesting client at least. Perhaps even a case where she could do some preliminary work. But there had been nothing. Until now.

"I need to see Mr. Granville," a firm voice with a hint of a Scottish accent was saying. "It's urgent."

Emily had to stop herself from rushing out into the main office. Professionalism was important.

"Very well," Laura was saying. "And your name?"

"McAndrews. Duncan McAndrews. I'm working with Mr. Granville on his current case."

"Please have a seat, and I will be right back."

Laura stepped sedately into the inner office, and closed the door behind her. Then she let the excitement she'd been suppressing dance in her eyes. "Emily! It's Mr. McAndrews, looking for Mr. Granville. What do you want to do?"

Emily grinned at her. "While they're out of the office, I'm his assistant. Please show Mr. McAndrews in."

Moments later a thin, bewildered-looking redhead a few years younger than Granville was being ushered into the office. He seemed to be trying to decide whether to shake her outstretched hand or bow over it.

"Mr. McAndrews," Emily said briskly. "Please have a seat, and tell me how I can help you."

"You're Mr. Granville's assistant? I mean, of course you are. I need to get in touch with him rather urgently." McAndrews unfolded into one of the chairs along the wall, turning slightly sideways to face her.

He steepled his fingers and touched them to his chin. It seemed to steady him. "I'm an accountant, you know."

"Go on."

"And he hired me. To look into Vancouver Permanent Investment & Loan, I mean. On a contract."

No, he was still rattled. It would be amusing, if it weren't so annoying. Women in business weren't that unusual. Or if they were, they shouldn't be.

But at least he'd told her what she needed to know. She smiled at him, which seemed to fluster him further. "Of course. And you've discovered something about Vancouver Permanent? Something you'd like me to make sure Mr. Granville is aware of as soon as he returns?"

She used the polished, professional tone she'd been practicing in front of the mirror, and was pleased to see it seemed to be effective.

"That's it." He met her eyes for a moment then dropped his. "You handle confidential information for him?"

"Yes, of course."

"Of course. Well, I've been investigating. Quietly of course. And it's a little hard to tell when things are selling so quickly, but I'm sure now that they're running a complicated fraud. And it's company-wide. All I have to do is prove it." The last was muttered, as if he didn't expect her to hear it.

"It sounds like you're saying the fraud is more complicated than a salesman could achieve?"

He nodded.

"You're sure?" Emily asked.

"Yes. Mostly sure. I've nothing resembling proof yet, though. When is Granville expected back?"

"Not until late this afternoon, I'm afraid."

McAndrews tightened his lips, and stared at his hands for a long moment.

"Can I tell him you called in?"

"The thing is, I don't know if this can wait," McAndrews said, leaning towards her. "I don't know how long we have until they decide to arrest my—I mean our client."

"Mr. Sinclair?"

"Yes. And once they do that, the evidence may vanish." He reached into an inside pocket and pulled out a folded page. "It's all here, Miss, everything I've found. If you could see that Mr. Granville gets it the moment he comes in?"

"Of course," she said with a smile, accepting the document but thinking fast. She had to know what was in it. "And there's nothing more you can do until he sees this?"

"I don't think I can prove it on my own. And there's no-one else I can trust."

"You can trust me," Emily said. "I'm Mr. Granville's assistant, after all. I can help you. It's why I'm here."

It was true. Granville had hired her to help him in his investigations. Even if this wasn't exactly the type of help he'd expected from her. She could do this. It was why she'd learned to typewrite and studied business so diligently.

"Can you tell me what you need?" Emily said.

McAndrews was looking at her a little oddly, but the question seemed to focus him. He nodded, his expression thoughtful. "I need more information, probably insider information, if I'm to prove what's going on."

"What is going on?"

"Exactly what Sinclair was afraid of. The company is framing him to take the fall for their own schemes."

EMILY STARED at McAndrews in shock. In the sudden silence between them, she could hear the rattle of Laura's keyboard in the outer office, the clatter of delivery wagons in the street below. The air still smelled of salt and roses, but she'd lost all desire to go to the park.

"So it's true?" she said. She hadn't considered the fact that if their client hadn't committed fraud, that someone had framed him for it. "Someone at Vancouver Permanent is really framing Mr. Sinclair for fraud. Deliberately?"

"Yes, I'm afraid so."

Emily swallowed. Hard. Took a sip of her water. She felt as if someone had suddenly wrapped her in cotton batting, unable to feel anything.

Then she picked up her pencil and a notepad. Leaned towards him. "But how did you find out?"

McAndrews had been watching her. She'd felt his eyes on her. Now his face brightened, and he leaned forward. "Sinclair said he was good at selling, and so I asked him who his buyers had been. I talked to a few of them. Who are still very pleased with him, by the way."

He pulled his chair forward a bit, the legs scraping against the wood floor. Pulled out his notebook, opened it on the desk between them. "They'd heard no talk of fraud. And several of those buyers boasted to me of the terms they'd been given—little or no down payment, with ridiculously low rates of interest."

Emily thought of what Granville had told her after his meeting with the man from Vancouver Permanent. He'd offered Granville similar terms, so it hadn't been just Sinclair's doing. "Then how is the company even making money?"

McAndrews gave her an approving look. "I see why Mr. Granville hired you. That is exactly what I asked myself. So I set out to find out. Do you know how these companies work?"

"They loan people money to buy houses or property. That loan is secured by the property being purchased. And the money for the loans comes from investors, who in return receive a percentage of the profits."

"That is exactly right. And those are the three places where money flows in this situation," he said, writing on a blank page in his notebook so that she could see.

"See here? It flows from the investor," he drew a large I, "to the company," a larger C, "to fund the mortgages. Then it flows from the company to the property owner," drawing a small P, "to pay for the property."

Emily leaned forward. Nodded.

McAndrews smiled at her. In rather the way a teacher would smile at a particularly bright pupil, she thought with amusement.

"And it flows from the purchaser to the company as mortgage

payments," McAndrews said, drawing arrows, "then on to the original investor in the form of repayments and interest."

"So then fraud could happen at any of those places?" Emily asked.

"Yes. The most obvious, and the one Sinclair seems to have been accused of, is mortgage fraud, where the interest rates are too high for the market."

Emily considered the lines and arrows he'd drawn, thought about what he'd just said. "And yet the buyers say they are paying very low rates of interest? Which is where the company would normally make money," she said.

" So if they are not doing so, and there is talk of fraud, either they are involved in the land sale, and pricing it too high, or…" she paused, tapping her pencil on one of the arrows. "Somehow they are defrauding the investors?"

"Precisely. And since most of the land in town is still owned by the CPR, and since the investors are primarily English and unable to check first hand, I suspect the latter."

"How would that work?"

"The simplest is that they are keeping all monies received themselves, and paying existing investors their share of the "profit" using the money from new investors."

"But could they do that?" Emily asked. "They still have to pay out mortgage money from the monies received from those new investors. How can there possibly be enough left to make it worth their while to risk everything?"

"I don't know."

"So how would you prove it?"

"We'd need to see what returns they promised investors. And ideally what returns they actually paid." McAndrews ran a hand through his wiry hair. "Though something showing a growth in the investor pool would serve the same purpose, I suppose, since investments would quickly drop off if a firm didn't pay as promised."

Emily thought for a moment. The Canadian Pacific still played a major role in local land sales, which meant her father would likely to have access to that kind of information. And she could trust the information he gave her.

"I think I might be able to get some answers," she said. "What, specifically, do you need to know?"

McAndrews looked surprised, but told her. "Anything detailing Vancouver Permanent's rates and projected returns."

Emily scribbled it all down, then looked up and smiled at the man. "If you return this afternoon, Mr. Granville will be back. And I may have some answers for you. Perhaps at four o'clock?"

"That quickly? That would be amazing. But there must be something I could be doing in the meantime?"

"There is. Can you find out anything about a connection between Vancouver Permanent and a lawyer named Carver?"

McAndrews gave her a sharp look. "Fellow who was murdered a few days ago?"

"Yes. You might want to be careful how you ask about him."

McAndrews grinned at her. "I'm an accountant. We're always careful."

With a grin like that, Emily didn't believe him for a moment. No wonder Granville had hired the man.

It was a lovely June day, with no sign of showers, though a few grey clouds were massed along the horizon. Emily caught the streetcar along Hastings, then strolled down Granville Street, enjoying the sunshine and the slight breeze off the harbor. The Canadian Pacific Railway terminal loomed ahead of her.

She took the stairs to the second floor, where Papa had his office.

After the clerk knocked softly on the heavy oak door and ushered her in, Emily settled herself into the leather club chair set for visitors and waited for Papa to look up from the letter he was writing. She took an appreciative sniff of the cedar-scented air, and took in the bustling view of the rail yards and the harbor beyond.

Eventually Papa signed his name and blotted his pen. Capping the inkwell, he dusted the letter carefully to set the ink, then placed it in the out tray on the corner of his desk.

Looking up at last, he seemed surprised to see her. "Emily. Are you in trouble?"

"Not at all, Papa. I hoped you might be able to assist me with a project."

"Oh? To do with your wedding, is it?"

"Not exactly." Emily wished he wasn't so fixed in his view of her. "You were recently talking to Mr. Granville about mortgage fraud. He told me a little and I found it fascinating. Since I have to do a project for my business classes..."

"Don't tell me. You want know about mortgages?"

She nodded.

He groaned softly and closed his eyes. "Why can't you be more feminine, like your sisters?"

That hurt, but Emily ignored it. She already knew there was no point in arguing. "It is for my classes."

One of these days she was going to have to tell Mama and Papa that she was now working for Granville. If she was very lucky, though, she'd be able to put that off until after she and Granville were wed.

Otherwise, Papa was likely to lock her in her bedroom again, and she hadn't appreciated the experience the last time. Not that it had done him any good, she thought with a fleeting grin.

Her father probably noticed, but he just sighed more deeply in exasperation. "Very well. What do you want to know?"

"How does a mortgage firm make money?"

"From the difference between the interest rate they charge and the amount they have agreed to pay their investors."

"And if the rate is too low?"

"Either the investors don't make enough to be worth their while, or the firm doesn't make enough to pay their expenses. Either way, the firm either raises rates or has to go out of business."

She nodded, made a few notes. "Is there any way I can find out what rate of return a company is offering to their investors?"

"You could request a prospectus from them."

She smiled at him. "I doubt that would work, don't you think?"

He forgot his disapproval long enough to smile back. "Coming from a young girl like you? Probably not. Look, I have several here you could borrow for a few days, if that would be helpful?"

"Yes, indeed it would. Thank you." As he passed them across the desk, she was pleased to see that Vancouver Permanent was one of the offerings.

"I do have a few more questions, though," she said.

Her Papa sighed, but signaled her to go ahead.

"Why would a mortgage company reduce the interest rates they charge?"

"In a rising market, like this one, higher prices may mean the firm can charge less interest and still make a good income. Low interest rates may also be a factor in convincing a purchaser to buy, especially if it keeps the monthly payments low enough to be palatable. More sales mean more monthly income. Sometimes companies will reduce the down payment as an incentive for purchasers instead."

"Or both?"

He laughed. "Not if they want to stay in business. Though less scrupulous firms sometimes charge very low rates on a shorter term contract—say a year or two—so that a purchaser has to pay much higher interest rates when the contract ends."

Emily nodded, her pencil flying, glad that she'd persevered in mastering shorthand. "I see. So it's a balancing act—charging enough to stay in business, but not so much as to lose all business."

He beamed. "Yes, you have grasped it. That course of yours might not be such a waste after all." Then he ruined it, adding, "Not that I can see how you'll use it."

"Thank you, Papa," she said quietly, and took her leave, resisting the temptation to slam the door behind her. This was a professional office, after all.

And she intended to begin as she meant to go on.

EMILY STROLLED TOWARDS HASTINGS STREET, enjoying the elusive scent of the roses blooming in nearby gardens, and thinking about what she'd learned. Then she caught the streetcar back to the office. Back at her desk, Emily reviewed the notes she'd taken, then put in a call to Mr. Marshall.

"Miss Turner," he said when the call had gone through. "How nice to hear from you. And your timing is perfect. Mr. Granville was just by this morning, and asked me to pull some listings for homes with a slightly different design than the ones you've seen so far."

His voice was impeccably polite, but there was something odd about it. He sounded almost—uneasy, that was it, Emily thought. She wondered why? Was it something to do with the case, or was it something Granville had said to the man?

She'd have to ask Granville when she saw him next.

"Yes, and I'd hoped to see a few of those listings after lunch. Would that be possible?"

"You would? Today?" There was a pause, and Emily could hear the rustle of paper. "I'll have to make a few quick calls, but I think that should be possible. Is there is a number where I can call you back?"

"Of course," she said, and gave it to him.

When Mr. Marshall called back fifteen minutes later, Emily was pleased that he'd lined up two houses, one for one-thirty that afternoon and the other half an hour later.

"Since both of the houses you'll be seeing are on Pendrell Street, that will give us more than enough time," he said.

"That's perfect," she told him, and arranged to meet him at the first listing. And it really was. Pendrell was only a block down from the new streetcar route on Davie, which gave easy access by streetcar to anywhere in the city.

It was rather a shame they weren't really in the market for a home—she rather liked the idea of a newer house in that part of town. She could see herself living there, taking the streetcar into town in the mornings with Granville, her husband...

With a smile at her own foolishness, Emily dialed Clara's number. While she waited for it to ring through, she winked at Laura. "I hope for both our sakes that Clara is home," she said.

"Otherwise, you'll have to come and look at houses with me this afternoon."

Laura grimaced, but didn't pause in her typing. Emily grinned, but both of them were relieved when Clara agreed that she'd love to go for lunch and then look at houses.

By one- thirty, Emily, Clara and Mr. Marshall were strolling along Pendrell Street. Emily was admiring the gardens as they walked, the holly bushes flanking the front walk, the scent of roses and lilacs. The gardens were newer than those along Blueblood Alley, but the yards were just as carefully laid out.

She felt very much at home here, though she hadn't particularly cared for the first house the real estate agent had shown her. It was too fussy, with all those details.

Then Mr. Marshall stopped in front of the second house he'd chosen to show her that afternoon. Unlike the Queen Anne styles she'd seen previously, this one was a narrow, two-story house in the newer symmetrical style. It had a hipped roof with a distinctive "cyclops" dormer window, and a wide porch supported by slender columns. Best of all, it was half the size of the houses Emily had looked at previously.

"It's so much simpler and more modern," she exclaimed, looking at the gleaming white paint on the columns. "None of that fussy scrollwork. What do you think, Clara?"

"It's quite darling. If a little small," was Clara's comment.

The real estate agent beamed.

It really was too bad she couldn't really live in this house, Emily thought. It was perfect. "This one has three bedrooms, which is more than enough for us. It's much more practical than the houses we saw on Friday. I really like it a great deal, and so I will tell my fiancé." Emily said.

"It is most unusual that a young lady looks at a house before her prospective husband has seen it," Mr. Marshall said, "but I see there is real value in it."

"Well, it seemed to make sense for me to look at some of these different listings before we do too much planning. We didn't want to lose time in our house search, and he was in agreement that it made sense for me to see some of the potential homes on my own. With Clara's input, of course."

Mr. Marshall nodded, and Clara made a face at Emily behind his back.

"I do have several equally unusual questions," Emily said. "I have an interest in business, and Mr. Granville supports that. He mentioned that you had recommended Vancouver Permanent, and that their rates were very low, with no down-payment. Is this an arrangement that other firms would also make?"

He looked startled, then smiled. "I see that the two of you have a very unusual relationship. And it is a good question. To put it simply, then no, Vancouver Permanent is currently offering the best terms in town. It is why we are able to send them so much business."

"And do they receive any kind of commission or discount from your firm?"

At this he did laugh. "No, not at all. That isn't how the business is done. They are compensated by the interest they receive on the loan they make to the purchaser. Mr. Granville, in this case, I hope."

Emily nodded. "Well, I really like this house, and I think Mr. Granville will agree."

"And do you have any further questions I could answer?"

Emily badly wanted to ask how much the two houses were, but she didn't want to shock the man too badly. And her behavior would reflect on Granville, too.

It was so annoying to have to consider such things, but she knew Granville would tell her what she wanted to know later.

"You mentioned how good the rates are for Vancouver Permanent right now," Emily said. "If Mr. Granville waits to purchase, might he receive a lower rate?"

"That is an excellent question. Unfortunately, the answer is no." Marshall sorted through a few papers in the leather folder he carried. He pulled out a hand-written chart and passed it to her. "I've been keeping track of their rates over the last year, and you can see that they're as low as they're ever likely to go."

He chuckled. "In fact, if they went any lower, the company would likely have to go out of business."

"Yes, I see," Emily said, thinking quickly. This was exactly the information she'd come for. "Might I have a copy of this, to show Mr. Granville?"

"Why, I suppose so," Mr. Marshall said. "I'll have my clerk make a copy for you and send it to you. And was there anything further that I can answer for you?"

"No, not for myself," she said. "Thank you. You've been most helpful. What about you, Clara?"

"I think I've heard enough, thank you," Clara said in smooth tones. Clearly she'd had enough of the business discussion.

Emily held back her smile through sheer willpower.

BY THREE-THIRTY, Emily was again back at her desk. Aside from Laura, still busily typing up reports, the office was deserted.

"Did I miss anything?" she asked.

"No, it's been very quiet," Laura said. "No calls, even."

"I suppose that's good," Emily said, and began to read through the four prospectuses that her father had loaned her.

It made for very boring reading, but the thing that surprised her was how similar all four were. Yet Mr. Marshall had said that they recommended clients to Vancouver Permanent because their terms were so much better than the other firms. Something was wrong here.

She heard footsteps approaching down the hallway and looked up as the outer door to the office opened. "Granville. Your timing is perfect."

"I'm glad to hear it," he said, hanging his hat and coat on the coat tree. "I gather you have had a productive day?"

"Very," she said, rising. "And I need to talk to you before Mr. McAndrews returns. He was here this morning, and will be back at four."

"Which is also perfect timing," he said with a grin, and stepped back so she could precede him into his office.

"Would you like a pot of tea?" Laura asked.

"If it isn't too much trouble, that would be appreciated," Granville told her over his shoulder. "And some of those biscuits, if we have them?"

14

"You've already seen two smaller houses?" Granville asked, looking across the desk at Emily. He thought how comfortable she looked there, perched on the edge of Scott's too-big chair, flipping through a notebook filled with squiggles that must be shorthand. "What did you think of them?"

"I liked them. Especially the second one, which was more modern than the ones we saw," Emily said, looking up at him. "Clara liked both of them equally. Though she thought them a bit small.

"I'm sure she did," Granville said, smiling at her. "But did they suit you?"

"Yes, they did. Much better than the second last house we saw on Friday, much as I loved it."

"What, even more than the mansions?"

"As if you'd be happy living in a mansion," Emily said.

Granville just smiled, and hoped she didn't see the house he'd been raised in until they'd been married a few years. It would fit four of the mansions they'd seen the other day. Easily. Probably with room to spare. And without his father there, it would no longer be a home.

But the house and the land, the obligations that came with them —those had owned his father, taken his time, his health. He didn't want that for himself.

"I did like both the houses I saw today," she said, apparently not expecting a reply. "They felt—cozy, I think is the word. Manageable. Big enough for us, with room for a cook and a maid, but not so big that I'd feel guilty for not wanting to be bothered with house matters."

"They sound perfect. Which one do you want to buy?" he asked.

"Oh! No, I didn't mean we should buy one of them." She blushed faintly, and he wondered what she was thinking. It wasn't like Emily to blush. "And certainly not without your having seen it first. Really, I just wanted to ask Mr. Marshall a question or two, and it was a good excuse to do so. And especially when you'd talked to him earlier this morning."

She paused, grinned at him. "Though I didn't ask him how much the houses were, which I really did want to know, because I didn't want to shock him too badly. But I suspect these houses would save enough to allow you to buy one of them and the office building as well."

He raised his brows. "And what questions did you ask him?" he said with a grin.

Emily quickly explained about McAndrews' visit and their conversation, and showed him the documents her father had loaned her and told him about the interest rate chart Marshall had given her, pointing out the differences in the terms.

"And Mr. Marshall said they use Vancouver Permanent because their terms are better," she concluded. "Something doesn't make sense."

"It certainly doesn't," Granville said, examining the documents with interest. If this was what they'd promised investors, he didn't see how they'd make any money, given the numbers Thompson had offered him. "This is good work, and ties in nicely with what I've been finding out. Now all we need is McAndrews."

There was a commotion at the door.

"And this should be him now."

But it wasn't. Trent burst into the inner office, with Scott right behind him.

"You'll never guess what we found out," he said.

"Probably not. So sit down and tell us," Granville said.

"It was murder," Trent said, too excited to sit down. "He was shot straight on. Made a mess of his face. And…" He drew the last word out until it was painful.

"And what?" Granville asked, winking at Scott. Knowing it was the fastest way to get Trent to tell him the rest.

"And they've arrested a suspect. Charged him, too."

"For what? Carver's death?" Granville asked.

"What else?" Trent said.

Right. Granville looked over at Scott, who was leaning back in his chair. "Why don't you tell it? I'd appreciate a few facts. And Trent? Sit."

A subdued Trent subsided into the nearest chair.

"Course you would," Scott said.

He grinned at his partner's dry tone. "So what do we know about Carver's death? I gather he was shot in the face? That makes a pretty strong argument for murder. They know who shot him?"

"Well, they've arrested a fellow, but I wouldn't put money on them having arrested the right man," Scott said.

"And why is that?"

"Because they've hauled in some sailor just hit port the afternoon of the shooting. Man swears he'd never set eyes on Carver, much less shot him."

Granville stared at Scott, thinking about what this meant to them. Was it possible Carver's death wasn't related to their investigation? Perhaps. But shot in his office by a visiting sailor? No. "And what does the town say?"

That was apparently too much for Trent. He bounced back up again. "Most believe the sailor. Carver wasn't one to hit the places along the dock, not ever. They say his tastes were more 'highbrow.'"

Granville fought back a smile. "And who is they?"

"I talked to his clerk, and then we hung around the Post Office some."

"Carver'd been in town a few years, and people knew him," Scott said. "He had the reputation of being a hard worker, and cautious with money. Apparently he was a poor judge of any kind of investment, though."

"I'd say that's an understatement," Granville said. "Considering he got involved first with one of Gipson's schemes, and then with Vancouver Permanent. Just what is his role with them, anyway?"

"With the Permanent?" Trent said. "That's what they call it, you know."

"Ironic name, isn't it?" came a voice from the door.

<hr>

GRANVILLE WAS SMILING as he turned to see McAndrews standing in the doorway, with Miss Kent behind him.

"I thought you'd want to see this gentleman as soon as he arrived," she said by way of explanation. "And the document Miss Turner was waiting for has been delivered."

"You thought right. Thank-you Miss Kent," Granville said as he stood and extended a hand. "McAndrews. Good to see you."

Emily had stood up, and was accepting an envelope from Miss Kent with a smile and a soft word of thanks.

"Granville." McAndrews shook hands, and nodded a greeting to the others as everyone reseated themselves. "But go on. You were talking about Carver's relationship with the Permanent."

"Actually, we were just about to not talk about it," Scott said. "As we didn't learn a single thing of value. Whatever that relationship was, they managed to play it close to the vest."

"Then my arrival is timely," McAndrews said. "Since I did learn a few things."

"Oh, good." Emily said. "You have contacts none of us do, so I was hoping you would have learned something. Can you tell us?"

"It appears that Putnam, their director, consulted with Carver fairly regularly."

Putnam had? "I thought the firm worked with Henderson and Pruitt," Granville said.

"Henderson and Pruitt drew up the documents that created the Vancouver Permanent's syndicate, and are called in on anything relating to that structure, or any dealings with the syndicate's investors. No more than four or five times a year, though, or so it would seem."

"That makes sense if the money is largely invested from Britain," Granville said, thinking of his last case, where his very English—and very opportunistic—brother had used Henderson and Pruitt to formalize their contract. "Henderson and Pruitt seem to have strong connections to England. What kind of work did Carver do for Putnam, then?"

"Excellent question, to which I have no answer at all. But Putnam and Carver met weekly, and Henderson and Pruitt were only called in occasionally."

"So the relationship with Carver must have dealt with operational issues. Perhaps he filed mortgage documents for them?" Granville said.

"No. The firm I work for takes care of that," McAndrews said. "We have a lawyer on staff for exactly that purpose, and our clients find it very convenient to handle the money transfer through us."

"Do you have access to the Permanent's records?"

"Not without being fired for it," McAndrews said. "And it would be a betrayal of my professional obligations in any case."

Granville liked that in him, even if it was inconvenient at the moment. "So Carver was an active part of the Permanent's operation. Was he an investor as well?"

"If he was, they kept it quiet," McAndrews said, and Scott nodded agreement.

"We couldn't find anything, either. And we found nothing to connect Carver's death with Vancouver Permanent or with Putnam," his partner said.

Granville looked at the dejected faces round the table. This case seemed to be dead end after dead end. So far they'd found nothing to help clear their client's name.

"Sorry I couldn't be more help." McAndrews' face looked drawn and tired. He was taking this case very personally.

"You've just begun," Emily said with a smile.

She spread out the various prospectuses on the table, and added the notations Thompson had made. "We were comparing Vancouver Permanent's prospectus for investors to what they actually offer clients. And it looks all wrong to us, but we can't see how they'd benefit in operating this way. Maybe you can see something we're missing?"

McAndrews dragged his chair over to the edge of the desk, and leaned forward so he could see more clearly. He began reading, flipping from one document to the other and back again, muttering to himself.

"I don't believe it," he said finally, slamming the Vancouver Permanent prospectus closed. "This confirms my suspicions."

"What is it?" Emily asked. "How are they making their money?"

"They aren't," McAndrews said. "What you have here is a house of cards. They are committed to paying their investors five percent on their investment. You can see that right here in the prospectus."

Emily was nodding, though Trent looked a bit confused.

"But they are only taking in three percent. At best."

"They offered me two," Granville said.

"Then why have the investors not put them out of business?" Emily asked.

"They must be using new investment money coming in to pay the interest on the older investments."

"But...but...Wait a minute." Trent said. "I know I'm not very good with numbers, but how can they keep doing that?"

"They can't keep doing that," Emily said to Trent. "Which is probably why somebody needed to frame Sinclair."

McAndrews was nodding. "Because it was all about to collapse on them."

She nodded, walking over to the desk and pulling a page towards her. "Unless they can keep the new investment money flowing in. And to do that, they'd have to show that their business is growing. It's the only way to justify the return they are paying."

She ran her finger down the column of interest rates the real estate agent had just sent her. "And to keep growing, they're offering better and better deals to potential clients, because our prices are rising and many buyers are nervous. Low rates entice them to buy now rather than wait to see if the market falls again. Just like they did with Granville.

You see here? Over the last month, the rates have fallen by almost a quarter of a percent. That makes no sense. Am I right?"

McAndrews nodded, and Granville smiled at her. Her head for business continued to amaze him.

"So they're caught," McAndrews said, moving so he could see over her shoulder. "In order to keep the investors, whom they can't afford to pay back, they have to accept lower and lower interest rates on the money they loan out. Which then means they need more and more investors to make up the difference."

"But who is behind this?" Emily asked.

Which was exactly what Granville had been thinking. "It has to be Putnam," he said slowly. "Doesn't it? If you're right about this, McAndrews, and they're defrauding the investors, then Putnam has to be behind it. It's too big for it to be anyone else. And Putnam's the one in direct communication to the investors."

"And the accusations against Sinclair are a smoke screen," McAndrews said, frowning in concentration. "That's why it didn't seem to make sense. And why I couldn't verify the complaints. Putnam's accusing Sinclair of a mortgage fraud that isn't actually happening to confuse things while he's busy defrauding his investors."

"What about Williams? The Sales Director?" Trent asked.

"He might be part of it, but if so, he's in league with Putnam, and probably working under his direction," McAndrews said.

"So if we expose Putnam for fraud, we break open the entire scheme," said Granville with satisfaction.

"But how do we prove it?" Emily said.

There was a little silence.

She was right, it was mostly guesswork at this point, Granville thought. How did they prove it?

"I don't get it. Why are they still in business if that's how they're operating?" Scott said. "What's in it for them? It's pretty easy for someone like Putnam to just disappear one night, along with whatever happens to be in the safe. They aren't likely to catch him, and with most of the losses being in Britain, the local law probably wouldn't even look very hard."

"Good question," McAndrews said. "Putnam and whoever else he's involved must be making money somewhere. Or there would be no point in keeping it going. They might simply be keeping all the interest themselves, while paying the investors out of the new money coming in."

"But why would they get themselves into such a mess?" Granville asked. "They must have started with a plan for making money, not losing it."

"Did Mr. Thompson tell you the term of the mortgage contract, or how long it would be before the interest rates had to be renegotiated?" Emily asked him.

"No, he didn't," he said. "Why does that matter?"

"My father said it's a trick some firms use," she said. "The mortgage firm takes a loss for a year or two, then raises the rates much higher."

"Which would create a solid cash flow in the longer term," McAndrews said. "But how did they plan to cover the short term loss?"

"When did they lower the down payment amounts?" Emily asked.

McAndrews eyes lit up. "Maybe when the market heated up? In order to get the sales to match the numbers on this prospectus, they had to keep people buying quickly. So they reduced the down payment as well as the interest rates. And found themselves without the money to pay their investors in the short term."

"So how would they be paying them?" Emily asked. "Would there be enough new money to provide both mortgages and the interest for the investors? Surely this whole scheme would spin out of control at some point?"

"You're right, it should," McAndrews said. "But without more detail on their finances, we're only guessing how this is working."

"What I don't understand," Granville said. "Is why they bothered to frame Sinclair. How does that gain them anything?"

"And how did Carver end up dead?" Scott added. "Is that coincidence, or has someone added murder to fraud?"

"I guess we have more work to do, then," Emily said. "And I suspect we'll be working late. Anyone for more tea?"

15

By evening it was raining again, and the dampness made it feel much too cold for June. A breeze off the harbor, smelling of brine and seaweed, sent the cold air straight down his neck. Granville turned up his collar and increased his pace. The street lamps lining Howe Street flickered on, buzzing madly as they warmed up.

Beside him, McAndrews matched his stride, though given the size of the umbrella the accountant carried, he wasn't getting wet in any case. Workhorses clopped by, iron shod hooves ringing against the brick of the streets, as the day's last deliveries were made.

"Why are we going to Carver's office, anyway?" McAndrews asked. "There wasn't anyone there earlier today, and now it's past closing time."

"Exactly," Granville said, shoving his hands into his pockets. He needed his fingers limber, not stiff with cold, for what he had in mind. "If Carver's death is connected to this mess that the Permanent seems to be in, then I'm guessing he did or planned to do something that Putnam found threatening. And he knew too much, so he had to go."

"How do you figure that?"

"Simple. If he worked with Putnam that closely, he had to know what was going on. And don't forget he was a lawyer, despite his questionable judgment in his business dealings. We need to find out what work he was doing for the Permanent."

"You mean what he was helping them hide."

"It seems logical, doesn't it? And keep that umbrella out of my eyes."

"Sorry. And yes, all too logical," McAndrews said, moving it to his other shoulder. "So why do I think I'm going to be helping you break into Carver's office?"

"Oh, you won't need to help me break in. I just need you to interpret what we find when I've done so."

"Oh, that's much better," McAndrews said.

"You might want to close the umbrella, too," Granville advised him. "We're getting close, and that thing is huge. It's too memorable."

In silence the two approached the alley running behind Carver's office. A rusting iron fire escape ran up the back of the four-story brick building, with a minuscule landing outside an oversize window on each floor. Granville tested the first step.

"Seems secure enough."

"What floor was Carver on?"

"Third."

"And you figure we'll get in that window?"

"Sure. It might be latched, but it won't be locked. We'll get in."

"Which puts us in a hallway. Then what?"

"Then your job is to follow me. Quietly."

McAndrews muttered something, but subsided.

Granville chuckled. "When we're done, the drinks are on me."

He was climbing rapidly up the rickety stairs before McAndrews could respond.

The third floor hallway was dimly lit by wavering emergency lighting at each end. Cheap electricity and the devastating fire of

'86 meant that the city took their fire precautions seriously. None of the offices had lights on, and the creak of the occasional floorboard was unsettlingly loud in the stillness. Number 316, Carver's office, was at the far end of the hall. That office was dark, too, and there was no sound coming from inside.

"We're in luck," Granville said. "I don't suppose you know how to pick locks?"

"You're joshing me, right?" McAndrews said. "And I suppose you do?"

"Unfortunately not," Granville said. "I've tried to learn a couple of times, but I'm hopeless."

"Then…" McAndrews was staring at the door, as if expecting it to open under his gaze.

Granville leaned back and, putting all his power behind it, kicked the door just below the handle. There was a loud crack.

McAndrews just stared. "I hope that wasn't your foot?" he managed to say, just as Granville repeated the motion.

The door swung inward.

"They built the building to last, but they went cheap on the doors," Granville said. "I noticed it the last time I was here."

He pushed the door open further and went in, pulling a candlestick and a box of lucifers out of his inner pocket as he did so.

"I wouldn't have taken that contract if I'd known what you had in mind…" McAndrews began.

Granville shushed him. "Later. When we're out of here."

He led the way through the reception area to Carter's office, one hand shielding the candle from drafts. All too conscious that the moving light, faint as it was, would attract attention if anyone happened to be looking up from the street below.

GRANVILLE TRIED the doorknob to Carver's inner sanctum, and it opened. Not locked, which was interesting.

The air smelt stale and a little musty, with the lingering stench of violent death underneath it, though the office had obviously been cleaned. Carter had only been dead for three days.

The blinds were down and closed. Good. Granville glanced out, and seeing no-one on the street, reached behind the blind to open the window an inch. The fresh, rain-laden air was welcome.

He let the blind drop and turned back into the room.

Closing the inner door, Granville drew out another candle. Lighted it, and handed it to McAndrews—who took it slowly. The man looked a little stunned, Granville thought with an inward grin. Obviously he hadn't expected this.

"Have a look through his files," Granville said, indicating the four-drawer wooden file cabinet on the wall behind him. "I'll see if there's anything in his desk."

"What am I looking for?" McAndrews asked.

"Anything relating to Putnam or the Permanent. Especially anything relating to the legal work he did for them or any financial details."

"There will be a number of files, so they should be easy to find."

"Assuming they're still here. If I was Putnam, I'd make sure whoever took care of Sinclair also cleared out those files."

"Oh." McAndrews carefully dripped some wax on the top of the cabinet and set the candle into it. Then he opened the first drawer and began methodically going through the file folders.

Granville watched as he pulled one file half out, flicking through a couple of pages, then putting it back. McAndrews kept going, and Granville turned to the desk, considering it for a moment.

There was a yellow legal pad on the right-hand side, with a couple of sharpened pencils beside it. The top page was half-covered with neatly drawn and shaded scrolls, winding together. Carver had been a doodler. Granville suddenly had a mental picture of the lawyer, pencil in hand, drawing these intricate patterns in the middle of a long and boring phone call.

Pushing the all-too-vivid image away, Granville focused on the search. He flipped through the legal pad, which was otherwise empty.

"If I was a lawyer, and I didn't trust my client, where would I…?" he muttered to himself.

His gaze taking in the heavy double pedestal oak desk, then the leather blotter, cut-glass inkstand and the angled metal lamp on the desktop. If he was going to find anything at all, he was probably looking for something small. A list of numbers, perhaps, or a safety deposit box key.

He quickly checked the desk drawers. Locked.

He lifted the blotter, checked beneath it, and under the blotting paper. Nothing.

Nothing under the inkstand, with its three engraved and lidded inkwells. Just ink in two of the inkwells, but the third was empty. No ink, but no notes or keys in the empty well, either. If it had ever been a hiding place, it had been too obviously so.

The lamp was equally unhelpful, as was the knee-well under the desk, though he carefully felt into every nook.

He glanced over at McAndrews, who was on the second drawer now, but seemed to be having equally little luck. He was frowning, and he hadn't pulled out any files or papers.

Granville scanned the room again. He checked behind the framed photographs, the landscape, the framed degrees. Nothing. He ran his fingers along the top of the molding, the door and window frames. Still nothing.

Returning his attention to the desk, he focused on the drawers. He likely didn't have time to break into all of them. So which one?

The two file drawers were too obvious. He looked more closely at the locks on those drawers. They bore signs of scratching around the edges. If there had been something to find, it was gone now.

That left four normal sized drawers, two on the left, two on the right. They all bore scratches around the locks, but perhaps the searchers hadn't known what to look for, or hadn't been patient—or devious—enough.

He started with the drawer on the top right. If Carver had been right-handed, it was the automatic choice. Pulling out his knife, he ran it between the desktop and the drawer. He felt resistance, and then, as he applied more force, a click.

He breathed a sigh of relief. Desk locks were much simpler than door locks. Pulling the drawer full out, he lifted it to check the underside, then scanned the empty box left in the desk. Still nothing.

Sitting down, he placed the drawer on the desk and methodically emptied it, checking each item carefully with his fingertips as well as his eyes before placing it on the desktop.

When the drawer was empty, he'd found exactly nothing. Examining the inside of the drawer, he saw nothing. He ran his fingertips slowly over the whole inside surface, paying particular attention to the area closest to where Carver had sat.

Behind him, he heard the rustling of files, the whisper of pages turning, and McAndrews steadily swearing under his breath. He suspected that the files the accountant had expected to find were missing.

Outside, Granville could hear the occasional carriage going by, the calls of the shopkeepers as they closed for the night, and a burst or two of rowdy singing from the bar down the block.

He almost missed the slight bump near the back of the drawer. Angling the drawer so he could see what his fingers had felt, at first he saw nothing. Then he realized he was looking at a bit of brown packing tape, that someone had inked with a fair facsimile of oak woodgrain.

He picked at the edges of the tape, and a small gold key fell out. Etched into it was the number 196.

Perfect. Now all he needed was the lock that the key fit into.

AFTER RE-ASSEMBLING THE DRAWER, minus the key and the tape, Granville looked to see what McAndrews had found. "Any luck?" he asked.

"A couple of interesting pages, but I suspect they won't yield much. You?"

"A key. Are you ready to go?"

"A key? Really?" McAndrews closed the drawer he'd been flipping through, and opened the bottom one. "I'll just be a couple of minutes. There's not much in this one."

While he waited, Granville walked to the window. As he got closer, he had a partial view of the street below. The street seemed deserted, but with the blinds closed, how was he seeing anything? Looking more closely he could see there was a narrow slice missing from one of the blinds. Just enough to give someone standing here a view of the sidewalk across the street. And just enough to let a passerby spot the glow from their candles.

"McAndrews, pack up. We're leaving. Now."

"But I'm nearly…"

"Now."

"Alright, alright." McAndrews slipped a slim folder into an inside pocket in his coat, then straightened up. "Why the rush? I don't hear anything."

Putting a finger to his lips and beckoning McAndrews to follow him, Granville tiptoed to the office door. He blew out his candle. He could hear the huff as McAndrews did the same.

Drawing his knife, Granville eased the door open. Listened hard.

Silence.

Poking his head out, he could see the reception area, full of shadows and faintly illuminated by the light from the hallway. He could see no movement in the hall. None in the reception area.

Beckoning McAndrews to follow him, he moved quickly through the main office to the door. There he stopped, senses alert. Waiting.

Probably he was being too cautious, but there was no point taking chances.

He eased the door open and waited. Listening.

Still nothing. Behind him, McAndrews hadn't made a sound. Good.

Granville risked a quick look around the doorframe. The hall was empty.

So was the fire escape.

There was no sign of anyone in the alley, either, but the shadows were thick there.

Granville braced himself. Knife ready. Eyes on the shadows. Alert for any motion, any sound.

He picked his way silently down the stairs.

Then McAndrews nearly lost his footing on a warped step and saved himself by grabbing the railing, which squeaked loudly. McAndrews froze.

Granville rolled his eyes. No point in caution now. He descended to the alley in a rush, to take anyone waiting by surprise.

Nothing.

There was no-one there. Granville let his knife drop into its sheath and took in his first full breath since they'd left the office. Behind him he could hear McAndrews stepping down onto the loose gravel of the alley. The fellow's foot slipped again. He grinned at the sound. Probably accountants didn't spend much time climbing fire escapes.

Then McAndrews let out a yell.

Granville spun around, knife drawn and ready. Only good instincts saved him. He leaned back, dodging the blow that came out of nowhere.

Bracing his right leg, Granville unleashed a kick with all his power behind it. His opponent hit the ground, clutching his privates. Moaning.

There had been three of them.

They must have hidden in the thick shadows under the fire

escape, waiting until he'd dropped his guard. The biggest of the three was now on the ground. The other two were making McAndrews' life miserable. He was holding them off, barely, with his longer reach. But the shorter, quicker men were getting in more blows than the accountant was.

Neither of the thugs seemed to be armed.

Sheathing his knife, Granville grabbed the closer of the two by his collar. He delivered a right hook. Felt the fellow's fist slam into his cheek.

Shook it off.

Followed it with a left that put the man down.

As the second man fell, McAndrews grunted under another blow, then closed on his opponent with a flurry of wild punches.

There was a crunch, and then there were three men on the ground.

"Ouch," said McAndrews, shaking out his hand and looking at their ambushers. None of whom was getting up. "I guess they wanted to talk to us."

"Especially you," Granville said. "I wonder why. Now, shall we get out of here?"

"Aren't you going to question them?"

"No point. I recognize the big one," and he gestured at the first man. "He's hired muscle. Won't know much."

"Hang on," McAndrews said, leaning over the man he'd just flattened. "I think I know this one. And I think we need to hear what he has to say."

"Right. You plan to hang out here until he comes to?"

"Nope. We're taking him with us," McAndrews said with a grin. "Poor man can't hold his liquor. We're taking him back to his place."

"Might work at that," Granville said, walking over and poking the fellow with the toe of his boot. "He's out cold, and likely to stay that way for a bit. Fine, we'll do it your way, as long as we can find a hack. On three."

With a grunt of effort, they hoisted the man between them, his arms draped loosely over their shoulders.

"Onward," Granville said.

McAndrews grinned at him, and the three of them staggered down the alley.

16

Against McAndrews's protests, Granville directed the hackney to one of the taverns along the wharf. The Beaver was disreputable enough to overlook the state of their prisoner. And between the him and McAndrews, thug number three wasn't going anywhere.

From what he could see of the fellow, Granville figured he was more likely to talk in a bar with a few whiskeys inside him than otherwise.

"So who is he?" Granville asked once the three of them were seated—or slumped, in their captive's case—around a small table in a back corner. The place was raucous tonight. The chance of being overheard was practically nil. "I gather he's not a thug by trade."

"Nope," McAndrews said, throwing back half his whiskey in a gulp. He seemed to have forgiven Granville for the break and enter earlier in the afterglow of a successful fight.

"In fact, this poor sap is an accountant. Or he thinks he is. Really, Fergus here is no more than a bookkeeper, which is why he's currently between employments."

"Interesting choice of a new career, then," Granville said.

McAndrews chuckled and downed the rest of his drink.

"Exactly. Especially when—as you pointed out—two of them were focused on me. If they'd asked around, they'd have known you were the better fighter."

"So maybe who-ever had them watching the office figured it would take an accountant to recognize what was valuable and what wasn't."

McAndrews nodded. "That's why I wanted to bring Fergus along."

"Because they must have told Fergus here enough for him to recognize whatever it is they were looking for," Granville said.

"That, plus the man's a coward. He'll talk."

"Ah." Granville swallowed a mouthful of his own whiskey. It was one step up from rotgut, but the burn was welcome after the damp alley. "That should be helpful."

"I thought so." McAndrews frowned at his captive. "If he ever wakes up, that is."

It was a good half-hour later before Fergus showed any signs of stirring. He groaned, shifted a little, then settled back into unconsciousness again.

"That's some blow you gave him," Granville said to McAndrews. "You do much fighting?"

"You're joshing again, right? No, I just got lucky this time. I don't know if I was more scared or annoyed."

Granville laughed. "That combination will do it, all right."

Fergus groaned again. Then blinked a couple of times.

"He's coming around."

McAndrews leaned over, slapped their captive on the cheek. "Fergus. Hey, Fergus."

Another groan.

Granville moved a glass of whiskey closer. "He'll be needing this. He's going to wake with some headache."

McAndrews was shaking his former colleague's shoulder. "Fergus, we have some questions for you. Wake up."

"Wha…? Whassup?"

"Who hired you?" Granville asked.

"Uh…? Hired? Fellow named Dagan. Why?"

"How'd you do that?" McAndrews asked in an undertone.

"He's not fully conscious yet. It works, sometimes. You ever heard of this Dagan?"

"No. He's not in accounting, though."

Granville nodded. "Fergus. Fergus!"

"Wha…a?"

"Where do I find Dagan?"

"The Black Bull, sometimes."

Granville glanced at McAndrews, who shrugged. He turned back to McAndrews' victim, but it was too late.

Fergus' head was up off the table, and he was blinking groggily from Granville to McAndrews. "I know you!" he said accusingly. "Where am I?"

"The Beaver," Granville said. "You weren't feeling well. We bought you a whiskey."

The fellow's gaze rested on the drink. He reached out a shaky hand, and downed it. "Thanks. My head hurts. What happened?"

"There was a fight," Granville said. "You got hit. Your friends left you behind."

"No friends of mine." Fergus said. "I need another."

"I'll get it," McAndrews said. "But we need more on Dagan, first. Why'd he hire you?"

Fergus eyes seemed to focus on McAndrews, and his gaze sharpened. "Wait, you're McAndrews. You're the one we—I need to get out of here." And he scrambled to his feet.

Only to find Granville's hand heavy on his shoulder, forcing him back down again.

"I think you want to talk to us first," Granville said.

"Like that, is it?" Fergus said, looking from one face to the other.

"Exactly like that. And since you're on the losing side right now, I think you might want to talk to us," Granville said.

"But Dagan…"

"Isn't here. We are. What did he want?"

Fergus shrugged. "Fine. I'll need another whiskey first."

McAndrews glanced at Granville, then headed for the bar. When he returned with the requested drink, Fergus reached eagerly for it and downed it in one swallow.

"Now...," Granville said.

"He figured McAndrews had something he wanted," Fergus said. "We were supposed to get it back."

"How did you know where to look for McAndrews?"

"They told us to watch Carver's office. If anyone I recognized went in there, then we were to attack them, take whatever they had."

"Any accountant, you mean?" Granville said.

"Well, yeah. See, that's who I know."

"And what were you looking for?"

"Numbers. Account sheets. That kinda stuff."

"What kind of numbers?" McAndrews asked.

"They didn't tell me, see?" Fergus said. "It wasn't like I was looking for them, just checking whatever you—or someone like you—took away with them."

McAndrews glanced over at Granville and nodded. So it was possible.

"Checking for what?" McAndrews asked.

Fergus blinked a little. "My head hurts," he said, rubbing at his forehead.

When that got him nothing but hard looks, he sighed gustily. "Checking they were real," Fergus said. "Not something cooked up for show, y'know. Like that."

"To do that, you'd have to know what industry the figures were for," McAndrews said.

"Well, yeah. Numbers. Financial stuff." He glanced over at Granville, then back at McAndrews and cleared his throat nervously. "Loans and stuff. Can I have another drink?"

Granville nodded at McAndrews, who stood up and went to the bar. While they waited for him to return, Granville watched Fergus in silence. By the time McAndrews returned with his whiskey and set it in front of him, Fergus was blinking rapidly.

He grabbed the glass, downed it. Then rubbed at his forehead again.

"What kind of loans?" Granville asked.

"Just loans."

McAndrews glared at him. "There's no such thing."

Fergus swallowed. "Real estate," he muttered.

And there it was. "So why did the man who hired you want these numbers?" Granville asked.

"What makes you think he'd tell me?" Fergus whined.

"You don't want to cross this man, Fergus," McAndrews said. "Trust me on this."

"But…" Fergus began, then cast a nervous look at Granville. "Look, I really don't know. I kinda owe them some money, so I didn't have any choice. They said I just had to do this, and not talk about it, and we'd be clear. So I tried. Only it didn't work."

And he gave McAndrews an angry look.

Granville nodded. It was probably true, unfortunately. And at least they had a name. Dagan, whoever he was. "Let's go," he said to McAndrews.

Turning to their former captive, he said, "I won't forget that you attacked us. If I hear you've told anyone—anyone at all—about this discussion, I'll come looking for you. And if I have to do that, what you may or may not know will be irrelevant."

Fergus nodded vigorously. "Yeah," he croaked out. "I won't talk."

"See that you don't. McAndrews?"

"I'm with you."

AS THEY EXITED THE TAVERN, McAndrews gave Granville a puzzled look. "I don't get it. Fergus is pretty useless, but he had to know more about whoever hired him than he was letting on."

"Maybe, maybe not. Could be he's more scared of them than of us. I doubt we'll get much more out of him, though. Which is why we're going to follow him, see where he goes."

Granville led the way to a dark corner where the alley met the street. "No-one coming out will see us here—it's too dark for their eyes to adjust. But we'll see them."

"Oh. No wonder I'm just an accountant."

"Hardly that. We all have our strengths, that's all. And you'll be able to analyze what Fergus did tell us in a way that I can't."

"What do you mean? He didn't tell us anything. Well, except that it's something to do with real estate loans."

Around them the only sound was hissing of rain on the street. It was foggy out on the water, but the streets were still clear. Checking that no-one else was in sight, Granville moved a few feet over so that he was mostly sheltered under the overhang of the roof. They had a good view of the door from here.

"It seems to me we have confirmation that they were looking for a detailed accounting record of a business dealing with real estate loans. One that hadn't been faked. Am I right?"

"Yes, but who cares?" McAndrews said, kicking at a rock, then wincing at the sound. "We already knew that."

"Well, we knew we might be looking for something of the kind. We didn't know they were. Whoever they are."

"Oh." McAndrews stood silent as the rain dripped from the eaves and bounced off the brim of their hats. "I'm hopeless at this, aren't I?"

Possibly. "Give yourself time."

"Yeah."

He didn't sound like he believed it. Granville didn't blame him. "Now all we need to do is figure out who they are."

"But it's Putnam, isn't it? It has to be."

"Does it? How do you know there isn't another player we haven't identified yet?

"I don't. But that seems far-fetched. Putnam's the one setting up Sinclair. Why wouldn't Carver set up Putnam?"

"He might have. Which would mean Putnam and Carver were at odds. Have you heard anything that would indicate that?"

"Well, no."

"Because if it was true, if Carver was collecting evidence on Putnam that Putnam is now desperate to get back, then that likely implicates Putnam in Carver's murder."

He watched McAndrews' face as the accountant absorbed the implication of just how desperate Putnam might be. "It can be dangerous to ask questions without having some idea what the outcome might be. And how you'd react if you found yourself in such a situation."

"Yeah," McAndrews said. "I—there goes Fergus."

"About time," Granville said, pulling his hat brim down and his collar up. "I was getting soggy. Slowly now. We don't want him knowing we're behind him."

———

AFTER A WASTED half hour following Fergus to his run-down boarding house on the edge of town, Granville and McAndrews walked back towards town. McAndrews turned off towards his boarding house, and Granville headed for his own rooms.

His thoughts turned to the houses he and Emily had looked at, and he tried to imagine how it would feel if he were heading for his own house tonight, with Emily there to greet him. It was a pleasant thought.

As he walked by their office, he was surprised to see a light in the window. He glanced at his pocket watch. Just after midnight, which meant it was probably Scott. He rotated his sore shoulder, wincing only a little. Not too bad, he decided.

He could find out if Scott had ever heard of Dagan. And it would be good to have a quiet drink together, just the two of them. Like it used to be. As he climbed the stairs to the third floor, Granville worked some of the stiffness out of his shoulders and hands. Just in case it wasn't Scott.

It was, though.

The big man must have heard him on the stairs, because he met him at the office door. "Granville? What happened to you?"

He grinned. "We got any whiskey left?"

Shaking his head, Scott turned and retrieved a bottle and two glasses from the cupboard behind the reception desk. Pouring a generous two fingers for each of them, he handed one glass to Granville. "Here you go."

"Cheers," Granville said, and downed half of it. "Ah, that's better."

"Bruises setting in?" Scott asked, as he matched the action, then led the way back into their shared office.

"Something like that," Granville said, settling gratefully into his deep leather chair. As long as the ache in his arm didn't mean he'd cracked the bone. A good night's sleep would probably fix it. Probably.

"I thought the plan was to get in, get the information and get out without being seen?" Scott said as he too sat down.

"That was the plan, all right."

"Uh-huh. So what happened?"

"We were expected."

"Expected? Isn't that what happens in your fancy drawing rooms?"

Granville let out a crack of laughter. "Yes. Okay, we were set upon."

"Attacked, you mean. I thought I broke you of talking fancy last winter."

"I thought you had too. Apparently Emily is a bad influence."

"I'll tell her."

"You do that. It will probably amuse her."

Scott chuckled. "So, did you find anything?"

Granville held out the key he'd found in Carver's desk. Scott reached out and took it from him, turning it over and over in his hand. "Bank box, you think?"

"Could be. Or a locker at the train station. I don't suppose you recognize the shape or the numbering system?"

"Nope. But it should be easy enough to ask questions tomorrow. Town's not that big. You want me to do it?"

Granville thought for a moment. "If you can find out where it's from without letting on that you have this key, then yes."

"Then you'll come in with the key as the rightful owner and empty the box?"

"Exactly."

"That'll do," Scott said, and tucked the key into his billfold and gave Granville a considering look. "So, what do the fellas gave you those bruises look like?"

"Worse."

Scott finished off his whiskey, stood up and retrieved the bottle from the other room. He held the bottle out, raised an eyebrow. Granville nodded, held up his glass.

"I guessed as much," Scott said. "You know you're working on a black eye, right? Your lady won't be happy."

That explained the ache. Granville touched the flesh around his right eye. Dammit. It was already swelling. He lifted his glass, drank. "Emily will understand. Cheers."

"Cheers," Scott replied. "If Emily will understand the way you look right now, you must have learned something from them?"

"I recognized the largest of the men. He was hired muscle, not likely to know anything. But McAndrews also knew one of them."

"Oh?"

"Hmmm. Fellow named Fergus, who's also something to do with numbers. According to McAndrews, he's not much good at it though. Not much of a fighter, either. After McAndrews knocked him out, we dragged the poor sap down to the Beaver. Got a couple of whiskeys in him, he started talking."

"Uh huh. Learn anything?"

"Well, they apparently brought Fergus along to verify that any account books we might have found were genuine."

"Huh. And who's they?"

"Ever heard of a fellow named Dagan?"

"Dagan? Who's he when he's home?"

"He hired this fellow and his companions to wait for McAndrews outside Carver's office. And then steal any papers—specifically real estate loans—he might have from him."

"Huh. So who's this Dagan work for?"

"Fergus didn't know. But apparently the man can be found at a place called the Black Bull. That's a new one on me. Ever heard of it?"

Scott frowned. "Yeah, it rings a bell. I know I've heard of it, but not where…" He sat back, contemplated his whiskey, then finished it off. "Whatever it was, it wasn't good."

"Where is the place?"

"Can't remember that either. I'll find out, though." He thought for a moment. "So did McAndrews have the papers with him? The ones this Dagan wanted, I mean?"

"I don't know if they're what Dagan was hoping for, but he found a few things that interested him in Carver's files. He'll bring them in tomorrow, after he's had a good look at them."

"Numbers and such?"

Granville nodded.

"Better him than me," Scott said. "And they were looking specifically for McAndrews, not you?"

"According to Fergus they were."

"Hmm. Wonder what they think Carver had that McAndrews could find? And how they knew he'd go looking for it?"

"They must have found out he's working with Sinclair," Granville said. "Maybe Sinclair's not imagining things. Maybe someone really is following him."

"Huh. Could be. Wonder if they've figured out that we've taken on his case." Scott picked up the whiskey bottle, silently offered more to Granville, who shook his head.

Scott half-filled his own glass and threw back the whiskey. "Want me to ask around about Dagan?"

"Why don't you hold off for now," Granville said. "At least until we figure out where the key fits. No point drawing attention to ourselves, in case they don't know we're working with Sinclair yet."

"Yeah, good plan."

"Meanwhile, I'll stop by Randall's office tomorrow morning. See if he's heard anything more about the murder. Maybe he's even heard of Dagan."

"Randall?" Scott said. "Doesn't seem likely. Why would you ask him?"

"I'd planned to visit him in any case," Granville said. "I've been wondering if he could ferret out what kind of work Carver was doing for the Permanent."

"Probably," Scott said. "He's pretty good at untangling the legal stuff."

"Yes, he is. But how did you and Trent make out?"

"We finished looking into Williams—the Sales Director—today. If he's dirty, he's hidden it well. And we couldn't find anything but praise for our client, either."

"So no help there. Did you find out anything useful about Carver's business practices?"

"Not much. Other than that lapse with Gipson last year, he seems to have kept his nose clean. According to Benton, the man was a competent lawyer, with a good reputation amongst the smaller firms in town."

"You talked to Benton?"

Scott shrugged. "It seemed logical. If Carver was crooked, he'd probably know. And he keeps track of the local talent. Says he needs to know the local players, and what the stakes are. Plus you haven't done anything to annoy him lately, so it was safe enough."

That earned him a grin. Challenging the town's premier gangster had become one of Granville's favorite pastimes—and so far, Benton seemed to enjoy their exchanges as well. Luckily.

Granville didn't make the mistake of assuming that amusement would buy him anything should Benton ever decide their interests conflicted with his own. "Any chance Benton was the one who told you about the Black Bull?"

His partner scowled at the widening crack running down the wall. "No. It wasn't him. Might be I heard about it as a place

Benton's got connections—which doesn't tell us much. That applies to half the town."

True enough. "Any idea how long Carver was associated with Vancouver Permanent?"

Scott shook his head. "No-one seems to have had any idea he was associated with them at all. They really did keep it quiet. Maybe Randall will know more when you talk to him tomorrow."

"Maybe. And if he doesn't know, I'm betting he'll know how to find out."

"Yeah, for a lawyer, he's a good sort. I'm glad he's working with us, not against us, though."

"Indeed," Granville said with a wry smile.

17

MONDAY, JUNE 18, 1900

It wasn't quite nine on Monday morning when Granville stepped into Randall's third floor office, shaking the rain from his hat and coat. He was somewhat surprised to find it not only open, but loud with the rapid rattle of typewriter keys. He had to clear his throat quite loudly before the clerk's fingers stilled, and the young man peered at Granville over his half-glasses. "I'm sorry, I didn't hear you come in."

"That's fine. Is Randall in?" he asked, nodding towards the closed door of the office. Expecting to hear a no, he was surprised to see the clerk spring sharply to his feet. "Of course. Is he expecting you?"

"No, but it's in relation to a case…"

"Mr. Granville, isn't it?" the clerk asked, surprising him again. "Just a moment, please."

He disappeared into the inner office, reappearing almost immediately to usher Granville in.

"Good morning, Granville," Randall said. Standing, he came forward to shake hands, then waved Granville to one of the two deeply upholstered leather chairs facing his solid oak desk. "What can I do for you?"

"How is the wrongful dismissal suit for Sinclair progressing?"

"We should be ready to file it by the end of the week," Randall said. "We'll know more about the company once I can get a look at their books."

"And have you heard any more about Carver's death?" Granville said. "Rumor is they arrested a foreigner, a sailor, but that was early yesterday. Do you know if it's true?"

"I heard the same. There seem to be no details yet, but Carver's death has left the city's legal community very shaken. Why do you ask? Does this connect to some case of yours?"

"And yours."

"Sinclair?"

"We think so."

"But who would benefit from Carver's death? Someone from the Vancouver Permanent?"

"Possibly. Carver was doing work for Putnam, but they kept it very quiet. Which raises an interesting question. Almost as interesting as the question of why Sinclair is the one being questioned about fraud, when everything we've learned so far points to the principals as the ones who are responsible."

"You've obviously learned more since we last talked," the lawyer said. "Fill me in."

Granville did so. Randall listened intently, making the occasional note on his omnipresent legal pad. When Granville was finished, the lawyer looked up, frowning.

"We're missing something."

"Yes, I know. I was hoping you could fill in some of the blanks. Like exactly what Carver might have been doing for Vancouver Permanent. And for how long?"

Randall glanced down at his notes, tapped his pencil against the desk. "I shall have to think about this," he said. "But I'll have my clerk pull some of the court records, see if I can find anything suspicious."

"Be careful. If Carver's death is related to this case, your actions may make you a target."

"I'm a lawyer. Caution is my middle name."

"Funny, that's what McAndrews said. Except he said accountant rather than lawyer. Right before he was attacked."

"Is the man badly injured?"

"He's a better fighter than I'd expected. And the odds were three to two, so it wasn't too bad."

"Ah. You were there also. I might have known."

Granville shrugged. "At least we're getting a reaction. We're getting close to something they don't want us to know about."

"Yes. But what?"

"That's what I'm hoping you can help us find out. By the way, does the name Dagan mean anything to you?"

"Dagan," Randall said thoughtfully, tapping his pencil against the legal pad. "Dagan? It almost seems familiar. In what context?"

Granville told him about their apprehension of and conversation with Fergus.

When Randall stopped laughing, he made a few quick notes. Then he glanced up at Granville. "I think you'd best give me a dollar," he said.

Granville stared at him for a moment, then reached for his wallet. Whatever Randall was up to, he trusted the man's quick mind and legal instincts. "Just out of curiosity, why am I doing this?" he asked as he handed the limp bill over.

Randall accepted it, pulled out a form and filled in a few lines. "Sign here, please."

Granville ran his eye over the form, raised an eyebrow in surprise, signed it.

Randall gave him a brisk nod. "I'm now on retainer to your firm. So I have to hold our conversations in confidence, and can't report your illegal activities of the previous evening."

"Ah." There was a reason he valued Randall, and this had just deepened his appreciation. Granville thought for a moment. "It's an excellent idea, actually. We'll have to discuss a more—appropriate —sum for the future. If you'd be willing to act for us?"

Randall smiled. "It would be my pleasure."

The lawyer paused, shook his head. "I still can't bring the connection with Dagan to mind, but I know it's there," he said. "But I'll have it for you in a day or two. If nothing else, the Vancouver Permanent filings may lead me to him."

"Just be careful," Granville said again.

Randall smiled, clapped Granville on the back as he saw him out.

———

TWENTY MINUTES LATER, Granville made his fourth visit to Vancouver Permanent Investment & Loan. To his surprise, he found himself being welcomed by the clerk as a valued customer, and shown straight to Evan Thompson's office. He wondered if Putnam had said something to the fellow.

"Granville. Nice to see you again," Thompson said, rising and holding out his hand. "Have a seat. Can I offer you a cup of tea?"

When Granville declined, Thompson picked up the folder that was sitting on the corner of the otherwise cleared desk. Granville could see his own name across the top.

"I took the liberty of making a few notes the last time we met, so that I wouldn't waste your time if and when you were ready to make a purchase," Thompson said. "Did you have further questions for me?"

He wasn't pushy, but he was organized and prepared. Granville liked that—in fact, he rather liked the man. Too bad he worked for a firm that was probably crooked. At best.

"Yes, actually. I'm considering a rather different purchase than the one we initially discussed, and I wondered how that would affect the mortgage terms."

"And what purchase were you considering?"

"In discussion with Marshall, I'm looking into purchasing an office building, to provide space for our firm to expand, as well as rental income."

Thompson was nodding as he jotted something down. "And your house purchase? Would that be delayed?"

"Not at all. I still intend to purchase a house for my bride, but I'd probably look for a smaller home. For now."

"I see. I see." Thompson was rapidly scribbling down numbers, and seemed to be calculating them on the fly. Granville was impressed by how quickly he did so.

"Well?" he asked when Thompson's pencil stopped moving.

"There would be no problem at all," Thompson said with a smile. "We could increase the amount you were approved for as needed, but the terms would stay the same. In fact, once you have found a building and know what the rents will bring in, that improvement to your income could allow you to borrow more, if needed. There might even be room to improve the interest rates a little."

It all sounded wonderful, too good to be true. Which meant it probably was. "Can you write that out for me?" Granville said. "I'll need to discuss it with our accountant."

And he was really looking forward to McAndrews' comments. He rather expected them to be rude, he thought with an inward grin.

"I could have it typed up for you in a day or so," Thompson said, making several notes in his file.

Granville nodded, keeping his expression neutral. "This is all very preliminary, as you know. I'd appreciate it if you could simply jot down a few key numbers now. I'd hate to see either of us wasting time on buildings that would prove too expensive for our firm."

"Or not expensive enough," Thompson said with a laugh. "Borrowing money can increase your return substantially, you know. But yes, I can put a few numbers together for you now. They'd be very preliminary, and the final numbers will definitely change."

"I'd expect that."

"Very well, this will just take a moment."

As he watched the man's pencil move across a fresh sheet of paper, Granville considered how to bring up Sinclair.

"I'm new to Vancouver, as you know," he said. "I don't think I ever asked how long your firm been in business here?"

"Only three years," was the answer. "But Mr. Putnam has been here since just after the city incorporated. Nearly fifteen years ago. It's still such a new city, with so much growth ahead of it. That's why what's building here is so exciting. You'll never regret deciding to live and invest here."

But he might regret it if he invested with Vancouver Permanent, Granville thought. "And you yourself?"

"I've worked here for three, nearly four months now."

"That short a time? Is there much turnover in your firm?"

"Not at all. But he business is growing—sometimes new hires don't fit in, so they move on, that's all."

"Didn't I hear that one of your colleagues left just last week?"

"Oh, Sinclair. Yes, that was unfortunate. A nice chap, but not everyone is up to the challenges of this kind of growth."

"You're planning on staying, then?"

"Absolutely. I plan on building my career here. And your mortgages will be safe with us."

Granville wondered how true that was. If Vancouver Permanent Investment & Loan folded, who knew which company would buy out the mortgages they'd held. And what their terms would be for the mortgagors.

And if Sinclair's allegations were correct, was Thompson blind to what was going on? Or was the fellow in on it, despite his very business-like approach?

"That's very good to hear. Thank you," he said, as Thompson handed over a page half covered with neatly written figures. "I'll be in touch."

"I look forward to it," Thompson said, standing to see him out. "And if you have any further questions, I'll be happy to answer them."

Granville could think of a few questions Thompson might not be so happy to answer.

Nodding to Miss Kent on his way through the front office, Granville rapped quickly on their closed office door and was through it before Scott could respond.

"Morning," Granville said. "How did you make out with your investigations of the key?"

Scott dangled the key from a piece of butcher's twine, and it glinted in the sun filtering in through the blinds. "This key?"

"Stop horsing around. Just tell me," Granville said.

Scott grinned at him. "Case getting to you, is it?"

"You're getting to me, you large idiot. We finally have a break, and you're wasting time."

"Didn't know there was a deadline on this one. It's not like anyone's been shooting at us—this time," Scott said, with a deadpan expression

"I'm afraid Sinclair is right and he's close to being arrested," Granville said. "And anything could happen to him once he gets into the system."

"Ah, the local cops aren't that bad."

"They're worse since the crackdown on police corruption started. It seems like everything is being covered up, whether it's legal or not, just on principle. Not to mention we now have one murder connected to our case. We don't need another one."

"Uh-huh," Scott said. "But are you sure it isn't your meeting with Pinkerton's boys that's really worrying you?"

"You mean am I trying to clear the case so we look good to the Pinkerton's Agency?" About to issue a hot denial, Granville paused and thought about it. Scott knew him pretty well. Was he pushing on this one so he could mark another case in the "solved" column?

"Not so fast with a reply, huh?"

"Shut up. I'm thinking."

"Oh, in that case, take all the time you need." And Scott sat back in his chair, and started making complicated motions with his fingers.

"Whatever are you doing?"

"Twiddling my thumbs. Isn't this how it's done?"

The comment, and the innocent face that accompanied it, caught Granville by surprise. He began to laugh, hard enough that he had to clutch the desk to stay upright.

Scott nodded. "There we go. You've been kinda tense lately."

Tense? "You're imagining things."

His partner shrugged. "I like what we had before. You sure you want us to affiliate with the big players?"

It was a fair question. "I'll think about it. Now, where did you find the box that Carver's key fits?"

Scott grinned at him. "Where's the last place you'd think to look?"

The last place? Not a bank, then. Carver was a lawyer. Where was the last place he'd expect a lawyer to hide something? "Train station?"

"They only have daily lockers. Try again."

"Scott."

"Yeah, yeah. Deadlines. I know." Scott leaned back in his chair, let out a sigh.

Sighing? Scott? Granville rolled his eyes at the performance.

Scott chuckled. "You're going to wish you were back digging in that frozen creek if you're not careful. You know that, right?"

Right. "The key?"

"Post office box."

Post office box? What had Carver been thinking? "That hardly sounds secure."

"Oh, they're not so bad. Especially if what you're hiding looks like regular mail. And you have to admit it's the last place you'd expect a lawyer to hide something."

True enough. So why did he? "Wonder who he's hiding it from?"

"You just met with Randall, right? Did he have any thoughts on the matter?"

"He's going to look into the work Carver did for Putnam."

"Good. He ever heard of Dagan?"

"Yes, but he couldn't remember in what context."

"Not much help. Still, maybe he'll remember."

"Just like you'll remember what you heard about the Black Bull?" Granville said. "Where's Trent at, by the way?"

"I've got him out looking for rumors about Carver's death. He's good at listening and not being noticed."

"When he stops talking long enough."

Scott grinned, tossed the key across the desk. "Maybe whatever's in the box will tell you something."

He grabbed the key out of mid-air. "I'll be back shortly. Main Post Office, right?"

"Yup. Happy digging."

Granville laughed and tipped the hat he'd just put back on. Picking up his seldom-used briefcase—hand-crafted of the best leather, of course. Appearances were sometimes important— Granville headed for the door, nodding to Miss Kent on his way out. Clattering down the stairs, he noted that the carpet was looking worn and the landings needed a coat of paint.

It surprised him how much the idea of being his own landlord, with responsibilities for his tenants, had begun to intrigue him. Though the weight of responsibility his father carried had seemed oppressive to Granville as a youth, his father's example must have had more impact than either of them had thought. The late Baron had been a caring landowner, one who paid attention to his tenants' concerns. He hated to think how those tenants were faring under his brother William, the current Baron.

Granville glanced at the key in his hand and laughed quietly. He was most likely about to expose as fraudulent the very firm whose generous mortgages would make becoming a landlord possible.

"I never did have much sense of timing," he muttered, earning a surprised look from a clerk who was puffing his way up to the second floor. "Scott and I might have to go prospecting again, at that."

IT TOOK Granville no time to empty out the narrow Post Office box. The steel cabinets that housed the stacks of rented boxes were set into a wall along one side of the large main room, and several marble columns stood between them and the main counter area. Half-hidden behind a marble pillar, no-one was paying any attention to Granville as he fit the key into box number 196.

Reaching into the narrow depths of the box, he removed two envelopes—a large, thin brown envelope with a typed label and a smaller white one addressed in a feminine hand. He'd rather expected the former, but the second envelope was a surprise.

He slipped both envelopes into his briefcase, then surveyed the busy lobby of the Post Office from beneath his hat brim. He might as well have been invisible. The hum of gossip and the clatter of boots echoed off the stone walls and floor as customers ebbed and flowed around the main counter.

The huge clock over the door read a few minutes before eleven. Plenty of time to visit Benton, and still get back to the office before lunch. Scott wouldn't even miss him.

AS HE'D EXPECTED, Granville found Benton in his ornate office, behind a desk that reminded him of a lake of frozen stone. "Nice marble," he commented as a clerk showed him in.

He sat down, ran a finger over the pale grey veining in the blue-white stone. "Italian, isn't it? New?"

Benton smoothed a hand over the gleaming surface. "I rather like it myself. Thank-you. And yes, it was delivered last week. I custom-ordered the desk and the color of the stone."

He gave Granville a wry smile. "I can afford it, after all."

Which was what Granville liked about the man, no matter how dangerous he might be. He didn't take himself too seriously, despite his power. Most of the men Granville knew who could casually order a desk like this thought that possessing such a thing was a reflection of their worth. Benton knew better.

Which was fitting, because the fellow had made a fortune stealing various of their possessions from just such men.

"Now what are you smiling about?" Benton said.

Granville fought back the urge to tell him. It wasn't worth the risk. This time. "I've been stealing from the Post Office," he said instead.

"You? Stealing from the government? This'd have to be a case you're working, right?"

"Yes."

"Ah. And that's all you're going to tell me about it? After a remark like that one?"

"Hmmm," Granville agreed. "But I've brought an impossible question for you, first."

"And whatever gave you the idea that I'm interested in answering your questions?"

"D'you know a place called the Black Bull?" Granville said instead of answering.

Benton opened the carved wooden cigar box on his desk, and took out a thick cigar. Ignoring Granville, he clipped the end of the cigar, lit it, then took several slow puffs, exhaling a cloud of pungent smoke.

"I know of it," he said at last. "It's a dive down at the foot of Westminster Avenue. You can buy or hire pretty much anything there. I'd recommend you avoid it."

"And if I can't?"

Benton shrugged. "Your loss. But what's so impossible about that?"

"I need to find a man named Dagan, who's apparently fond of the place."

"Dagan," Benton said, and drew in a lungful of smoke. He chuckled. "I wish you luck."

"Thank you," Granville said. "Why do I need it?"

"Dagan is a penny ante thug, though he thinks better of himself. His ego makes him dangerous. You'd be best advised not to tangle with him."

"And why is that?"

"He's violent and nasty with it. Plus you'd be outnumbered. Badly."

Good to know. "And if I have questions for Dagan?"

"Bring a gun. You'll most likely have to take out his men, first. And he usually travels with six or more of them. All good shots."

Granville nodded. "Thanks. I'll be going, then."

"Not before you tell me what you're doing stealing from the Post Office, you won't."

Granville settled back with a grin.

18

The rainclouds had cleared by the time he got back to their office, and the air smelled of summer. Granville sauntered into the room he and Scott shared, whistling a fragment of some song that had stuck in his head.

"You sound cheery," Scott said, looking up from a page of figures. "I gather you found something?"

"I did indeed. Are you free this evening?"

Scott glared at him. "You're changing the subject? Without telling me what you found? Now I call that poor sportsmanship."

That earned him a grin. "I thought I'd pay a visit to the Black Bull tonight, have a chat with Dagan and his men," Granville said. "It might be good if you came along."

"His men? How many?"

"Six or more, according to Benton."

"So you decided to ask Benton after all, did you?"

"Hmmm."

Scott just shook his head, muttering something about a death wish. "Yeah, I'll come with you. Sounds like you need the backup. But what did you find at the Post Office?"

Granville opened the briefcase and pulled out the two envelopes, placing them on the desk between them.

"That's it? Those hardly look worth killing for."

"Let's see, shall we?" Reaching across the desk for his paperknife, he slit open the larger and thicker of the envelopes and pulled out a thick stack of folded sheets of paper.

Granville reached for them, flipped them open. Glanced through them. There were more than a dozen pages of columns, full of figures and notations. He scanned the first one, then passed it to Scott.

"These look like ledgers of some kind. With any luck, they'll be related to Vancouver Permanent."

His partner took one look and passed it back. "Not me," he said. "Looks like a job for McAndrews. I'll have Trent take them over to him. What's in the other envelope?"

"I suspect these are something to do with the loans," Granville said, examining a third sheet. "There are no names, though—some of these notations may refer to clients, but we'd need a master list of some sort to decipher it."

"McAndrews can figure it out," Scott said again. "Pass me that other envelope, will ya?"

With a laugh, Granville folded the ledger sheets and put them back in their envelope. Picking up the smaller white envelope, which was neither addressed nor sealed, he opened it. Two sheets of lavender paper fell out, along with a waft of scent.

Scott's nose wrinkled. "Think that's supposed to be lilac," he said as he stood up. "Knew a woman who practically bathed in the stuff, once. Can't think what I ever saw in her."

Striding to the window, he wrestled it open, accompanied by squeaks and groans as the window frame resisted.

"I thought that one didn't open," Granville said as he watched the struggle.

"Well, it does now. And a good thing too," Scott said, flapping his hands in front of his nose.

Granville laughed. "I take it you're not a fan of scented letters?"

"Not that scent, anyhow."

"I'll make sure to tell any lady friends you might somehow acquire."

"Funny, Granville. Real funny." Thumping back down in his chair, Scott gave him a mock-glare. "So what does it say, anyway?"

"The ink is purple, too," Granville said as his eyes scanned the pages.

"Figures. What's it say?"

"It's a statement verifying that her husband borrowed money from Vancouver Permanent in order to purchase a house for her in town. When he was killed in a logging accident, they took the house."

"Huh. Think the gent in question was really her husband?"

"Probably not. But does it matter?"

"Might do. So what's the problem?"

"Apparently he'd paid for some kind of insurance that would pay off the mortgage in case of his death."

"Logging's a pretty high risk profession. But I never heard of that kind of insurance before."

Granville shrugged. "There are firms that'll insure almost anything. Not unlike gambling, if you think about it."

"And the insurance was with Vancouver Permanent, too?"

"It was."

"And they won't pay out?"

Granville scanned the letter again. "Not exactly. Supposedly they were willing to pay, but she couldn't prove she was his wife."

Scott leaned back in his chair, swung his legs up on the desk. "Uh huh. Can't say I find that surprising. So why would Carver have locked this letter away?"

"I suspect it was proof."

"Proof of what? Fraud? But where's the cheat?"

"She says the marriage lines shouldn't matter, since she's his legal heir."

"Wait a minute. He named her in his will?"

"Apparently."

"Was the house in his name, or hers?"

Granville turned the sheet over, squinted a little. "Both names, I think. I think she's written it was joint ownership."

"Then they should have paid the claim."

"I tend to agree, but we'll see what Randall has to say."

"Good idea. Does she say who her—husband—dealt with?"

Granville turned to the last page. "Seems to have been Putnam himself. That should help."

"Help what?"

He grinned. "Help us prove whatever kind of fraud we're about to prove."

"I think I liked searching for gold better," Scott grumbled.

"Never mind. We're going to cheat a thug tonight. That should be exciting."

GRANVILLE STRODE into the Black Bull just after eight that evening, Scott at his side. Already crowded, the place was huge—an old warehouse from the look of it, with corrugated tin walls that didn't keep out the heat, exposed wooden joists supporting the roof, and a cement floor covered with a few inches of sawdust. Under the smell of beer and unwashed bodies, Granville thought he caught a tang of diesel oil, as if it had soaked into the floors over the years of the place's former existence. Likely it had.

A long wooden bar stretched along the near end of the building, rough-cut from some enormous tree. It looked nearly as battered and worn as the men lined up along it. Tonight's crowd was rowdy and loud, already half-drunk.

They each grabbed a pint of ale, then Granville headed for a spot along the back wall where they could watch the noisy crowd without being too obvious about it. At the far end, three musicians were setting up, two guitar players and a fiddler. Granville couldn't imagine how the music could be heard over the din. Or that anyone would listen.

"We'll have a job finding Dagan in this lot," he said.

"Especially since you still don't know what the man looks like," Scott said. "And even if you did find him, how do you plan on getting him to talk?"

"Thanks for the vote of confidence," Granville said. "I'll think of something."

Half an hour later, both men were working on a second pint, and still no closer to finding Dagan. Several parties of revelers had come in in the meantime, and the noise level was approaching a roar.

"Third shift must have let out," Scott hollered in Granville's ear. "Over at Hastings Mill."

"Just what we needed," Granville muttered. "Why would Dagan choose this place?"

"Huh?" Scott said.

Granville shook his head at him, and went back to watching the crowd seething around the bar. For a moment it looked like a fight was about to break out, as one tired looking man knocked over another's drink in the crush. But a new drink was quickly ordered, and before long the two almost-combatants had joined arms with several others and were singing a rousing chorus of a bawdy song Granville had never heard before.

Just as he was about to suggest this was a waste of time, there was a ripple of movement by the door, as if everyone standing near the door was stepping back, making way for something. It was odd behavior for this crowd. He nudged Scott with an elbow to get his partner's attention, and fixed his own gaze on the door.

Seven men walked into the space created by the ripple. They were large men, all of them, not just tall, but heavily muscled. Longshoremen perhaps, or former wrestlers. All were nattily dressed in homburgs and cheap dark suits—which hung oddly on their bulk. They looked nothing like Granville's previous experience of local thugs. But he'd be willing to bet this was Dagan and his men.

The man in the center—likely Dagan himself—was dark, with thick, heavy brows, a pock-marked forehead and a sneering look about him. His bearing didn't match his looks, though. He held himself like a lord, as if he was afraid that touching anything might sully him or at least soil his attire.

"Get him!" Scott said in Granville's ear. "Thinks he's something, don't he?"

Benton had mentioned something of the kind. "Hmm. I wonder why."

"Why what?"

"Why he has such an opinion of himself. And why it's tolerated, here of all places. I'd have thought these fellows would be quick to take him down a notch or two." He glanced at the crowd surrounding Dagan and his men. Despite the crush of bodies in the room, the seven newcomers stood alone in a cleared space, with no-one paying any obvious attention to them.

"It's odd, for sure. But given the size of them, they're probably just the meanest in a nasty lot."

"Could be. Let's go have a chat with them."

"What?" Scott said.

But Granville had already begun to make his way towards the door. He knew his partner would be right behind him. Probably muttering to himself the whole way, too, he thought with a grin, then focused on his target.

Approaching Dagan like this was risky, but he hoped the element of surprise would work in his favor. He doubted very many men challenged Dagan on what was obviously home turf for the fellow.

"Dagan?" he asked as he got to the edge of that cleared space near the door. The sneering man turned towards him.

"Yeah?"

Voice and accent matched the face, but not the clothes or the manner. Interesting. Who was this fellow? "Name's Granville. I run an investigation firm."

Dagan grinned, showing off a set of truly disreputable teeth, then laughed loudly. "Yeah, so?" he said. "What d'you want?"

"I want to know why you set a trap for McAndrews," he said. Behind him he could hear Scott's groan. "And who you're working for."

"Huh. I just bet you do." Dagan nudged the man beside him. "Hear that? He wants to know what we want with McAndrews."

All six of Dagan's followers laughed along with him.

Granville smiled genially. "I also wondered if you found what you were looking for in Carver's office?" he added. "Because if not, I might be able to help you."

Dagan's laughter stopped abruptly. "Oh? So what makes you think the likes of you c'n help me?"

"Because I know what we took from there."

"I think we'd best take this conversation outside, don't you?" Dagan said. "Kinda noisy in here."

"Fair enough."

Dagan led the way outside, two of his men by his side. The other four hung back, then followed Granville and Scott outside. Granville could feel Scott's tension, but his partner stayed at his shoulder, though a half-step back so he could keep an eye on the four men behind them.

Dagan walked part-way around the building, stopping out of sight of the street, and turned to face Granville, leaving three feet of uneven ground between them. He still had a man on either side of him, with the other four falling into a rough half circle behind them. Scott moved up to stand beside Granville.

Dagan looked him up and down. "So it was you with McAndrews that night, was it?" he said. "Whyn't I just get my boys here to beat what you know out of you?"

"You could try. But," Granville said, holding out a hand in a 'stop right there' motion, "It would be easier and much quicker to make a trade." He could feel Scott's tension at the mention of a trade, but nothing showed on the big man's face.

"Trade? What for?" Dagan said.

"You tell me who you're working for, and what you were looking for, and in exchange I'll give you what we found."

"And why would you do that?"

"I don't need what we found. It's useless to me," Granville said. "But I do need the information you have."

Dagan squinted at him, as if hoping to see through his words to the truth. "Why should I believe you?"

"You shouldn't. But there's seven of you, and only two of us. It would be a long fight—we'd make sure of it—but in the end, I wouldn't get the answers I need, and you wouldn't get the ke—whatever we took."

He saw the flash in Dagan's eyes at the mention of the key. He was gambling that in addition to any papers McAndrews removed, Dagan had been hired to get the key itself. Putnam wouldn't have trusted him to retrieve the contents of the post office box.

Looks like he'd guessed right. But would Dagan be so focused on the job that he was oblivious to the implications?

"I work for myself," Dagan said. "And we're looking for a key. So hand it over."

Apparently he was exactly that focused. No wonder Benton didn't take him seriously. But that wasn't the answer he needed.

"I already know you work for yourself," he said, letting impatience color his voice. "I need to know who hired you to search Carver's office. And to attack McAndrews."

Dagan took a step forward, and the two men flanking him did the same.

Granville watched them approach. He didn't move.

"You have the key. We'll take it," Dagan said. "Shake it out of you, see?"

"Wouldn't it be easier just to give me the name? What can I do with it, after all? I've no proof of anything you say."

Dagan stared at him for a long moment.

In the distance a horse and buggy rattled by, and beyond that came the slow sound of a train's whistle, cutting the night. "Yeah. That's right, you don't," Dagan said finally. "I get the key, my job's done. Yeah, Okay. It's a bloke named Putnam."

So it was Putnam. "Charles Putnam?" he said. They needed to be absolutely sure they were looking at the right man.

"Yeah. Happy now?"

Yes, he was. Granville had been fairly sure it was Putnam behind all this, but confirmation was good. And might prove useful. Randall wouldn't be able to use it in court, but the lawyer wouldn't have been able to use the key in court, either. Not given that they'd essentially stolen the thing.

He nodded at Dagan, and reached into the inner pocket of his blazer—slowly, so they could see he wasn't reaching for a weapon. Dagan's henchmen had their hands resting on illegal revolvers.

Drawing out a sealed white envelope, Granville held it up where they could see it. "I also need to know who killed Carver."

"I look stupid to you?" Dagan asked, scowling. "Some sailor, wasn't it, boys?"

The six thugs rumbled something that was probably agreement.

It had been worth a try. Granville passed the envelope to Dagan. "What we found," he said, trying hard not to sound smug.

They'd even put a reasonable facsimile of the documents in the first envelope back in Box 196. It seemed that Miss Kent was an accurate copyist, with an uncanny ability to match handwriting. McAndrews had coached her in making just enough changes to render the document useless. Let Putnam make what he would of that.

Dagan ripped the envelope open, and tipped the tiny key into the palm of his hand. Grinning, he tucked it into his pocket, waved towards the bar. "Buy you a drink?"

Granville nodded. "Two whiskies," he said, after a glance at his partner, now standing a little behind his left shoulder, ready to cover him if needed.

Scott was looking a little pale. The whiskey would do his partner good, Granville thought with an inward grin. And he wanted to know more about Dagan. He had a feeling it might come in useful later.

19

TUESDAY, JUNE 19, 1900

As Emily hung up her cloak and made her way to her desk the following morning, she couldn't help but feel the simmering tension between Trent and Laura. An evening away from the office had clearly made no difference to these two.

Laura wore her usual calm expression, but her back was painfully straight and her shoulders were tight with tension. For his part, Trent was scowling as he leafed through some files. Pulling one out, he slammed the file drawer shut and stalked back to his desk in the converted storage closet.

They really were going to need more office space, and soon. Emily glanced at her friend, who rolled her eyes, without interrupting the smooth flow of her typing. Emily envied Laura's level of skill, then remembered that she didn't need to be a superlative typist any longer. She raised her brows in silent question, but Laura just shook her head.

They exchanged smiles, then Emily gestured towards the closed door of the inner office. "Are they in?"

"Mr. Granville is. Mr. Scott hasn't come in yet."

Emily nodded, then tapped on the door, opening it without waiting for a response.

"Good morning, Granville," she said, and made herself at home in one of the plain wooden guest chairs beside his desk.

As he swiveled his chair so that he was facing her, she smiled at him. Then she glanced around the office. "You know, you and Scott really need new desks. Having a partners' desk might be helpful when you're working together, but it makes it unnecessarily awkward for clients when they come in to discuss their cases."

"Hello, Emily. And yes, you're right, but we haven't room for two desks. Which is why we bought this one, remember?"

She did. "Yes. But I think now it was a mistake. Your business is growing now, and you and Scott *are* the firm. You'll need to think about the impression you make on clients, and especially potential clients. It might be time for each of you to have an office. An impressive one."

Emily watched Granville carefully, judging his reaction. He wasn't quite frowning, but he didn't look happy. Yet he'd seemed quite persuaded by the notion of expanding their offices the last time they'd talked. And she knew she was right about what a growing business needed, especially one that needed to inspire confidence in their clients. Had she gone too far, too fast?

"You're talking about new premises."

"Yes. If you're considering buying an office building, then this is the time to think about what kind of offices you'll be needing as the business grows. Have you given any more thought to buying this building?"

He grinned at her. "Other than becoming increasingly annoyed with the repairs our landlord hasn't bothered to do? No. First we have to close this case. And if we do our job well, we'll put Vancouver Permanent out of business."

He tapped a finger on the figures he'd been reading. "Which will answer the question for us, because without the insanely low interest rates that firm's been offering us, I doubt Scot and I will be able to afford the mortgage on any office building, including this one."

Emily suspected that Vancouver Permanent wasn't the only

company that would be willing to finance the purchases Granville had in mind. The only challenge might be the difference in the monthly interest between what Vancouver Permanent was offering to what another, more honest firm could offer. She was sure it was the right decision, and the right time to make a move, before prices rose any further. But she'd probably said enough for now.

"You went looking for Dagan last night, didn't you? How did it go?" she said instead.

He smiled at her, and she felt a sudden warmth. "We got confirmation that Putnam hired him. Not much else, though."

"You traded him the key for the information? With Laura's forgery in the box?"

"We did indeed. Putnam will likely accept it, because I suspect he isn't certain what the document he's looking for actually looks like. And Dagan is unlikely to admit to Putnam where he got the key from, in any case. So we're in the clear."

It was a risky move he'd made, but she suspected he was right. "Was it worth it, just to get confirmation that Putnam hired Dagan?"

He shrugged. "Putnam's hidden his trail pretty well so far— except for hiring Dagan—so yes, it was worth it. And we also got a better sense of Dagan and his gang, which could prove useful."

"Mr. Scott wasn't hurt, was he?"

"Because he's not in yet?"

"Well, he's usually in before you are."

Granville laughed. "No, Scott's fine. There was quite a bit of posturing, but no damage on either side."

"Good. I'm glad," Emily said. "How did they know to look for McAndrews, do you know?"

"No, not from anything that was said. But I'm guessing they'd had Sinclair followed, and took note when he met several times with McAndrews. It seems he was wise to meet with Scott and me in an obscure location. They didn't know about us until last night."

Before Emily could ask Granville any further questions, there were raised voices in the outer office. Granville's door was flung open and Mr. Scott strode in. He was scowling.

"Granville, this expansion of yours isn't working. We have to do something about those two."

Emily's gaze flew from Scott's face to Granville's. He seemed to be taking Scott's outburst remarkably calmly.

"I assume you mean Trent and Miss Kent?"

Scott nodded. "Yeah. They've been feudin' all week. It can't go on like this."

Emily wanted to say something to ease the situation, but she couldn't think what. Scott was right. It was uncomfortable, and it didn't seem to be easing.

"I tried to go along with your ideas," Scott said. "But you have to let Miss Kent go. Then we'll get back to how it used to be."

Oh no.

"I don't think going back is the answer," Granville said. "It worked when we were small, but as we grow..."

"Yeah, I know. We're joining Pinkerton's, so we have to grow. And once we're an empire, you'll have so many staff you won't even have to work," Scott said. "Meanwhile, I can't stand coming into the office anymore. I'll be at the Beaver if you need me."

And he stomped out, slamming the door behind him.

The room felt as if a tornado had swept through, leaving them devastated. Emily closed her eyes for a moment, then looked at Granville. His face had hardened, and his hand was clenched on the desk.

She swallowed hard and hoped she could find the right words. "You know we need to do something about this, and soon. Don't you?"

He laughed, but there was no humor in it. "That's become very clear. And what do you suggest? Firing your friend? Or maybe Trent?"

"No. We simply need more space. I was wrong to stop you leasing another office for Trent."

He stared at her. "What?"

Okay, this might work. At least she'd caught his attention. "I was thinking too much about the money. And I hadn't thought about what happens when there isn't enough room to work."

"So you think a bigger office will somehow make them able to work together? When things are already tense?"

She had to convince him. "Yes. Laura and Trent do need to learn to work together, but the real problem is that there isn't enough space for them to develop new ways of working. Everything was set up for just Trent doing everything in the outer office, with you and Scott in here."

"And you think we've outgrown that." It was a statement, not a question. And his voice was flat, with harsh edges.

Emily met his eyes. He didn't agree with her, but he was still listening. She had to get through to him. "Yes. Let me show you. I'll consult with both Laura and Trent, and come up with a plan for an office design that I think will work. It will be worth it, Granville, I promise."

"And if we don't affiliate with the Pinkerton's?"

She could see the tension in the set of his broad shoulders. Scott's sudden doubts had shaken him. "You're becoming known in this town. You still need a bigger, more professional office."

"Which we'd have trouble justifying."

"Not if you owned the building, had the rents coming in."

"More complexity. Maybe Scott's right, and it would be better if we kept things small and simple. That worked for us. Especially when we were all out of the office, as we were last month."

"But if you had enough staff…"

He held up a hand. "Emily, we're talking in circles. And I need to meet with Randall this morning."

He was shutting her out. "But…"

"Look, McAndrews should be in later. If he comes in before I get back, can you work with him on the numbers?"

"Of course," Emily said. At least this meant he was trusting her to work on a key element of the case. Didn't it?

But he was hurting, she could tell. And he wasn't seeing the solution to his problem, not the way she was. And she wasn't giving up. There must be something she could do to help.

Granville stood up, gathering a few papers and his notebook into his briefcase. Getting ready to meet Randall. Emily sat watching him, knowing she should leave.

There was nothing more she could do, but oh, she wished there were. She'd never seen him so upset. If only she could find the right words…

A quick rap on the door saved her from trying. And probably saying the wrong thing, she thought wryly.

Trent poked his head cautiously around the door. Usually he'd just waltz in, Emily thought. Scott's anger had unsettled all of them.

"Yes?" Granville said, glancing over at Trent.

Granville's tone was curt, his face closed. Emily was suddenly glad she hadn't thought of anything else to say.

"Umm, McAndrews is here." Trent sounded uncertain.

Now Granville was looking at her. Should she offer to meet with him now, so that Granville could meet with Randall? Emily opened her mouth, then closed it. Sat there feeling uncertain. She didn't want to make things worse for Granville.

But she didn't know how to make them better.

Was she wrong to want to work with him, if her ideas were only causing him more stress? She stared at his tense face, bit her lip.

For the first time since they'd returned from Hazelton, Emily wondered if she was truly ready for this marriage.

She didn't know what he'd seen in her face, but Granville smiled at her. "Show him in," he said to Trent, and his voice was back to his normal tones.

Emily sat back with a silent sigh of relief.

Maybe McAndrews would have some good news.

20

Granville shook hands with McAndrews as Trent ushered him into the office, and waved him to the chair beside Emily. Maybe Emily was right. This office wasn't well set up for meetings. But at the moment he didn't seem to have any clear options. In any direction. He dismissed the thought, and focused on McAndrews, who was pulling files out of his briefcase.

"Thank you, Trent," he said to the boy, who was still hovering in the doorway.

Trent looked disappointed, but gave a quick nod and left, closing the door behind him.

"Well?" Granville said to McAndrews. "Did you find anything useful?"

"No. Or at least, I don't think so." McAndrews sounded almost as frustrated as Granville felt.

"Oh?" was all Granville said.

It drew a reluctant grin from McAndrews. He pulled his chair nearer to the desk, and spread out the contents of the top file. "Look," he said, pointing at the first sheet.

Emily pulled her chair closer so that she could see too.

The sheets on the desk were legal sized, and looked like they had come from a ledger of some sort, though the left edges were smooth, not ragged. The pages were ruled, and had been carefully divided into columns. Each line was covered with neatly written numbers or letters. Leaning forward, Granville realized he recognized them. These were the pages from the post office box.

"These figures seem straightforward," McAndrews said, gesturing at the first columns. "Income, expenses. Everything looks fine. And these ones,"—he pointed to the next columns—"these show their profit and where it went. You can see the money flowing back to the investors, here." And he tapped a finger on the pertinent column.

"But these numbers contradict all the assumptions we made earlier," Emily said, leaning forward so far she looked in danger of falling off her chair. "According to this, the company is doing very well."

"These are the documents from Carver's post office box?" Granville asked.

"You mean the one you sent over with Trent? Yes."

"Anything to tie them to Putnam?"

"No, not a thing, unfortunately. And if these figures are correct, then Emily is right," McAndrews said. "Vancouver Permanent is doing very well. I can't even find any hint of fraud."

"Then why would Carver have hidden these documents away?"

"Would these figures be enough to get your client acquitted if he is charged with fraud?" Emily asked. "Maybe that's why."

"On the face of it, you might be right," McAndrews said. He sighed. "It depends, though, on what evidence the company has against Sinclair. And whether it contradicts these statements."

"You think they're keeping two sets of books?" Emily said.

"My guess? Yes. But I can't prove it, dammit." He glanced at Emily. "Sorry."

She smiled at him.

Granville was only half-listening to the two of them. The complexity of accounting didn't interest him much—Scott had been right about that much. He leafed through the other pages

McAndrews had laid out. More columns of complex numbers. But the interesting thing to him was that the handwriting changed. Looking just at that factor, he had several sets of documents here.

"What do you make of this?" he asked, interrupting the other two in an increasingly complex discussion to point out what he'd just seen. "Are these separate documents? Or just several clerks working on the same document?"

McAndrews and Emily examined the pages. McAndrews muttered to himself as he looked at them, but it was Emily who spoke first.

"These pages are all numbered in their current order," she said, "So what would we see if we re-arranged them according to hand-writing?"

She glanced over at McAndrews, who looked thoughtful but didn't protest. A quick re-shuffling, and she had four sets of documents. She handed one to McAndrews, one to Granville, and took one herself. After they'd each examined their set, they passed it on, until each of them had looked over all four sets.

For the next five minutes there was no sound but the ticking of the clock, the occasional thump from that fan overhead, and the whisper of pages being turned.

"I'm sorry," McAndrews said finally, leaning back in his chair. "Looking at it as four separate ledgers—there's something here. There seem to be slight differences between each set. It has to be to fraud. But I'll be da…" he broke off, glanced at Emily and colored a little. "But I can't see it. Makes me feel like an incompetent dolt."

Emily just sighed and sat back, still staring at the documents.

"And then there's this," McAndrews said, pulling out the second file. There were three sheets of plain legal size paper, all of them covered both sides with columns of figures and percentages, written using brown ink and a fine-nib pen and in a meticulous hand.

"The paper looks hand-ruled," Emily said. "Not from a ledger journal. This was also in the envelope from the post office box?"

McAndrews nodded. "Yes. And it's a different hand, as you can see. And I can't see what the columns relate to."

Granville looked from one to the other, reading the frustration on their faces all too clearly. Right now, he was regretting ever taking this case on. "And the document you found in Carver's files? Is that here?"

McAndrews nodded, pulling out another file. "It looks like more of the same. Though again there seem to be slight differences from these," and he tapped the first folder. "I suspect we'll have to compare all five sets against each other to see what we have."

"Then we still have no proof of fraud against Vancouver Permanent?" Granville said.

"Nothing more than a feeling. Not yet at least." McAndrews' pale face was flushed, and his mouth was tight.

Granville just nodded. "Emily?"

She looked through the last document. "It almost looks like shorthand, with numbers added. So it could be someone's personal code. Which means it may be useless to us without that code."

She passed the document to McAndrews, who grimaced and stuffed it back in the file.

"So to summarize, we're nowhere with any of the evidence we have found so far," Granville said, standing up. "You'll have to excuse me. I've an appointment with our lawyer to see if he's made any progress on what work Carver was doing for Putnam. Perhaps he's found something."

He gave them a nod, and left before he said something he would later regret.

RANDALL'S OFFICE was as organized as ever, with his legal pad and writing implements neatly aligned on the heavy desk. Granville glared at a very plain fountain pen, irrationally wishing it were lying crookedly across the page, or had spattered ink everywhere. Anything to match the disarray of his current case. And the havoc it was making of his life.

"When was Sinclair arrested?" he asked.

"Early this morning," Randall said. "I'm working on arranging bail."

"And you've found nothing helpful in the court filings?" Granville said.

Randall's long fingers reached out, aligned that pen a fraction of an inch closer to the yellow pad. "No, I'm afraid not. My clerk couldn't find any filings that Carver made on behalf of Vancouver Permanent."

"None at all?"

"No."

So whatever Putnam and Carver were up to, Carver wasn't taking anything to court. Granville gripped the chair arms tightly, then forced himself to release them. "I see. In our recent meeting with Dagan, he gave us Putnam's name as his employer, in exchange for an— item—that once belonged to Carver. Which we happened to have."

Randall gave him a sharp glance, but didn't say anything.

"I assume that will not be admissible in court?" Granville said.

"That's correct."

He'd known that. So why did it make him furious now? He glanced at Randall, who was keeping his expression carefully neutral. Which was a good trick, for a lawyer, and one Granville appreciated now. But it wasn't Randall he needed to be talking to. It was Scott.

"Is there anything at all about our meeting with Dagan that you could use?"

"I'm afraid not. And I've not managed to remember why I know his name, either."

Granville stood and buttoned his suit jacket. "Thank you for your time. I'll be in touch."

"Granville...?" Randall said. There was a question in his voice that Granville couldn't answer. Yet.

He smiled at his lawyer. "I'll be in touch," he said again. And strode out of the office.

After the door shut firmly behind Granville, Emily glanced at McAndrews, who didn't seem to know where to look. She considered the mess of ledgers they'd spread out on the desk. Would going through them yet again get them anywhere? She doubted it. But she had a better idea.

"If you could wait a moment, I'll just ask Miss Kent to join us," she told McAndrews as she moved to the door. "She might bring a different perspective, see something we have all missed."

Closing the door behind her, she looked around for Trent, spotting him through the narrow doorway of his office, the one that used to be a closet. She caught his eye and beckoned him over to where she stood by Laura Kent's desk. He scowled at her, obviously still out of temper from his earlier run-in with Laura, but stood and joined them.

"Trent, I'll need you to cover reception here, while Laura joins Mr. McAndrews and me in Granville's office. We…"

"What?" Trent exploded. "It's not enough that my job is taken away? Now she," and he glared at Laura, "gets to be involved in investigations, too?"

"Oh, and you're qualified to compare ledgers and tell us which ones are fraudulent, are you?"

"I can do ledgers," he said.

Emily looked at Laura, who'd begun straightening the items on her desk, and wouldn't look up. Just as well. They'd both seen the state of Trent's "ledgers," and Laura was the one who'd had to redo them. "I think not."

"I can too," he said through gritted teeth.

Emily glanced at the closed door to Granville's office behind her, hoping McAndrews wasn't hearing any of this. "Look," she said, her voice soft but fierce. "I don't know what is going on between the two of you. But if it doesn't stop? Between you, you're going to put this firm out of business."

Laura looked up at that, her lips forming around a protest, and Trent bristled, clearly about to make another hot rejoinder. Emily glared at both of them.

"You're serious." It was Trent who spoke. He sounded stunned.

"Yes. I am. Your inability to work together is already causing problems between Granville and Mr. Scott. Unless something changes, they'll give up on growing the business and go back to how things were six months ago."

"Good," Trent said, while Laura went white. Emily knew her friend needed this paycheck, but even more, she needed a job with a future. Women typewriters were at the bottom of the list when it came to both.

"You really think so?" Emily asked Trent. "Granville and Scott are becoming known for their abilities, and more people will be coming to them for help."

"They already are," Trent said with a grin, as if he'd just disproved her argument.

The idiot.

"So they'll need someone here handling those requests while they are out solving cases." She met Trent's eyes. "If they don't expand, that someone would be you." Just in case he hadn't worked that out for himself.

"But..." he began. Then stopped, and stood there, hands dangling loosely at his side, and frowned at her.

Emily hid her smile. When Trent had nothing to say, it meant she'd won the argument. Time to move on.

"This case is a mess right now," she said. "They need our help, not more problems. Because it would be very easy to grow discouraged and re-think the whole business model if things don't start working out."

Trent made a face at her use of business language, but Laura compressed her lips tightly together.

"You're right," Laura said softly. "What can we do?"

Laura wasn't the real problem in this, and Emily was pretty sure she knew it. But she suspected that Trent had annoyed her friend to the point where she'd started to take satisfaction in making their interactions just a bit more difficult for him than they needed to be. And when it came to protecting his place here, Trent was young enough—and defensive enough—that it wouldn't have taken much.

"We need to make sense of what evidence we do have," Emily said. "And we need to find new evidence. Right now, that means making sense of a series of ledgers. Mr. McAndrews, Granville, and I have all worked on them, and found no answers. We need a fresh viewpoint, and since Laura is the one with business training, it means that Trent covers reception."

"Why do you need me out here?" Trent asked. "Wouldn't a second viewpoint help too?"

At least he'd stopped arguing that Laura should be left out here. "Why do you think?" she asked him.

He muttered something under his breath, then straightened. "Because that's what a professional firm—like this one—does."

She grinned at him. "Exactly. And when we've finished with Laura, then you need to get out there and keep looking for witnesses that might have seen something the night of Carver's murder."

"Something pointing to a different murderer than the sailor the cops have arrested," Trent finished for her. "Maybe someone connected to Vancouver Permanent? Yeah, I can do that."

He moved over to the desk, looked down at Laura. "I'm sorry. I kinda made it harder for you than I had to. I won't do it anymore."

Laura looked up at him for a moment, as if judging his sincerity, then stood up and held out her hand. "Thank you. Same for me."

Trent looked a bit taken aback, but accepted her hand. They shook.

Emily just hoped they truly meant it.

But she didn't even try to hide her smile as she ushered Laura into the office where Mr. McAndrews waited for them.

McAndrews SEEMED TOO ENGROSSED in what he'd been reading to even notice when the three of them walked into the inner office. Emily cleared her throat.

"Oh, there you are. I think I might have found something," McAndrews said as he looked up from one of the sets of ledger pages.

He'd made himself at home in Scott's chair, spreading the various sets of ledgers out over most of the double-wide partners' desk. As they walked towards him, he held out the sheaf of papers he'd been peering at. "See for yourself."

Emily noted that he'd been making notes on a yellow pad, the top page of which was covered with tiny scribbles. She felt a lift of hope.

They needed to solve the puzzle hidden in these numbers, they really did. And soon. Otherwise she was afraid she'd have to watch Granville and Mr. Scott's partnership—and perhaps their friend-ship—fracture under the strain.

And that would break her heart. Just as she was afraid it would break Granville's. Though he'd never show it.

Emily laid down the pages along the near edge of the desk so Laura could see them too. Her friend seemed reluctant to join her at first, or perhaps merely felt awkward in this new situation, because she certainly reached for a page eagerly enough. Together they scanned the four sheets of cramped entries. Emily noted that the one she held had been written by the clerk who used a dark blue ink.

Try as she might, she couldn't see anything significant in the pages.

Nor could Laura. After spending several minutes with her forehead scrunched into vertical lines, Laura took a step back and shook her head. "I'm sorry," she said softly. "I don't seem able to help with this."

"Don't worry," Emily said to her. "I don't see it either." She looked to Mr. McAndrews. "What did you find?"

He stood up and came around the edge of the desk to where they were standing, sweeping the sets of pages with him.

"These all looked the same," he said, laying the sets down along the length of the desk, then walking from one end to the other. "A record of mortgage loans, rates and profit margins. And they all seem to refer to different properties, with different rates and profits. But look here. This first set..."

Dark grey ink, a tidy hand but larger writing, Emily noted.

McAndrews' bony first finger stabbed at a very narrow column two in from the right margin, "...this column has no apparent meaning. I assumed it listed the salesman responsible."

"Some form of identification number," Laura said with a nod. She'd moved closer to the table, her earlier hesitation forgotten, and was examining a second set of pages with something that looked like fascination.

Dark green ink, small writing, but with an open character to the numbers, Emily noted absently.

"The column is here, too. But the numbers don't repeat often enough to be individual salesmen," Laura said. "They must be something else."

"Yes, exactly. But what?" McAndrews tapped on the ledgers he'd first handed them.

Blue ink, Emily thought.

"Same column again," he said, handing a page to Laura, who quickly placed it against the one she'd been looking at.

"Yes. And they match, somehow," Laura said slowly. "Even though the numbers aren't the same. I can't say why yet, but I'm sure they match. Do you see it?"

McAndrews leaned closer, as Laura's finger traced from a number in the blue column to a number in the dark green. "Yes," he said. "You see it too. It's what I saw earlier, though I'm not sure, either, what it is we're seeing."

Emily was watching the two of them in fascination. She couldn't see whatever it was they'd seen, but these two were clearly caught up in the same quest. Perhaps Laura's innate ability to organize the messiest files and documents was something more than a need to keep things orderly—despite her habit of straightening everything in sight whenever she was uncomfortable. This looked to Emily like an ability to see underlying patterns, one that McAndrews obviously shared.

And she didn't.

Emily looked more closely at the sheets they were so focused on, considering every detail of the various columns. Nothing.

Yet Laura had now picked up the last set of pages—brown ink, very upright writing—and was tapping excitedly on the brown version of the column they were so interested in. McAndrews was nodding rapidly, reaching for the first set of sheets, the grey ink ones. They compared them, grey and brown for a moment, then Laura ran her finger across the sheet to a second, slightly larger column, two in from the left margin.

Emily couldn't see why it was significant, but it set McAndrews and Laura to comparing that column across all four sets of sheets. They were clearly seeing something, and increasingly excited by it. The annoying thing was that they hadn't said a word in the last fifteen minutes, seemingly communicating through pointing out numbers in various columns to each other.

Finally she'd had enough. "Excuse me," Emily said. "But would one of you mind telling me what you think you've found?"

Laura and Mr. McAndrews looked at each other. He gave her a subtle nod, and she turned towards Emily, her face lit with excitement. "There's a pattern, and it recurs in all of these. There can be no doubt about it."

So she'd been right, Emily thought. Laura had an ability to see patterns in numbers—and perhaps other things?—that Emily herself lacked. She tucked the information away for future use. "And what does that pattern tell you?"

Laura and Mr. McAndrews exchanged glances. "That these aren't four separate ledgers," he said. "I think these are four versions of the same books."

"Then this is definitely fraud," Emily said.

He nodded. "On a massive scale."

"Can you prove it?"

They looked at each other.

"Not yet," Laura said, picking up the green set of pages and looking at it for a moment before handing it to Emily. "We don't think we have the original set yet. So we don't have a starting point. And we can see the pattern, but we can't break it, just see that it's there."

Emily handed the green-inked pages back to Laura. Stood back a little and looked at the four sets of books. Looked at Mr. McAndrews, who returned the look uneasily. He probably expected her to ask how long proving it would take, and he was unlikely to have an answer. "Where did these pages come from?" she asked instead.

"These were in the post office box."

"Which opened with a key Mr. Carver had carefully hidden. And where did you find the document you took from Mr. Carver's office?"

He looked startled. "In his files. It wasn't hidden. Just filed in his filing cabinet."

"Hidden in plain sight?" Laura said. "Like in *The Purloined Letter*?"

Laura read detective stories? Emily thought with surprise. And she had a mind for patterns?

Granville might just have hired another detective without realizing it. She hid a smile at the thought of his expression when he eventually found out. And she looked speculatively at Laura as she wondered what else she didn't know about her quiet but determined friend.

"Maybe he needed access to the document he kept in his office," Emily suggested. "But how does it relate to these patterns?"

"Oh," said Mr. McAndrews. "Now that's an interesting question. I wonder…" And he was rushing towards his briefcase, with Laura right behind him.

Mentally crossing her fingers, Emily sat back to watch the fun.

Even this early in the day, the Beaver Tavern was thick with smoke and smelled of spilt beer and cheap tobacco. Scott was sitting at a back table, hunched over a nearly empty mug of ale. Granville had never seen his large friend look so diminished. Or so miserable.

Getting two ales at the bar, he crunched across the peanut shells on the floor, and stood in front of Scott's table. He slid the fresh mug across to Scott, then pulled up a stool, and sat down.

After a while Scott looked up. Pushing his empty mug aside, he drank off the top half of the one Granville had just brought. Wiped the foam off his beard. Thumped the mug down on the table.

Didn't say a word.

"Look, Scott. We need to talk about this."

"Nothin' to say."

"Why not?"

"It's your business, your call. Told you that." And Scott buried his face in his mug.

"We're partners. The business is half yours."

"Well, the money is, anyway."

"Scott." Granville stopped, drained half his own ale. "I've just been to see Randall. Sinclair's in jail. And we can't use anything Dagan told us as evidence."

Scott let out a crack of laughter. "Figures. I was asking around, earlier—before I came into the office. The cops are no further on Carver's murder. Still saying that sailor did it."

"Wonderful. This case is going nowhere."

Behind him, there was an explosion of curses, then sound of fists hitting flesh. Granville glanced over, assessed the situation. Only two men fighting, over by the door. It was unlikely to spread this far. He ignored them, turned back to Scott.

Who had an oddly satisfied grin on his face. "Yeah. I don't know why we took the case, anyway. It's not our kind of job. Not my kind, anyway. Mostly just numbers—pretty boring stuff."

"Plus a murder," Granville said, but he knew what Scott meant. It wasn't the kind of job they'd taken in the past, and it seemed to be defeating him at every turn. "And it's better than playing bodyguard."

"Speak for yourself," Scott muttered, draining his mug.

He'd never seen Scott like this before. "At least we're not getting shot at."

"Yeah. But if they're shooting at us, we can shoot back. When they throw numbers at us—what do we do with those? We're running in circles, gettin' nowhere."

Scott was right. And there wasn't a damn thing Granville could say.

"Why'd we take this one on, anyway?"

Because McAndrews had asked, and he liked the man? Because he thought it might be time to expand their business? Those were both part of it, but Granville knew the upcoming meeting with Pinkerton's had been at the back of his mind all the time.

He'd thought, more than once, that it would be satisfying to prove he could handle this kind of case, before he met with them.

"This the kind of case you plan on taking in future?" Scott added.

It was a good question. And not one Granville had an answer to.

Last week, it would have been an easy yes. They needed cases like this to grow, to build their reputation locally—maybe even nationally if they affiliated with Pinkerton's.

For a heady moment, he'd envisioned their small investigative firm growing to attain international recognition. That would show Brother William, who'd always treated his youngest brother like a wastrel, a gambler who liked his drink too much and would never account for anything.

But now? With the case falling apart around them, and his newly enlarged team at odds with each other? With Scott—Scott!—feeling left behind, and questioning their new direction?

Now Granville had no answers. Except that he didn't want to build a business that didn't include Scott. They'd been partners a long time, tested and honed on the creeks through a long Klondike winter.

"I think you might be right. We were doing fine when it was just the three of us, you, Trent and I," he said slowly. "Maybe we need to go back to that."

"Four of us. Emily's been very helpful."

Granville smiled. "Four, then." He raised his mug, swallowed half the remaining contents. It went down too easily.

"Another?" Scott asked. At Granville's nod, he disappeared towards the bar.

When he came back it was with two whiskeys as well as two brimming mugs. "You looked like you could use a whiskey," Scott said, plunking the drinks down on the battered table.

"Yeah. Cheers," he said, raising his glass.

Scott did the same. Both whiskeys vanished.

"So what now?" Scott asked, before taking a hefty swig of his ale.

"First we need to solve this case. We can decide on the rest later."

"And your meeting with Pinkerton's?"

"Our meeting. You need to be there."

"But…"

"I need you there."

Scott shrugged. "Yeah, okay."

"And I need a steak—a thick, bloody one."

Scott's laugh said he too was remembering the steak he'd once ordered for Granville, a much-needed meal that had begun their detective business. "Mary's?" he asked.

"Of course. We can figure out our next step over lunch."

MARY'S WAS AS CROWDED and noisy as ever. With the warmer weather, it was also hot, the few ceiling fans losing the battle against the heat of the grills. But the welcome was warm and the food was cheap but good. The aroma of frying bacon and grilling steaks would have drawn him from three blocks away and the taste of it all kept him coming back.

Granville and Scott took their time over their steaks, helped along with another whiskey or two, and too many cups of Mary's excellent coffee. They discussed the case from every angle, eventually concluding that they needed to re-examine every piece of evidence and every conclusion they'd reached to date.

"We must be missing something," Granville finally said. "Probably something small, or seemingly so."

"Yeah." Scott drained his coffee, signaled for more. "Maybe we've been too interested in all those numbers."

Granville stared at him, suddenly seeing connections he'd been missing. "You know, I think you're right," he said, then drained his own cup as the waitress came by with a steaming pot of coffee. "You've been saying this isn't our kind of case. But what if we treated it like it were?"

Scott's brows drew together, but he added three spoons of sugar and a healthy dollop of cream to his coffee before he spoke. "Let McAndrews figure out the fraud, if there is one," he said slowly. "We look for Carver's killer."

Granville had been watching Scott adulterate his coffee. Even after more than two years, he couldn't quite believe his friend would do that to good coffee, much less drink it like that. He took a sip of his own black coffee, savored the rich bitterness.

"Yes," he said as he put the cup down. "We find the killer, then tie him back to Vancouver Permanent."

"You seem pretty sure they're involved."

"Aren't you?"

Scott's broad shoulders rose and fell. "Dunno. Maybe we've leaped to that conclusion."

"Without judging the facts that we had?"

Granville drank his coffee, the taste now bitter in his mouth. This was on him. He'd been quick to assume that Carver's death was related to his work with Vancouver Permanent. Still thought it had to be, in fact.

Especially given Dagan's connection to Putnam. But they didn't have proof Dagan and his thugs were responsible for any more than breaking into Carver's office after the lawyer was already dead.

And that wasn't how they worked. "Yes. You're right. We need to focus on Carver's death, but without any assumptions."

"You still think Dagan was involved?" Scott asked.

"Yes. But we couldn't get anything out of him, and there's nothing to connect him to it yet."

"Except the break-in."

"Which is hardly conclusive. We've got work to do." Granville gulped down the last of his coffee, signaled for the check. "And we should get started."

He wasn't looking forward to going back to an office still steaming with all the tension he'd left behind earlier, but it had to be faced. And for the first time he wondered how much of that tension had been caused by his and Scott's own issues with this case. If they found their sense of direction again, would things settle down in the office?

"What's the rush? We still don't have any leads."

"We have a case to solve. Before our client spends the next ten years or so in jail."

Granville picked up the check that had been dropped on their table, glanced at it then slapped a half dollar and three quarters on top. "Ever think how much this meal would have cost us in the Klondike?" he asked Scott.

"From our mine? At least a day's worth of gold. And that's on a good day," Scott said with a laugh. Then he sobered. "You figure Sinclair's case will come up for trial pretty fast?"

It was good to be reminded of the odds they'd faced in the past. And survived. "It should be a few weeks, since he's being held for fraud. But if Carver was murdered because he knew about the fraud at Vancouver Permanent…

"And Sinclair's already in jail for defrauding the Permanent," Scott said heavily.

"I only hope whoever's really behind the fraud doesn't find a way to blame Carver's murder on Sinclair, as well."

"Then we'd better get busy proving who did kill Carver," Scott said. "Let's go."

A few hours later, Emily sat in Mr. Marshall's tidy but not extravagant reception area, her gloved hands folded neatly over each other, her back straight. Her mind was racing as she tried to choose the best way to approach this meeting. She'd already discarded several potential approaches, and it had to be done right...

"Emily!"

Emily started at the hissed word, then turned to look at Clara, seated beside her in a pale pink dress of printed organdy that would have looked more appropriate at a garden party than in a real estate office. Emily straightened her own plainly cut navy jacket and skirt. Had she chosen correctly, or did she simply look too business-like?

She was Mr. Granville's fiancée, after all, and unfair though it might be, people would judge him by how she presented herself. She glanced at Clara's lovely summer dress again. Perhaps she should pay more attention when Clara wanted to go shopping, after all?

"Emily?"

From Clara's expression, she had been trying to capture Emily's attention for several minutes.

"I'm sorry, Clara. What is it?"

"Emily are you sure about this?" Clara said in a low voice. A small motion of her hand indicated she meant being here, in a real estate office, which was fairly busy for an ordinary Wednesday afternoon.

Emily hastily summoned up a smile, and nodded cheerfully. "Of course. I've thought it through." And through. And through again. And this was still the best solution she could see. But if she didn't carry it off perfectly, she'd be making everything much worse for Granville…

"Emily."

Clara's voice brought her attention back to her friend, who was looking concerned. For her? Emily's breath caught a little. It wasn't an expression she was used to seeing on Clara's face, and she was afraid it meant her nervousness was showing.

And she so wanted to be calm, polished—a true partner to Granville. And someone who could be as at home in the business world as he was.

Clara's hand on her arm almost made Emily start. Her eyes were concerned. But then Clara knew her well. Others might not see what she did.

Clara's eyes held hers for a moment, then moved ever so slightly to the left. Emily's gaze followed them, to see Mr. Marshall standing there. Giving Clara's hand a slight squeeze in thanks, Emily stood up with a bright smile, shaking out her skirts as she did so. "Mr. Marshall. Good afternoon."

"Miss Turner. And Miss Miles. This is an unexpected pleasure. What can I do for you?" And he was gesturing them into his office, closing the door behind them.

Once they were all seated, he leaned forward a little. "May I offer you tea?"

"Thank you, but no," Emily said. "Our time is a little short." And she wanted to be back at the office when Granville returned, if possible.

"Of course. How may I help you? Did you have further questions about the houses you saw last Friday?"

Of course he'd think that was why she was here, and with Clara, too. "Not exactly," she said. "In fact, it is the other part of my fiancé's business with you that I wanted to discuss."

"The other part?"

Emily took in a breath for courage. "I know you were discussing several purchase options with Mr. Granville," she said. "Including the possibility of purchasing an office building."

"Yes, that's correct."

Mr. Marshall's expression was hard to read, but Emily thought she saw a mix of reluctance and interest. She smiled at him. "I don't imagine this is a conversation you have with many prospective brides."

The real estate agent's face had turned very neutral. Probably not a good thing. But he met her smile with one of his own. "No. I'd have to say this is a unique experience for me."

"In your dealings with Mr. Granville, did he give you any reason to believe he would be upset if you discussed such matters with me?"

He rubbed at the corner of his right eyebrow with one finger as he considered her words. It looked like an unconscious move on his part, Emily thought. She sat back and waited for his response.

Beside her Clara sat almost too still. Emily wondered what her friend was thinking, and hoped she wouldn't choose to say the wrong thing at the wrong moment. This was delicate enough as it was.

But she'd had to include Clara—she couldn't have come on her own. And Clara had an ability to read people that Emily sometimes envied.

"Actually," Mr. Marshall said, after a pause that had gone on almost too long. "Mr. Granville gave me quite the opposite impression."

Well, at least the man had understood what she was really asking without a lot of tedious explanation. Which was a promising start. Now for the challenging part. She drew in a calming breath.

But then Clara leaned forward a little. Emily held her breath, tried not to flinch.

"I think you will find your client most appreciative of your ability to work with his fiancée. If you are able to do so, of course," Clara said, then sat back with a slight smile on her face.

Really, it was almost a smirk, Emily thought, in the quick moment she glanced at her friend before turning her attention back to the real estate agent.

Who was leaning back in his chair, and seemed to be considering both of them very carefully. And by the look on his face, she rather thought he shared her opinion of Clara's smile.

But Clara's words seemed to have dissolved the last of his doubts.

Mr. Marshall gave Emily a quick nod and opened a lower drawer in his desk. He removed a file. Flipping it open, he ran a finger down the top page, then glanced at her. "Was there a particular building you wanted to discuss?"

Her opinion of Mr. Marshall rose again.

"Not exactly. I believe you were looking into several office buildings, similar to the one Granville currently rents in, which are, or could be, for sale?"

"Yes indeed." He flipped over several pages in the file before him. "I have three or four here that seem suitable."

"Then I'd like to request you prepare a comparison between the office building where Granville currently rents, and whichever two of those you have found that seem to you to be the best choices. What interests me most is the projected income versus expenditure for each building."

Clara reached over and squeezed her arm. In approval? Or warning? For the moment, Emily didn't care. She was focused on Mr. Marshall's face, trying to read every hint of a reaction.

She had to get this just right—they couldn't afford to have any rumors that Granville didn't trust Vancouver Permanent. Not yet.

Mr. Marshall had blinked twice when she'd begun talking—surprise?—but he'd quickly started making notes. Now he was again flipping pages in the file on his desk. Would he ask the right question?

"These figures might take a day or two," he said, tapping his pencil on the page of notes he'd just taken.

Emily nodded. Waiting.

"And of course, the mortgage rate would be important." He glanced up at her. "I know that Mr. Granville has been talking with Vancouver Permanent Investment & Loan, and since they have the best rates, would you like me to use those figures?"

He'd asked it. Now she had to get words and her tone just right.

"My father has always believed in looking at the long-term costs of major investments," Emily said carefully. And it was true, even if they weren't conversations he'd have had if he'd known she was listening.

"He's never fully trusted mortgages, says the rates fluctuate too much, and you can't count on low rates staying low. So would it be possible to take an average of all the rates currently being offered by various firms, and use that? If you have access to them, of course. Or perhaps simply take the highest rate being offered? The rates for comparable buildings, I mean."

She held her breath. Was it reasonable enough?

But the real estate agent was scribbling notes, nodding to himself. Apparently it was. Emily collapsed back in her chair, feeling limp.

Clara reached for her hand, squeezed it, and gave her a small smile. Approval then, not warning. Good.

Mr. Marshall looked up, smiled at both of them. "I certainly see why Mr. Granville chooses to include you in these discussions," he said. "And your father is a very wise man."

If word got back to her father, he'd be pleased, but more than a little confused, Emily thought with an inward grin. As far as she knew, he'd never advocated using a higher rate of interest in any of his projections.

Then again, his employer, the CPR, mostly sold land. The railroad had plenty, gained as concessions when they chose Vancouver as the terminal city for the cross-Canada line. They'd no need to buy more land, much less mortgage it.

But it was plausible that her father might have said such things, and that gave her the reason she'd needed for her unusual request. Now, would the real estate agent make things difficult for himself, or would he do the human thing, and convince himself the easier option was actually the best one anyway?

Emily was hoping for the latter—she wanted the projections based on the highest possible mortgage rate, because she suspected that nothing less would convince Granville. She watched Mr. Marshall twisting his pencil between his stubby fingers. Which would he choose?

"Averaging out the rates will give you a more accurate projection of long-term profitability," the real estate agent said slowly. "I'm not sure why we don't do it for all our clients."

Because it would keep too many of them from buying, Emily thought. It was the low rates that drew people in, when no-one pointed out to them the long term consequences of their decisions.

"However..." he looked down, tapped his pencil against some figures he'd scrawled on his notepad. "I believe that for your purposes—assessing long-term viability of your investment—that making projections based on the highest of the current rates is the right choice. It will give you the best margin of safety. And given a property with excellent rental returns, long-term profit should not be unduly affected by the higher mortgage rates."

Yes! Emily thought.

She looked down at the hands she'd just folded together in her lap. Anything to keep from showing her elation. "Thank you. I appreciate your help, and I know Mr. Granville will as well."

"It has been my pleasure. And I do mean that," he said with a broad smile.

"Thank you," Emily said, smiling back. "And I know you said it might take some time to prepare the figures. But if it would it be possible to have them by Friday morning? That would be very helpful to Mr. Granville in making his decision."

She handed him one of Granville's business cards. "You could send the documents to that address. Or simply call the number and we will have someone collect it."

"I'll be happy to. And since it is important to you, we'll do our best to meet your deadline. And of course, I will be including the figures on the houses you looked at last time we met."

"Thank you," Emily said, rising and placing her reticule over her left arm. She held out her right hand, and after a momentary hesitation, he shook it.

"It's been a pleasure," he said as he showed them to the door.

Clara held her silence until the two of them were safely out on the street.

"Well, what did you think?" Emily prompted her, as she tucked her hand into her friend's arm.

"I think you handled that extremely well," Clara said. "And that your Mr. Granville has no idea what he's letting himself in for, in marrying you. Now, shall we go shopping? If you intend to keep having these kinds of meetings, you need a different outfit."

She looked over at Emily's navy outfit and sniffed. "Preferably one that is better cut. Your outfit needs to draw the kind of respect that your words do, rather than making you look like a dowd who doesn't know how to dress."

Speechless, Emily found herself being towed in the wake of her determined friend. She might have been successful with Mr. Marshall, but no-one could argue with Clara when it came to clothes. She wondered what her new look was likely to be, and what Granville would think of it.

As they climbed the creaking stairs to their third floor office, Granville thoughts turned from their stubborn case to the intriguing question of real estate. Vancouver Permanent aside, perhaps there was still a way to become a landlord, as much of a stretch as that seemed for someone who'd been down to his last dollar less than eight months before.

"What do you think of being on the third floor?" he asked Scott, who was ahead of him on the stairway.

"Compared to what?" Scott said.

"Do you think our clients appreciate climbing all these stairs to get to our office?"

"Probably not."

"If we were on the second floor, or even the main floor, it would be easier for them." Granville frowned at the dingy tan walls, which he'd been quite pleased with a few months before. "And these stairs are too narrow."

Scott grunted. "Higher is better, for those folks wanting to consult us quiet-like. We're investigators, after all. And I thought higher floors had more prestige."

"They do, but these stairs undo any benefit of being higher."

"So, we need a building with an elevator?"

Scott was kidding, but he might be right, Granville thought. An elevator had never occurred to him, because the buildings that had them charged much higher rents. But if they owned the building, perhaps that would be an asset.

Granville was annoyed with himself at the oversight. He'd been thinking small-scale, instead of large.

He'd heard his father, more than once, talking to his estate agent about the benefit of spending more money on repairs and upkeep for the farms and tenants. It resulted in a higher profit and fewer expensive problems along the way. But you had to be able to afford the initial outlay, or the costs would send you straight into the receiver's arms.

It had happened to more than one neighbor when times grew hard.

"You aren't seriously thinking about moving us to a building with an elevator?" Scott said.

"I hadn't thought about it, no." But he was now.

Apparently his partner could read him better than he'd thought.

"Granville, even with the gold we took from the mine, you'll bankrupt us," Scott said. "We might need a couple more staff, but a new location? Rents are high in Vancouver, and our rent comes due every single month. Sure, we're making money, and we've got the gold, but only the amount we already took out of the lost mine. We won't see more until that mine's being worked again. Which might be never."

All of that was true enough, but Granville could still picture his father's face as he worked with his agent. And he suddenly realized that Brother William was right—he was a gambler. Probably always would be.

He was good at games of chance, at cards and dice—but he'd never get Edward's ugly death out of his mind. The price for that kind of gambling was too high. Chasing half-way around the world after Klondike gold had been another huge gamble, and he'd failed miserably at that one. And nearly died in the process.

This business he'd started with Scott was a gamble, too, and it remained to be seen if they held a winning hand. But it hadn't occurred to him that investing in real estate was another kind of gamble, and that he'd had the best example of what a winner looked like in his father, the late Baron.

And remembering his father's expression, he thought that this might be the kind of gamble that was worth the risk.

"I won't do anything that might cost us the business," Granville said. "And I'll talk it over with you before I do anything. But I am interested in investing in real estate for myself, whether our business chooses to make an investment or not."

And wasn't that an interesting thought.

Scott muttered something Granville suspected he wasn't meant to hear, and opened the door to the third floor hallway.

Granville gave the hallway door a critical look, noting that it needed paint, then followed Scott half the length of the hallway to their office door, trying to see it from a client's perspective. It would be appealing to a client without much money, he thought, because their detective agency didn't look too successful. But was that the kind of client they wanted for their business?

He thought about their past cases. Most of their clients hadn't had much money, just like Sinclair. But they'd needed help. Would moving to a different building, one with an elevator, lose them those clients? He didn't want that.

On the other hand, could they affiliate with an outfit like Pinkerton's with the shabby offices they had now? But if they lost those clients who couldn't afford much, would it be worth it?

He knew the risk of making big gambles, especially when the stakes were too high. If he played too deep now and lost, it wasn't just himself who would pay for it—it was Scott, and Trent, and Miss Kent, and Emily. Most of all Emily. Was it worth it?

SCOTT OPENED their office door and Granville abandoned that line of thought, bracing himself for the tense mood he'd left that morning.

But all was quiet. Miss Kent sat at her tidy desk, her fingers flying over the keys of the old Royal typewriter. With her typing speed, they'd have to invest in a better machine for her, Granville noted as he glanced around the office.

It was bright, with sun pouring in through the open window, and a faintly sweet scent wafting in. He wondered what was in bloom. Emily might know. Whatever it was better than the usual smell from the city streets below.

There were no files dumped on the floor, no angry words being hurled around, no-one sulking at their desk. In fact, there was no sign of Trent. Or Emily. Or McAndrews.

Miss Kent looked up and turned away from her typewriter as the door closed behind Granville, and gave them both a bright smile. "Good afternoon. Would you care for tea?"

He nearly groaned at the thought of drinking anything more. "Not at the moment, thank you. Where is everyone?"

She pulled an open appointment book closer to her, glanced up at the large clock on the wall. Granville followed her glance. It was quarter after two. He and Scott had been talking for longer than he'd thought.

"Mr. McAndrews had appointments at his office this afternoon," Miss Kent said. "He is hoping to be back here by five o'clock. Miss Turner had a few errands to run, and had hoped to be back no later than three. Trent was heading for Mr. Carver's office building. I believe he was looking for information about the day of the murder."

Granville and Scott exchanged glances. "An excellent briefing, Miss Kent."

She gave them a composed smile. "Thank you. Miss Turner is always careful to make sure I have information when everyone is out of the office."

That sounded like Emily. He wondered where she'd gone this

afternoon. "And do you know why Trent decided to visit Carver's offices again today?"

"I believe Miss Turner suggested it."

Of course she had.

"Scott? Shall we?" And he indicated their private office. To Miss Kent, he said "I'd like a meeting with all of us once Mr. McAndrews arrives. Can you close the office at five, then stay on?"

"You'd like me there?"

"Please."

She glanced at the appointment book, and nodded briskly. "Of course. There are no appointments booked for this afternoon. And I put several messages on your desk." But she couldn't hide her smile.

Granville followed Scott into the inner office, closing the door behind him. He'd left an office in disarray, with everyone at odds and no obvious next step.

He'd returned to find a perfectly organized office, and a team that seemed to be working together, with each off on their own tasks. Miss Kent was back to her usual calm self. He'd even glanced into Trent's cubbyhole, and seen orderly stacks of paper rather than the disaster he'd expected.

What in blazes had happened in his absence?

"Well?" he said to Scott, who'd sat behind his desk and was staring at the neatly stacked pile of messages on his desk.

"What happened to the chaos I left this morning?" his friend asked. "Did you do something?"

Granville shook his head, and sat down. "It was worse by the time I left. McAndrews had arrived, with more questions and no answers."

He picked up his own stack of messages and was rapidly flicking through them. "I suspect Emily had something to do with it."

Silence. Granville glanced up. Scott had flipped through his own messages, and he was frowning heavily. "What is it?" Granville asked him. "Bad news?"

Scott shook his head. "Maybe I was wrong," the big man said at last. "I wanted to stick to what we're good at, just me 'n you. And Trent. But with just three of us, things were usually pretty much a mess."

"Nice to be able to find things, isn't it? But it's early days yet. We don't need to make any decisions today," Granville said.

"Yeah. Anything you want to talk about?"

"Other than the independence that our front office suddenly seems to have developed, you mean?"

Scott chuckled. "Yeah. And the way they're suddenly working together. Could'a cut the air in here with a blunt knife this morning."

"I know. It's one of the reasons I started thinking about a new office. We really do need more space."

Scott's eyebrows drew together. "We've still got a lot of talking to do first. If you meant what you said at lunch."

"I did. And I agree that we've some talking to do. But I realized a few things on our way over here. I need to think about them further before we have that discussion."

"Fair enough." Scott glanced through his message slips again, stacked them neatly, then stood up. "Think I'll go find that apprentice of ours. Make sure he's not getting into any trouble."

"Good idea. You'll be back by five?"

"Yeah. We need that meeting. And with any luck, Trent and I will have some new information by then."

"Good luck. I've a couple of calls here that I need to return." Especially the one from Marshall. He wondered what the real estate agent was calling him about. Surely there weren't rumors floating around about Vancouver Permanent already?

"Marshall? Granville here," he said when the other man answered.

"Granville," came the hearty tones of the real estate agent, clear despite the crackling of the phone line. "I've been able to pull together the figures your fiancée requested more quickly than I'd expected. She said you'd send someone over when they were ready?"

Figures? What had Emily been up to?

Before he could respond, Marshall added, "Her request happened to be a timely one. I'm sure Vancouver Permanent will survive their recent crisis, and any mortgages you took out with them would be fine, but it's always wise to be prepared, just in case."

Crisis? "Yes, that's always been my view," he said. "And I am very lucky that my fiancée shares it."

"I'll say," Marshall said, chuckling. "I mean no insult, of course," he added hurriedly. "It was just—I was very impressed with Miss Turner's grasp of my business. Her request was not only well thought out, it was clearly presented."

Granville heard the surprise in his voice. Emily had really impressed him. But what did Marshall know about a crisis at Vancouver Permanent?

It wasn't a conversation he wanted to have over a party line.

"Look, I have an errand downtown this afternoon," he said "I'll stop by and pick up the figures myself. If you'll be in, I'd appreciate the chance to discuss the situation with Vancouver Permanent with you."

"Be happy to," Marshall said. "I'll be available until four."

It was just past three.

"I'll see you shortly, then," Granville said, and rung off. Stared at the phone for a moment, thinking.

He'd go into the meeting blind if he had to, but it would be helpful to know exactly what Emily and the real estate agent had discussed.

He strolled into the outer office. "Any word from Emily?"

"I'm afraid not," Miss Kent said, looking up from the notes she'd been making. "She wasn't sure what time she would return."

"Do you know where she went after she met with Mr. Marshall?"

Miss Kent's face showed a hint of surprise before she managed to jam her professional mask back in place. So she had known where Emily had gone. Interesting. That detail had been left out of her otherwise thorough briefing earlier.

"No, as far as I know she and Miss Miles were planning on coming straight back here."

So Clara was with Emily. Which should have been reassuring, but the two of them had taken risks before, and were more than capable of doing so again.

He considered Miss Kent, wondering what, if anything, she knew. But with her mask firmly in place, it was unlikely she'd tell him. He'd have to talk to Emily about that. Secrets could undermine the best office.

As he turned back to his own office, he realized that Miss Kent had been working with several very familiar ledger sheets. And she'd also had several folders on her desk with McAndrews' handwriting on the labels. What was that about?

Their meeting at five was going to be an interesting one.

As Granville was shown into Marshall's office, the real estate agent came forward to wring his hand. "Please, have a seat," he said, as he handed Granville a sealed manila envelope that was nearly half an inch thick.

"Here are the figures, as promised. I'll be most anxious to discuss them with you—or you and Miss Turner, of course—once you've had a chance to review them. As I told your fiancée, I'm most impressed with her approach—that is, your joint approach. I'm considering using it with more of my clients. And once I saw the results of the comparisons she'd asked for, I was even more impressed."

Granville was tempted to tear open the envelope and see what Emily had been up to. He hid a grin. Whatever it was, she had certainly made an impact on Marshall.

If the fellow had felt any reluctance about discussing business with Emily, he'd definitely got over it. Granville had the feeling he'd quite happily do business with her again, whether he was there or not.

He felt faintly uneasy at the thought. Much as he appreciated Emily's skills, it was distinctly unsettling to see her so successfully breaking with convention. The last thing he wanted was to hold her back, but he hadn't expected quite this level of success so soon.

"Thank you. We'll review these, and get back to you," he said. "But it was Vancouver Permanent I'd wanted to talk about at the moment."

"Of course, of course," Marshall said, leaning forward. "I'll admit, it was a shock to hear that one of their employees had been arrested for fraud."

So that was the crisis he'd been referring to. "What happened?"

"I don't yet have all the details," Marshall said, tapping a pencil softly but increasingly rapidly against the desk. "The arrest just happened this morning. But I gather Putnam had known about the fraud for some time, and had been putting together evidence."

The agent seemed to notice what he was doing and put the pencil down. "The company has been around for a few years now, and has a good reputation. I've never heard even a rumor to the contrary. I'm sure this arrest will have little if any impact on their business."

Granville said nothing. He'd been learning in the course of this investigation just how unstable some Vancouver businesses could be. Unlike the centuries old firms he'd dealt with in London, the local companies had mostly been in business less than ten years. They had enthusiasm and energy, but no history. Which wasn't surprising in a city that hadn't existed before the railroad built their terminus here less than fifteen years ago.

Marshall had to know there were few—if any—local businesses that a run of bad luck couldn't put under. Even if Vancouver Permanent were legitimate—which Granville was nearly positive they weren't—one embezzling employee might be enough put them out of business.

Marshall had been watching him carefully. "Since you haven't arranged a mortgage with them yet, you don't need to worry," he said quickly. "Which may be for the best, at least for now, as it means you aren't caught up in any of this."

"And these figures your fiancée requested," he added, tapping the envelope, which Granville had placed on the edge of the desk. "These are based on a much higher rate of interest than Vancouver Permanent was offering. And the numbers still work."

So that was what Emily was up to. Apparently she'd decided to prove to him that buying an office building was feasible with or without the Vancouver Permanent. And from what Marshall was saying, she'd been right.

"Thank you. We'll look forward to discussing these figures with you, then," Granville said. "I'll call you in a few days."

———

GRANVILLE WAS BACK in his own office just after four, and was disconcerted to find only Miss Kent present. "Miss Turner has not returned?" he asked her.

"No," she replied, looking up with a small frown. She seemed not to have heard him come in, her attention focused on the notes she'd been making. He glanced at her notepad, but the random arrangement of figures on the page made no sense to him. She still had McAndrews' files open on the desk.

"I'll be in my office," he said.

She nodded, but she was already running a finger down another column of figures. Shaking his head, Granville left his office door open, in case they had visitors and Miss Kent didn't hear them, either.

Then he tore open the envelope Marshall had given him, and began reading. He saw immediately what Emily had done. She'd asked for a comparison of three office buildings—including this one—with all costs, in and out. And the calculations had been done at a rate of interest almost triple what Vancouver Permanent had been offering.

With interest rates that high, he'd have thought the whole thing a waste of time, but—and he glanced down at the final figures— she'd been right. Even with a small down payment, the rents coming in more than covered all costs. With a reasonable down payment, they'd be making a tidy profit. And getting office space for free.

He stared at the numbers, his mind racing. Emily was a genius.

These numbers meant he and Scott could find new offices in any building they chose. Assuming it was for sale.

Or they could fix up this building and expand their current office space. It just depended what kind of business they wanted to be in.

He was still wrestling with that question when he heard a clatter of running footsteps in the hall, the outer door slammed open. The noise got through Miss Kent's preoccupation as well as his own thoughts. Both their heads snapped up as Trent burst into the office.

"Granville. I need Granville. Is he here?" he was saying, between pants.

Miss Kent gestured towards his office. Trent followed the line of her hand, caught sight of Granville through the open door, and raced in.

"You need to come. Now. Scott's in trouble, maybe shot. I couldn't help him. You…" And he broke off, too short of breath to continue.

Granville was already standing, clapping a hand to his hip to ensure that his knife was there. He pulled his revolver from the back of the desk drawer. Checked that it was loaded. Slid it into the pocket of his overcoat and grabbed his hat.

"Come on, you can tell me on the way," he said, grabbing Trent's elbow and ushering him out of the office.

Miss Kent watched wide-eyed as the two of them dashed out.

"WHICH WAY?" Granville demanded as they reached the street level.

Trent, still too winded to talk, pointed in the direction of Carver's building. He barely matched Granville's long strides as they ran.

By the time they reached the building, a huge crowd had gathered on the sidewalk out front, standing six deep on a four-foot wide sidewalk. They were looking up at the windows of the building.

Granville slowed down, trying to work out what was happening.

Trent grabbed his arm. Pulled him towards the corner.

"The alley," he said, between breaths. "Shoot-out."

It was the last thing Granville had expected to hear. "Slow down," he said, forcing the lad to do so by slowing his own pace. "Tell me."

"No time," Trent said. "Hurry."

They rounded the corner and headed down the alley.

Granville could make out two groups of dark figures facing each other. They stood the width of the alley apart. Their rounded hats and billy clubs marked the first group as police. But who were the second group?

And where was Scott?

It was darker in the alley. The height of the buildings on either side cut the sunlight. Granville blinked several times against the sudden dimness, trying to sharpen his vision.

He could just make out a dark clump, lying still and too silent halfway between the two groups.

Scott? His every muscle tensed, ready to attack.

Trent seemed to sense it, and put a hand on his arm. Held him back. Pointed to another dark clump, in the shadows a couple of feet behind the policemen. The shadow seemed to be moving a little. Trying to stand?

"Scott?" he demanded, remembering to keep his voice low with an effort.

Trent nodded.

"Then who's that one?" Granville said, indicating the first dark patch. The one that still wasn't moving.

"Dunno. Wasn't there when I left," Trent said. He'd got his breath back.

"What happened? And who's in the second group?"

"It happened pretty fast. I was going from office to office, asking questions, like," Trent said, keeping his voice low.

Granville nodded, holding on to his patience with an effort. Racing in there now would just get them all killed.

"I found this old guy, cleans the offices? He said Carter was working late the night he was killed. He's Chinese, doesn't speak very good English, but wanted to help. He told me he thinks he saw a couple men in the alley, then heard them on the stairs."

"Did he recognize anyone?"

"No. And he couldn't describe 'em. Anyway, he's just started talking when a couple of those guys,"—and he pointed at the group who weren't police—"came along, and started giving both of us grief.

Then Scott came, and he was making 'em back off. But then there was more of 'em, and then somehow the police were there, and clearing out the building. Something about a bomb."

Which probably explained the folks out on the sidewalk. "How did everyone end up out here in the alley?"

Trent shrugged, the move barely visible in the cool shadows. "The cops herded us here. Then one of the other guys started crowding me, and Scott pushed him off, and there was a lot of yelling, and one of the cops shot him."

"They shot Scott?"

"Yeah. I think so, anyway. There was a gun flash, and I couldn't see, but Scott dropped. They dragged him over there by the wall, and he was just lying there and I got away and came for you."

"You did right," Granville said, his eyes on the dark bundle by the wall. The shadows were deep there, but his eyes had almost adjusted to the dimness. He thought he'd seen another flicker of movement, but he couldn't swear to it. He had to get his partner out of there, get him to the hospital.

His eyes moved between the two groups. Rapidly considering, then eliminating options.

"We need a distraction," he said to Trent. "You know how to shoot a revolver?"

Their apprentice was a crack shot with a rifle, but he'd never seen him with a smaller gun.

"Course," Trent said. "What d'you need me to do?"

"Go around to the other end of the alley. Get them to focus on you for a few minutes. Don't get caught. And don't get shot."

"You can count on me." Trent said. He grabbed the revolver Granville held out, and was gone.

Two minutes later, there was a loud crash from the far end of the alley, followed by another, even louder crash. Granville watched as all heads turned that way.

Then he moved rapidly forward. Hugging the wall, he stayed in the deepest shadow he could find. Until he stood eight feet from where Scott lay.

Granville slowed. Every movement cautious. He couldn't afford to be spotted now. Not when he was out-numbered this badly.

A rolling crash from the other end of the alley—bless Trent— sent two of the policemen down the alley towards the sound.

It gave him the cover he needed to creep up beside the large, Scott-shaped bundle lying on the ground.

Another crash from down the alley. Everyone's attention was focused on the noise Trent was making. No-one noticed as Granville put a hand on Scott's shoulder. His partner's eyes opened.

Not dead, thank God.

But he still had to get him out of there. And Scott was heavy.

An exchange of shots. Granville thought he recognized the sound of his own pistol, being answered by another gun. At the sound both parties—still eight feet apart—moved further down the alley.

The noise covered his grunt of effort when he heaved the big man upright. And Scott's groan. Now he just had to get them out of there.

Draping Scott's arm over his own shoulders, Granville sent a quick prayer for Trent's safety. He began to half-drag Scott towards safety. No-one was paying attention to them.

To his relief, Scott's feet started moving almost immediately, though he was leaning heavily on Granville. Another round of gunfire. Then they were on the sidewalk and out of sight.

Pushing Scott to one side so he rested against the building, Granville gave him a quick once-over. He was pale, but his eyes were alert. If a little blurry. There was no sign of a bullet hole. He didn't seem to be bleeding, either. Except for a trickle of blood on the right side of his forehead.

Granville stared at that trickle with horror, remembering the poor soul in the Klondike who'd been shot in the head and not even realized it. Until he'd collapsed and died of the injury several days later.

Carefully, holding his breath, he pushed the hair back from Scott's forehead. And let out his breath in a whoosh when he saw the shallow graze along Scott's skull.

The bullet had missed him. Mostly, anyway. No wonder he'd gone down like a felled moose. He'd probably been out cold for a bit.

Scott should be fine, once he shook off what was probably a mild concussion.

"You're fine, thanks to your hard head," he said. "But let's get you checked out anyway."

It was half past five by the time Granville, Scott and Trent dragged their way up the stairs and into the office. Scott insisted he was fine. The doctor hadn't found anything more than the abrasion and a concussion.

But his partner was shakier on his feet than Granville had seen him since the time they'd been ambushed in Dawson City, back in '88. He made sure he kept within arm's reach of Scott the whole way back. Just in case.

Luckily Trent was also fine—fit as a fiddle and twice as cocky, as the old-timers would say. He'd tracked them down at the hospital, bubbling over with his success in providing the distraction that had probably saved all their lives.

"Did I tell you I was behind some boxes, and they couldn't find me?" he said for the third time. "Rotten shots, the lot of 'em."

"Yeah, you told us," Scott said. "And I thanked you for it. It took courage—and probably saved my life."

Trent grinned even wider at that. "I wasn't scared," he said. "Course, I wasn't sure it would work. Hiding like that, I mean. I got lucky."

They both had, Granville thought, unlocking the door to their office. He shoved it open with a thump when the warped wood stuck a bit. They really needed to get that fixed. "You did well," he said, and Trent stood a little straighter.

The outer office was empty, but he could hear voices, including Emily's, coming from their inner office. So she was back. And she sounded fine.

They all seemed to be arguing about something, and probably hadn't heard the door open. Nor did they notice as he, Scott and Trent moved to stand in the doorway of his office.

McAndrews, Emily and Laura Kent were grouped around the big partner's desk, on which they'd spread out a series of ledgers. Miss Kent—Miss Kent?—was pointing to a column of figures and arguing loudly with McAndrews. Emily was standing to one side, looking from one set of documents to another, but the tilt of her head said she was listening hard to everything that was being said. On the far side of the room, Clara sat quietly, her hands folded, her eyes watching everything.

He hadn't expected to see Clara. What was she doing here?

Clara was the first one to notice them, looking up with a smile that encompassed all three of them. "I'm very glad to see you're alive," she said in polite tones that didn't fool him for a second.

Emily turned around with a little shriek. "Granville. You're well?"

Her eyes, like Clara's, checked the three of them out thoroughly before flying back to his face. "Laura said—I was so worried."

"We're fine," he said, stepping more fully into the room and standing beside her. Trent and Scott crowded in after him, Scott dropping into his chair with an imperfectly hidden groan.

Granville was amused to see that McAndrews and Miss Kent, still arguing, hadn't even looked up from the ledgers. Which looked very much like the ones McAndrews had discussed with him and Emily earlier that day.

"What is going on here?" he asked, then took another look at Emily. There was something different about her. Was that a new suit?

Emily's suit was still a dark navy with few embellishments, as it had been that morning. But now it seemed more polished, and more flattering. He glanced over at Clara in her very fashionable day dress. Apparently the two of them had been up to more than real estate transactions.

Emily tucked her hand into his arm and leaned against him for a moment. "Mr. McAndrews thinks he's found something important. Laura doesn't agree."

"I can see that," he said, watching the normally reserved Miss Kent with fascination. "What I don't understand is why she's been working on those ledgers all day.

"How did you…?" Emily began, then grinned up at him, and gave his arm a squeeze. "Of course you'd notice. I should have expected it."

"Does she have accounting training of some sort?"

"No more than I do," Emily said, reminding him of the figures the real estate agent had given him, on her request.

Which he'd left spread across his desk in his hurry to depart. His gaze went to the papers spread across the desk, but he didn't see the real estate agent's figures. Emily's eyes followed his, and she seemed to know exactly what he was thinking. "They're in your desk drawer," she said. "Perhaps we can discuss them later?"

"You've looked through them?"

She nodded. "I didn't think you'd mind."

"Quite the opposite," he said. "I'm looking forward to our discussion. Though I suspect it will have to wait until tomorrow. And by the way, I'm impressed."

She flushed a little. "I'm glad."

"But about Miss Kent?"

Emily met his look, her green eyes determined. "I asked her to join Mr. McAndrews and me earlier. I thought someone uninvolved might see something we'd all missed in the ledgers."

He glanced at the young woman, still arguing vehemently with McAndrews. Whose red hair was now standing on end, as if he'd been running his hands through it. "I gather she did?"

"Yes. She focuses on the underlying order of things." She paused, gave him a quizzical look. "You do something like that, only you see patterns in what people do, how they act."

She was right. It was why he liked investigating so much. "And Miss Kent sees patterns in—what exactly?"

"In how things fit together. Especially documents and numbers. I think that's why she's so organized."

"Because she has a sense of which things belong together?" Granville said slowly, thinking about it.

He had found a certain logical order in the files Miss Kent had straightened out, one which seemed to make it very easy for him to find the documents he was looking for. "Yes, I can see that, but how does it apply to the ledgers that none of us could make sense of?"

"I don't know," Emily said with a grin and a nod towards the arguing couple. "And I'm not sure they do either. But as far as I can tell, there's something in the ledgers that feels wrong to her. The problem is, they can't seem to relate her feeling to his knowledge of accounting."

"That is a problem," Granville said. "Maybe between us, we can help."

HALF AN HOUR LATER, Granville was regretting his optimism.

McAndrews and Miss Kent were still arguing. They seemed to be getting nowhere. No-one else had been able to contribute anything meaningful, though Emily at least seemed to be following what they were discussing. Clara was watching all of them with a small amused smile.

Granville could see Scott's growing frustration, Trent's impatience. Which wasn't surprising. This was exactly what he and Scott had talked about at lunch.

The three of them needed to focus on the actual investigation, and leave the numbers to the others. Who would find their answers eventually. He glanced at McAndrews, nose to nose with Miss Kent, both arguing in raised voices. Maybe.

The fact that they were all trying to work in such cramped quarters didn't help. They really did need a large meeting room of some sort if they were to work together as a team.

He motioned Scott and Trent to follow him, leaving the three of them to their numbers. In the outer office, he pulled out a chair for Scott and half-pushed his stubborn partner into it. "We need to talk about what you found out this afternoon," he said.

"Since we're clearly useless with the numbers," Trent muttered.

"Never mind the numbers," Granville said. "You were telling me earlier about the second group of men in the alley. You said two of them interfered when you were talking to the janitor?"

Trent was nodding. "That's right."

"Did you recognize either of them? And what were they doing there?"

"I don't know why they were there—they sure weren't going to tell me. And I didn't recognize anybody."

"I did," Scott said. "One of Dagan's boys. The lantern-jawed one we met the other night."

Granville nodded. He remembered. "Dagan again? So I'm assuming all of the second group were Dagan's men?"

"Seems likely." Scott was leaning against the chair back now. He looked pale under his thick beard. "It all happened pretty fast, though, so I didn't recognize anyone else."

"Doesn't matter. It's too much of a coincidence for this not to be related to Carver. And quite probably Putnam. I wonder what they were looking for?"

"Maybe Putnam expected to find more in Carver's post box than the fake documents you left there?" Trent said.

"That's possible."

"You think they're still looking for the evidence McAndrews took?" Scott asked, his eyes on Granville.

"Probably. They're looking for something. It would be interesting to know who called in the bomb threat."

"You think it was a fake?" Trent asked. He'd gradually leaned more heavily against the wall as they talked.

"I think that's pretty obvious. And the police weren't too convinced either, given that they cleared the building but not the area."

"Huh. You think it might've been them?" Trent said, his thoughts obviously still on Dagan's gang. He was unconsciously rubbing his shoulder as if it ached.

Granville wondered where the boy had picked up the injury, and how many others he was hiding. He knew better than to ask.

"I think they wanted access to something," he said. "Either the building or the people in it. And I think it would be useful to know where the call came from."

"I can find out," Trent said. "I know some people."

"That would be helpful," Granville said. He looked at Scott. "Think it would be worth our while to talk to Benton again?"

"Doubt it. Dagan's not causing problems for Benton."

"True enough. Just for us."

"Yeah. And Benton won't care about that," Scott said, his face solemn but his eyes glinting.

He grinned, glad to see Scott was recovering. "No, he won't at that. I wonder…"

Scott gave him a suspicious look. "What?"

"Just something I might follow up tomorrow."

"Uh-huh," Scott said. "That look means you're about to get yourself into a whole pile of trouble."

Scott knew him too well.

"Trent, had the janitor you were talking with told you everything, do you think?" Granville said.

"Dunno. Maybe not. I can talk to him tomorrow as well, if you want?" Trent said. "And I never finished talking to the others in the building. I could do that too."

Granville nodded. "Scott, what about you?"

"Trent could probably use some company. And I think we might get him a revolver of his own."

"You are remembering that carrying a gun is illegal in town?"

"Yeah. What of it?"

He had a point. And Trent had made good use of Granville's revolver today, seemingly without even injuring anyone. "You up to it?"

"Wouldn't suggest it if I wasn't."

Right. Scott was tough. And he had a pretty hard head. He'd survived today's incident without even a concussion.

"So we've got our jobs," Scott said, watching him closely. "But what're you up to?"

"I was planning to follow up with Randall," he said. "See if he can get McAndrews in to see our client. Sinclair might make some sense out of those ledgers. And someone needs to talk to the woman whose letter was in Carver's post office box. Nothing too dangerous."

Scott muttered something, but didn't repeat it when Granville raised an eyebrow at him. It had probably not been complimentary, Granville thought with amusement. "But I've rethought that plan," he added.

Trent started to say something, but Scott beat him to it. "What d'you mean, rethought it?" he growled. "What're you getting yourself into now?"

"I'm not the one who got shot," Granville pointed out. "Now am I?"

Scott glared at him, then the corners of his lips twitched, and a laugh rolled out. "Maybe not. But you're about to step straight into trouble. I know that look."

Now Trent was looking from him to Scott and back. He looked worried and determined all at once. Terrific.

"I can go with you," Trent was saying. "After I get my gun, I mean."

He grinned at the pair of them. "As I was about to say, I think we should stick together, the three of us. I suspect we're getting close to the end of this thing, and whoever's behind it will be getting desperate."

"Now you're talking sense," Scott said with a grin. "You still think it's Putnam? Behind it, I mean?"

"I do. Though it will be hard to prove."

"Yeah. So do we go after him?"

"No, we keep the focus on Carver's murder and on Dagan. The attacks seem to have grown bolder. Putnam seems to be increasingly desperate to recover whatever it was that Carter had. And we can't let him suspect that we might have it."

"Even if we don't know what to do with it," Scott said.

"Why not?" Trent said. "We can take them. And if they go after us, then we know who they are."

"But Miss Emily and Miss Kent can't defend themselves," Scott said, echoing Granville's own fears.

Trent scowled. "But…No. That can't happen. What can we do?"

"I think questioning that janitor is important," Granville said. "The fact that Dagan's men attacked you when they found you talking to him suggests we have more to learn."

"So what do we do next?" Trent asked.

"We get them before they figure out anything more," Scott said.

"And since you two need a good night's rest, we'll meet at Mary's for breakfast at seven," Granville said.

Trent looked ready to argue, but Scott was nodding. "Makes sense."

"Let's see how the others are doing," Granville said.

McAndrews and Miss Kent were still poring over their sheets of figures, but they seemed to be working together now, instead of arguing. Emily and Clara were chatting quietly. They all looked tired, and they had to be hungry by now.

"Any luck?" he said.

That was met with head-shakes from everyone.

"McAndrews, might Sinclair be any help in making sense of those ledgers of Carvers?"

McAndrews was slouched in Scott's armchair, tapping a pencil against his chin. He had a smear of ink on one cheek, and another on his cuff. He looked like he'd been through a whirlwind. Backwards, Granville noted with weary humor.

"It's a good idea," McAndrews said slowly, straightening up. "He might be able to supply the missing piece. We're almost there, but we're still missing…something. Can you get me in?" he asked with real enthusiasm.

"I can try. But for now, we'll call it a day, and start again tomorrow."

He glanced at Miss Kent. "Scott, Trent and myself will be out of the office for most of the day tomorrow."

She nodded.

"Emily, I'll see you and Clara home." He glanced at Trent, who was looking slightly better. "Trent, can you see Miss Kent home?"

"We'll both do so," Scott said.

WEDNESDAY, JUNE 20, 1900

When Granville arrived at Mary's Diner far too early the following morning, the restaurant felt warm and bright after the chill mist clinging to the streets outside. He shivered and hung his damp coat and hat on the hooks outside the booth. There was no sign of Scott or Trent. He checked his pocket watch as Betty brought him a cup of coffee and a grubby menu.

"How many?"

"Three."

She slapped two more menus on the table and tapped him on the shoulder. "It ain't often you're the first one here."

No, it wasn't. Trent tended to oversleep, but Scott was an early bird. He returned the waitress's grin as he wondered if his partner had been concussed after all, despite what the doctor had said.

He'd nearly finished his coffee when the door creaked open and he looked up to see Scott and Trent saunter in, tendrils of mist eddying around them. They looked fine. As they divested themselves of coats and hats, Betty brought over another coffee and a soda for Trent.

"You're both late," Granville said.

Scott grinned at him, landing on the black oilcloth covered seat opposite him with a thump. "You worried about me?"

"Nah," Granville said, after a quick glance had told him Scott still looked tired, but he'd regained his usual ruddy color. "Just afraid you wouldn't be in fighting form. We've a lot of work to do today."

"Then why aren't our breakfasts on the table?" Trent asked cheekily as he slid into the booth beside Granville.

He subsided quickly when Granville gave him a look and passed him a menu.

Scott chuckled. "This should be fun," he said to no-one in particular. "I'll take a Mary's Breakfast," he said to Betty, who was now standing with pencil poised over her order pad.

"Same for me," Granville said. Trent nodded.

Over heaping plates of flapjacks, eggs, bacon and sausage, they discussed their next steps. The cafe was crowded, and noisy with the buzz of conversation in several languages, which made it a good place to talk without being overheard.

"We should start by getting a revolver for Trent," Granville said to Scott. "That was a good idea of yours."

Trent looked smug, and Scott just raised his eyebrows.

Granville laughed. "Slow of me," he said. "You've already taken care of it. That's why you came in together. And why you were late."

Trent moved as if to reach for a gun at his hip, and Granville stopped him with a hand on his shoulder.

"Not here," he said. "No need to ask for trouble."

Trent's hand fell, but he looked disappointed. The gun was important to him.

"But tell me what you bought," Granville said. "And where, at this time of day?"

Trent's smile was bright enough to burn off the fog that still lingered outside. "It's a double-action revolver, a 32-calibre Iver Johnson. And it's got a three-inch barrel." Then as if doubting Granville's approval, he added, "It's a really nice piece, and Scott says it's got a good trigger action. I know it's not a Smith and Wesson, and it's a little battered, but I got it for two dollars. With bullets."

"Sounds like a good choice."

"I think so. And Scott knew a guy, so it was a good deal."

Granville looked over at Scott, who was pouring still more syrup on his flapjacks. He grimaced at the thought of all that sweetness. "Oh?"

Scott grinned at him, cutting off a huge piece, and swirling it in the syrup until it practically disintegrated. He took his time chewing, too. "We don't have time to get a gun through regular channels," he said at last. "Might be questions about the lad's age, too. This guy I know has access to reliable weapons. And he's an early riser. Seemed best to get the matter dealt with first."

It made sense. "Fair enough. Eat up. And then we'll go and find your janitor?" he asked Trent.

Who nodded.

"And in honor of Trent's first revolver, I'll pay for breakfast," Granville said, putting the money on the table.

EMILY HUNG up her coat and hat, and glanced around the quiet office. Laura's coat was there, but she wasn't at her desk, which was unlike her. A low murmur of voices came from Granville's office. And he hadn't expected to be in this morning.

She pushed the inner door wider, and wasn't surprised to see Laura and McAndrews with their heads bent over pages of figures. "What have you found?" she asked.

Both of them started, but Laura's face showed alarm. "What time is it?" she asked.

"Just after nine," Emily said.

Laura stood up quickly. "I...the office should be open now. I'm so sorry."

Emily patted her arm. "It's fine. What have you found?"

"Still nothing," McAndrews said with a sigh. "I…we hoped that looking at it again this morning we would see something we missed."

"But we haven't found a thing," Laura said.

"I can only hope Sinclair will be able to shed some light on it," McAndrews said. "If Granville can get me in to see him." He glanced at his watch. "And I'm late too. I must run."

He gave them both a nod, and departed.

Laura quickly gathered the papers they'd spread out, and carried them to her desk.

Emily followed her, watching her friend's face. "This is really bothering you," she said.

Laura glanced at her. "Yes."

"Why?" Emily asked.

"You mean aside from there being a man in jail who has done nothing wrong?"

"Yes. Aside from that."

Laura wouldn't meet her eyes. "It's nothing."

"I don't believe you."

"I…thought I could help. That's all."

Emily didn't try to comfort her. "I know. Sometimes we can help. Sometimes we can't. But they were all listening to you, did you notice?"

Laura stared at her for a moment. Smiled. Then took the cover off her typewriter and got on with her day.

The mist had burned off and it looked like it was going to be a warm day as Granville, Scott and Trent approached Carver's building. Delivery carts and buses were jammed along Hastings Street. Granville could see the police wagon pulled up out front. A pint-size newsboy was holding the reins for two large black Clydesdales with magnificent white manes and feathered hooves. They'd used horses like that on the home farm as long as he could remember.

"Not again," Scott said with a groan.

"At least this time the sidewalk isn't jammed with people," Granville said. There was no sign of the police officers, but the bronze double doors at the front had been barricaded off.

"Doesn't mean much," Scott said. "It's too early for most of the offices to be open."

"Hmmm." Granville ignored him and walked over to the boy holding the reins. He flipped him a quarter, which the boy caught dexterously and without ever losing hold of the reins. "Can you tell me what's going on here this morning?"

"Not for sure, but ten minutes or so ago the cops came pounding up. These fine fellers"—he waved an arm at the horses

—"were all lathered up. Apparently some poor sap came in early, and found a body."

"Any idea who's dead?"

"Dunno. But that gent over there in the brown suit is the one found the dead guy. Maybe he knows something."

"Thanks. I'll have a word with him," Granville said, and sauntered over to where a rather short, gaunt faced man was leaning against the stairway railings. From his pallor, and the glazed look in his eyes, Granville rather thought the fellow was leaning there through necessity rather than affectation. He looked around for Trent, beckoned him over.

"Are you all right?" Granville said. "I gather you found a body this morning?"

A half nod was his only response.

"It must have been a shock. Can I get you coffee? Tea?"

"Tea," the man croaked out.

He glanced at Trent, who nodded and sped off in search of the tea. The lad was becoming a real asset. "Where did you find the poor man?"

"Collapsed on the landing halfway down between the second and third floors."

And Carver's office was on the third floor. "Was the fellow dead when you found him?"

"No." It was said on a moan. "Breathing hard, and bleeding too much. I tried—tried to stop it." He waved blood-stained hands. "But it was too late. He died a few minutes later."

Looking at those hands, and the smears of blood on the fellow's jacket, Granville wondered that the officers—who didn't have a reputation for investigating too thoroughly—hadn't arrested the man on the spot. Or at least handcuffed him to something heavy until they'd had a chance to investigate further.

"Do you know who the man was?" Granville asked. From the corner of his eye, he could see Scott walking over to talk to the newsboy.

The man in the brown suit nodded, and swallowed hard. "Yes,

I'd seen him around. He was the building's janitor. I—I think he worked nights, and opened up in the morning. Maybe locked up at night, too."

So they were too late. Granville wished he'd insisted on coming back the night before to ask his questions. "Did the fellow say anything before he died?" Granville asked.

"Yes. He…seemed almost desperate to tell me something."

Granville leaned forward. "What did he say?"

"I'm sorry. I can't tell you. It was in Chinese. Or at least it sounded Chinese."

Trent popped up at Granville's elbow just then, a thick mug of hot tea in his hand. Granville took it from him with a smile of thanks, and passed it to the man in the brown suit.

"I made it milky and sweet," Trent told them both. "It's what my mam used to do for shock. I hope it's okay?"

"Thank-you," the fellow said with a shadow of a smile, and drank deeply.

Granville turned to the lad. "The old man you talked to yesterday. The janitor. Did he seem frightened when you talked to him?"

"No. I don't think so, anyway." Trent frowned as he thought about it. "But he did look worried when those other guys took out after us."

"I think he got nervous as soon as he caught sight of the second guy," Scott said. He'd quietly joined them when Trent returned. "He said something then, but I didn't catch it."

"Yeah, that's right," Trent said. "He started speaking Chinese. I was going to ask Bertie about it. But then I forgot in all the excitement."

Bertie was Emily's parents' house-servant. He'd come over from China only the year before, and though his English was still broken, he seemed to have little difficulty understanding it. Trent apparently considered him a friend—he'd been working alongside Bertie at the Turners when Granville had first met him.

And Bertie had helped them on several previous cases. "Do you think Bertie could figure out the janitor's last words, if this gentleman can remember them?" Granville asked.

"Probably. He's plenty bright, even though he doesn't talk so good yet," Trent said.

Granville hid his grin at that mangled statement, and turned to the man in the brown suit, who was listening with interest. The fellow had finished the tea Trent had brought him, regaining some of his color in the process. "Do you think you could remember the late janitor's last words well enough to sound them out to a Chinese speaker?" he asked him.

"I could try," was the answer. "I might just be able to do it, too, since he only said about three words, but he kept repeating them."

"If you'll stay here, I need to have a quick word with the police. Then we'll bring our translator to you. Trent, can you stay with him? Scott, with me?"

All three nodded.

Granville made his way into the building, Scott beside him, both of them stepping over the flimsy barrier the police had put in place. He didn't expect any conversation with the police to go well, especially if they recognized Scott from last night, but he was hoping they'd see or overhear something that would make the risk worthwhile.

IT DIDN'T QUITE work out that way.

They found the police on the third floor—Carver's office had been ransacked again. Granville could see the resultant mess through the open doorway. It looked as if every single item of furniture and piece of paper had been tossed.

Despite the evidence, most of the policemen were unwilling to admit that there had been a break-in, much less give them any details about it.

Several of the officers recognized Scott immediately from the day before, and were inclined to arrest him "on suspicion." Suspicion of what wasn't clear.

It took a lot of talking on Granville's part, and a cool head from one of the officers, Daniels—who hadn't been present the previous day—to keep them from getting a beating. Granville recognized Daniels as one of the new crop of officers hired to clean up the force. The fellow seemed open to sharing information about the break-in, at least until the others stared him down.

He might be worth looking up in future.

No-one had anything to say about the janitor's death, except that it was a police investigation, and they were to stay clear of it. Or else.

"So, what did you find out?" Trent wanted to know when Granville and Scott rejoined them.

"Someone broke into Carver's office," Granville said, after a thoughtful glance at the man in the brown suit.

Who blinked twice, then said, "And maybe the janitor saw them? That's why he was killed?"

"You think it was the guys from yesterday?" Trent asked.

"Perhaps," Granville said to both of them. "Trent, do you think you could fetch Bertie?

"Yeah, okay," Trent said. He picked up the emptied mug he'd brought earlier, and was gone.

"He won't be long," Granville said to the man in the brown suit, who shrugged.

"The police said I had to wait for them, anyway," he said too quietly.

Granville gave him a sharp look. If he was any judge, the fellow was still in shock. He seemed glad of his and Scott's company, though.

Within twenty minutes, a winded Trent was back, Bertie in tow. "He can't stay long," Trent said, nodding towards Bertie. "He has to finish clearing up after breakfast."

Bertie bowed. His long plait fell neatly down his back, his grey tunic and trousers were immaculate. "Trent say you need help," he said.

"We do, and thank you for coming," Granville said, and quickly explained the situation. "We're hoping you might be able to translate what the dead man said."

As he watched Bertie bow to their witness, Granville realized how unlikely it was that this would work. From the little he knew of the Chinese language, the rising and falling intonations were critical to the meaning of the words. Unless the man in the brown suit knew something of the language, which was doubtful, how could he convey the janitor's last words?

He watched as Bertie leaned closer to where their witness sat. The man in the brown suit sat up straighter, said something in what sounded to Granville like Chinese. The rising and falling tones sounded right, but who knew what he'd actually said. Bertie's smooth face registered no emotion, but he stepped back a little, as if in shock, then repeated the words.

They sounded the same to Granville.

The man in brown nodded, and repeated his words.

Bertie turned to Granville. "He say that my countryman tell him "dead man come back.""

Scott's eyebrows rose at that.

"You're sure?" Granville asked Bertie. "It couldn't be other words that he mispronounced?"

"No. His words, he say exactly." Bertie glanced over at the man in the brown suit, nodded. "Exactly," he said again.

It sounded like a compliment. "How did you get the tones right?" Granville asked their witness. "Do you speak Chinese?"

The man in brown shook his head. "I sing," he said. "In a barbershop quartet. Always been told I have perfect pitch. And their language—well, I've been kinda fascinated by the musicality of it."

He wasn't sure musicality was the word he'd have chosen, but Granville knew what the fellow meant. And it was thanks to him that they knew the poor janitor's dying words.

But what had the dead man been trying to communicate? What were they to make of "dead man come back?"

He turned to Trent. "You said you were going to ask Bertie about what the janitor said when he saw Dagan's men breaking in. Do you still remember what that was?"

Trent nodded. "I think so."

He turned to Bertie, who'd been listening quietly, and said something in liquid syllables.

Trent spoke Chinese? It sounded authentic to Granville, but who knew what it sounded like to a native speaker. Certainly Bertie's calm face didn't tell him anything.

"Again," Bertie said to Trent, who repeated the words.

It sounded no different to Granville, but Bertie shook his head. "Again," he said. "Slow now."

Trent closed his eyes, and his expression went blank. He was silent for several moments, then a quick river of Chinese flowed from his mouth.

Bertie nodded, his pigtail bobbing with the movement. He seemed—pleased? Granville guessed.

"Again," Bertie said.

Trent's eyes were still closed. The lad drew in a shallow breath, and repeated the words.

"Yes," Bertie said. "Okay."

Trent opened his eyes and his face resumed its normal inquisitive expression. "Did I get it?"

"I think so. Yes," Bertie said. "It same two, nearly three times."

"And?" Granville said. "What did the fellow say?"

Bertie looked at him. His face didn't show it, but he seemed sad, somehow. "He say—these bad men, they here too much."

Granville wondered how often the old man had seen the thugs, and what he'd seen that cost him his life. And what on earth he'd meant by "dead man come back."

Had the fellow been seeing ghosts? And whose ghost?

It took Granville, Scott and Trent fifteen minutes to walk to Randall's office, and less than three minutes to talk their way past his clerk. Randall looked surprised as the door opened and the three of them crowded around his desk. His clerk hovered in the door behind them, trying to explain, but Randall waved him off.

"It's fine, it's fine. Sit down, all of you." He looked at Granville. "I assume there's a reasonable explanation for this."

"Well, I'm not sure how reasonable you'll find it," Granville said. "But we need your help in freeing your client."

"That is my job."

He sounded so prissy as he said it that Granville had to grin. If there was anything Randall was not, it was prissy.

Randall shook his head at him, but smiled back. "What is it you need?"

"Other than to prove Putnam's the one behind all of this, you mean?"

Randall said nothing.

"We need you to get McAndrews in to see your client."

"That shouldn't be too difficult," the lawyer said. "Though I still haven't been able to arrange bail."

"Good. But McAndrews also needs to show Sinclair a number of documents, get his opinion on them. In confidence."

"Ah. That could prove more challenging. Let me see what I can do."

"And it needs to be today," Granville said.

"Naturally. If I can arrange it, I'll need—McAndrews, is it?—to be available immediately."

Granville handed him McAndrews' card. "You can reach him at this number today," he said, scrawling it on the back.

"Very well." Randall glanced at each of them. "I'm hearing rumors that the sailor they'd arrested may be released soon for lack of evidence. Are you any closer to finding whoever killed Carver?"

"There's been another murder, and it's probably related. The janitor for Carver's building was murdered this morning, on the stairs leading to Carver's office. And someone ransacked Carver's office around the same time."

"We suspect a hired thug," Scott said. "One of Dagan's men. But we can't prove that, or who hired him. Not yet."

"Though Putnam seems the most likely choice," Granville said.

"I see." Randall looked a little sick. "This is a bad business."

"It is indeed. Have you had any success in determining exactly what Carver was doing for Putnam?" Granville asked him.

"Not yet. I'll keep looking."

"Us too," Trent said, leaning forward earnestly. "We'll get him. We have to."

For a moment Granville was afraid the boy was going to pull his revolver and prove how serious he was. He didn't, though, just sat back with a determined look on his face.

This case was getting to all of them. They needed proof, which they didn't have. And they were used to action, not relying on columns of figures.

"There is one other matter," Granville said, and handed the lawyer the letter that had been in Carver's post office box. "This document is one that Carver had kept in a secure location. I'm hoping it might be useful in proving fraud against Putnam."

The three of them waited silently while Randall read the letter, then read it again.

"It doesn't prove anything, in itself," Randall said. "Though it is an interesting situation."

Interesting. Granville hated that word. "You think she has a case?"

"If everything she says here is true, I think it quite likely. Though we'd have to get Putnam in front of a court on fraud charges in order to prove it." He scanned the letter again. "Someone needs to speak to her."

"I agree. But should that be you? Or should we do so?"

"Hmmm." The lawyer glanced at the letter again, then handed it back to Granville. "I think it should be you, since I'll need to look into getting McAndrews in to see Sinclair. But when you talk to her, you'll need to find out what proof she might have of these statements. Most particularly, was there a will? And does she have a copy of it?"

Granville made a note. "We'll talk to her this afternoon, then."

"Can I see the letter?" Trent asked.

Granville passed it to him.

Trent glanced down at it, wrinkling his nose at the scent. "We might have to find her first. Look at the address. I think this was written while she was still in the house."

Scott glanced over his shoulder. "The lad's right. She could be anywhere by now."

IT TOOK MUCH LONGER than Granville would have liked, but it was still only ten-thirty when they tracked the woman down to a rundown apartment block on the east end of Powell Street. The three of them crowded around the door on the third floor, trying not to touch the walls, which were painted with black mold.

Agnes Pospischil opened the door on a waft of scent, and smiled up at them through heavily darkened eyelashes. "And what brings three such fine gents to my door?" she cooed.

She was dressed from head to toe in pale lilac, with purple ribbons. Mourning colors. The style wasn't a good choice for her, Granville thought, holding his breath to keep from choking on the cloud of cheap lilac perfume that surrounded her. She wasn't as young as she clearly wanted to seem, and had passed the age where makeup could hide it.

"Mrs. Pospischil?"

"Yes, that's me."

"I'm John Granville. We're here to talk about the house you say was stolen from you," he said as he handed her his card. "If you're willing to discuss it with us?"

She took a moment to read his card, then looked up with a smile. "Willing? I'll say," she said, opening the door wider and stepping back. "Come in."

"Thank you," Granville said as he walked into a tiny but scrupulously neat apartment. It smelled faintly of lilac, but there was no odor of mold.

"Please, have a seat," she said, gesturing towards a sagging sofa. "Would you like some tea?"

"No, thank you," he said, lowering himself cautiously onto the sofa. It held up under his weight, and without the cloud of dust he'd expected. Trent sat beside him, but Scott stood behind the sofa. Probably wise.

Mrs. Pospischil sat opposite them on a faded chintz armchair and waited. She looked tired, and resigned, Granville thought. She had probably had very little good news since her logger had died. He obviously hadn't left her much money, if this sad room was any indication.

"We're looking into a number of accusations of fraud against Vancouver Permanent Investment & Loan," he said. "But you need to understand that this might not come to anything."

"So don't expect to get my house back," she said bluntly. "You needn't worry. I know too much about how the law works for people like me. But I'll help you anyhow. I'd like to see the folks at Vancouver Permanent get theirs."

"Thank you," Granville said. "Can you tell me who you dealt with at the firm?"

"Putnam, his name was. Charles Putnam."

Granville and Scott exchanged glances. "Putnam himself? Pardon my asking, but why would you have dealt with him directly? It isn't usual for the General Manager to work with clients."

"Specially small ones like us, huh?" she said, examining him with shrewd eyes.

"He strikes me as a man who values the prestige of his position," Granville said diplomatically. One look at her mocking smile told him he hadn't fooled her for a second.

"Well, I don't owe him a thing after what he pulled over this," she said. "Charlie was a—friend of mine—from the old days, like. I called, asked him about mortgages. Said he was happy to do me a favor." She snorted. "Some favor."

Which information might undermine Putnam's standing in town, if it became known. "And he sold you the mortgage insurance as well?"

"He sure did. Told me how it would protect me if anything—happened—to my husband." She closed moist eyes for a moment, then blinked twice. Met Granville's eyes. "The liar."

"Did you contact him afterwards? When the mortgage insurance had been turned down?"

"Went and sat in his office myself, when I couldn't get him to take my call."

"And?"

"He was so very sorry, but rules were rules. He'd love to help, but there was nothing he could do. Then his clerk forced me out. As if I was nothing."

It was said with venom.

And her words tied Charles Putnam directly to fraud. "Thank

you," Granville said. And meant it. "Would you be prepared to testify to that? If it came to it?"

"I sure would!" She gave a savage smile. "I'd like to be face to face with old Charlie again."

"I have just a few more questions, if you will?"

She nodded.

"We have your letter, with the details of what happened. But can you tell us more about the insurance your husband took out on the mortgage?"

"I can do better than tell you," she said, rising and walking over to a small writing desk. She rummaged inside for a moment, then brought out several envelopes. "I have the paper he signed. Also his death certificate. The purchase agreement, in both our names."

She laid each one on the small table beside the sofa as she spoke. "And I have his will. The only thing I don't have is my marriage lines. And that was the only thing they were interested in."

Granville picked up each document, scanned it, then passed it to Scott without a word. When he'd finished reading, she looked him in the eye. "Well?" she demanded.

She was tougher than she had seemed.

"These are exactly what we had hoped for," Granville said. "And what our lawyer told us we would need to prove a case of fraud against this firm."

"Even without the marriage lines?"

"The will seems clear. But I'm no lawyer. Ours will need to examine these documents in detail before we can proceed. Will you let us borrow them? We'll keep them safe, and return them to you in the same condition, I promise."

She stood up and gathered up her documents, gave him a hard look. "I like your style. And these here documents aren't much good to me now. But I'm not much for just handing things over, so I think I'll come with you to see this lawyer of yours. Just to be sure."

And that was that.

30

To say Randall looked surprised to see them at his door would be an over-statement. He was too good a lawyer for that, Granville thought with quiet amusement. But he was clearly annoyed.

"Yes, I've spoken with the police, and yes, I can get McAndrews in," he said testily. "Though not until tomorrow. I'm surprised to see you couldn't wait for my call."

Granville stepped into the office and to one side, which meant Randall could see the lady standing in the doorway behind him, with Scott and Trent behind her.

"Mrs. Pospischil has been kind enough to bring the documents you need herself," Granville said. "And she is prepared to testify that it was Putnam himself who sold her the mortgage insurance, then refused to honor it. Mrs. Pospischil, let me introduce our lawyer, Mr. Josiah Randall."

As she walked towards the desk, Granville's eyes met Randall's over her head. "And I believe Mrs. Pospischil herself will need a lawyer's advice in this matter. If she is to get her house back." Randall looked a question at him, and Granville nodded. They would pay her costs.

"Then of course I'd be happy to take on her case," Randall said.

The lady in question looked startled. "You mean you think I have a case? You haven't even seen my papers."

"I've seen the letter you sent. If you have the documents in question," he glanced up to catch Granville's nod, "then I would say you definitely have a case. Quite a good one, in fact."

Granville watched her face, the smile that reached her eyes, then vanished as suddenly. "There's no point. I can't pay you," Mrs. Pospischil said bluntly.

"You won't need to," Granville said. "Your documents and your testimony are central to a case we're working on. Proving that your house was fraudulently taken from you could help prove our case."

"Maybe. But that doesn't get my house back."

She was a realist, had probably had to be, Granville thought. "No. That's why Randall needs to be your lawyer, as well, to take the additional steps to get your house back. Or to ensure that you receive adequate compensation, if getting your original house back isn't possible."

"I've told you, I can't afford it."

"Most of the work will be done as part of Granville and Scott's case, so the additional cost is a small one," Randall assured her.

"And my firm will pay it," Granville said, "as a token of thanks for your help here."

"I won't take charity."

"It isn't charity," Scott said. "If we can't prove Charles Putnam and Vancouver Permanent a fraud, we don't earn our fee. And without your papers, we might not have enough evidence. So if we prove the fraud, you deserve to get your house back. It's simple."

"It's too generous," she said, after a moment during which a lace-trimmed handkerchief came into play. "But I can't refuse you."

"Good," Scott said.

"Then why don't you all come in and have a seat," Randall said. "Instead of clustering in the doorway like this. We have work to do."

ONCE THEY'D LEFT the lawyer's and seen Mrs. Pospischil onto the streetcar—over that lady's protestations—Granville, Scott and Trent headed back along Hastings toward their offices.

"So what's next?" Scott asked, stepping over a large crack in the wooden sidewalk. "Randall said he can't get McAndrews in to see Sinclair until tomorrow, so I'm guessing that leaves us focusing on Carver's murder?"

"It does. But first I'm going to take Emily out for lunch," Granville said.

"Does she know that?" Scott asked with a sideways look.

"Of course she does," Granville said, hiding his grin. Scott knew him too well. "We have some business matters to discuss," he added, raising his voice over the rattling of a grocer's delivery cart going by.

That drew a snort of laughter from Trent, and Granville stared the boy down. "Afterwards, I think I'll have another chat with Benton."

Scott just shook his head. "A man'd think you've a death wish or something, you're so fond of talking to Benton. What do you hope he'll tell you?"

"Dagan and his gang are everywhere we look in this case. And there's something I'm missing about the fellow. Something we need to know."

"Such as?"

"Such as why Benton seemed so amused when I mentioned his name. Dagan has his own group of thugs, his own little kingdom at the Black Bull. Why doesn't Benton take him more seriously, or at least consider him as a potential threat?"

"Good question. You sure you want to know the answer?"

"No," Granville said. "But I suspect I need to know it."

"What about the stuff the janitor said?" Trent wanted to know. "We going to find out what he was talking about? I never did finish talking to people in the building yesterday."

"That's a good idea," Scott said. "Trent and I are going to get a bite to eat, discuss some business," he said with a chuckle and a sideways glance at Granville. "After which, we can wander on over to Carver's building, see what we can find out."

"Don't get shot," Granville said, pulling open the front door and starting up the stairs to the third floor.

31

Emily glanced up from the simple hand-written menu, considered Granville's face. He looked tired. She knew he was frustrated with this case, worried about their lack of progress, with two people dead and their client in jail. One thought followed another. "You don't think they'll try to frame Mr. Sinclair for Mr. Carver's murder, do you?"

"No. There's no evidence to support it." He put his menu down. "Unless that's what these latest break-ins have been about."

Around them the hum of conversation rose, bouncing off the plain wooden walls. Granville had asked if she minded eating here, since Mary's had the best seafood in the city. He'd been right, too. The salmon steaks she'd seen go by had been a deep, succulent pink. But her favorite thing about the place was its anonymity.

This was where the fishermen and the dockworkers ate. No-one her family knew would ever come here—and no-one here would carry tales that she and Granville had been seen dining together, just the two of them. Nor would anyone here care what they talked about.

The waiter came by and took their order, then hurried off.

Emily leaned towards Granville. "You mean Mr. Dagan's men

might have come back to plant evidence that would implicate Mr. Sinclair? So it's possible, then?"

He picked up his cup of tea, and regarded her over it. Then nodded slowly. "I hadn't considered it, but it might just be possible. And it's more clever than I'd given them credit for, if it is."

"Clever? It's horrible. They're not only ruining that poor man's life, they're planning to end it."

"Like they ended Carver's."

"Yes," Emily said. "I know. But imagine being stuck in a jail cell, and then accused of killing someone."

"We're working on it," he said. "And Sinclair hasn't been accused of the murder."

"Not yet," Emily said.

"And not soon, I hope. Scott, Trent and I are focusing on finding Carver's murderer. Meanwhile, Randall has arranged for McAndrews to see Sinclair tomorrow. Perhaps Sinclair can cast some light on how the fraud was worked."

"What can I do to help?" she asked.

He paused, eyes on her face. She suspected he couldn't think of anything, but didn't want to tell her she couldn't help.

"I mean, what did you want to discuss, when you suggested meeting for lunch?" Emily added quickly. She hadn't meant to embarrass him.

He smiled at her. She suspected he'd guessed her thoughts, and felt her cheeks heat. She hoped she wasn't blushing too obviously.

"I wanted to talk about the figures Marshall sent over yesterday," Granville said. "Were they what you had expected when you talked to him?"

"Actually, they are better," Emily said, leaning towards him. Then sat up straight again while the thick white plates piled with food were put in front of them. She'd ordered the salmon steak, which came with fried potatoes, a slice of lemon and a sprig of parsley. It looked and smelled delicious. But Granville's fried fish and chips smelled even better—the smell of hot oil, fish and potatoes all combining with the sharp scents of malt vinegar and tartar sauce were enough to make her mouth water.

"You don't mind?" she asked. "My asking him for the figures, I mean."

"No. Your request was quite brilliant."

This time Emily knew her blush was obvious. She looked down, re-arranged the potatoes on her plate, took a bite of salmon. Which tasted as fresh as it looked. When her face felt cooler, she looked up.

"Thank you," she said. "But what did you think of the numbers Mr. Marshall came up with?"

He finished a chip. "I think it's clear we should be buying an office building, not renting one."

She nodded. "Yes, that is what I thought, too."

"And after reading the report, which building would you suggest we buy?"

He'd surprised her enough that she nearly spilled her tea. "You really want my opinion?"

"I will always want your opinion." His eyes were warm on her, and Emily felt her face grow hot.

"Then, I would choose your current offices," she said, and was relieved she could get the words out without stammering. "Or at least the current building."

"You would?"

She seemed to have surprised him, and Emily wondered why. From her limited experience, men didn't like change, and certainly not a major move. Wouldn't staying where they were appeal to him? Apparently not.

"You would choose it because it's the lowest priced?" Granville asked.

He seemed to be struggling to understand her choice. Suddenly Emily felt nervous for a whole new reason. Had she missed something? Misunderstood something?

"No. Or at least, that isn't the first consideration," she said slowly, thinking hard. She began to tick her reasons off on her fingers as she spoke. "The building is centrally located, and easy for your clients to reach. It's not too fancy, which suits a business that is just starting out. And while the building itself is sound, the current owners have allowed the interior to become a little run-down, which means it's under-valued. So there is still room to bargain. And once it has been fixed up a little, the rates could be increased."

"You don't think having our offices on the third floor is detri-mental to the business?" he asked.

Why was he concerned about that? But Emily didn't even have to think about that one. "No, not at all. It is an investigative busi-ness, and will feel more private to your clients."

"And the lack of an elevator?"

"Says that yours is a solid firm, not a flashy one."

He looked thoughtful, and she wondered what he wasn't saying. And why. But before she could ask, the waiter stopped by with fresh tea, and the moment passed.

"How is your mother progressing with our wedding plans?" he asked.

Emily looked up at him and grimaced. "The guest list grows longer and the plans more elaborate each day," she said. "I fear that it will be a day-long event before she is done."

Granville chuckled. "Perhaps we should move up the date."

"Oh, could we?" Emily leaned forward in excitement, reaching for Granville's hand, then thought of her mother's reaction and sat back. "No. That wouldn't work."

"If we had already found a house, and I needed you to travel back to England with me it might."

England? Really? But the house was just one step. If the wedding was to be moved up, there were so many details she'd have to address first. Or they'd both be stuck with her mother's version of a 'proper wedding'...

"But can you afford to purchase both a house and an office building?" she asked him.

"I think so. But perhaps you could speak with Marshall again about preparing those figures for us, based on buying the office building we currently rent in. And you should choose a house you would want to live in, so that his figures will be accurate."

Emily narrowed her eyes at him. Was he just suggesting this because there was no place for her in their current investigation?

Granville must have read her mind, because he smiled at her. "There will always be urgent cases needing to be solved. Our business still has to move forward, even when we're in the middle of a case. Can you do this for me?"

She nodded. It made sense. "Yes. I'll set up another meeting for tomorrow to discuss the figures further. Perhaps I'll ask to see the house I liked the most again. And you know I'll enjoy doing so."

"I was counting on it."

AN HOUR LATER, Granville sat across the gleaming marble desk from Benton, who was watching him with a slight frown.

"Thank you for seeing me," Granville said.

"And what can I do for you today?" It should have been a helpful remark, but Benton's tone turned it into a warning.

Since he'd already annoyed the fellow, Granville figured he had nothing to lose. "I want to know why you find Dagan and his gang of over-muscled thugs so entertaining."

"What?"

The air of menace in the room thickened.

"Dagan is everywhere Scott and I turn on this case. If I hadn't talked to you first, I'd assume the fellow was a real power in this town. And yet you not only dismiss him, he seems to afford you some private amusement."

"And that would be your business... why?"

He could see the predator lurking in Benton's eyes.

"It isn't my business. But Scott and I are getting nowhere on this case of ours. If we can't sort it out, they're likely to charge our client with a murder he didn't commit. Then hang him for it,"

Granville said. "Dagan is the link. And I'm missing something about the fellow. I think you know what that is."

Benton considered him for a moment. "I see. Well, if you're finding the poor fool so hard to read, then it's probably a good thing I never hired you."

Granville let out a crack of laughter. "I told you as much, if you recall."

"You did. But I thought I saw glimmerings of competence." Benton tapped his fingers impatiently on the edge of his desk, but the frown was gone. "I don't suppose kicking you out would work."

"I don't suppose it would," he said with a grin. "I'd just come back. I'm persistent."

"But foolhardy," Benton said. "Very well. Dagan. I've been keeping an eye on him for some time."

"He sees himself as a potential rival to you, doesn't he?" Granville said. "I saw as much when I met him."

"As I said, the man's a fool," Benton said. "A poor leader. And remarkably incompetent, for all his airs."

Granville thought about that for a moment. "His men did a poor job of searching Carver's office, and have been creating havoc while trying to fix it ever since."

Benton smiled coldly. "He'll self-destruct before too long."

"Which is why you find him amusing."

"True. But it's also what makes Dagan dangerous, which is what I told you the first time you asked about him. He's far too anxious to prove himself, and that makes him more violent, because violence is the only way he can deal with most situations. And his style of violence tends to cause more violence."

And Dagan probably wouldn't self-destruct fast enough to keep him out of Granville's case. His mind went to Putnam—who had hired Dagan. "It would take a desperate man to hire someone like that."

"Likely it would."

"So why is Charles Putnam so desperate?" Granville said.

Benton didn't answer, but then Granville hadn't been

asking him.

THE TERMINAL CITY Club seemed even more welcoming now that he was a member, Granville thought with an amused grin as he strolled down the dark paneled hallway towards the bar. With any luck, O'Hearn and his fellow reporter, Draper, would already be there. He'd been turning the question of why Putnam had been desperate enough to hire Dagan over in his mind since he left Benton's office.

Reaching the bar, he glanced around the thinly populated room, spying O'Hearn's red head at a corner table. Draper was with him. Good.

He hadn't been sure O'Hearn could convince the senior reporter to join them on such short notice. Signaling to the bartender to bring a round of whiskies, he joined them.

"It's good to see you both," he said, shaking hands. "And I have a favor to ask."

"Good to see you too," O'Hearn said. "Ask away."

"I need some information," Granville said. "And it will probably take a fair bit of digging to uncover."

"Is there a story in it?" Draper asked. He leaned forward and tapped the ash off his cigarette, deceptively casual, but Granville could see the intensity in his eyes.

"Yes, and a good one. But I'd need the same agreement from you that O'Hearn has given me in past cases. Everything I tell you is confidential until the case is closed, and the story stays under wraps until then."

Draper glanced at O'Hearn, who nodded.

"You can trust him," O'Hearn said. "And if he says it's a good story, it will be worth your while to wait on it."

"He's the source for the front-pagers you've been publishing lately?" Draper asked.

The younger man nodded. "Most of 'em."

Draper looked from one to the other, drew deeply on his cigarette, then smiled. "Then I accept your terms. And O'Hearn, if you want to work with me on this, we can share a byline. Just don't tell your editor till we're ready to publish."

O'Hearn looked surprised, but was quick to agree. "Sure. But you know I don't have much experience on business stories."

"Best way to learn," Draper said. "And you're the one brought me the story."

"Thanks," O'Hearn said.

Draper winked at him, and turned to Granville. "What do you need from us?"

"You've heard there's been an arrest made for fraud over at Vancouver Permanent?"

"Fellow named Sinclair, isn't it? I've been following that, but the story's none to clear." He took a final drag on his cigarette, and stubbed it out in the ashtray. "And you were asking about Charles Putnam when you were first at the club. I assume that's the case you're working? Is Sinclair your client?"

"I'm afraid the identity of my client is confidential," Granville said. "But yes, that's the case I'm working. I suspect Putnam's behind the fraud, and they've got the wrong man in jail. Though I don't have enough to prove it. Yet."

"What've you got?" Draper had pulled out his notebook and pencil.

"Only speculation on the fraud itself," Granville said. "But Putnam is suddenly making some moves that smell of desperation. Whatever scheme he's running, I suspect he's gambled too deep, and was close to being discovered. So he made Sinclair the scapegoat and had him arrested for fraud."

"You think the police are in on it?" Draper asked.

"No. I think Putnam is that believable. Though he probably has influence, too. And I also think Putnam is responsible for Carver's death, and that he hired some thugs to do the deed. And probably to recover some papers from Carver's office. Which they haven't managed to find yet."

Draper's eyes narrowed. "I've heard that Carver did some work for Putnam's firm."

"I've heard the same," Granville said.

"So what information d'you need from us?" O'Hearn asked.

"Putnam's actions are those of a desperate man. I want to know what he's up to. Why is he making these choices? And why now?"

Draper finished scribbling his notes and looked up. "We'll look into it. I assume you don't want to alert Putnam?"

"He knows I'm looking into it. Best not let on that you are too."

"Fair enough. That shouldn't be hard, given that there's already a suspect in jail for the fraud. It's a natural story for me to cover." Draper finished his whiskey and stood up. "We'd best get on it. O'Hearn?"

O'Hearn stood and shook Granville's hand. "We'll be in touch. You'll let us know if you learn anything more?"

"Count on it," Granville said, finishing his own whiskey. The three men walked out together.

As Granville walked away from the Terminal City Club, he pondered what additional resources he could call on. He'd not admitted it to himself, but he'd hoped that Draper would have some information for him immediately, not just offer to look into the matter. Helpful though that was, he needed answers now, before things got any worse for his client.

What about Gipson? Weasel or not, the fellow also dealt in mortgages. He'd admitted to working with Sinclair occasionally. And Putnam had called him a "colleague." He knew more than he was telling, he had to.

Much as Granville hated dealing with the man, he was running out of options.

So how to get the truth out of him? Gipson wouldn't help Granville in any way, not if he could avoid it. But that attitude of his might be used against him, if Granville played it right.

He checked his watch. Gipson's office would be closed. Tomorrow, then.

32

THURSDAY, JUNE 21, 1900

The following morning, Granville was alone in his office, scowling over his notes from the previous day. The idea of visiting Gipson again, and worse, being polite to the man, didn't sit well. Especially since it was likely to be a waste of time. His phone rang, providing a welcome distraction.

"Granville here."

"McAndrews won't be able to talk to Sinclair today." It was Randall's voice, but there was an edge of frustration that Granville hadn't heard from the normally imperturbable lawyer before.

Not another delay. "What's happened?"

"They've charged Sinclair with Carver's murder."

"What? Why?"

"I don't know. I'm on my way to the police station now. I'll call you as soon as I know something."

"It doesn't make any sense," Granville said. "Look at the murder of the janitor yesterday. It has to be related to Carver's death. And Sinclair was in jail yesterday—he couldn't have done it."

Randall's sigh echoed down the line. "You said yourself the janitor's death was likely the work of a hired thug. Anyone could have hired him. Even Sinclair."

"From jail?"

"I know. But this is the argument we can expect."

"Right. Look, when you see Sinclair, find out where he was the night Carver was killed," Granville said. "We might be able to prove he couldn't have done it."

"Yes. I'll get what I can."

"They haven't charged Sinclair with the janitor's murder, have they?"

"No, they haven't," the lawyer said. "Not yet, at least. Look, I'll be in touch as soon as I know something."

As he hung up, Granville fumed. Now their client was being framed for murder, or maybe multiple murders, as well as fraud. The poor fellow would never get bail now. And any chance of him assisting McAndrews in understanding the extra sets of ledgers was gone.

He thought about the janitor's body lying crumpled on the stairs, in a pool of his own blood. Someone needed to pay. And it wasn't Sinclair.

His office door creaked open, and Granville looked up to see McAndrews standing there, breathing hard, hair ruffled and an odd expression on his face. Had he run up the stairs?

"McAndrews? The visit to Sinclair is off. He's been..."

"Charged with murder. I know." McAndrews came into the room, slamming the door behind him. "May I?" he asked, pointing at Scott's chair, then sinking into it without waiting for Granville's reply.

"McAndrews? What's wrong?"

"I was there. When they arrested—I mean charged—him." McAndrews swallowed hard. "Granville, I was there."

"At the police station? You'd already gone in for the meeting?"

"Yes. I mean no. I mean—" McAndrews struggled to get a grip on himself. "Yes, I'd gone in for the meeting. But I was in his cell, not the station. When they charged him, I mean."

"You were *with* Sinclair when they charged him?" He stared at

McAndrews. "What did they say—wait. Did you get a chance to talk to him? Before they charged him?"

McAndrews nodded. "Yes. I—I was early. For our meeting."

He stopped, took a deep breath. When he spoke again, his voice was calmer. "I showed him the ledger pages we found, and we talked about them. We'd be talking for, oh, twenty minutes or so, I guess, when there was a lot of shouting in the corridor leading to his cell."

He paused again, then said in a voice Granville had to lean forward to hear, "I've never been so scared. It sounded like a riot, like we were all going to be murdered right there."

Granville reached into the bottom drawer of his desk and pulled out a bottle of whiskey. He passed it to McAndrews without a word. The fellow gave him a grateful glance then took a couple of deep pulls. He didn't hand the bottle back, though, but held it as though it were a weapon.

"What happened?" Granville asked.

"It went on for a few minutes, just yelling. Sinclair and I sat staring at each other, waiting. I think he might have been even more scared than I was—he'd been locked up in that dark cell for three days, after all. Who knows what he'd heard already."

McAndrews lifted the bottle as if to take another slug, but apparently changed his mind and put it down again. "Then they came thundering down the hallway, four or maybe five cops, their batons drawn. They hauled me out of the cell, slammed the door behind me. Told Sinclair he'd better never expect to get out again, after murdering Carver."

"Wait, that's how they put it?"

"Something like that. One of them was shaking his baton at Sinclair and yelling about how Sinclair had been wasting all their time by not admitting he'd even known Carver."

"What?"

McAndrews shuddered. "It didn't make much sense to me. Maybe Randall can help him. All I know is I felt like they were going to turn on me any minute. All I wanted was to get out of there before that happened."

Granville ran a quick eye over McAndrews. He was pale, but there were no obvious bruises. And he hadn't moved like he was injured when he walked in. "How did you get out?"

"One of them, a new guy I hadn't seen before, he helped me. Just walked me out, calm and quiet, like I had nothing to worry about. Funny thing is, I think I recognized his voice as one of the ones who'd been yelling earlier. Trying to stop the others from doing something."

Probably beating a confession out of their prisoner, Granville thought cynically. "This was one of the policemen?" he asked. "The fellow who helped you?"

"Yeah."

It sounded like he'd be a fellow worth talking to. "You get a name?"

"Daniels."

Granville nodded. That was the new fellow he'd noted at the recent murder in Carver's building, the one who'd seemed competent. Definitely a man worth talking to. "You want another whiskey?"

McAndrews looked at the bottle as if he'd forgotten it was there, then handed it back to Granville. "Thanks," he said. "But don't you want to know what Sinclair had to say?"

"Yes. I would very much like to know what he told you," Granville said.

McAndrews seemed to miss the dry humor, which wasn't surprising given his recent ordeal. He leaned forward earnestly, and let the story pour out.

They'd been examining each ledger sheet, comparing one to another. "Sinclair hadn't seen any of the ledgers before," McAndrews concluded. "But he thought he recognized some of the transactions on one of the sheets as ones he'd been involved in, and he was able to give me details on them."

"So does that mean you have answers?" Granville asked.

"No," McAndrews said, then hastened to correct himself. "I mean, no, not yet. But I believe, or rather I hope, that the details Sinclair has given me will serve as our Rosetta Stone, and allow us to decipher the rest of the ledgers. I've called in sick from my place of work, and plan to work with Miss Kent all day today, to see if we can't work it out."

He glanced at Granville, reddened a little. "If you don't need her for your work, of course."

"Not at all," Granville said. "As long as the phones are answered. Since there will be no-one else here."

"Yes, of course," McAndrews said. "You're going out?"

"I'm off for a chat with a certain police officer," Granville said with a smile.

GRANVILLE WAS IN LUCK. As he strode towards City Hall, a squat brick building that also housed the Police Department, he recognized Daniels leaving the building. As the officer strode briskly towards him, Granville stopped and held up a hand in greeting.

Daniels gave him a nod and slowed his pace as he approached. The new officer was smartly turned out in the navy frock coat and tall, rounded hat of the Vancouver Police force. His shoes shone, his buttons and buckle gleamed, and his expression spoke of professionalism and pride in his position.

Granville hoped for Daniel's sake that he'd be able to keep that promise, to himself as well as to his community. It wouldn't be easy, being an honest voice on a force that had been largely corrupt since its founding.

"Mr. Granville, isn't it? You wanted to talk to me?" Daniels said.

"I did. But you seem to be in a hurry. May I walk with you?"

"Of course," Daniels said as they turned onto Cordova. "What can I do for you?"

The clatter of an approaching streetcar drowned all hope of

conversation for several minutes. Granville matched his stride to the other's and waited.

"The murder of the janitor the other day?" he said when the tram had passed them. "It ties into a case I'm working on, and I hoped to discuss it with you."

Daniels cast him a sideways glance. "When I'm not with my colleagues, you mean."

"Yes," Granville said bluntly. "I can imagine some of the difficulties you must face in your new role, and I'm sure you can imagine the challenges I face as a private investigator."

"You aren't a police officer, and can't expect to be treated as one," Daniels said.

"No. But I am as committed to justice as you are," Granville said. "I have no intention of hampering your investigation. But perhaps we can assist each other."

"You'd share information?"

"I'd exchange information," Granville said. "Within the bounds of protecting my client's confidences."

A shouting match between two deliverymen attracted their attention, and Daniels slowed his stride to listen. The two wagons were stopped at angles, and the horses were uneasy, one of them neighing in protest. Whatever had happened, there didn't appear to be any damage.

Granville sensed that Daniels was poised to intervene, but after a final round of name-calling the two men returned to their wagons and drove off. They resumed walking.

"Protecting your client's confidences could mean you'd share nothing at all," Daniels said, as if they'd not been interrupted.

"That isn't my intention. But you have no reason to trust me."

"No reason to distrust you, either." Daniels glanced over at Granville again. "I'm willing to see how it goes on this case, if you are."

"That will work for me."

"Then we need to meet. I'm off shift at seven tonight," Daniels said. "Do you know Mary's Diner?"

"I know it well. I'll meet you there at a quarter after seven?"

"Make it seven-thirty. I'd rather not be in uniform for this discussion."

"I'll see you there," Granville said, and reached out a hand. They shook, and as Granville watched the other man stride off, his back very straight, he wondered what would come of this discussion.

"Has Randall called yet?" Granville asked Miss Kent as he strode into the office.

"No," she said, looking up from the ledgers that she and McAndrews were poring over. "I did take one message, though. He said you'll know what it's regarding, and that he'd call back at ten."

Granville accepted the message slip. Draper. Maybe he had some information on Putnam's financing.

"Put either Randall or Draper through as soon as they call, then," Granville said as he hung up his hat and coat. "Is Scott in?"

She nodded, pointing to their shared office.

"And Trent?"

"Running errands. He said he'd be back in an hour or so."

"Thanks," he said. "Any luck with the ledgers?"

Miss Kent's mouth turned down and McAndrews scowled.

He almost offered to help, but knew it would be a waste of everyone's time. "Well, let me know if you find anything. I'll be talking to Scott."

They needed a break on this case, or their client wouldn't have to worry about the fraud charges, because he'd be hanged for a murder he hadn't committed.

Scott looked up when the door opened.

"You heard?" Granville asked.

"Yup. McAndrews told me. How bad is it?"

"We won't know until we hear from Randall. But we're going to have to prove Sinclair couldn't have murdered Carver."

"That might be difficult."

"Well, from what McAndrews heard at the station, Sinclair may not even have known Carver."

"That won't be easy to prove, either."

"Let's look at it from another angle," Granville said. "What motive could he have?"

Scott shrugged. "Carver's a lawyer. Putnam's accusing Sinclair of fraud. Carver finds the proof. Sinclair kills him and destroys the proof. Pretty easy to figure out."

He was right—the scenario was all too logical. "Thanks, partner. Whose side are you on, anyway?" Granville said, but couldn't quite manage the lightness he'd been aiming for.

The sound of the outer door opening distracted both of them. "Now what?" Scott muttered.

"Go right in," came Miss Kent's voice, and their office door opened. Randall.

Granville stood up and strode forward to wring the lawyer's hand. "I'm glad to see you," he said. "What's going on?"

"They've definitely made the connection between Carver's murder and the janitor's, and tied it to the ransacking of Carver's office," Randall said as he took a seat. "It's my guess that Sinclair will be charged with a second murder before the week is out."

"And being in jail at the time isn't a sufficient alibi?"

Randall smiled thinly. "He could have hired someone. In fact, it's likely from what you've told me that the real killer did hire someone."

"Dagan," Granville said. Unfortunately, from the police perspective, it all made sense. It was six kinds of wrong, but it made sense.

"I gather Sinclair says he didn't know Carver, and they don't believe him?" Granville said.

"Yes. It seems to be undercutting everything else he says. But how did you know?"

Granville explained what McAndrews had seen and heard at the jail. "Why are they so sure he knew Carver?"

"They won't say. I suspect that means Putnam has told them something—probably that he had Carver work with Sinclair on some project or other."

Granville glanced over at Scott. That fit nicely into the scenario they'd been discussing, and made matters worse for their client. "Did Sinclair tell you where he was the night Carver was killed?" he asked.

Randall nodded. "Yes, but it won't help us. He was at home, and alone.

Scott rolled his eyes.

Randall almost smiled.

"Even if he'd had a solid alibi, it probably wouldn't help him," the lawyer said. "If it was a hired killing, an alibi is worthless in any case."

Scott thumped a meaty fist on his desk. "No. There has to be something we can prove," he said. "What if we get one of Dagan's thugs to talk?"

Randall raised his brows. "And confess to murder?" he said skeptically. "It still wouldn't clear your client, unless you could prove someone else hired them."

"Fine. So we get Dagan to talk."

"How?" Randall said. "He'd be signing his own death warrant."

"We'd have to prove Dagan and his gang committed both murders," Granville said slowly. "Then we could get Dagan to roll over on Putnam."

"How?" the lawyer asked, while Scott started to grin.

Granville just shook his head, still thinking. "Or if we can prove fraud, we can put pressure on Putnam, get him to point the finger at Dagan. Then we get Dagan to implicate Putnam."

"What would be strong enough to make Putnam even admit he knows Dagan, much less implicate him for murder?" Randall asked.

"We'll come up with something," Scott said, nodding at Granville.

"There's more than one way to dig for gold," Granville said with a grin for his partner. "I'd been forgetting that."

Randall rolled his eyes. "Just get me evidence," he said. "The kind I can use in court."

ONCE RANDALL HAD LEFT, still shaking his head, Granville and Scott looked at each other.

"So what do we do first?" Scott asked.

"We have two scenarios," Granville said. "And we can improve our chances by working both at the same time. Then we focus on whichever one gives us the best odds for clearing our client."

"And you say you've given up gambling," Scott said with a wink. They were back on track, and they both knew it. "So we're looking to prove that Dagan and his gang killed both men. And to prove Putnam committed fraud, then hired Dagan to cover it up."

"That's it," Granville said.

"Trent should be back soon," Scott said. "I'll take him back to Carver's building, see what we can scare up about the break-in or the murders. Maybe we missed something. We need to finish interviewing the other tenants, anyway."

"Then I'll focus on Putnam himself." He glanced at the clock on the wall. "Draper is supposed to call in fifteen minutes. He may have something on why Putnam might be committing fraud."

"Sounds pretty dull. I'll leave you to it," Scott said. "We'll be back when we've found something."

Since there was little he could do until Draper called, Granville pulled out the telegram from the Pinkerton's Agency, offering a meeting. He glanced at the calendar. Now just over a month away.

He still wanted to explore the possibilities of aligning with such a well-known firm, but was that the right thing for any of them? Scott's reaction had made him take another look at all the changes he'd instigated lately—from new staff to the potential for new premises. Was it too much, all at once?

He'd begun to realize he had a vision for the kind of firm he wanted to be part of—he glared at the fan overhead, which seemed to be squawking at him this morning—and he hadn't realized how much he'd admired the care his father took of his people and his properties.

At the moment, with Scott and Trent busy interviewing and Emily off looking at houses, the offices felt rather empty. And more than big enough. Was he suffering from pride, thinking he needed bigger offices and better amenities?

And what about Emily?

He could hear the phone ringing in the outer office, and then the phone on his desk rang once. He picked it up to hear Miss Kent's voice. "Mr. Draper has called back. I'll put him right through."

The switchboard was another innovation, and one he was none too sure of. Still, it was supposed to be more efficient in the long run. "Good. Thank you."

He heard several clicks, then Draper's voice. "Granville? You there?"

"I'm here. You have something for me?"

"I might have. It's complicated, but I think I might have found a few things that relate to what's going on with Vancouver Permanent. And explain Putnam's increasing desperation. In fact, this could be key to unraveling the whole mess."

He sounded like McAndrews. "Can you hold a moment?"

"Certainly."

Putting the receiver down, Granville strode into the outer office. McAndrews and Miss Kent were still bent over the ledgers, which they'd laid in four ordered rows across the two desks. "Are you getting anywhere?"

McAndrews looked up. His red hair was standing on end, as if he'd been running his fingers through it, and it took a moment for his eyes to focus on Granville. "Um. I think so. It's slow going, though."

"I've been working with Andrew Draper, the business reporter. He thinks he might have found out what drove Putnam to frame Sinclair. I'd like him to come here, see what the two of you are working on. Any objections?"

"Umm. No?" McAndrews glanced at the pages, looked over at Miss Kent. "You?"

She shook her head. "It might be the missing piece to this puzzle we have. But he's a reporter. He'll keep this confidential?"

It was the right question, though he hadn't expected her to ask it. Granville wondered if the business school Emily and Miss Kent had attended was exceptional, or if they both simply had a real aptitude for the business world. He suspected it was the latter.

"Yes. He's agreed not to publish until the case is over. And he's working with O'Hearn, whom I've worked with before."

She nodded, and he smiled at her. "I'm impressed that you asked," he told her as he walked back into his office.

"Draper?" he said, picking up the phone. "We have some information here that I think you should see. Can you bring whatever you have and come over to our offices?"

He heard some rustling over the phone, and a murmur of voices. Then Draper said, "Sure. O'Hearn and I can pack this up, and be there in half an hour. That suit you?"

"Yes. And you'll be working with two of our associates, Mr. McAndrews and Miss Kent."

"Not yourself?" Draper asked. If he was surprised to hear he'd be working with a woman, he didn't let on, which was to his credit.

"I'll be here as well," Granville said. "Though I'm afraid I don't have a head for ledgers."

Draper laughed at that. "We'll be there shortly," he said.

GRANVILLE HAD JUST INTRODUCED Draper and O'Hearn to Miss Trent and McAndrews when the outer door flew open and Scott and Trent rushed in. In the resultant hubbub of greetings and interactions, Granville looked at the sudden throng of people in their office.

There really was no question that they needed larger offices, he realized. They couldn't work as a team without a meeting room, for one thing. One large enough to hold all of them, and a client or two as well. He'd need to talk to Emily about it.

In the meantime, he needed to get the team back on track. "We need to move into Scott's and my office," he suggested, and Miss Kent was quick to gather up the ledgers and herd the others into the other room. She was definitely turning into an asset.

In the other office, Miss Kent spread the papers out in order on the large double desk, and Draper, O'Hearn and McAndrews gathered around her. McAndrews was pointing something out, making a low-voiced comment, and Draper was nodding.

Granville was just about to move closer to find out what they were seeing when Trent tugged at his elbow. He hadn't even heard the lad come in.

"We need to talk to you," Trent said, practically jittering in his eagerness to get Granville's attention.

Granville glanced over to see Scott, standing behind Trent. His partner nodded. It was urgent. He followed them back into the outer office.

What had they found out?

"Carver had a partner," Trent burst out as Scott quietly closed the door between the offices.

That was news. He'd never heard any mention of a partner.

"Not a partner," Scott said. "A junior associate, he called him. Not a lawyer, though. More like a legal assistant, I think."

Trent started to say something, and Scott just gave him a look, then continued. "Man was English, like Carver—a few years older than Carver. A bit too fond of his drink—but Carver seems to have given him a lot of latitude."

"And we think—you'll never guess…" Trent all but sputtered in his excitement.

Granville looked at him, thought about the janitor's dying words, as Bertie had translated them. "Carver isn't dead?"

Trent's face fell. "How'd you know? It took us half of yesterday and most of this morning to even begin to suspect it."

Scott chuckled. "You'll have to get used to that. Granville here gets hunches, and he's either spot on, or spectacularly wrong."

"Hunches?" Granville shook his head. "You wound me. They're well reasoned judgments, please."

"Tell that to the idiot you got arrested for fraud in Dawson City," Scott said.

Granville grinned at him, then turned back to Trent, who was frowning at them. "How did the police make the error?"

"The dead man was found in Carver's office," Trent said, with an uncomfortable looking half-shrug. "And they were the same height, similar build. People said they looked alike from a distance."

"He was shot in the face," Scott said. "The bullet did enough damage that they assumed the body was Carter's."

"Poor fellow. What was the other man's name?"

"Joseph Heller."

"And why haven't we heard anything about him before?"

"Apparently Heller was the quiet type," Scott said. "The neighbors didn't notice his absence for a while, especially in the confusion of a murder. And their clerk isn't talking."

"And did this Heller have any enemies?"

"Not that we found," Trent said. "He really kept to himself."

"If he was a drinker, did he have a favorite bar?"

"Nah," Scott said. "Drank at home, from what we could tell."

"And do you know for a fact that it's Heller who was murdered, and not Carver?"

Scott shook his head. "No. But neither of them has been seen since that night. And a fellow down the hall from their office saw Heller working late the night of the murder."

"Yeah, and Carver left early because he had a date with the

mayor's daughter," Trent said. "They went to the Opera. But she was home by eleven."

"So Carver could still have gone back to the office?"

Scott and Trent nodded.

Granville began to pace as he thought. "Heller as the corpse seems the more logical choice, since he was working late, but it could still be either of them," he said. "But if it's Heller who's dead, and Carver is still in town, where has the fellow been hiding for the last week?"

"And if it was Carver the janitor saw the night he was killed, why was Carver there?" Scott said. "And who killed the janitor?"

"Also, who broke into Carver's office that night?" Trent added. "Even if Carver was there, looking for something, he'd have had his keys."

Granville turned to Scott. "You get an address for Heller?"

"Sure. It's on Alexander, just past the ironworks."

"Interesting part of town."

"Cheap, too," Trent said.

All too true. "If Carver is alive, we need to find him now. Before he gets himself killed, too," he said striding across the room and grabbing his hat from the coat rack.

He opened the door to the inner office, "We'll be out for the next hour," he said to all of them, then left the door open.

"Let's go," he said Scott and Trent.

"So I guess we're going to Heller's place? But why? If he's dead, I mean," Trent asked from behind them, a little breathless from keeping up with Granville down the stairs.

"We don't know he's dead," Granville said.

"And if it's Carter who's alive, that might be where he'd hide," Scott added. "Dumb move, though. The police will find out about Heller eventually, and go looking there. Or Dagan will. If Carver stays in town, he's as good as dead."

Granville didn't answer, his gaze focused on the crush of carriages and delivery vans on Hastings Street. When he saw a break in the traffic, he made a quick dash across to the other side of the street. Scott and Trent raced after him, Scott cursing fluently the whole time.

But they were in time to catch the streetcar.

Heller's small apartment, when Granville, Scott and Trent finally found it at the back of a run-down three-story building, was shabby, scrupulously clean—and deserted.

"Looks like it hasn't been empty long. The ice hasn't fully melted in the ice box yet," Scott said, lifting the rusting lid to check.

"No dust, either," said Trent in the knowing tones of one who knew something about dust.

"And nothing to tell us where he might have run," Granville said, prowling around the single room.

Aside from the ice box, there was a battered hot plate with a top plate of scratched aluminum, an old pine table and chair—that looked like it also served as a desk, judging by the stack of newspapers and the glass jar holding pencils—and a narrow bed frame under the small window. The lavatory would be down the hall.

A room like this one would quite be a come-down for a high-flying lawyer. And for Heller, too, if his suspicions were right about the fellow.

He flipped through the newspapers, noting the same scrolling pencil patterns he'd seen in Carver's office scribbled on the edges of some of the pages. So it had been Heller who'd died.

"Carver's been here," he said. "And recently. He's got the *News-Advertiser* from the past week. Today's paper isn't here, though, so he could have left yesterday."

He sat down to sort through them, looking for anything to tell him what Carver had been thinking, planning. He found the chair solid under him. Everything here was old and well-used, but it had also been kept clean and in working order.

Heller might have been a drunk, but he'd kept up at least some of the standards he must have been raised with.

There was a deep pencil mark against the brief article detailing the death of the janitor from the previous day's paper. It would have been easy to miss if he hadn't been looking for it. There was a small tea stain on another page, which held mostly ads.

Granville considered it for a moment, his gaze landing on the list of the following day's arrival and departure times for the railroad. Was Carver planning on leaving town? Perhaps he'd gone to his office that night to retrieve something to take with him? But why would he wait for nearly a week after Heller's murder before leaving?

Setting the page aside, Granville worked his way methodically through a week's worth of papers. He found a pencil mark on an article on housing prices and another faint mark on the article about Sinclair's arrest for fraud—noting with interest Draper's byline on both articles. He found nothing else of importance in the newspapers, but caught between the pages was a half sheet of paper torn from a yellow legal pad, with a few penciled notations on it.

Granville tried to decipher it, then walked to the window, hoping better light would help. It didn't. Carver's writing was either worse than most doctors, or this wasn't English.

He glanced around the room. Trent was checking the few cupboards, and Scott was going through Heller's meager wardrobe, which was hanging on hooks behind a piece of gingham fabric nailed up in a corner. "Anything?" he asked.

"Not much," Trent said. "Some stale crackers, a little salt. No whiskey. Either Heller didn't keep much, or Carver's running and he's taken supplies with him."

"I suspect both are true," Granville said. "Scott?"

"Not a thing. Even the pockets are empty except for the lint. No empty hooks, though, so nothing's been taken."

"Is there a coat?" Granville asked.

"Don't see one. But maybe Heller was wearing it when he was killed."

"Or maybe Carver took it. It was pretty warm out, the day Heller died," Trent said.

"I think Carver's running," Granville said. "And he can't do it as himself. I suspect he took the coat, maybe a few other things, and boarded a train out of here. Trent, can you go to the depot, see if anyone resembling Heller or Carver bought a ticket yesterday or today?" And he showed him the newspaper listing.

"But if Carver stayed in town this long, why's he running now?" Scott asked. "If he's got the goods on Putnam, he could get him arrested. Or just blackmail the man."

"I suspect it was the article on the janitor's death," Granville said. "He may not have realized how blood-thirsty Putnam and his hired thugs were becoming until that moment."

"So he ran?" Trent said. "Gave up everything, just like that?"

"At least he's alive," Scott said. "Heller isn't."

* * *

EMILY SAT across from Grant Marshall in his office, waiting for him to complete a telephone call. Clara was sitting beside her, and Emily was trying to keep from smiling at her friend's expression.

Clara had been thrilled when Emily suggested they take another look at the second house they'd seen on Monday. She was less thrilled to be included in the business discussion that followed, but she'd agreed to be here and promised confidentiality on what she heard about Granville's business dealings.

Just then Mr. Marshall finished his conversation and hung up.

"My apologies, ladies," he said. "It was an urgent matter, or I'd not have taken the call." He steepled his hands on the desk in front of him. "Now, did you have any further questions about the house we saw today?"

"No, I think you answered everything," Emily said, then glanced over at her friend. "Clara, did you have anything you'd like to ask?"

Clara gave her a little sideways smile that had Emily regretting the question. Apprehension turned to amusement when Clara turned the smile on the real estate agent and she watched him melt.

"Yes, actually. I was wondering why such a new house is on the market," Clara said, leaning forward a little.

"Uh, the previous, I mean the owner—well, he cannot make the payments," Mr. Marshall managed to say.

"And are there problems with the house that a buyer should know about?"

"No, no—not at all. Nothing of the kind," Marshall said quickly, and then seemed to lose his train of thought under Clara's regard. "Well, except that perhaps the furnace wasn't as well built as it should have been." He frowned as he said it.

"The furnace? I see." Clara bit her full lips with small white teeth. "I don't know anything about furnaces, and such, but that sounds terribly difficult to fix."

"Not at all. A new furnace would easily solve the problem."

Mr. Marshall seemed to have forgotten that she was even in the room, Emily thought with an inward grin as she waited to see what Clara would make of this bit of information.

"Oh, good." Clara smiled at him, then bit her lip again. "But wouldn't that be rather expensive? I mean, when you're buying such a new house, it seems rather a waste."

"Well, of course the price could be adjusted to reflect that requirement," Mr. Marshall was quick to say.

"Could be? Oh, I should think it was of the first importance, to a buyer, I mean," Clara said, brushing the curls back from her forehead. The real estate agent's eyes were fixed on the motion.

Emily watched in awe as her friend bargained with the real

estate agent for the best price. She'd known that her friend's love of shopping was partly about getting the best deal, but she hadn't expected it to extend to real estate transactions.

When they'd finally reached a number Clara seemed happy with, Emily squeezed her friend's hand and beamed at both of them. "Mr. Marshall, that sounds perfect. Now, if you could just put together a package calculating the purchase and operating costs of that house at that price, together with the office building that Mr. Granville currently occupies, that would be very helpful."

Mr. Marshall looked a little stunned as he nodded agreement, Emily noted with amusement.

But the poor man went pale when Clara turned to her and said, "Mr. Granville is thinking about buying his office building? But Emily, there are so many problems with it. And wouldn't it be quite expensive to fix?"

"So what happens if we find Carver?" Scott asked Granville as they climbed the stairs back to their office. "He must have something against Putnam, if the man was willing to have him murdered.

"But what?" Granville said. "Even if Carver could prove that Putnam committed the fraud that Sinclair's been charged with, Heller and the janitor are still dead."

"But what's Sinclair's motive?" Scott said. "He had no reason to kill Heller."

"Nor did Putnam," Granville said. "Whoever killed the poor man likely intended to kill Carver, so that argument won't help us."

"So we're no further ahead?"

"It depends on what Carver knows. If we find him."

"We'll find him," Scott said. "But it might be too late, depending on how far he ran.

"But we know that the wrong man was killed and that Carver is alive. That could provide a lever with Putnam. Or even with Dagan, if we play our cards right."

"Bluff 'em, you mean?" Scott asked as he reached for the door handle. "Yeah, that could work."

"Or perhaps Draper found something that would help us pin Putnam to the wall," Granville said as he followed Scott into the office. "The man deserves to pay for what he's been doing."

The office was ominously quiet. The reception area was deserted, and there was no sound coming from his office. "Anyone in?" Granville called.

A whoop broke the silence as McAndrews rushed into the reception area.

"Granville, we did it," he cried, wringing Granville's hand. Finally noticing Scott, McAndrews nodded a greeting, grinning like he'd just won a poker pot.

In McAndrews wake, Draper, O'Hearn and Miss Kent trooped in, all smiling broadly.

"Congratulations," Granville said. "What did you find?"

"The key to Putnam's little scheme," Draper said. "Come back into the office and we'll show you."

They did so. Granville stood in front of the partners' desk, now covered with paper, and Draper stood beside him. O'Hearn stood just behind Draper, while McAndrews took up a position on Granville's other side, with Scott beside him. Miss Kent moved to stand beside Draper. All of them focused on the documents spread out in front of them.

"This is the information I got from my contacts in England," Draper said, pointing to a page of figures that Granville hadn't seen before. "Which is where most of Putnam's money is coming from. There are a couple of investors in Toronto, but he's been fairly honest with them. Maybe three thousand miles, and in the same country was too close for his comfort."

"Whereas London's five thousand miles and an ocean away," O'Hearn put in.

Draper winked at him, and continued. "He promised the Brits," then hesitated, glancing at Granville. "Sorry, I forgot. I meant his English investors..."

"Don't worry about it," Granville said. "Just get to the point."

Draper nodded. "Sure. Well, Putnam promised them a return

based on a booming economy. Only he over-estimated how fast the local real estate market could grow. And he must have assumed it would keep growing at a steady rate."

"But it didn't." McAndrews said.

"In England, Putnam's been drawing in new investors at a steady rate, based on the handsome sums his earlier investors have been raking in," Draper said. "And knowing our local real estate market, that makes no sense at all. Unless he's cheating."

"Which he is," O'Hearn put in.

"And based on the figures your colleagues here have been showing me," Draper said, "Putnam did exactly what you all have been speculating—he used the new investors' money to pay off the interest he owed to the earlier investors."

"Thus ensuring himself a steady influx of investors," McAndrews said. "Only when it seemed to be working, he took it a few steps further, and started paying himself rather large sums first, and then paying his investors. That's why we couldn't make sense of these ledgers."

"How long has this been going on?" Granville asked.

"A couple of years, based on the figures McAndrews and Miss Kent showed me," Draper said, turning to give the latter a smile.

"So what changed that made Putnam set Sinclair up, and then have Carver murdered?" Granville asked.

O'Hearn looked up sharply. Draper went pale. "Murder? You didn't mention that before," the older reporter said.

"No."

"And who is Carver?"

Granville explained, then said, "What set Putnam off?"

"That's the other piece that I learned this morning," Draper said. "Putnam's investors asked for an audit of his books. It's scheduled for two months from now."

"And that explains these ledgers," McAndrews said, tapping a finger on the nearest set of pages. "He was trying to create a version of his books that would pass the audit."

"We couldn't find a logical pattern because there isn't one," Miss

Kent said. "There's been nothing logical about the way Mr. Putnam has been running his firm for several years now. And it looks like he hasn't yet found a way to explain it."

"So these," Granville indicated the four sets of figures they'd spread out. "Are the failed attempts?"

Both she and McAndrews nodded.

"Then why would Carver have them?"

"Insurance?" O'Hearn suggested.

That made sense. "And the set of figures you found in Carver's office?" Granville asked McAndrews.

"Yet another set of false books," McAndrews said. "Possibly the one he used to frame Sinclair."

Draper nodded. "It seems to be the only set that has enough money unaccounted for to require a fraud to explain it."

"Which is why he set Sinclair up," McAndrews said. "It was clear to me when I talked to Sinclair this morning that he didn't recognize any of the ledgers I showed him. And he couldn't even see the difference between them.

Sinclair had been the perfect patsy, Granville realized. Putnam had apparently given him just enough access to make him look guilty, but not enough for him to spot what was going on."

"I don't get why Putnam needs fake books at all when he's got a guy accused of fraud," Scott said.

"The extent of the true fraud is probably too vast for anyone below Putnam himself to have pulled off," McAndrews said.

Now that made sense. "Then what is the fifth set of figures that Carver had hidden in the Post Office box?"

"We haven't figured those out yet," McAndrews said. "Possibly a comparison that Carver himself made."

"Then he should be able to explain it to us, when we find him," Granville said. The others gawked at him.

"I thought Carver was dead," McAndrews said.

Scott chuckled. "So did we," he said. "But apparently it was his associate that was killed. Carver's been hiding out, high-tailed it out of town yesterday morning. Trent's trying to track him now."

As Granville watched their reactions, he was thinking through everything he'd just heard. "Never mind Carver," he said abruptly. "When did Putnam begin squirreling away large sums for himself?"

Draper's eyes narrowed, but it was Miss Kent who answered.

"Nearly a year ago, we think," she said, tucking a strand of blond hair behind her ear. "You're thinking he was planning to leave town?"

Just before he hired Sinclair. Granville smiled at her. "That's exactly what I was thinking. Putnam must have known that he couldn't pull off this scheme of his forever. It was bound to come out eventually."

"That makes sense," McAndrews said thoughtfully. "Especially if he never planned to embezzle money in the first place. The original business looks legitimate—though ambitious, given the returns he was promising. And everything seemed fine until the market softened and he had to find the money somewhere."

"Or declare bankruptcy," Draper said. "You know, you might have something there. Perhaps he thought the market would turn around and he'd be able to pay everyone back."

"That was stupidity on his part, if he did," McAndrews said, his voice tight with annoyance. "And if he'd had an accountant worth his salt, they'd have told him so. No business can pay back that kind of money. They just dig themselves deeper the longer it goes on. By the second month, or the third, at the worst, he should have folded, declared bankruptcy if he had to. That was the turning point."

"Instead he kept going for almost two more years," Miss Kent said quietly.

Draper nodded. "Even after the real estate market improved. But he hadn't started siphoning off amounts for himself, yet, had he? Didn't he see it?"

"Probably not," McAndrews said. "There was more money coming in—Putnam must have thought he'd be able to make it all good."

"And it took him another eight months to realize he couldn't do it," Miss Kent said. "Which is when he started paying himself first."

"And looking to hire the perfect patsy, just in case questions were asked and he needed to buy himself more time to wind up his scheme," Granville said thoughtfully. "That's when he found Sinclair. The question is, how much more time does Putnam need before he vanishes into the night?"

"Probably not much," Scott said. "If he was willing to have Carver killed to buy himself that time."

"Sounds right to me," McAndrews said. "He must have a fair amount put away by now. More than enough to run on."

"So how do we get Putnam arrested?" Granville asked. "Do we have enough to have him charged?"

McAndrews and Draper looked at each other, shook their heads.

"Not with a suspect already in jail for the fraud. And murder," McAndrews said.

"What do we still need?"

"To clear Sinclair and charge Putnam? Besides a jury made up of accountants?" Draper said. "We'd need an audit, and a judge to order it. These,"—waving at the various documents spread across the desk—"are probably not enough. Not without someone who knows the whole story to explain them."

"Then we need to find Carver and convince him to tell that story," Granville said. "But first I've a call to make." He was on the telephone to Randall when he heard the outer door open and Emily and Clara came laughing into the office.

EMILY HAD BEEN LAUGHING at Clara's reaction to the numbers she'd been discussing with Mr. Marshall, but one look at the somber group gathered in the inner office drove all thought of the meeting out of her head.

"Granville, what's wrong?" she said in alarm. She hadn't seen him this stern since his last case, when he'd begun to doubt he'd find his client alive. "Has there been another murder?"

Clara gave her a horrified look, but Emily ignored it, her attention focused on Granville. Belatedly she noted the telephone receiver in his hand and gave him a look of silent apology. After a few more quick words, he hung up and smiled at her.

"Randall will be joining us shortly," he told the all, and then to her, "Emily, I'm glad you're here. It's been an interesting afternoon."

"What's happening?" Emily asked, looking from face to face.

Mr. McAndrews, after a quick look at Granville, introduced Mr. Draper to her and Clara, and Draper began to fill Emily in on what he'd learned.

As she listened, Emily noted that Granville and Scott were conferring quietly in one corner. Clara had moved to Mr. O'Hearn's side, where they too were talking in low voices. Making a mental note to ask Clara later what was going on between the two of them, she focused on Mr. Draper's explanation.

She'd just begun to make sense of Mr. Putnam's elaborate scheme—which made her recent discussion with Mr. Marshall of the best way to finance and office building and a home seem trivial —when the door burst open and Trent rushed in.

"I found him!" he said.

"Good going," Scott said.

"Where?" Granville asked, moving towards the boy with an intent expression on his face. "How far did he run?"

"He never left town at all," Trent said. "Took me forever to figure it out, though. First I tried the train station, but nobody seemed to have seen him, and there was no record of him buying a ticket under Heller's name."

"Go on," Granville said sharply.

"Who are we talking about?" Emily asked Mr. Draper in an undertone.

"Carver," Draper said, his eyes fixed on Granville and Trent. "Supposedly the man who was killed was his associate. They looked somewhat alike."

Emily nodded her thanks, wondering what this would mean to the investigation. If they'd found Carver, did he know enough about Mr. Putnam to put the man behind bars? And would he testify?

"So I tried the coach lines to the Interior," Trent said. "Nothing. He owned a carriage, but all of his horses are accounted for. He hadn't rented a horse anywhere, either. And those are the main ways to get out of town.

Then I figured it meant that maybe he hadn't left. So I started to think about where he might go, where he figured no-one would look for him."

Granville was looking amused now. "And where had he hidden himself?" he asked.

"In a whorehouse."

Granville's smile had vanished, Clara looked like she was about to faint, and Emily had to fight back an embarrassing urge to giggle. Trent looked up, realized she was watching him, and reddened.

"And how did you find him?" Granville said.

"I asked Miss Frances," Trent said, with a quick glance at Scott. "Mr. Scott's sister knows what's going on in her part of town. And what she doesn't know, she knows who to ask. Didn't take her long to find out that Carver liked to frequent Madame Sal's establishment."

"I thought he was dating the Mayor's daughter," Granville said with a sideways glance at Scott, who chuckled.

Mr. Draper looked up sharply, then grinned. "The one doesn't necessarily affect the other," he said. Then he glanced from her to Clara, and looked uncomfortable. "My apologies."

Emily wondered how many men thought like that. When she announced her engagement, her mother had given her some advice about looking the other way, and men having interests outside the home, but it seemed wrong to her.

Granville didn't seem comfortable with the idea either, she thought, watching him. Or maybe he just didn't like her hearing it? Except he could have stopped Trent from saying anything further, and he hadn't.

"They have an attic," Trent was saying. "Hot, and not very comfortable. But not the place anyone would look for a fancy lawyer like Carver. Especially when he's supposed to be dead."

"Must be a pretty good customer," Mr. Draper muttered under his voice, but Emily heard him anyway.

She couldn't decide if she liked the reporter or not. He seemed intelligent, and those intent grey eyes didn't miss much, but she suspected he didn't like very many of his fellows very much. She wasn't quite sure what he thought of women, and just how far that cynicism of his went.

"You talked to Carver?" Granville said.

The harsh note in his voice seemed to startle Trent, who stammered out, "N-no, I didn't want to spook him. I didn't go anywhere near Madam Sal's, just in case. This is information Miss Frances gave me. And she knows how to keep her inquiries quiet-like."

Granville just nodded, but the smile he gave Trent had the boy beaming.

Good for him, Emily thought. For both of them, actually. "Will Carver be able to help our case?" she asked.

"That depends on what he knows," Granville said.

"And what he's willing to share," Draper said. "It's likely that at least some of his recent dealings were illegal. He's not likely to implicate himself."

"Depends how badly he wants to stay alive," Scott said. "That attic can't be any too comfortable with the weather so warm today."

Emily heard the front office door opening.

"That will be Randall," Granville said. "Let's see what he has to say about all of this. And what he'll be needing in court."

Twenty minutes later, Granville, Scott and Trent were hot-footing it from the streetcar stop on Hastings towards Dupont Street, where Madam Sal kept her house. All three of them were armed, though Granville wasn't expecting any trouble. Not once he'd talked them past the madam, at least.

He'd never met the woman, but he'd heard the rumors.

Madam Sal was as well known for her fiery temper as for the luxuriant red hair that accompanied it. She had the reputation of being as protective of favored patrons as she was of her "girls". Together with the fact that she ran a clean house, that fierce loyalty had kept her business profitable for a number of years, and showed no sign of ending.

He'd have to convince her that he meant Carver no harm. Which shouldn't be too difficult, since it was true.

Randall had been less convinced that he'd succeed. Granville's lips quirked as he thought of their last conversation.

It had been a brief one. Randall had come in clutching his hat, and declined to sit down. He'd carefully examined the evidence that Draper had managed to gather, but as soon as he heard that Carver was still alive, he lost interest in everything else.

"I need to talk to the man, and as quickly as possible," he'd said. "Find him, and bring him to my office. I'll be working late, so I'll be there for the next three or four hours."

"But he's at Madam Sal's," Trent said.

"I don't care if he's… Madam Sal's?"

Trent had nodded.

Randall had swallowed hard. "I still need to talk to him. You need to get him out of there. And Granville?"

"Yes?"

"Good luck," the lawyer had said, putting his hat back on. "I'll be in my office if you need me."

And that had been that. The two reporters had wanted to accompany them, Draper in particular making a strong argument for the back-up they could provide, but Granville had held firm. Even if five men had not been too many to take when visiting a whorehouse, he'd seen the gleam in Draper's eye, and didn't know the man well enough to know if it was amusement or avarice. Either could be dangerous to this mission.

With Carver's life at stake—and Sinclair's too, if they couldn't clear his name—it wasn't a chance he was prepared to take.

He'd managed to convince them and McAndrews to see the three women safely home, instead. O'Hearn hadn't been difficult to convince—Granville suspected he carried a bit of a torch for Clara —but Draper had glanced at Miss Kent and agreed readily as well.

It didn't fit with what he'd observed of the man. Glancing over at Emily, he saw she was watching Draper thoughtfully. So she'd noticed too. Still, it solved his immediate problem.

They were approaching Dupont Street, Granville noted. "How far?" he asked Trent.

"Three doors down," the lad said. "The grey one, with pink curtains at the windows."

It was a better-kept and more welcoming building than most of the ones down here. The pink curtains, back-lit with lamplight, gave off a welcoming glow. As Granville ascended the front stairs, he noted that they were freshly painted and in good trim.

A black clad doorman, whose heavy musculature said he served in more than one role, ran an assessing eye over the three of them, then ushered them into a parlor filled with piano music, light laughter and the smell of good whiskey. Despite the early hour, business was good. Granville noted half a dozen or so black-suited businessmen being entertained by painted doves in colorful gowns.

A statuesque redhead in an emerald green gown with velvet trim, her maturity masked by careful makeup, glided forward to greet them.

"Welcome to my house," she said, waving a fan gently back and forth and surveying them with the same assessing look as the doorman had. Apparently she approved of what she saw, because she smiled, and asked "What is your pleasure tonight?"

"We're looking for a friend of ours," he said. "Who I understand may also be a friend of yours."

"Oh? Well, if he's a friend and has recommended us to you, then I'm sure he'll be along eventually." This time her smile was calculating. "You're welcome to wait here for him. What refreshments can I offer you in the meantime?"

Trent's eyes were huge, and fixed on a slim blonde wearing a nearly transparent dress of blue and silver. Granville saw the madam take notice and smile a little, and had to bite back a smile of his own.

"I'm sure we can find something each of you will appreciate," she said smoothly.

But he'd lost his patience with this game. "I think we'd prefer to wait elsewhere. Perhaps you have a quiet room in the attic."

"Unfortunately our attic is unfinished," she said. Her voice didn't change, but her hand clenched on the fan and her eyes glittered. "But we have a private parlor. Perhaps you'd prefer to wait there?"

"That might be preferable," Granville agreed. "It might be—safer —for our friend to join us in a more private setting. One where he could remain unseen."

He smiled at her. "I'm assuming your private parlor has a separate entrance?"

Her expression hadn't changed, but she was watching him carefully now. "And why did your friend suggest that you meet him here tonight?"

Scott stepped forward, gave her a little bow. "Actually, a mutual friend passed on the message that it would benefit both us and our friend if we came here. My sister, Frances Scott?"

She scanned his features. "Samuel?" she said.

"He nodded."

"Follow me," she said, crooking a finger at him.

———

GRANVILLE, Scott and Trent were standing by the fireplace—the chintz upholstered chairs scattered about the room had proved far too soft—when Madam Sal returned fifteen minutes later. She ushered Carver into the window-less parlor, then stood silently beside him like a bodyguard while he stood staring at them. Granville could see why she was so protective.

Robert Carver was tall, dark-haired and had once had a commanding presence. Granville had seen him in court, and he'd been impressive. Now he was drawn, grey-faced, and looked like he hadn't slept well since the murder.

Carver's pale blue eyes darted from one to the other of them, and he licked dry lips. "Who are you? And how'd you know to look for me?"

"We're investigators. We talked to a few people," Scott said. "Wasn't too hard to figure it out."

Carver blinked once, as though he'd been in the dark too long, drew in a breath.

"Heller was your brother, wasn't he?" Granville asked before the fellow could say anything.

Carver blinked again, nodded. "How did you guess?"

"His resemblance to you. It was good enough that he was taken for you. And the name, of course."

"Heller." Carver half-smiled. It looked like it hurt him. "He got called that, you know. In his drinking days. I tried to talk him out of naming himself so, but he wanted the reminder. Said he'd change it once he'd proved himself, and that he could control his drinking."

Carver looked down at his hands, which were shaking slightly, and caught one hand tightly in the other. "He was beating it, he really was. And it cost him. I saw what it cost him."

He drew in a harsh breath. "And then they killed him. Just like that. Not for something he'd done. For something I'd done. My brother paid for my crime." It was a cry of anguish.

"Then help us get the man behind it," Granville said.

Suddenly shrewd eyes studied him, and when Carver spoke, it was in flat tones that had left denial behind. "Putnam."

Granville nodded. "He hired Dagan's men, but he's the will and the money behind your brother's murder. He needs to pay."

"Yes. He does. But what's in it for you?"

"Our client's been charged with your murder," Granville said.

"Now that's ironic, given that I'm not dead," Carver said. "Which is a defense even I could win with, despite the fact that I mostly do business work."

"Except someone killed your brother," Scott said. "I'm guessing they'd just charge our client with that instead."

"And there's always the fraud charge against him," Granville said, watching Carver closely.

"Putnam," said the lawyer heavily, and he sat down in a nearby chair as if he hadn't the strength to stand any longer.

Madam Sal looked from one to the other of them, then her gaze fell on Carver. "I don't think I'm needed here. Ring if you need me."

It wasn't quite a question, but Carver nodded anyway. She gave him a small smile and left them with a swish of satin skirts.

"Putnam's framing your client?" Carver asked as the door closed behind her.

"He is," Granville said. "While building his own wealth and continuing to defraud his investors. As you know all too well, I suspect."

Carver groaned.

"I don't get it," Trent said, stepping forward. "When you left Heller's place yesterday, why didn't you run? We saw the train schedules there."

"Dagan's men were there, checking departures."

Dagan's men had been at the train station? Granville's gaze flew to Trent.

Dagan's men had seen Trent before, at Carver's building. And if they'd noticed him at the station—and made the connection that he was looking for Carver—the lad could've been killed. He should never have sent Trent out on his own. And he'd make sure he didn't do so again, not until this case was done with.

Granville focused on Carver. "Who were they looking for?" he asked.

"I don't know, but I couldn't take the chance it was me," Carver said.

"How'd you know about Dagan?" Scott said.

"For my sins, I helped Putnam pay him, off the books," Carver said. "Though it was just threats, the occasional bit of damage to a property. Not murder."

"And now it's murder, twice over," Granville said.

Carver's shoulders bowed. He groaned, quietly this time, then looked up at Granville. "And I'm paying for that now."

"It was your brother who paid," Granville said, his eyes on Carver's face. "So what are you going to do about it?"

Carver looked up at him and straightened his shoulders, looking for a moment like the take-charge lawyer he'd been. "It's on me. I'm the one that should have died. So I'll do whatever you need me to do. To make it right."

RANDALL LOOKED up as the four of them walked swiftly into his office, closing the door behind them. "What...," he began, then spotted Carver. "Ah. You found him."

"Randall. Nice to see you again," the other lawyer said, his voice laced with irony.

"I'm sure it's anything but nice, but I'm certainly glad to see you," Randall replied.

"Yes, you'll want that client of yours vindicated," Carver said with a grimace.

"I don't like to see innocent men hang," Randall said quietly. He nodded to Granville, Scott and Trent. "Please, have a seat, all of you."

As they seated themselves in a row in front of Randall's over-sized desk, which was covered with paperwork even at this late hour, Carver elegantly crossed one leg over the other, then winced.

"You've been beaten," Granville said. He'd been watching Carver closely since they left Madam Sal's. Partly he wanted to be sure the fellow stayed alive in their care. Partly he didn't trust him.

And partly he didn't think they'd yet heard the whole story. Perhaps they'd hear more of it now.

Carver frowned at him, perhaps realizing he couldn't hide it any longer. "Yes."

It was a curt response, and not nearly enough. "Where and when?" Granville asked.

"At the train station. One of Dagan's men saw me, tried to hold me. Much to my surprise, I was more desperate than he was, and I got away at the expense of a good drubbing. It was more than worth it, I assure you."

"Why didn't you tell us this earlier?"

"It was none of your business."

Who was this man? Granville wondered. At one moment he was heartbroken over his brother's senseless death, the next he was an arrogant idiot, out to prove his superiority to the world. "So they know you're alive, then?"

Carver nodded. "It's why I went to Madam Sal's. I knew she'd take me in. And they wouldn't look there." He gave a bitter laugh. "Hell, Dagan's an occasional client there. He'd never question them."

Granville thought he was wrong, and that he'd probably put Madam Sal and her household at risk. Unless he could get Dagan arrested first.

"What do you know about Dagan?" he asked. "We need anything that's illegal and easy to prove if we're going to keep you alive."

Carver just glared at him. Maybe it was Randall's presence that had brought out his arrogance, Granville thought. Confessing to a fellow officer of the court had to be a humiliating position to find himself in.

But Carver had brought it on himself. And they didn't have time for this.

"If Dagan has even the slightest suspicion that Madam Sal gave you shelter, you know what he'll do to her. And to whichever of her girls was your favorite," Granville said. "Neither of them will be completely safe until we put Dagan behind bars"

Carver began to protest, then he met Granville's eyes, and his voice died away. He nodded. "I can give you what you need," he said, his voice barely audible. "And on Putnam, too."

"We're going to need the police in on this," said Randall.

"Leave that with me," Granville said. "I might have a plan."

"Good." Randall pulled his legal pad closer, picked up his pen. "Go ahead."

As Granville walked into Mary's Diner, he scanned the room for Daniels, but he was also looking for trouble. This case wasn't making them many friends, and now that Dagan knew Carver was alive, he'd be desperate to find him.

The place was half empty, but noisy, and he could smell Mary's spicy meatloaf—it must have been the special of the day. His mouth watered. With so much going on, he'd forgotten to eat lunch. In fact, it seemed like yesterday he'd spoken with Daniels, rather than just this morning.

The policeman hadn't arrived yet, but Mary nodded at Granville from behind the cash register. Lifting a hand in greeting, he strolled towards his favorite booth on the far wall. He'd just added cream to his coffee when Daniels hung his coat on the hook outside the booth and slid onto the bench opposite him.

"Sorry I'm late. Been a busy day."

For all of them. "No matter. Thanks for meeting me."

Granville still hadn't decided how far he could trust Daniels. He hoped they could work with him.

Daniels nodded. "You eaten?"

"Not yet."

"You like meatloaf?"

"I like Mary's version of it," he said, though he'd be surprised if there was any left—Mary's specials tended to disappear pretty quickly.

Daniels glanced over his shoulder and signaled the waitress. Moments later, two steaming plates of meatloaf, mashed potatoes and green beans appeared on the table, followed by a cup of coffee for Daniels.

Granville was impressed. "You're known here."

Daniels grinned. "Two things matter when you're a cop. Good shoes, and a good diner."

"I can imagine," Granville said. Then got down to business. "About the murder of the janitor the other day."

"Old Joe Wong?" Daniels said. "What about him?"

The words confirmed Granville's impression of Daniels—he couldn't think of another policeman he'd met since he arrived in Vancouver who would have bothered to learn the janitor's name, much less remember it. "I believe his death is related to the murder of Robert Carver, since Carver's office was ransacked that same night."

"And Walter Sinclair is charged with Carver's murder," Daniels said.

"Indeed. And I'm already hearing rumors that Sinclair may be charged with this murder as well. I also hear you have other ideas."

Daniels' expression was carefully blank, and his eyes gave nothing away. "I might have raised some questions I thought hadn't been fully answered. No more than that."

That wasn't how it had sounded to him, but Granville liked Daniels' diplomacy. And the loyalty he displayed towards his colleagues. "Sinclair is innocent of both deaths."

"That has yet to be proven."

"True. What if I tell you I can prove it?"

"I'd need more than your word."

That was reasonable. "Are you assigned to the case?"

"I've been re-assigned. Elsewhere."

He didn't sound too happy about it. It seemed Daniels might have disagreed with his colleagues once too often. That was telling.

And unfortunate, but they could work with it. Besides, it increased Granville's confidence in working with the fellow—that he'd stand by his principles regardless of cost. "And how hard are the police looking for the killer?"

Daniels drank some coffee, didn't reply.

Which was an answer in itself. Time for a different approach. "I also heard that Wong might have seen a burglary the night he died," Granville said.

Daniels looked up, and his eyes fixed on Granville's face with an intensity that made him a little uncomfortable. "I'd like to know who your sources were, though I doubt you'll tell me," the policeman said. "But the fact that there was also a burglary in the same building that night does not mean it had anything to do with the murder."

"You're saying it could have been a coincidence?"

"No. I'm saying we need to be focused on the facts of the case. Not speculation."

It was clearly a sore spot for the officer. "What about the facts your witness gave you?" Granville said.

"Witness?" Daniels seemed startled, though his face still gave nothing away. His eyes never left Granville's face.

"The man in the brown suit," Granville said. "The fellow who found Wong."

"He didn't have anything useful to say."

"No? I found what he said to be very interesting indeed," Granville said. "I don't suppose you questioned him yourself, though?"

Daniels watched him thoughtfully for a moment, then a slow smile slid across his face, and his eyes warmed. "All right, all right. Enough fencing. Clearly you know what you're talking about. You tell me what you know, and I'll do the same. Perhaps working together we can clear Sinclair. Get the right man behind bars."

"Do you mean it?" Granville asked him.

"I never say things I don't mean."

"You're willing to take the risk of your fellow officers finding out? They wouldn't take it well, you know."

"Yes, I know. And yes, I'll take the risk. If it gets the real killer behind bars, where he belongs, it'll be worth it. Then the judge can decide whether to hang him or not."

"Good, then," Granville said, putting his knife and fork down decisively. "You need to come with me."

"And where are we going?"

"To my lawyer's office. Joshua Randall. And we need to go now"

"Why?"

"To prevent further murders," Granville said bluntly.

That was enough for Daniels, who stood and reached for his coat and hat. "I don't have my badge," he warned Granville as they strode out of the cafe.

"You won't need it," Granville told him. "Just your wits."

As Granville exited the stairwell, he knocked twice on Randall's outer door, and waited until Trent came and unlocked it. As he strolled into Randall's inner office with Daniels in tow, he glanced around.

While he was at dinner with Daniels, someone—probably Trent—had obviously gone out for food, because the remains of thick beef sandwiches had been stacked on top of a glassed-in bookshelf and half-drunk cups of tea sat in front of each man. Randall, Scott, Trent and Carver were all focused on some document Randall was writing, and it took them a moment to notice Granville's entrance.

"Any tea for us?" he asked, aware they'd all jumped a little and turned, but he kept his eyes on Daniel's face. He wanted to see the fellow's expression when he spotted Carver. Who was supposed to be dead.

Daniel's control was impressive.

He lost a little color, and his eyes widened a bit, but that was it. "Mr. Carver?" he said calmly. "I hadn't expected to see you here."

"Well, you wanted proof," Granville said, grinning. "And we're here to provide it."

Impressed with his policeman, Granville performed the introductions and sent Trent to find another chair for Daniels. Once the six of them were seated, he and Daniels with fresh cups of tea in front of them, Granville looked over at the policeman and nodded.

It seemed that was the cue Daniels had been waiting for. Placing his notebook and pencil in front of him, the policeman looked around the table. "I think someone had best explain," he said. "Who was murdered at Carver's establishment last week?"

"My elder brother," Carver said bitterly. "They mistook him for me."

"So you were the intended victim, Mr. Carver? Are you sure?" Daniels said.

"Oh, yes. I'm sure."

Daniels made a note, then turned to face Granville. "And how long have you all known Carver was actually alive?" he asked, his tone bordering on accusing.

At least he knew better than to ask why they hadn't reported it.

"We found out today," Granville said. "It was actually Mr. Wong's last words, which your witness was able to reproduce well enough for a translator to interpret, that set us on the trail."

Daniels looked bemused, but his pencil didn't stop moving. "Who else knows he's alive?"

"Carver?" Granville said.

"Only a friend," Carver said. "And, as of yesterday, one of the hirelings of the man who tried to murder me."

Daniels looked up at that. "You know your killer? I mean, your brother's killer?"

Carver nodded, his expression drawn.

"Who was it?"

"You mean, who were they. A thug named Dagan and a couple

of his henchmen shot my brother," he said. "But they were hired to do so by Charles Putnam."

Daniels' head flew up and his pencil stilled. "I see. And have you proof of this?" His voice was very bland.

"Not exactly."

"What makes you think Mr. Putnam wants you dead?"

Carver stood up, took a turn around the room, as if he couldn't stand to sit still any longer. "I did a fair bit of work for him. I know too much."

Daniels hesitated, as if wondering which question to ask next, Granville thought. Had he judged the man right?

"Would this be related to a possible fraud at Putnam's firm?" Daniels asked, and Granville released the breath he'd been holding. He'd chosen the right man for this.

Carver nodded, still pacing.

"And I'm assuming your actions on his behalf were illegal?"

"Not at first. Initially, they were perhaps questionable, but no more than that."

"Initially," Daniels said, his pencil flying. "And over time?"

"Once Putnam got his business into trouble, he started looking for creative ways to recover," Carver said, "They were supposed to be temporary measures, until the economy recovered. But he kept digging himself deeper."

Carver paused in his pacing, reached over and grabbed his teacup. Drank deeply.

"And I allowed myself to be dragged down with him. Allowed? Hell, I encouraged him," he said, giving a bitter laugh. "The money was too good. And I thought I was a better lawyer than I am. A better judge of people, too."

"So you knew what he was up to?" Daniels asked.

"I thought I did," Carver said. He stopped pacing and stared blankly at the lowered blinds. "I thought I was smarter than him, too. But I was wrong."

Carver took a gulp of cold tea, forced the words out. "I completely misjudged the man, and where his greed would take him. Oh, I knew some of it, but towards the end I started to figure out the extent of Putnam's fraud. It was going to come out—it was too big not to. But it also became clear to me that Putnam was preparing to make a run for it."

"He's planning to run?" Daniels asked sharply.

"Yes," Carter said, and sat down again. "I think he'd been planning for months before I noticed. His timeline's pretty short now, so he's clearing up loose ends. And he's lost any scruples he might once have had. Putnam will do whatever he has to do to buy himself the time he needs."

"Even murder?"

Carver nodded. "It's why he's framed Sinclair for fraud, too."

"I take it you're ready to challenge him on what you discovered?"

"Yes. And he knew it, too. I told you I misjudged the man."

Daniels glanced at Granville, then back at Carver. "Assuming I can believe you, how soon do you expect Putnam to run?"

"There's an audit of his business scheduled for early September," Carver said. "He'll have to be gone before that. And with two murders already, I'd guess he'll run before the end of the month."

"This month?"

"Yes."

"Does anyone know you're here?" And he indicated the lawyer's office with its shades drawn, the door locked.

Carver glanced at Granville, shook his head. "No."

"Carver's clothes are different and his hat was pulled well down when we brought him here," Granville said. "We weren't followed."

"Good." Daniels tapped his pencil against his notebook for a moment, his eyes on Carver's face. "Are you willing to testify?"

"In exchange for…" Carver began, then sat back with an oath. "Sorry, old habit. Yes, I'm willing to testify against him."

"Even though you may end up in jail for your part in this?" Daniels eyed him curiously.

"He killed my brother."

"I could arrest you, right now," Daniels said.

Carver just nodded.

"But I'm not sure you'd survive until the trial. And frankly, you're a minor player in all this." Daniels glanced from Granville to Randall. "Off the record, I'm not sure Putnam will be brought to book for his crimes. He's got some powerful friends."

Randall steepled his hands on the table in front of him and leaned towards Daniels. "We might have a plan that would see Putnam pay for what he's done."

"Good."

"But it means we have a lot of work to do in a very short time-frame," Randall said.

"We'll have to call in some markers," Scott said to Granville. "You and I need to talk to Benton."

Daniels' eyebrows went up at the gangster's name. "I didn't know he was part of this case."

"He's not," Scott said. "He owes us a favor, that's all."

Daniels gave them an odd look, but to his credit he didn't ask why the crime kingpin owed them anything. "I assume you have a role for me somewhere in this discussion?" he asked.

"Of course," Granville said.

"Then I'm listening," the policeman said.

38

MONDAY, JUNE 25, 1900

The court was crowded and noisy as Walter Sinclair, in handcuffs, was led to the prisoner's dock. Judge Tobias Hardy, in his curled white wig and splendid robes, sat behind the elevated judge's bench, blowing his nose into an oversized white handkerchief. Police Chief Stewart and two of his senior officers sat in all their uniformed glory—however undeserved—in the front row, looking smug.

The room was set up with the jury on the Judge's left, nearest the dock, and the prosecutor's table on his right. The witness stand was also on the left, right beside the Judge's bench.

There were rows of low-backed benches for the onlookers— two on each side of the aisle—running from behind the defendant's and prosecutor's tables, all the way to the double exit doors at the back.

Granville sat near the center of the room and two aisles back, with a good view of all the players in this drama. Sinclair was there, and both lawyers. The jurors had all filed in. Everyone was in place.

It was almost time for the judge to ring up the curtain.

He glanced at Emily, sitting beside him, white-gloved hands tucked neatly together in the lap of her new green suit. It suited her, bringing out her green eyes. She looked demure and very calm —all things he knew full well she was not. Only her dancing eyes and the little curve at the corner of her mouth gave her away.

Beside her sat Clara, who looked bored, though he suspected that was a front, also. Beside Clara was O'Hearn, then Draper. Scott and Trent were on Granville's other side, with McAndrews beside Trent.

He didn't see Officer Daniels, which worried him for a moment. He hoped the fellow had been able to keep up his end of the bargain.

Within moments the stolid bailiff called the court to order, and the buzz of gossip died away. A few people shifted uncomfortably on the hard wooden spectator benches, and there was a cough or two, then silence.

Into the quiet rolled Judge Hardy's deep tones. "We are here to consider a most serious charge today. This poor soul in the dock before us is charged with murder, and for gain. There can be few sorrier charges a man can face." He sighed deeply and turned to Sinclair. "How do you plead?"

"Not guilty, M'Lord," Sinclair said. His voice was strong but he looked terrified.

Randall, sitting beside Sinclair as his defense lawyer, squeezed his client's arm.

For strength, Granville wondered. Or courage? He couldn't imagine being in Sinclair's place.

Beside him, Emily put a gloved hand on his arm. She'd never attended a trial before, and this was a difficult one to be starting with, but both she and Clara had insisted on attending. And there was a scattering of other women in the courtroom, he noted, glancing around, several of whom he recognized as friends of Emily's mother.

Surely they didn't know Sinclair. Did they know Carver? Or was it curiosity, a morbid desire to hear the death penalty pronounced? He put his hand over Emily's, glad she was here out of concern for their client—and for him. If this didn't work—but it would. It had to.

He and Scott had lost a client, once, but not to the law. And the fellow hadn't been innocent, as Sinclair was. Still, he hoped never to repeat the experience.

Granville pulled back his attention when the prosecutor began his opening remarks, and Emily gripped his arm.

THE TRIAL HAD DRONED on half the morning, with the prosecution making a case so dire that Emily wondered how Mr. Randall would find an argument to counter it at all. Was that why he hadn't cross-examined a single witness, but had sought permission to recall them later?

Was he biding his time?

As the prosecutor hammered out statement after statement, Emily began to doubt. Surely that many facts couldn't be wrong. And any man who had done what they said Mr. Sinclair had done deserved to hang.

Only he was Granville's client, and Granville believed in him.

"It's all circumstantial evidence," Granville had said quietly at one point. Likely he could see how worried she was. "Even if Randall didn't have a surprise in store for them, they don't have enough to convict."

Still, even with the surprise she knew was coming, she couldn't see how Randall hoped to win his client free.

She glanced at him, but Randall seemed to be listening attentively to his counterpart, while making little notes on a legal pad in front of him. His face showed no expression.

His client's face, on the other hand, was too pale.

Sitting in the dock with his back straight and shoulders back, Sinclair's lips were pressed tightly together, as if to keep back words of denial.

Emily gave a little shiver, and gripped Granville's arm more tightly.

Finally the prosecution had called its last witness and it was Randall's turn. He stood, shaking out his dark robes, and strode to the front of the court.

"M'Lord," he said, nodding to the judge. "Gentlemen of the jury. My client is accused of heinous acts, which he is alleged to have committed. These acts have been proposed to you as fact, and in great detail, by my honorable colleague."

He paused, looking towards the jury, as if considering their reactions. Two of the men shifted uncomfortably in their seats.

"Now you will hear the truth," Randall said simply, and Emily saw the black look the other lawyer sent his way.

But Randall was already turning to the bailiff.

"I'll call my first witness, please. Mr. Gregor Dagan," he said.

DAGAN WAS HALF-DRAGGED to the witness box between two policemen, his hands shackled behind him. Emily noted that the man was wearing a fairly well-cut suit of some cheap material. Even in his present circumstances, the angle of his head and shoulders suggested he expected admiring eyes to follow him.

Emily leaned in towards Granville. "Is that the man you captured the other night?" she asked in an undertone.

"That's him. And the policeman on his right is Daniels," Granville said. "You should have seen it. It was a perfect operation. We waited till late Sunday night to avoid alerting anyone who supports Putnam."

His quick glance at Chief Stewart, sitting stiffly upright in the front row, told Emily exactly who he had in mind.

"Benton helped us set up Dagan up by dropping a fake tip in his ear about the arrival of a costly Hudson's Bay shipment. Scott and I took care of the three henchmen Dagan had brought along. Daniels and another officer he trusts arrested Dagan for attempted grand larceny when he tried to rob the warehouse."

He grinned. "You've never seen anyone look so surprised."

"He looks mean," Emily said after studying the man's face.

"He's not so much mean as he is uncaring. Other people simply don't matter to him."

Emily tried to imagine that and shivered. "Nothing would stop such a man, would it?"

"No," Granville said, putting his own hand warmly over hers. "But he thinks too well of his own abilities. And he's arrogant enough that he couldn't refuse a challenge."

She knew Granville meant that he and the others had challenged Dagan.

And defeated him, too, in what she suspected had been anything but a fair fight on Dagan's part.

She glanced from the man in the witness chair to Granville.

Her fiancé didn't look injured. There wasn't a mark on his face. But she'd noticed him wince a little earlier when he'd turned too quickly.

His ribs, perhaps?

"Why would Mr. Dagan testify, though? He's not going to expose Mr. Putnam, is he?"

"Dagan's dangerous to himself, as well as Putnam, because he isn't nearly as smart as he thinks he is," Granville said. "And he has no loyalty to Putnam. Quite the opposite, actually. Men like him will always protect themselves first.

"But surely he can't betray Mr. Putnam without betraying himself?"

"Just watch. Randall will handle him."

And he did.

Emily could feel her eyes widening as Randall skillfully led Dagan deeper, until the man was confessing to pulling the trigger while blaming Putnam for planning it.

"So you're telling me that you yourself fired the gun that killed Mr. Carver?" Randall said.

"It wasn't really me, see," Dagan said, leaning forward in the witness stand. "It was Putnam wanted him dead. I was just the—the instrument. That's what I was. Like the bullet went direct from Putnam and into Carver."

"Through you?"

Dagan grinned, glanced around the court as if looking for approval of his cleverness. "Yeah, that's it. I was the instrument that the bullet passed through to get to Carver."

"And who pulled the trigger?"

"Yeah, that was me. But you gotta see it was Putnam's plan. He's the reason Carver's dead."

"And it was Putnam's money, I assume, that paid you for being his instrument?" Randall said. "For pulling that trigger that put a bullet into Carver?"

The spectators began to realize what was going on.

A hush fell over the courtroom.

Emily glanced at the jurors. Every one of them sat alert, their eyes fixed on Dagan. Several of them were frowning heavily. One looked rather sick.

"Yeah, that's it. He paid pretty good, too. But it wasn't up to me, see? I didn't care if the fella lived or died. But Putnam did. Oh, he did!"

Dagan glanced at the jury, then spoke directly to the ones whose eyes were fixed on him. "He wanted that Carver gone, permanent-like. And for us to look for anything he might have hidden. But then the police came too soon. So we had to go back."

"You searched the office several times, did you not?" Randall asked.

"Putnam wouldn't listen to reason, would he?" Dagan said, thumping a fist on the edge of the witness stand.

Which made the two policemen step closer and earned Dagan a warning look from the judge. "Man refused to pay us until he got that paper. The one he thought was so important," Dagan said witheringly.

"Which is when the janitor got shot?"

"Janitor? Oh, the Chink. Yeah, that was when he got in the way. We didn't have no choice. Putnam didn't give us one."

Emily shivered at the ugly words, and Granville silently took her hand.

She squeezed it in gratitude.

A movement in the front row caught her eye.

She glanced over to see Chief Stewart, his face nearly purple, being held back by his officers. What was he trying to do?

Then her eyes followed his gaze towards the prosecutor.

Who was sitting with his lips pressed so tightly together they'd gone white. His eyes were fixed on the police chief. Oh.

This trial was going to send ripples through the city.

"Thank you, Mr. Dagan," Mr. Randall was saying, moving back to his seat. "Your witness."

The Judge looked at the prosecutor. "You wish to cross-examine the witness, Mr. Peabody?"

The prosecutor's heavy cheeks flushed and he shook his head.

Glancing around the tense courtroom, the judge checked his pocket watch. Then he called for an early break for luncheon. They would reconvene at one p.m.

39

By a quarter to one, the courtroom was already crowded with spectators and noisier than ever. It was standing room only at the back of the courtroom. Word had obviously spread about the surprising revelations of the morning, Granville thought.

He watched several youths, clerks by their attire, pushing and shoving to make room for themselves in the throng. No-one wanted to miss out.

He spotted Daniels, still in uniform, take an inconspicuous seat in the back and smiled a little. He was glad the policeman had made it back.

Randall was about to make both the wait and the crowded conditions worthwhile. The defense lawyer knew how to put on a show for the jury. And Daniels deserved to see what he'd helped make possible.

"I'll call my next witness, please," Randall said at exactly one o'clock, looking as professionally calm as ever. "The brother of the deceased, Mr. H.J.R. Carver."

There was a little ripple of surprise through the courtroom as the bailiff went out to fetch the witness. Emily saw a number of matrons putting their heads together, could hear several of them expressing surprise at the unknown brother while commiserating over the loss the poor man must feel.

She waited, watching the door, watching the court. This was Randall's moment. But how would he play it?

The door opened and Robert Carver walked in wearing a very well-cut black business suit. Her father would have approved. Carver looked every inch the successful lawyer. And rather handsome, in an exhausted kind of way.

She could hear indrawn breaths all across the courtroom.

"But that's Robert Carver," she heard someone mutter.

"It can't be! He's dead!"

"Maybe they're twins," a different voice said in a loud whisper.

The judge glared at the courtroom. Picked up his gavel and pounded it on the bench. "Order! I'll have order here. Or I'll empty this room."

Satisfied with the silence that fell, he turned to the bailiff. "Swear in the witness."

The prosecutor stood up as if to object. The judge glared him into silence as well.

Once the oath was taken, the judge turned to Randall. "Go ahead."

"But...I object," began the prosecutor.

The judge cut him off. "He hasn't said anything yet. Now settle down before I have to find you in contempt."

Judge Hardy was known for his fondness for sending lawyers who disagreed with him off to jail. Emily smiled to herself as the prosecutor hastily sat down.

"Mr. Randall?" Judge Hardy said. "Please continue."

"Thank you, M'Lord," Randall said, standing up and striding over to the witness box. "Good afternoon, Mr. Carver."

"Good afternoon."

The sound of Carver's voice provoked an immediate reaction. Emily could see several men in the front rows stiffening, and staring at the witness. They must know him well enough to recognize his voice. But siblings could sound alike. How was Randall going to handle this?

"By what name are you known, sir? Or do you go by your initials?" Randall asked.

"I go by Robert," was the answer.

"But you can't be. He's dead!" Chief Stewart exclaimed. The judge glared him down.

<hr>

EMILY'S EYES were glued on Sinclair. He looked increasingly confident, she thought, sitting arrow straight in the dock.

"You are Mr. Robert Carver, a lawyer in this town?" Mr. Randall said.

The judge glanced at the details on his docket, stared at the witness. "Remember you're under oath," he cautioned.

"Thank you, your honor," Carver said. "Yes, I am that Robert Carver."

There was a gasp that ran throughout the courtroom. Emily noted the women's fans coming out, the men shaking their heads.

She was particularly interested in the prosecutor's reaction. A rather corpulent man of middle age, he'd flushed red, and clutched the arms of his chair. She hoped he wasn't apoplectic, or he'd never make it to the end of the trial.

"Then who was killed in your offices on Thursday last?" Randall asked.

"My brother was killed there. My elder brother."

"And what was his name?"

"He went by the name of Joseph Heller. Though his real surname was Carver."

"And can you tell the court why your brother would have been in your offices alone at that time of night?"

"He was working as my assistant. He—often stayed late to finish up tasks I had assigned him."

"And did you and your brother resemble each other?"

"Yes, especially in dim light. He'd borrowed my office, as he often did at night if I was out." Carver paused, swallowed hard. "His habit was to use only a desk lamp for light, since he was the only one there. From a little distance—he could easily have been mistaken for me by one who didn't know us both."

Randall nodded and began to ask the next question. "You're certain…" he managed, when the prosecutor sprang to his feet.

"Objection! Leading the witness."

The judge glanced at him. "Over-ruled. Sit down, Mr. Peabody."

The prosecutor stayed on his feet. "Judge, permission to approach the bench."

The Judge frowned at him, but said "Permission granted. You too, Mr. Randall."

As the two lawyers approached the bench to confer with the judge, the whispers spread across the courtroom.

Emily glanced at poor Sinclair, who still looked petrified. She switched her attention to the judge. Not for the first time, she wished she could lip read. What was going on up there?

She leaned closer to Granville, whispered, "Can you tell what's going on? And what will Mr. Randall do?"

"Randall expected something like this," Granville said in a low voice. "The prosecutor will be arguing that it doesn't matter that the wrong victim was named—that Sinclair is still guilty because his intent was to kill, and he did kill. The fact that he killed the wrong man without realizing it—that doesn't take away from the fact that he planned the murder and executed it."

It seemed a strong argument to her. "But how will Mr. Randall counter it?"

Granville smiled. "That's the brilliance of Randall's strategy. He never intended to challenge that line of reasoning, since the best it would result in would be a mistrial, and new charges in the real victim's name."

"But wouldn't that be double jeopardy?" She thought about the London case she'd read about a few months before. Her father would have been horrified if he'd known she read every gruesome detail. But she'd been unable to believe such a horrible crime could go unpunished, simply because key evidence hadn't been found until after the trial. "Surely Mr. Sinclair couldn't be charged again?"

"It doesn't matter, because either it is the same case—and this trial can go forward—or it isn't—which means it can't be double jeopardy."

Emily wasn't entirely sure a determined judge wouldn't find differently, but since it wasn't Randall's strategy in any case, it probably didn't matter.

"So how is Mr. Randall planning to proceed?" she asked.

"They're coming back," Granville said, and the moment was lost.

Granville had been right, though, Emily noted with interest as the prosecutor went back to his seat, looking smugly satisfied. She sat forward to see better. This was going to be fascinating.

The judge made a note on his docket, and addressed the court. "This trial will proceed, but the name of the murdered man is stipulated to be Joseph Carver, also known as Joseph Heller."

And the judge motioned at Randall to proceed.

Which he did. Turning to Carver, the lawyer said, "You're certain it was your brother who was killed?"

"I saw the body," Carver said with a grimace of pain, and dropped his eyes for a moment. A rustle ran through the courtroom."

"How was that possible? You were presumed to be dead, yet no-one noticed you?"

"They never saw me. It was a dark night, and they had other concerns."

Carver mopped his brow, and continued. "I was going into the office late that same evening, and I saw the police cart in the alley. The body had already been brought down, and the driver was occupied in holding the horses. I don't know where the other policemen were, but the back of the van was open." He swallowed hard.

"There is a streetlamp there, and the light was good enough to see him. I know my brother. Even in that light. Even in death." He paused, looked down.

The court waited, silent. After a moment Carver resumed.

"It was he. He was wearing a suit that I'd bought him. And he carried our father's pocket watch. The case caught the light, and the shape is unusual." His voice broke on the words. "I didn't know he'd kept that watch."

"Thank you," Randall said.

Gesturing towards his client, the lawyer asked, "Do you recognize this man?"

"Walter Sinclair? Of course. He and I both worked for the same man, Charles Putnam. Putnam spoke of him often."

"Oh? In what context?"

"Putnam spoke to me of noticing Sinclair's enthusiasm and lack of business experience. He was determined to use them to frame the young man for fraud. To distract attention from the fraud that Putnam himself was committing."

At these words, a murmur of startled voices spread through the courtroom and the prosecutor bounced to his feet as if he was made of India rubber. "Objection, M'Lord. The witness is expressing an opinion," he yelled.

"Over-ruled. I want to see where he's going with this," the judge said. "But I warn you, Randall, this needs to relate to Carver's murder."

Randall nodded. "Of course," he said, and turned back to his witness. "You realize that you have just accused Mr. Putnam of fraud. Under oath."

"Yes, of course," Carver said, then leaned forward. "And I don't say it lightly."

Randall considered him gravely. "I'm sure. However, you heard the judge. This trial is with respect to the murder of your brother.

As a lawyer yourself, you know that any statements you make must be relevant to this heinous crime."

"Yes, indeed I do. The subject is relevant, however."

He paused. It seemed to Emily the whole courtroom held its breath.

"Putnam's extensive fraud is the reason he hired a man to kill me," Carver said. "And my poor brother was murdered instead."

At this revelation, all the spectators began to talk at once. The judge banged his gavel hard until quiet descended again.

Emily clutched Granville's arm. She hadn't expected such a blunt unfolding of Putnam's crimes.

"I knew too much, you see," Carver finished matter-of-factly.

"Let me make sure we are all clear here," Randall said. "You are saying that Charles Putnam hired a man to kill you?"

"Yes, that's correct."

At this the prosecutor sprang to his feet. "Objection."

The judge didn't even look at him. "Overruled."

"And are you saying that my client, Walter Sinclair, was the man so hired?"

Emily could see the sudden glee on the prosecutor's face. Surely he didn't think Carver was about to accuse Sinclair. Had the man not listened to Dagan's testimony that morning?

"Of course not," Carver said. "I'm certain that he hired a gagster named Dagan to do the shooting. Dagan's the fellow that Putnam used for all his dirty work."

The Judge hammered away with his gavel to silence the reaction of the gallery to this statement.

Emily looked over at Peabody, who seemed to be deflating where he sat.

Then she looked from the faces in the gallery to those in the jury box. Dagan's obvious lack of moral fiber had been so evident in his earlier testimony that they'd been reluctant to believe him. They certainly hadn't expected this confirmation from a prominent lawyer, and their attention was riveted on the drama unfolding in front of them.

But however would Randall proceed from here, she wondered? And would it be enough to clear Sinclair?

RANDALL PACED to the juror's box, stopped. Looked back at his witness. "Can you prove these allegations?" Randall asked.

"I have irrefutable proof of the fraud Putnam committed," Carver said. "These documents are part of the reason he wanted me dead."

"If it please the court, the defense enters the following documents as exhibits A through F for the record," Randall said, passing copies to the judge and the jurors. "Proceed, Mr. Carver."

"Thank you. The first four documents were provided to me by Mr. Putnam, for safekeeping. The fifth document is a comparison I created, based on the first four documents. The sixth is the final document that Putnam created, the one he put forward as proof of fraud on Sinclair's part."

"And what do these documents represent?" Randall asked him. "To the best of your knowledge, of course."

"It is my understanding that the first four are duplicate ledgers. Variants on a second set of books, if you will. Mr. Putnam created these versions in an early attempt to hide the massive fraud that he has been perpetrating on his own investors over the last two years or more."

"Did I understand you correctly?" Randall asked. "You have stated that this is proof that Mr. Putnam himself perpetrated the fraud of which he has accused Mr. Sinclair?"

"Yes," Carver said. "These were his first attempts, created before he decided to frame young Sinclair. He discovered that he couldn't hide enough of the missing money, so he had to admit to some fraud and find a scapegoat."

"And that scapegoat was Sinclair?"

"It was. Sinclair had no part in it at all, which is clear when you compare Exhibit F with the first four exhibits."

"And we are to understand that Mr. Putnam never used these first four documents?" Randall said. "Why are they relevant here?"

"Because when compared with Exhibit F, they detail the extent of the fraud," Carver said.

"And why Mr. Putnam entrust them to you, rather than burning them?"

"He probably did burn the originals. These are copies he had made and entrusted to me for safekeeping as they were developed. Before he realized he couldn't use them."

"So you have proof that Mr. Putnam masterminded the fraud that he has accused Mr. Sinclair of. Have you also proof that Mr. Putnam hired Mr. Dagan to murder you?"

"I have payment records proving that Putnam had a pattern of hiring Dagan and his henchmen for any number of unsavory tasks over the last few years."

"For the record, these are exhibits G through J," Randall said, passing copies of these document to the judge and the jurors. "And did these unsavory tasks include murder?"

"No, or at least not to my knowledge," Carver said. "Intimidation, mostly."

"So you have no proof that he hired Dagan to murder you?"

"No, but you'll find it if you get a search warrant. Putnam will have left a paper trail somewhere. He always does."

Randall nodded. "Thank you, Mr. Carver." He looked over at Peabody. "Your witness."

The prosecutor leapt up and approached the witness stand. There he stood, legs apart, arms behind his back, considering the witness.

He looked far too confident. Emily held her breath. What was he planning?

Peabody began by questioning the documents that had been admitted as Exhibits A through E. Only to abandon that approach when it became clear that Carver had detailed answers, and a better grasp on the subject of fraud than the prosecutor did.

Emily grinned as the prosecutor paced from the witness stand to the jury box, giving the jurors a significant look, and back again. But he still looked confident. Now what?

"Why are you only coming forward now, Mr. Carver?" Mr. Peabody asked with a barely restrained smirk. "You vanished for a week after the murder, let people think you dead. And all that time you say you had information about the killers. Wouldn't you, a lawyer, call that obstruction of justice?"

"I was afraid for my life," Mr. Carver replied. "If Putnam had known I was still alive, he'd have sent Dagan after me again."

"Why didn't you go to the police, then?" Mr. Peabody said.

"With everything I've seen in my practice? I didn't trust them."

His reply left Mr. Peabody searching for a response. He probably hadn't expected the honesty.

"I see," the prosecutor said heavily, as if hoping to express doubt through his tone. "So. This Dagan you keep mentioning. How could you know that he killed your brother. Were you there?"

"No, to my sorrow," Carver said. "But I arrived just after the police did, and spotted Dagan and several of his men loitering across the street, watching. He had no reason to be there. His business is on the East Side, not in that neighborhood."

"I'm sure the police questioned them and cleared them," Mr. Peabody said dismissively.

Which was a mistake.

"No," Mr. Carver said clearly. "The police never noticed Dagan and his henchmen, much less questioned them. I've read the police reports."

Which Daniels had provided to him. Emily glanced around the courtroom, pleased to see the officer in a back row.

Mr. Peabody had frozen for a moment, and Emily had to fight back a nervous giggle. It seemed he didn't dare ask how Mr. Carver had read those reports, for fear the answer would be even more detrimental to his case.

She took a calming breath.

"No further questions, Your Honor," the prosecutor said.

4 0

———————

After a short break, Randall recalled Putnam, who had testified earlier for the defense. A wave of murmurs swept through the crowd. Granville watched the man walk to the witness stand, and wondered if he had any idea what he was going to be facing here.

Granville glanced at Emily beside him, her face tense. Was it a mistake to have brought her? She was seeing the ugly side of her world unmasked, and it wasn't easy for her. But she'd wanted to see Putnam brought to justice.

And if she was going to be working with him, she had to know what they faced. She'd not be safe, otherwise. In any case, she wouldn't thank him for trying to wrap her in cotton wool—she was too much her own person for that.

He glanced over at Clara, who was also watching intently. Her eyes were narrowed a little, but she showed no other signs of strain. For all her seeming frivolousness, Emily's friend wasn't one to hide from the world, either. Though he noted that she was clutching O'Hearn's arm nearly as tightly as Emily was holding his.

Putnam seated himself in the witness box, looking calm, distinguished even, with his well-shaped silver beard. He obviously had no idea what had gone on the courtroom that day, smiling calmly as he reiterated his oath and returned Randall's greeting.

"Mr. Putnam. You pointed out my client this morning, stated that he was a former employee of yours." Randall pointed out Sinclair where he sat in the prisoner's dock.

As if the fellow wasn't capable of recognizing the man he'd slandered that morning, Granville thought, suppressing a grin.

"That is correct," Putnam said.

"You stated that your former employee, Walter Sinclair, had been fired for fraud, is currently under arrest for the same. And that you believed a person capable of fraud on that scale is more than capable of murder."

Randall paused, looked at the witness in silence for a moment. The jury members craned to hear. "Would you say that is an accurate summation?"

Putnam smiled blandly. "Accurate indeed. I commend you."

Randall ignored the insult. "And has your opinion on the subject altered in any way?"

"Since this morning? I should think not!"

"Good, good." Randall smiled at him.

"Now if I could draw your attention to Exhibit F," and he handed Putnam a copy of one of the documents he'd submitted that afternoon. "I believe this is one of the documents you provided for the police, in order to prove fraud against your employee, is it not?"

"It is," Putnam said. Granville thought he looked slightly puzzled, though he masked it well.

"Objection!" Peabody cried. "Where is this meandering questioning going? I assume it has a purpose?"

"Indeed it does," Randall said, looking at the judge. "If you will indulge me for a few minutes, M'Lord, I can assure you that you will find this line of questioning relevant."

"Very well," Judge Hardy said. "But I'll caution you against wasting the court's time."

"Of course, Your Honor," Randall agreed, before turning back to

Putnam. He handed him another document. "And can you identify Exhibit A for the court?"

Putnam examined the page and turned a little pale. "No, I cannot."

"But would you agree this is also fraudulent?"

"How should I know? These numbers could be anything."

"Ah," Randall said, retrieving the document. He compared it to Exhibit F, which he still held. "But the similarities between F and A...?"

He glanced at Putnam and seemed to change his mind. Randall put both documents back on his desk, and handed Putnam three others.

"Exhibits B, C and D. Do they mean anything to you?"

"Nothing," Putnam said curtly.

"Are you sure? Perhaps if you looked a little more closely? And I'll remind you that you are under oath."

Putnam glared at the lawyer, then at the documents for a long moment.

The court was silent, waiting.

"Nothing," he said at last, handing the exhibits back to Randall.

"I see." Randall walked over to the jury box, making eye contact with each juror, as if he was about to say something momentous.

Then, with a slight shake of his head, he strode back to the witness box. "You do still stand by your assertion that a person capable of major fraud is more than capable of murder?" he asked Putnam.

Putnam's face was tense, but his voice was strong. "I do."

"I see," Randall said.

He walked to the exhibit table, picked up Exhibit D again, and showed it to the jury.

Then he handed it to Putnam. "Please have another look at this document. Does it bear any similarity to any document produced by your company?"

Putnam accepted the page from the lawyer. If Randall had

hoped he'd react in some way, he didn't know his target, Granville thought, watching Putnam's calm expression.

The man had himself well in hand.

"I'm sorry," Putnam said. "But I don't recognize any of the elements of this document. At all."

"I see. Thank you," Randall said.

Accepting the page, he walked in silence towards the jury box, meeting the eyes of individual jurors.

After a moment, he walked back to face Putnam.

"Would you please tell the court about any interactions you may have had with a man named Gregor Dagan," Randall said. Letting the words fall as if they had little importance.

"Dagan?" Putnam repeated slowly. His voice and face remained calm.

Whatever emotion Putnam might be feeling, he hid it well, Granville thought.

The jury waited avidly for Putnam's answer.

"I don't believe I know the man," Putnam said. "Though the name seems slightly familiar. We may have been introduced at some time. I don't remember."

"Yet the man says he knows you, has done work for you. How do you respond to that?"

Putnam stared at the defense lawyer. "Since I don't know Dagan, I don't know what kind of man he is. He could be a man of character and honesty, one with a business that is respected in the community. Or he could be a common thug. The jury will have to decide for themselves which of us to believe."

It was a masterful answer, as the murmurs throughout the court bore witness to.

The judge had to bang his gavel loudly to restore order.

"I see," Randall said. "So Mr. Dagan lies when he says that he killed Mr. Carver on orders from you?"

Putnam leapt to his feet. "What? What nonsense is this?"

He looked angrily about him, then his eyes settled on Chief

Stewart. "Chief? You can't allow this travesty to continue. They have no proof of these wild accusations."

Judge Hardy banged his gavel.

Putnam jumped at the loud thunking noise a foot from his ear.

"The witness will sit down," the judge ordered. "Now."

Pale, sweating lightly, Putnam did so.

It was beginning to look as if Mrs. Pospischil would get her day in court after all, Granville thought. Right after Sinclair was set free.

Randall approached the witness stand. "Does Mr. Robert Carver lie when he says you hired Mr. Dagan on numerous occasions?"

"Carver? Carver's dead," Putnam said.

A murmur ran through the courtroom.

"Luckily for him, the shooter mistook his target," Randall said. "Robert Carter is very much alive."

Putnam sat rigid, his eyes locked on his opponent.

"And Robert Carver was happy to testify in this case," Randall added. "He had quite a bit to say, too."

At this, Putnam turned ghost pale.

He put a shaking hand on the edge of the witness box. Then thought better of it and leaned back against the chair.

Granville immediately glanced towards the jury box. Not one of them had missed that byplay.

Twelve pairs of eyes were glued to Putnam's drawn features. There was speculation on at least half of their faces.

And Randall's expression was as bland as if he hadn't noticed a thing.

It was the prosecutor's cue.

Peabody leapt up. "Objection! Counsel is badgering the witness."

"I've heard enough. From both of you," Judge Hardy said.

He fixed a stern eye on the prosecutor, transferred it to the now quiet witness.

The courtroom was silent, waiting for his next action.

"It's become clear to me, and likely to every thinking man in this court, that Mr. Sinclair's arrest for the murder of Mr. Carver is a serious miscarriage of justice."

He frowned down at Chief Stewart, who turned the color of a pomegranate. "I trust you agree, sir?"

Stewart nodded hastily.

"Mr. Peabody?"

Under that unrelenting eye, Peabody's shoulders drooped. He ducked his head, mumbled something.

"What's that?" Judge Hardy demanded. "Speak clearly, please."

"The city drops the charges against Walter Sinclair."

"What charges?" the judge asked, his eyes fixed on Peabody like gimlets.

"All charges," Peabody muttered.

Then again, more clearly, "We drop all charges against Mr. Sinclair."

"Thank you," Judge Hardy said. "This trial is over. Members of the jury, I thank you for your service. You are free to go."

"Uncuff the prisoner, will you?" he said to the bailiff.

He glanced around the courtroom, then spotted Daniels near the back, still in full uniform, and nodded at him. "And you. Daniels, is it? Put this man in handcuffs and take him away, please," he said, waving towards Putnam.

"I'm sure you can work out the appropriate charges," he told the prosecutor and the police chief.

That night, Granville and Scott took everyone out for dinner. The five of them, plus McAndrews, their client, their lawyer, Clara and the two reporters enjoyed a boisterous celebration dinner at Mary's Diner, helped along by several pitchers of beer, and after dinner, glasses of the remarkably decent brandy Mary kept for special occasions. Granville had offered to take all of them to the best restaurant in town, but he'd been voted down. The consensus was that they'd have more fun at Mary's.

And they did. Everyone was a little stunned and very relieved that they'd actually won, Granville thought, looking at the flushed faces around the table. McAndrews and Draper had taken turns giving Miss Kent a moment by moment re-telling of the trial, with a little help from Trent. As the drama built, Miss Kent was gasping aloud, and the others stopped talking to listen in. There were a few moments where Granville's heart was pounding as he listened, realizing just how many risks they'd taken, and how narrow a path Randall had walked.

It wasn't just the corruption within the police force they'd faced —it was the influence Putnam wielded through the money he controlled. The fellow was a respected presence in the business community, and had loaned money—likely on very favorable terms —to a number of the town's key players. Those men would not have wanted him exposed, even if they'd believed him a fraud. Luckily Judge Hardy was not one of them.

He looked from smiling face to smiling face. Had they not taken the risks they had, and called Putnam to account in open court, Sinclair might well have hung for a murder he'd had nothing to do with. Putnam would have fled, taking some part of the city's economy with him, and Dagan would still be in business. Well, until he annoyed Benton too much, he would be.

Granville signaled Mary for another round of brandy, and when she'd poured them, raised his glass. "To us," he said with a grin. "We took down Putnam, and I for one wasn't even sure it could be done."

"It couldn't," Randall said. "Not without an extraordinary effort from all of you. And a very devious plan."

There was laughter and much clinking of glasses around the table. Everyone looked happy to be there—Trent in particular—and Miss Kent looked as if she couldn't believe she was part of the group. He'd have to ask Emily later how her friend had stood up during the crisis.

He'd been impressed with their new clerk's calm demeanor and ability to keep everything organized, but he'd learned early from his younger sister Elaine that sometimes what mattered was what didn't show on the surface. Emily would know, though.

"Here's to a great team," Scott said, raising his glass with a broad smile.

"I'll drink to that," Granville said, pleased to see that his partner meant every word. Just a week ago, he'd never have predicted the case would end so well, nor that they'd all find a way to work together so quickly. He just hoped that the camaraderie survived their next case, whatever it might be.

LATER, Granville walked Emily home along Pender, glad of a chance to be alone with her, and to talk over the day. They walked in silence for a time. He noted she kept stealing glances at the houses they passed, and wondered if she was having second thoughts about the home she'd chosen.

When they reached Burrard, they cut down to the beach. It was a warm evening, with just a hint of breeze, and the lights of the city gleamed in the twilight. The air smelt of salt and roses, and the reflection of a quarter moon shimmered in the small waves. He reached for her hand, and she smiled up at him.

"Thank you for dinner," she said. "That was truly fun. And did you notice how everyone was bonding over our success?"

"Even Trent and Miss Kent?" he asked with a sideways grin.

"Especially them. And she said something to Mr. Scott, and then he thanked her for keeping the office open while everyone was at the trial. And she blushed! I've never seen Laura blush before."

"Is that good?"

Emily laughed, and the breeze caught the ringing sound, echoing it off the water. "Yes, indeed it is. I don't think many people appreciate what Laura does, much less tell her so. It would have meant a good deal that Mr. Scott did so. She knew he didn't really want her there at first."

"Miss Kent did? She knew?" He hadn't expected that, and he didn't want to lose her. Not when it had been nearly impossible to convince Scott to hire her in the first place.

"Yes. But that's changing, and she knew that too." She glanced up at him. "Don't worry, Laura isn't going anywhere. She's loving the job, especially when she got to work with Mr. McAndrews and Mr. Draper on interpreting the fraudulent ledgers."

"Good. I like her, and she's turning into a real asset. I'd hate to see her leave just as the team has figured out how to work together."

Emily was quiet for nearly half a block, then glanced up at him. "Granville? Did you and Scott sort out your issues?"

"I think so. He's willing to see us expand, but I'll need to take it in steps. Give him time to adapt."

"And Pinkerton's? Will we affiliate with them?"

He grinned at the eagerness in her tone. Emily wasn't one to take things slowly—one of the many qualities he loved about her. "We're planning to meet with one of their representatives in August."

"Oh!"

"We're just exploring the possibilities for now. This won't be a quick decision on either side. But Scott will be at the meeting with me—this isn't a decision either of us will make alone."

"I'm glad. You make good partners," she said. Then, thoughtfully, "Have you thought about hiring Mr. McAndrews? Having an accountant as part of our team has been really helpful."

"I've noticed. And yes, I'm considering about some kind of part-time position as the firm's accountant, if he's open to it. It could be a situation where he takes on other clients, and also contracts with us on specific cases. I'll need to discuss it further with Scott, but what do you think?"

"I think it sounds ideal all around. And we'll need another office. Which reminds me…"

He glanced down at her. "You met with Marshall yesterday, didn't you? And how did you make out with your house and office hunting?"

"I have the figures for you back at the office. And I think you'll like them," she said, smiling. "Even at the worst rates in town, you can easily afford both the office building and the house. In fact, the office building revenue will pay for all of it."

"So you'd recommend moving forward?"

"Yes, of course."

"Then we'll do it. Though I'll have to discuss the figures with Scott," he said slowly, to tease her. "He wants the firm to buy the building, and I think that makes the most sense."

"It probably does. The revenues would carry the business through slow times," she said. Then she squeezed his arm as her excitement bubbled through again. "But if we keep winning cases like this one, there won't be any slow times. You should have heard the gossip about our firm in the courtroom!"

"That still leaves the question of the house," he said, keeping his voice neutral with an effort. "You found one you liked for Marshall to run the numbers on? And they were good?"

Her face lit up. "Yes, I did—it's the one Clara and I looked at the other day. Not too big, but big enough for what we'd need. And the street is lovely. But the numbers are even nicer—very manageable."

"It sounds as if you could picture us living in that house?"

"It's funny, but you're right. That's what I liked best about it—it felt home-like."

"You really liked it? You're sure?"

He could see her eyes fill with questions, but she nodded, and said, "Yes. I'm sure. I really liked that one."

"Then we'll make an appointment to sign the papers tomorrow, shall we?"

Emily gasped. "Sign? But—you haven't even seen the house!"

"If you're happy there, it will be the right house for me. Unless you'd like to change your mind and look at a larger house?"

"No of course not! But shouldn't we wait until closer to the wedding to buy a house?"

"I thought we'd agreed that once we found a house we could move up the wedding," said Granville, feigning disappointment. "And thus avoid your mother's version of the perfect wedding day."

"But…" Emily said, then pulled her hand from his arm and turned to face him, arms akimbo, her heels sinking a little into the sand. "John Granville! You're teasing me!"

"Perhaps a little," he admitted. "But not about the house. And not about moving up the wedding."

He took her both her hands in his. "Emily, I'd like to be your husband this year, not two years from now. If you agree?"

"Oh," Emily said, blinking away a sheen of tears. "I do. I do indeed." And she melted into his arms, there in the moonlight.

In writing this book, I have been particularly fortunate in the number of original source documents that are now available online —so different from when I first started researching *The Silk Train Murder*, when practically everything was either in print or on (sigh) microfiche. I keep being surprised by things I thought were modern, only to discover they were in use, in some form, in 1900.

I was intrigued to discover that in 1900 British Columbia, you couldn't get a mortgage from a bank—it was illegal until 1954. This resulted in a number of mortgage lending firms of various configurations, many of them funded by investors looking to make a better return than the banks would pay. (Sound familiar?) In the real estate boom that accompanied the influx of money to Vancouver in the wake of the Klondike Gold Rush, it was a situation ripe for fraud. And murder.

The Vancouver Permanent Investment & Loan company didn't really exist, and nor did their General Manager, Charles Putnam— but a number of similar firms came into existence at the time. And the fraud? Who knows. Anything is possible when in a real estate boom.

I hope you enjoyed reading the further adventures of Granville and Emily as much as I enjoyed writing them and exploring the times in which they lived!

Particular thanks go to my first readers for insightful comments on early drafts of the manuscript, and to Linda Roggeveen for her exceptional copyedit. Any errors or omissions are mine.

I am also indebted to the resources and helpful staff of the Vancouver Public Library Special Collections and History divisions. A number of historical works and on-line sites have been invaluable to me in researching this book; many of them are listed on my website at www.sharonrowse.com

THE CANNERY ROW MURDERS
A John Granville & Emily Turner Mystery

1

TUESDAY, AUGUST 7, 1900

It was a hot day, even for August, and the faint breeze carried the reek of kelp rotting on the beach a few blocks away. John Lansdowne Granville strolled down Hastings Street, noting the rush of businessmen hurrying from some appointment or other—all formally dark-suited and hatted in defiance of the heat.

He himself was no better, he thought with a grin as he glanced down at his own well-cut suit. Good thing he didn't wear the thick beards so popular now. Or even a mustache.

Crossing the street, he waved off the driver's good-natured cursing as he narrowly avoided being clipped by a furniture-delivery wagon. He laughed aloud at the incongruous sight of an oak china cabinet, finely carved, swaying in time with the clop of the job horse's hooves.

Between two mansions looking out over the harbor, Granville found his destination. The Vancouver Club was an ivy-clad, two-story building of brick, with a gabled roof and a heavy stone arch over the doorway. He found it too heavily imposing for a house, and too chateau-like for a club. Whatever had the architect been thinking?

Pushing open the heavy walnut doors, he swiped at the sweat beading on his forehead as he gladly passed his hat to the attendant at the door and glanced around. The place was clad in warm wood-paneling, custom-built in a style that would be found in many of London's best clubs. Which was undoubtedly the intent of the members, many of whom were English themselves, and still spent time there on their frequent trips 'home'.

Two years digging for gold in the frozen ground of the Klondike had given Granville a different perspective on such clubs —and while he still felt at home in these environs, he found them a little stifling.

The formality of the Vancouver Club felt odd to him here—in this newly built city carved out of the wilderness—in a way it never did in London, with its long-depleted forests and centuries of existence. Still, it was an excellent place to do business. Its members represented most of the businesses in the city—and most of the money.

If the Terminal City Club was a place for the up-and-coming businessmen, the Vancouver Club was home to those already well-established.

Granville took the stairs to the first floor, his feet sinking into the thick pile carpet. Turned left, towards the so-called wine room, which served as the bar. He paused in the doorway, scanning the sparsely-filled room.

"Granville. There you are," Angus Turner said, walking up to him and holding out a pudgy hand. His future father-in-law looked like he belonged here, with his full beard, expensively tailored dark suit, and satisfied expression. "Come along, there's someone I want you to meet."

Following the portly figure across the room, Granville wondered what Turner was up to. They had agreed to meet here for a drink to celebrate Granville's acceptance as a member of the club, since his future father-in-law had sponsored him.

Apparently Turner had another motive.

His suspicions were confirmed when Turner marched over to a tall, fairly thin man with a full beard and a commanding presence. He'd been sitting in one of the leather club chairs near the window, but stood as they approached.

"Alexander, this is my daughter's fiancé, John Granville. John, Alexander Ross-Murray."

Inclining his head in acknowledgement, Ross-Murray held out a hand, one equal to another. "Pleasure," he said, a faint burr of his Scotland in his voice.

Granville shook hands. Ross-Murray? The family was a good one, from the Scottish borderlands, he thought. And he'd heard of Alexander Ross-Murray.

He was one of the city's most influential businessmen, and a stalwart member of Vancouver's upper class. He was also an acknowledged leader in the canning industry, managing the British & Canadian Packing Company.

In fact, Granville remembered hearing that the fellow had founded the company some years before, raising the money to consolidate nine canneries, seven of them near Vancouver. It had made Ross-Murray's fortune.

Why would a canneries magnate want to meet with him? Granville knew very little about the industry.

But like Ross-Murray, he was the son of a good British family— his late father had been the 5th Baron Granville. And he'd found Vancouver's businessmen to be surprisingly class-conscious, for all the city's declared independence from the colonial mentality. And that included his prospective father-in-law. Angus Turner was definitely impressed by his genteel background.

Did the same hold true for Alexander Ross-Murray?

"I've been hearing good things about your firm's investigative work," Ross-Murray said. "And Turner here tells me you're trustworthy."

Good to know, Granville thought with an inward grin. He inclined his head in acknowledgement. And waited for the man to come to the point.

"Please, have a seat," Ross-Murray said, gesturing to the empty leather-covered club chairs clustered around a heavy coffee table. "Can I offer you a drink? Whiskey?"

Granville nodded, and Ross-Murray motioned to the uniformed attendant, holding up three fingers.

Turner beamed at both of them as they sat down and the whiskey was served on a silver tray.

Ross-Murray raised his glass to them. "What do you know about the local canneries?" he asked.

"Other than the recent fisheries strike?" Granville said. "Not a great deal."

Ross-Murray nodded. The answer didn't seem to concern him. "What you need to know is that salmon canning is now British Columbia's major industry. The output from our canneries grew one hundred and sixty percent last year alone."

Those were impressive figures. Granville wondered if they were sustainable. He'd learned about salmon's four year cycle from the Indians in the north, whose lives had depended on the size of each year's salmon run. As did Ross-Murray's fortune.

"Go on."

"In a very real sense, the success of the province—and this city —depends on the success of the fishing season. We have already lost most of July to the fishermen's strike—no salmon were caught, and none canned. And the salmon will run for only another two, two and a half months, at most. We must make up our losses in the time we have left."

He looked hard at Granville. "Nothing can be allowed to prevent that."

Interesting. Ross-Murray clearly spoke for his fellow cannery owners as well as himself. And he was undoubtedly right about the impact on the economy if the canneries did poorly.

And on the fishermen and the cannery workers as well, though Ross-Murray hadn't mentioned them. They too must need to make as much money as they could in what was left of the short fishing season.

"I see. And why come to me?"

"I have a job that needs doing," Ross-Murray said. He paused a moment, watching Granville's expression. "It's a sensitive issue, one that will have to be very carefully handled. Otherwise, we're likely to be facing another strike, and as I said, neither the city nor the province can afford that."

"Go on."

"I'd like to hire your firm to handle it for us," Ross-Murray said. "And I'm speaking on behalf of the B.C. Salmon Packers' Association."

So that explained Ross-Murray's involvement.

Granville had heard of the newly-formed association, which represented all the canneries in the province. But what kind of situation could require this kind of build-up?

"I'm flattered," Granville said smoothly. "What is the job?"

"They've found a body at the Gulf of Georgia Cannery in Steveston. Or rather, they've found the bones."

Even on the mining fields of the Klondike, Granville had heard stories about Steveston's infamous Cannery Row.

But still. Finding a human skeleton? At a cannery?

How was that even possible?

Granville raised his glass—of heavy crystal, he noted absently—as he considered Alexander Ross-Murray's matter-of-fact offer. The rich taste of good single malt whiskey coated his mouth. Around him the low buzz of quiet conversation mixed with the clink of glasses as drinks were served. Sunlight poured in from clerestory windows, in direct contrast to the dark subject of their conversation, while slow-turning ceiling fans kept the room comfortable.

Beside him, Granville's future father-in-law sat alert, sipping his own drink, his eyes slipping from one to the other of them. He looked rather like a playgoer at a particularly interesting performance.

Across the table, Ross-Murray was leaning back, seemingly relaxed, but his long, slender fingers played with his whiskey glass.

"Whose bones?" Granville said.

"One of the workers, most likely."

"Then it's a recent death?"

"So it would seem." Ross-Murray waved an impatient hand. "But coming so soon after the strike was settled? We can't afford to have any rumors of this unfortunate fellow's death re-igniting the tensions that are still simmering in the wake of that action."

Probably he meant the fact that the government had called in the army—specifically the Duke of Connaught's 6th Regiment— against the strikers, Granville thought. Urged on by the cannery owners?

The official reason had been to prevent further threats against the Japanese fishermen, who had settled with the canneries and gone back to work. The real story was unclear, but the newly formed Fishermen's Union had cried foul.

Granville remembered reading about it—during what proved to be the last week of the strike—and wondering how the fishermen had felt, facing an armed regiment. Not surprising that there was still tension between the cannery owners and the workers with their new union.

And that the cannery owners were worried.

"It needs to be handled quietly," Ross-Murray was saying. "Which is why we haven't brought in the Steveston police."

"You know we'll have to bring the police in, if we take the job." Granville wasn't compromising on this one.

Ross-Murray's face was impossible to read, until he broke into a smile. "A man of honor, then, are you? Good. That's what we need."

He leaned forward. "And what will it take for you to decide to accept this job?"

'To start, I'll need more information," Granville said. "Who was found, where, and when."

"The dead man, or rather his bones, were found early yesterday morning. In the lye bath at the Gulf of Georgia Cannery. We have no idea who he was."

In a lye bath? He grimaced at the thought. "Could it have been an accidental death?"

Ross-Murray shook his head. "I'm afraid not."

Which meant they were looking at a murder. And one with no body—and presumably no witnesses. Just bones.

This would be a difficult case. And different from anything his investigative agency had yet attempted. Granville and Scott Investigations had been in business less than a year, but they were slowly becoming known for their ability to take on complex cases—and solve them. He wasn't ready to risk that reputation on a hopeless case.

On the other hand, it would be a challenge. And he'd never been able to resist a challenge, even one with long odds.

And if they succeeded, it could only help their reputation. And in the right quarters, Granville thought, glancing at the old-world elegance around him.

"And who knows about this discovery?" he asked.

"The only ones who know so far are the shift foreman, the cannery manager, myself and several of my fellow cannery owners, and now you," Ross-Murray said. "None of us will talk about it. We can't afford to have word getting out."

"None of the workers know?"

"Just one. A Chinese who maintained the lye bath. He's been let go, and the Chinese contractor will make sure he doesn't talk."

"The Chinese contractor?"

"Also known as the China Boss," Ross-Murray said. "All the canneries hire them. A China Boss is paid a per head fee to provide all the Chinese workers for the season. He's responsible for them.

Makes sure they show up, feeds them, takes care of any complaints. And since the China Bosses are Chinese themselves, they know the language, the customs. It's a good system."

It sounded like a convenient one, at least for the cannery owners. And maybe for the workers, too, since most of them wouldn't speak English. "And what are your expectations on this case?"

"That you will find out who was killed, by whom, and why. I trust that you will do so in a discreet manner."

He raised his whiskey glass, glanced at Granville over the top of it. "And I sincerely hope that your finding will be that this man's death had nothing to do with the strike, or with tensions between the Japanese and the white workers," he said, and drained the glass.

"And if the death proves to be related to the strike?" Granville said. "What do you expect of my firm then?"

"Then it will be up to you how you choose to handle it. Which is why I needed to hire an honorable man."

That decided him. He hoped Ross-Murray meant what he was saying, because once their firm took on a case, they followed it through. "Then we accept the job."

"Good."

"I'll need to see the cannery where the bones were found."

"Yes, of course. Someone will be in touch later today." Ross-Murray stood and shook hands. "I'm glad you've decided to take this on. You're one of us."

Beside him, Turner had nodded. In approval?

Granville couldn't decide how he felt about Ross-Murray's statement. Was he was flattered to be treated as a peer by this very successful businessman, or appalled?

What did "one of us" mean in a murder investigation?

Enjoyed this preview? THE CANNERY ROW MURDERS
is available through retailers everywhere